ELEMENTAL TRUTH

CELIA LAKE

Cover design by Augusta Scarlett.

Formatted with Vellum

THE MYSTERIOUS FIELDS TRILOGY

Need a reminder of what happened in *Enchanted Net* (book 1 of the Mysterious Fields trilogy) and *Silent Circuit* (book2) ?

You can find it on my website at https://celialake.com/en-summary or at the end of this book. (Look for "Enchanted Net Summary" and "Silent Circuit Summary" after the Author's Note if the link doesn't work on your reader.)

These three books follow Thessaly Lytton-Powell and Vitus Deschamps through their lives in 1889 and into 1890.

Curious about how these events play out in the Fortier family over time? In 1947, Ursula Fortier (Laudine and Dagobert's granddaughter) picks up some of these mysteries in her search for ways to strengthen the land and land magic. *Grown Wise* will be out in May 2025.

I

OCTOBER 13TH AT ARUNDEL

Thessaly thought the entire day was inauspicious even without considering the numerological superstitions around the number thirteen. It was a Sunday, which was suitable enough for this sort of announcement, but that was perhaps all the day had going for it. She had, in fact, done the somewhat tedious maths required to draw up a basic timing chart of the stars, to look at the influences on the ritual. It was not promising, entire collisions in the sky, the movement of the planets entirely antagonistic. Even if they'd done whatever ritual there was a couple of days ago, that wouldn't be much better.

On the other hand, Lord Clovis Fortier needed a new and formally named Heir. He had a remaining son. Anyone watching Dagobert, Lord Clovis's younger brother, would understand there was trouble there, even if they had no idea what or how deep it ran. Thessaly had a sense of the depth, but no idea about the cause, and that still bothered her.

And of course, it was also entirely inauspicious for Thessaly, who had assumed that with Childeric's death, she would no longer be required to appear at these Fortier events. She was no longer betrothed to him; she was no longer at his - or his family's - beck and call. This time, Lady Maylis had at least sent a letter explaining why they wished her to attend, which was more than Childeric had ever bothered to offer. Not that the explanation was compellingly coherent, but rather merely a gesture at wanting to both include Thessaly in the family and perhaps wanting to increase the guests in attendance without being too crass.

That change would have been far more persuasive if it weren't for the past six months, including the entire span of that entirely unpleasant betrothal, in which the Fortiers had told her next to nothing, repeatedly. She had danced to their tune because she hadn't had much choice. Now she had more choice, but matters were still delicate. She had slipped out of the cage Childeric had wanted to put her in, that his family had helped him build and strengthen. But she was not yet, apparently, actually free.

Now, Thessaly was a heiress in her own right, more than enough money to support whatever choices she chose to make, including becoming a recluse. Which, frankly, continued to seem like an excellent option, especially if she were a recluse with Vitus beside her. She would much rather have had her Aunt Metaia back, alive, laughing and teasing. But if that wasn't possible - and it wasn't, after Aunt Metaia had been murdered - she would take the protection her aunt had given her.

And yet, by a different count, it was only a fortnight since Childeric had made his Challenge for the Council and died in the attempt. Thessaly did not actually have access to the full list of such things, but she had gathered that what had happened was unusual. Certainly, Childeric had been soaking wet, as if he'd been out in a fearsome storm. He'd had marks on his skin that Vitus had said came from lightning. No one talked about that. No one had during the days before the funeral, when the Fortiers - and Thessaly - had kept vigil. Certainly, no one had mentioned it since.

Worse, the fortnight had brought other gossip. Thessaly had wondered, when she'd heard a bit of it, if it might encourage the Fortiers to leave her alone. Instead, Vitus visited her last Tuesday, cautiously, and told her what he'd heard, then shyly added that his mother knew about his affection for her. They had not got carried away in demonstrating that affection. The mood had been too unsettled for that. But Thessaly had reassured him that she would be glad to see him again when he got a chance. And that she still wanted to figure out how to go forward.

Vitus was nothing like a Fortier at all. He worked for a living, for one thing— that was part of what was so delicate. He'd had three new commissions for talismans since the last time they'd talked, all of them for people who might become more regular clients. Of course, that was taking much of his time and attention. She'd hoped to have time with him now, but here she was, at Arundel, waiting for the Fortiers to do what they were going to do.

Another thing she liked rather a lot about Vitus was that he asked her what she wanted. And he did rather well at offering it. That was also definitely unlike a Fortier.

She might not have come, but the Fortiers had written to her parents, as well. And parents— even living a fair distance away, as the crow flew— still had a lot of influence over Thessaly. And they had more over her younger sister. It was not a duel Thessaly felt she could confidently win, and losing would have been worse than conceding.

Today, the great hall was set up for a small gathering. The Dowager Lady Chrodechildis's chair— near enough a throne— was up at the front, with two chairs to one side for her son, Lord Clovis, and his wife, Lady Maylis. There was a chair on the other side, for Sigbert, the variation making things look unbalanced.

Dagobert and his wife had chairs in the first row, facing the front of the room, their son Garin beside them. Bradamante, who was the sister between Lord Clovis and Dagobert, and her family were on the other side. All three daughters were there along with their husbands, and a good handful of small children of varying ages. Thessaly counted them up in her head, four of them, including the babe in arms with accompanying nursemaid.

Behind, on each side, were a dozen or so others in total, all key allies for the Fortiers. The family was in mourning, and for a son, social gatherings were against all the codes and strictures of mourning. But the passing on of the land magic was an even older set of expectations.

Thessaly occupied herself considering the guests. Henut Landry was seated toward the back on the opposite side, also in deepest mourning and veiled. Of course, her elder son had died, three and a half months ago, right at the same time as Aunt Metaia. The Landrys had been closely tied to the Fortiers for nearly two decades. Henut had come begging refuge in the wake of her husband's death, with Philip not quite ten and Alexander not yet born. She was like a statue, or perhaps a gargoyle, watchful and solid. Or she had been a solid presence, and now, as Thessaly considered her, there was something different Thessaly couldn't name. It was like the leading of stained glass, strongly defined lines and edges shaping spaces that needed light from the proper angle to show what was there. She offered no illumination herself, nor any hint of what light might bring out the colour of what her presence implied.

Finally, though, the four key figures came out, from the rooms at the back, Lady Chrodechildis's private rooms, and her sitting room. She came first, alone, then Lord Clovis and Lady Maylis, with Sigbert trailing behind, looking a little like a lost duckling. All four were in stark black, and with the women firmly veiled. Thessaly was too, though hers was light enough to let her see easily, with just a wisp of illusion making it harder for others to see her expression. She might be here, but she saw no reason to cause trouble for herself by letting her face slip at the wrong moment.

Her mother nudged her, lightly, with one elbow, treating her as if she were a small child who needed to be told to pay mind. Thessaly held still, focused on the Fortiers. Lord Clovis had settled his wife in her chair, and he stood, reading something that sounded florid and formal. It was also in French, an older form of it. Thessaly caught about one word in four, enough to be fairly certain it was a family history full of bragging and exaggeration. No one moved, no one dared pretend they weren't enraptured, even if Thessaly was fairly sure that perhaps only Bradamante and Dagobert were following much of it, besides Lord Clovis. He droned on, a good fifteen minutes, before clearing his throat and accepting a jewelled goblet from his wife's hand.

"We come here today to formally and ritually acknowledge Sigbert Thibaud Fortier as my Heir. He has pledged blood to the land and his magic to tending the estate, from now until the hour of his death." That had an unpleasant echo to it. Childeric had, she knew, made the same vows at twelve. The ritual could not have been too damaging. Probably. She was fairly sure her calibration of the Fortiers' sense of such things was still askew. "Stand, Sigbert, and make your oath."

This was also in French, but there was a card for him to read from, and Sigbert at least had a pleasant voice to listen to. He gave it in French, then in Latin - Thessaly followed that one more easily, and then in English, he ended with a simple "I so swear on my magic." Thessaly could see - they all could - the shiver of magic and fear that passed through him, at the touch of the Pact that was the bedrock for all such oaths in Albion.

Lord Clovis waited a moment, then spoke clearly. "We are, of course, completing the proper paperwork for our own Ministry, and for the necessary offices in London. There can be no question of the line of inheritance. My sister and brother have confirmed that in magic and in writing." That was, Thessaly thought, jabbing a knife in at Dagobert particularly.

Then the thing was over, and people were released to light refreshments. It was still pleasant enough outside that these were served on the lawn, and Thessaly trailed her parents out there, while the Fortiers talked a little amongst themselves. Thessaly had drifted away from them - Father was talking to one of the other guests - towards the side garden.

"Thank you for coming." The voice behind her sounded shy, and she turned to see Sigbert. It kept startling her to look at him. He was dark-haired, like his father, not Childeric's golden hair that he'd got from his mother.

"Congratulations." Thessaly offered, turning to face him fully. "It was clear, from your oath, you mean to do the thing properly."

His mouth turned up slightly. "It would be a bad idea to swear by the Silence and intend the opposite, wouldn't it?" Then he nodded. "I'm glad you came. It made Maman pleased, and not much does right now. Me included."

It must, on the whole, be rather horrible to be Sigbert right now. Childeric had always been the shining one, certainly his mother's pet. Sigbert had been younger, lesser, trailing along in his older brother's wake. Another mother might have doted on her remaining son. Thessaly wasn't sure whether not doing so was better or worse. Thessaly considered what she could say, settling on "I hope things ease soon." She glanced back toward her parents. "And I understand that sort of response, of course."

Sigbert ducked his chin. "You would, yes. They didn't force you to come?"

Sigbert might be speaking more to her than Childeric had about what was going on, but that was not actually very difficult. Since their betrothal, Childeric had given orders and made pronouncements, but not much else. But force was a blunt term. What Thessaly felt had a lot of possible names. Implication, certainly. Pressure was entirely valid. Obligation absolutely applied. None of that was force, the way Thessaly would think of it in a duel, or in this context. No one had marched her here under charms. They had not compelled her. They had instead made the consequences of failing to do so visible.

All right, technically it was force, but it was not a sort of force any legal or practical judgement would do anything about. "I was clear about what would happen if I didn't. And there was no need of that. I was glad to be here to hear it myself." Before she could say much else, there was a gesture off behind Sigbert, that rescued her from the need for further conversation. "I think that's your aunt?"

"Oh." Sigbert turned. "Aunt Bradamante, yes. Do excuse me, perhaps we'll get a moment later?" He lifted his right hand, and Thessaly saw a flash of turquoise on his hand, the same as she'd seen on Childeric. A family ring, maybe something worn by the Heir, though Thessaly didn't remember it from before the summer. Thessaly nodded, watching him disappear into the small crowd again. Before she could bring herself to go back into the fray, her mother came up beside her.

"You should be speaking with the others." Mother sounded terse, but of course, Thessaly couldn't read her face well under the veil.

"Mother." Thessaly inclined her head. "Sigbert wanted a word."

"And now he is back talking with people." Then Mother glanced around. "Your father is casting around for possible directions for a betrothal to come. So you are aware. Not here, not directly, but making it known he will consider suitable offers."

Thessaly grimaced, glad her own face was hidden properly. It was one small freedom. "There aren't many likely." She knew the ranks and status of the potentials as well as anyone.

"He is reconsidering his priorities." Mother tilted her head. "Go on and do your duty. I want a word with Laudine."

That also was not actually terribly reassuring, but Thessaly knew that ducking the problem further would just cause difficulties. Instead, she took a breath, and went to go speak with Lady Maylis. Maybe it would ease things for Sigbert a bit more this evening if she did, and at least have some use for someone.

2

THAT AFTERNOON

Thessaly finally escaped from the gathering by the simple expedient of murmuring in five different ears - one of them Sigbert's - that she'd like a little quiet time at the cemetery. He offered to escort her. She firmly declined, saying gently that she'd prefer to be on her own. It was enough to slip away, promising her parents she'd go to the portal from there. It was a risk, but bringing Emeline as companion and bodyguard had not been possible, and Thessaly was having to trust to her own skills and training to keep herself safe. That said, she did not particularly fear the kind of interference that might require duelling today. There were too many other people still around.

Why she was promising her parents anything was another question, but habits held, even though she was a grown woman, with property of her own. She was not, however, a married woman, and that still mattered more than it ought. Thessaly wondered, not for the first time, how Aunt Metaia had managed it, to hold on to her own independence without perpetual interference. She was clear now her aunt had done some of it simply by not telling her sister - Thessaly's mother - at least half of what she was up to. Maybe only a tenth. She hadn't told most of the rest of the family much, either, except perhaps Cousin Owain.

At any rate, Thessaly made it to the cemetery with no one following her. And that meant she spent some time staring at Childeric's grave. Part of her wanted to dig down and reassure herself he was actually there, but she knew perfectly well that he was. She had seen him dead. She had sat vigil watching him for hours. She had seen him buried. There was no doubt.

Even if she'd already had a nightmare or two about it. Thessaly knew that was normal enough, or what passed for normal. She had been under great strain, wondering what Childeric would do, what he would threaten next. She'd begun to fear what the marriage would bring, even if she did everything as perfectly as anyone could wish. Now she was free, but it was taking her emotions a bit to catch up, and certainly her dreams were none too speedy about it.

More of them, at least, had been more a sort of lurking dread than anything specific to Childeric. The dread was easier to deal with. On the whole, it was less specific. It was frustrating, of course, nothing she could duel or even get a grip on. And the worst of it was, she couldn't even let it go. After all, here she was, invited to an intimate gathering of the family. Not the most intimate, but invited. Not that most of them had actually been remotely informative about anything which would have encouraged Thessaly to consider further invitations in a more generous light.

And on the third hand, whatever Thessaly had thought of Childeric by the end, his family did appear to love him. His mother and brother certainly did. Both were looking deeply distraught when not actively engaged in conversation. Thessaly had been less sure how to read Lord Clovis. Losing his son and Heir must be a terrible blow. She suspected he was making use of potions to present the proper stoic mien to the world.

She had been standing there at the graveside for maybe five minutes at the outside when she heard a rustle of silk. Thessaly looked up, her hands in front of her. Fortunately, she was just as well trained in not letting her thoughts show on her body as any young woman of Fox House might wish to be. It was not, however, Lady Maylis. It wasn't even Laudine, who Thessaly had wondered about. Instead, it was Henut Landry.

Her veil was now pulled back from her face. That made her look even more like a statue than she had inside. It was as if her mien had changed, subtly. She was at rest, in a particular way that Thessaly did not understand. Now she was taking small steps forward, the silk of her dress rustling. "Thessaly." Her voice was like her expression, hers, but altered, lower in pitch, maybe.

Thessaly inclined her head. "Magistra Landry." She would be polite. She was inclined to be polite anyway, but all of her sense of caution was prickling. Something about the woman was even more uncanny than it had seemed before, in a way that made her duelist's senses very attentive indeed.

"I came to tend to Philip's grave. Perhaps you will join me?" She nodded down toward the far end of the cemetery, not the favoured spots.

"Of course, if you would like." Henut walked on. Thessaly fell into place beside her, then let her go first into the row with Philip's tombstone. The older woman stopped in front of the memorial, unlike any other in this place, a square pillar covered in hieroglyphs and images. Henut produced a small bottle of water from within her skirts. She must have a good-sized pocket underneath. Setting it down for a moment, she pulled out a small incense holder and a cone of incense. The last pieces were a tiny loaf of bread, made of clay, and a pinch of actual bread, the size of the tip of Thessaly's thumb.

Thessaly watched this, because while offerings were common enough, these were more elaborate than she had expected. Henut placed each in what was clearly its proper place on the memorial itself, a flat ledge that served as a table, then lit the incense. Once that was done, she straightened up. "It is our custom to bring food and drink to the tomb every day, day upon day. The incense is more a, how do you say it? It acts as a clock."

"Oh." Thessaly rather liked that idea, though going out to Aunt Metaia's grave would be rather arduous. "That is not our custom, but I find it soothing to think about, in some way." She glanced back toward Childeric's. "That was not why I had come out here, though."

"Of course not." Henut inclined her own head again. "You are still coming to terms with the meaning of the death. And you have seen more than a young woman ought, in just a few months."

"Yes." Thessaly couldn't argue with that. "I don't know when I will be here again, but would it bother you if I came to pay my respects to Philip?" There was certainly nothing tying her to the family anymore, other than Childeric's memory. She'd struggled with what to do with the betrothal ring and the other tangible gifts he'd given her. Custom was that those were hers to keep, and the ring was not a particular family heirloom. She'd dithered over it for the fortnight, and at this point, she was set on finding a suitable ocean cliff and hurling it in.

Now Henut turned to her, a slow and unnerving smile. “I would be grateful for it. We believe someone continues, so long as their name is remembered.” She stepped forward, her fingers brushing the carving on the stone. “This is his name in our language, the ancient one of our people. Here is his name in French and English.” She fairly obviously would not attempt to teach the first. “If, for any reason, I could not continue on my own, especially before Alexander returns from his travels, it would please me to know someone thought to care for Philip.”

Thessaly nodded. “If I have the chance, then. I cannot make oath or promise on it. I...” She turned, gesturing behind her. “I don’t know what the future holds.”

Henut’s eyes narrowed. She looked around, and then there was a shift of magic. It was the sort of enchantment that would take most people a proper ritual and an hour’s time, and Henut drew the threads of it to her in an instant. “An effective privacy charm.” Once she’d given the explanation, she went on, “I would not wish you brought closer here. For all Sigbert is in many ways the better brother, that does not mean good. Do you understand?” Her eyes flicked back toward the house. “Last evening’s rite and today’s announcement continue the family, but they are further steps down a particular road. One that would not be kind to you, certainly.”

That was a message that had more layers than Thessaly could sort out in a moment. She swallowed, looking back through the cemetery, then at Henut. “I would be grateful for whatever you might tell me. I do not know what I could possibly offer in exchange.”

“I like your friend, the one gifted at talismans. He is honest, he is whole-hearted, his magic bubbles up like the water at an oasis, to be treasured and stewarded.” She obviously meant Vitus. There was no one else in Thessaly’s life who fit that description. "I wish him well, and I wish you well. Perhaps together?" Before Thessaly could react to that, Henut went on. "There is a great deal wrong in the house and the estate. There has been for some months, if not years. Since Vauquelin's death."

He had died five years ago, and Thessaly had known him far more by reputation. A strict patriarch of the family, he'd been known as a match for his wife, Lady Chrodechildis. Lord Vauquelin had been a gifted ritualist. She knew that too, people still talked about some of the rituals he'd led, workings to enhance the magic in the heart of Trellech, or the rituals that stabilised part of the land magic here. He had drawn on tremendous power. He'd terrified a number of people, but he'd most visibly used it for the common good.

Thessaly hesitated, trying to decide how to play this duel she found herself in. Or rather, she had to decide whether to trust she was right, that Henut was somehow on her side of that duel against the Fortier family. The older woman did not rush her, she barely moved an eyelid. Finally, Thessaly said, "They have not treated me well." Then she added, in all honesty, "Laudine has been kinder and certainly more informative."

"I wish Laudine well," Henut said, evenly. "And her husband, who I suppose has sufficient correction for his past choices. Dagobert is listening more to his wife now. That is wise of him." She considered, weighing something. "I have always thought a husband and wife should improve each other. That has not been the case for Maylis and Clovis, alas." There was a note there that Thessaly could only read as a decision made, a line of action committed to, in some unseen duel. Certainly, Thessaly had no desire to face her there, she was entirely overmatched.

It was also startlingly informative, and Thessaly had

not expected that. She nodded, first murmuring a thank you.

Henut let that settle, before she said, quietly, "What would you like to do with yourself, now you will not marry Childeric?"

"Take a bit of time before making any decisions." That was easy enough to say. "If I have my way, and I hope to. I am still exploring Aunt Metaia's home, her library. I must finish my apprenticeship. Once I'm done, I might at that point consider other work. I hadn't thought to tend in the direction she had, ensuring spaces are protected, ignored by those without magic. But now I find it intriguing."

Henut nodded. "That would be a good use of your skills, yes, and the way you think." Thessaly felt her eyes widen at the compliment implied there. "I wish you well in it. If I can be a help, please let me know. I do not think an introduction from me would be of benefit. But if I can advise on the practical aspects of dealing with clients, I would be glad to do so. Though I am sure Vitus has learned much of it already."

That mention made Thessaly blush. "I suspect so, yes." Then she swallowed. "I beg your pardon, but I think most of the others have left. I should probably go to the portal before anyone thinks to come talk to me."

"An entirely sensible tactical decision." Henut nodded at the incense, half burned down, to indicate she would remain. "My best wishes."

"And mine, to you." It felt flat, somehow, but it would have to do. Thessaly turned, making her way out of the cemetery. She turned along the road toward the portal, without going back near the house. When she got almost to the fence, though, she found Laudine and Dagobert, and their son Garin. Dagobert was sitting, his hands folded on the cane. "Laudine, Dagobert. Hello, Garin." She offered him a slight smile.

"We wondered if we'd missed you. Garin wanted to see you, just for a moment, and we wondered," Laudine nodded at Dagobert, "If you might at some point wish to visit us in Essex. I remember I'd offered to talk about managing an estate with you, what seems like a long time ago."

Thessaly remembered the conversation as well. "It's kind of you to think of me, especially today." She hesitated. "Not just at the moment, if you don't mind? I still feel rather shaken by everything, and being on my own at Bryn Glas is restorative."

Laudine offered a slight snort. "Oh, I understand that. We'll be returning to Essex tomorrow, thankfully. There is no rush. We will be glad to have you whenever you do wish to be more in company. And I think Garin would like to learn a little more duelling from you, if you might be willing. The salle needs some tending there, but we are thinking to have that done in the next month or three. Master Bolton, senior, is considering when he'll be available for the work."

"He is much in demand, and with good reason." Now Thessaly was wondering if he'd agreed before or after Childeric's death, and how to weigh that information. She glanced down at Garin, who was watching her silently. "I would be glad to spend a little more time, Garin, showing you what I know. When I'm properly dressed for it, not like last time."

"There. In due course, that will give us all something to look forward to. We won't keep you, of course. You must be tired from the day." Laudine smiled.

Dagobert nodded. "And we must go back into the fray ourselves, I think. Have a good evening." He pushed himself up on the cane, Garin offering his shoulder on the other side, which seemed a remarkably direct bit of help. Thessaly smiled at them, added "Good evening" for good measure, and turned for the portal. She had a great deal to think about, especially with what Magistra Landry had implied about the family.

3

OCTOBER 14TH IN TRELLECH

"In conclusion, in addition to the comments in the pamphlets provided to those interested, I am honoured to note that Council Member Marchant has offered to speak on behalf of some of my recent work. I will, of course, be glad to take questions once she has spoken." Vitus could see the end approaching.

It had taken a fortnight to reschedule his presentation to the Talisman Maker's Guild. He'd originally been meant to present right after the Challenge. Of course, putting it off had made sense after the chaos of Childeric's death, but it had just made him increasingly nervous. Theirs was not a large guild, especially when seen as distinct from the Jewellers. Vitus had earned his journeyrank on that side before his trip to Europe, thankfully, so it was only the magical competency that was at question here.

The presentation had taken half an hour. Now he could move to one side, turning the podium over to Magistra Marchant, and getting a chance to sit and take a drink. Almost all the guild members were here, and most of their senior apprentices, making it a room of about fifty.

There were about another fifty associate members, people who worked in various of the workshops, but who were not responsible for the entire design of a piece.

He thought it had gone well. As was the custom, it had three parts. He'd presented about seven talismans he'd made that could be discussed. Not the one for Theo Carrington, of course, though he had discussed the lion piece the Carringtons had bought, though without saying where it had gone, naturally. He'd talked about the pieces he'd done to support the Council challenge spaces. Both Niobe and Council Head Rowan had encouraged him to include those. And he'd had five other pieces.

He'd also prepared the exercise he'd been set. That afternoon, he'd been given a prospectus, details as if taken from a possible client. The guidelines were that he could use any materials in his workshop, or if he did not have a suitable stone, he could indicate how he would acquire one. Then he had had to create sketches and the design work, including identifying potential weaknesses. Here, the assignment had been a piece to deflect curses sent toward the wearer. Of course several of the most likely stones had a tendency to shatter if hit at the wrong angle. Designing a talisman that would work better and that could be worn more safely was an interesting challenge.

Of course, this was all design work, not crafting - one couldn't expect a complete piece to be made in an afternoon. And the Guild was stringent, but not so much as to ask for weeks of work for no remuneration from someone so early in their career. So the frantic four hours of the design and the extant pieces he submitted were considered sufficient. Well, that and the oaths from people familiar with his work, including Niobe.

Vitus was listening to what Council Member Marchant said, which was all rather flattering. But she'd told Niobe in advance what she intended to say, so there were no surprises. She praised his ability to create matched pieces to specifications, his understanding of the priorities in the work, and his timeliness, as well as their efficacy. He listened more closely as she added, "It is no secret - without getting into details - that it was a difficult night. I am certain that the quality of the talisman work assisted in making sure that we could respond in the best ways possible to rapidly changing events and be certain that we were giving all possible aid to those affected."

That was a delicate way of saying 'those still alive to care'. Vitus kept a pleasant smile on his face. There were one or two questions for her. Council Member Marchant wasn't a regular at the guild meetings, though she remained in good standing. Her primary focus was on using talismans to anchor additional enchantments, the sort of thing that was built into a house or fence or warding. She wasn't a skilled gem cutter herself, or a carver.

There were one or two questions for her, and then she ceded the podium to him again. Vitus looked out at the assembled group, and at the catering staff who were lurking by the doors to the kitchen hall and preparing to bring the meal out. He wished Thessaly could be here, but of course, she was not a member of the Guild. His parents weren't here either, or Lucas, but they'd celebrate on Sunday. Assuming that celebration was in order, but he hoped it would be.

The Guild Master cleared his throat. "A question from Harold Tambleton."

Vitus inclined his head. "Master Tambleton." The man was competent - he'd earned his mastery - but not so skilled that he got the additional honour of being called Magister. That rankled, Vitus suspected, but he would be correct. That was an expectation here as well as his skills in working with stones and their magic.

"Could you take us through your decisions that led to using Forsythe's Third on that piece of topaz, your second example? And why you didn't use Hemmingsmith's First?"

Vitus had in fact gestured at that, albeit briefly. Niobe had warned him this would be likely. There would be a couple of difficult questions. And she and Vitus had talked about who they'd likely come from, and what they'd focus on. Tambleton liked to make everyone feel small and lesser than he was, treat them like they were barely out of Schola and only nominally able to lace their own shoes.

He took a breath, then explained in more detail. "If you examine the details on the piece in the pamphlet provided, sir, you'll see that there's an inclusion. That made it likely that the Hemmingsmith approach - any of the First, Fourth, or Sixth - would interact with that. Rather than make the pieces significantly smaller, perhaps two-thirds of the size, I decided to use Forsythe's Third, which preserves the inclusion through a much larger number of facets . In practice, we've found the inclusion adds to the utility, rather than detracts, though I admit it's not the most beautiful piece to look at."

There were various murmurs throughout the room. He thought he'd answered that well enough. The Guild Master cleared his throat. "Antonius Whitesnake."

Vitus braced himself for this one. Whitesnake had a reputation for nastiness. Now he looked for him in the room. "Master Whitesnake." The man was sitting next to his current apprentice, Daniel Rollings, and Rollings was clearly dancing attendance, making his attention floridly visible.

"You did a piece for the most recent Council Challenge. Can you share your approach to that?"

"Sir." Vitus pulled his hands behind his back. "I follow - as I have been trained to, by Magistra Hall - the customs of this Guild, allowing privacy to clients. I am glad to discuss the process I followed, but not to describe the details of the piece. Is that acceptable?"

Oh, yes, that had been meant as a trick question. He got a nod from Whitesnake. Vitus went into the overview of the process, the questions he had asked, how he had presented multiple stones. Once Carrington had selected the peridot, Vitus laid out how he'd thought through how to do the talismanic work. None of the details of what it was for. He didn't mention the specific stone, nothing that would indicate the focus.

He thought Whitesnake seemed a bit displeased, and that was all right then. The Guild Master looked around. "Any other questions? Yes, Florent Montague."

Vitus had not expected that. Florent Montague was the father of Laudine, Dagobert Fortier's wife. He didn't know the man well. But of course he'd been at the funeral, and he suspected also at whatever Thessaly had been at yesterday, a gathering of the family of some kind. "Magister Montague."

"I suspect you might enjoy this one a bit more. That piece you did with the carnelian and the lion's head. Could you go into the details of the carving? I had a chance to see the piece in person last week. You have not, I think, spoken as much to the artistic impression it makes as might be useful here."

It was, in fact, something of a gift. It meant Vitus had a chance to talk about that aspect, and how he'd designed it to fit with the carnelian, but also with the goals for the talisman. He added that he had some larger pieces of amber he was intending to do similar work with. That was an easier material to carve in some ways. But he'd also laid in several other varieties of chalcedony and of clear quartz. He finished up, "I am still learning my skills as an artist in this form. But I do like the idea of creating pieces that speak to the beauty of the stone beyond a pendant, ring, brooch, or some other jewellery item on a smaller scale. Much as I also enjoy those."

There was a silence, then there were apparently no further questions. Vitus was permitted to sit, as the tallies for his membership went around. These were small stones, charmed in the hand to black or white, one of the simplest methods of voting, then placed in a deep opaque jar.

Vitus waited while that was circulated, then the Guild Master and two others withdrew to count them, coming back almost immediately. The Guild Master came up on the dais, and Vitus stood.

The words, when they came, almost felt anti-climactic. He'd been working for this for so long, and yet this actual step felt tiny. But he was pleased - and absolutely relieved - when the Guild Master began. "Vitus Deschamps, we are delighted to welcome you to our company, as a full member of the guild with all the rights, privileges, and obligations that apply. We know you have been taught well, as you will teach in due course when you take your own apprentices. We recognise and thank Niobe Hall for her time and effort, and we look forward to seeing what you will make in the months and years to come." Then he smiled, offering the proper medallion, slipping it over Vitus's head. "You are expected to have a fitting for the robes promptly, they will be needed by solstice. And no getting out of the mummer's play in the spring, of course." Those were two of the more socially obvious obligations.

"Thank you, Guild Master. And of course, I will make arrangements for both." He bowed his head, and the applause started up. After a minute, he was released to join

Niobe and the others at their table, bringing his notes and papers with him.

The conversation was most agreeable. People did not linger too much on Vitus's presentation, other than a comment about one thing or another. Instead, they settled into a rather fascinating conversation about variations based on the source of a stone, and the idea of doing another round of deliberate testing about that. Apparently there had been some done thirty or forty years ago, but of course there were newer mines for some minerals now, or the quality had shifted. Vitus got in a comment about working a little with some of the small Burma rubies, and his experiences.

It wasn't until the end of the meeting - there were, of course, more discussions after the meal - that people drifted off. Some were obviously going to smaller gatherings elsewhere. Vitus had expected to walk Niobe home for a celebratory drink and to figure out where to go with his family on Sunday, when she'd be joining them. As they were finishing talking to a few people, Vitus turned to find Florent Montague standing next to him. "A word in slightly more private, perhaps?" Florent nodded at a corner, currently clear of people.

"Of course, sir." Once they had moved there, Vitus waited, not sure what the man wanted.

"I had an opportunity to talk a little with my daughter yesterday. Sigbert, her nephew by marriage, was named Heir to his father." That part was not entirely unexpected, but it made Vitus wonder if that was what Thessaly had attended, or what she knew of it. Florent went on. "She mentioned that she and Dagobert were considering asking you to do some work for them. I didn't want you to feel awkward about it."

That was a kindness, because Vitus certainly did not to

draw the attention of anyone in that family in a dangerous way. "Given your own expertise, sir, I am surprised to be considered." Florent Montague was certainly competent. "I've enjoyed the conversations with Laudine about her own knowledge, actually, though she has mentioned her sister more than you directly."

"Ha." That seemed to amuse Florent. "In this case, I got the impression that it is not a problem she wished to bring to her father, that someone a little more distant from the situation might have a more useful perspective. Should it make sense, I am certainly glad to consult, but you bring a fresh line of thought to it. More creative than I usually run to, especially around materia choices. I think that's a fine thing. If we want the art of making talismans to improve, it is certainly necessary. Perhaps sometime, in a fortnight or two, say, we might have a drink or supper and talk more?"

That was a generous gesture, and the sort that could lead to referrals from Florent, for pieces he didn't want to take on. Naturally, Vitus was going to say yes. "I'd be delighted, sir. And for your daughter and her husband to join us, if you think they'd enjoy it."

"We will see." Florent looked pleased. "I'll send a note around. Where's the best place to send it?"

"Oh, yes." Vitus pulled out his calling card case and offered a card. "Those are my consulting rooms and workshop."

"Excellent. I'll look forward to it, absolutely. And now I see Niobe's waiting for you, I won't keep you. Congratulations, young man."

Vitus let Florent go first, and then rejoined Niobe. Once they'd made their own farewells and were out on the street, he offered her his arm. "Are you pleased?"

"Absolutely, and especially in how you handled yourself. I had several other inquiries about whether you'd be interested in private meetings. There will be notes in the coming days. Do come and discuss. I have a few ideas on several of the ones I expect you'll get."

Vitus smiled. "You're going to keep looking out for me, then."

"Oh, absolutely." Niobe snorted. "I intend to make sure we keep having tea regularly. Well, tea and gem cutting. Now, when we get back, tell me how that piece you were working on is going." Of course, they wouldn't discuss details on the street for all sorts of reasons. Vitus chuckled and instead asked her a few questions as they walked about what other gossip she'd heard recently.

4

OCTOBER 15TH AT BRYN GLAS

The next afternoon, Vitus came through the portal at Bryn Glas to find Thessaly waiting for him. She was still wearing the brightest clothes she could find, aggressively refusing to be in mourning for Childeric Fortier when at home. These suited her better than the last set. They were a vibrant medium blue with a robe over, open down the front with draping sleeves, of a blue-green silk embroidered with twists of waves.

It was noticeably cooler here, up in the north of Wales, than it had been in Trellech, down in the south. It was a sign of the fading of the autumn and the coming of the winter. Vitus knew that Snowdonia - looming to the east - often got a fair bit of snow. That name for it, from the Old English, meant 'snow hill' of course. Vitus had looked it up. Though he knew Thessaly preferred its Welsh name of Eryri. Either way, sunset was marching on, even though it was only quarter to five.

He held out his hands, and again, somehow, Thessaly flung herself into his arms. Vitus hugged her tightly, swinging her around once so he didn't topple over, before setting her down on her feet. "Glad to see me, then?"

It wasn't exactly that he thought she wasn't, but the reassurance mattered unreasonably to him right now. Thessaly beamed at him. "I have been pining all day. And hoping yesterday went well. It did, didn't it? You'd have told me if it didn't?"

Vitus grinned. "It went very well. I'd have sent a note, but I was at Niobe's until midnight, had an early client call, and it went from there. I want to tell you all about it. How are you doing?" She took his hand, tugging him along into the protections of the full wards. Her companion and bodyguard, Emeline, waited just inside the fence. As she had the past few times Vitus had visited, Emeline disappeared back across the lawn as soon as Thessaly closed the gate.

Instead of answering or following Emeline, Thessaly stopped. "Would you come out to the grove with me? I wanted to take the chance before it gets too cold. Or dark. We can go in and have tea after?"

"Of course." Vitus wasn't entirely sure what he was agreeing to. He'd seen only a limited part of the estate so far. "Inside the warding?"

"Oh, yes. Especially so. A different part of the warding, but I don't need to tell Emeline. This way." She tugged his hand, leading him off to the right of the house, through a different gate in the fence, and then down a long meadow. She had picked up her skirts with her free hand, obviously sure of her footing. "This is where I practise duelling, when the weather permits." Thessaly added it. "I'm thinking about what it would take to build a proper salle. But the ground slopes and there's the problem of someone to duel with and all the construction, and the wards. The barn's not big enough, really, it's long and narrow. We'd have to tear it down and rebuild."

Vitus was glad that she had ideas for the place of some kind. "You can think about it over the winter?" He wasn't sure what went into building a salle. Architecture was not his gift, other than knowing what was needed in his own workspaces, but he was fairly sure no one was going to start a major building project this far north so late in the calendar year. Magic could only do so much. At the end of this meadow, Thessaly kept going into a grove of trees. He could see a small orchard, what were probably apple trees, then the foliage got more dense. Thessaly went straight down the path in the middle, only stopping at a ring of trees.

She reached with her free hand to touch one of the tall trunks beside her, then nodded. "Here. I left a blanket down here. I was reading until you came." There was, in fact, a picnic blanket spread out in the centre. "This is why the house stays in the family. It's not a Fatae grove now, but it needs people paying a little attention to it. Just a little. And letting the Council know if there's a problem, promptly enough."

"Which wasn't a problem for your aunt, or did she live here before that?" Vitus wasn't at all sure of the timeline.

"She moved here the same year she challenged." Thessaly let go of his hand long enough to lower herself to the blanket and pat it. "Come sit, please? Tell me how it went. I want to hear all of it."

Vitus snorted. "I'm fairly sure you don't want to hear all the technical details, at least without enough light to see some of the sketches and diagrams that make them make sense." He settled into telling her about it, with enough specifics to make her happy. When he got to the end, the conversations after supper, he told her about Florent

Montague. Thessaly did a thing with her mouth that he was fairly sure meant she wasn't saying about six things.

He was never sure how far to press her and he didn't want to be clumsy about it. She'd had more than enough of that already. At the same time, he wanted to know what she was thinking. "Kiss for your thoughts?" It seemed more pleasant than a coin of whatever size.

That made her laugh and turn her toward him. "That's a fair trade." He didn't linger as much over the kiss as he might have in other circumstances. It was getting darker, especially under the trees, and if they were going to have a bit more of a romp together, like they had a fortnight ago, he was hoping for less in the way of clothing. That would be tedious outside even without the cold. He was not fond of grit in sensitive places.

"Sunday, when I'd rather have been with you, that was the announcement of Sigbert as the Fortier heir. It wasn't a large gathering, not by their standards, thirty people with the immediate family. I saw Florent and Aline Montague both, but not to talk to. Aline was mostly staying near Laudine." Thessaly pursed her lips. "They talked to me - Laudine and Dagobert - right at the end. After Henut Landry."

Thessaly got part way into the explanation of the conversation with Henut, before Vitus coughed. "Did that strike you as odd, then? What did she say?"

"At the time," Thessaly said, "I was nervous about our having been obvious. Though when I thought about it after, I don't think she meant any of the things about you as a threat. Not to us, anyway?"

"I feel like Henut Landry could make a simple 'good morning' into a threat any time she wanted to." Vitus said with some force. "I am grateful to her - the flat continues to be excellent, her easing the way was a gift. But I do not know what she wants." He hesitated, then added, "I returned a few sheets of paper that had slipped behind Philip's desk, but they did not seem to be more than ordinary notes on something he was reading."

"I have no idea either. Except that it pleased her to have someone want to remember Philip. It must be horrid for her, really. None of the Fortiers have been paying her much mind at all. Except maybe Laudine and Dagobert. She was different about them, said she wished them well. Or at least she wished Laudine well and did not wish Dagobert ill now that he's listening to his wife. As if maybe she did not have the same wish for the rest of them. She specifically told me not to consider Sigbert."

"And the rest of the family?" Vitus was trying to figure that out. "Laudine wasn't at the Challenge."

"Oh!" Thessaly shook her head once, a wisp of hair coming down. Vitus reached out to brush it back, almost instinctively, and she smiled at him. "She's expecting. It's very early yet, but no portal travel for her, unless it's entirely urgent."

Vitus blinked. "Not the sort of thing they generally tell unmarried and unrelated men. We are meant to sort it out by guesswork, I think, without ever commenting on it." It came out of his mouth before he could think of anything more sensible. "I hope that goes well, then. I suppose that's why her parents were more visible?"

"Probably," Thessaly agreed. "I'm envious of that. Probably? But Laudine seemed to appreciate them being there. It's the rest of it I don't know about."

Vitus thought about what Thessaly had said so far. "Henut warned you away from Sigbert. Did you need warning?" His voice got an odd note in it at the end, wrong somehow.

Thessaly twisted a bit, reaching to touch his cheek.

"Are you jealous? Are you worried you should be jealous? I don't really know how that works."

Vitus tried to look away, but her hand meant he really couldn't, not without making it much more of an issue. "Yes? No? I don't know. I don't much like feeling whatever this is."

"I find Sigbert - at least at the moment - definitely an improvement over Childeric. But Childeric was charming until we were betrothed, and I am not remotely inclined to make the same mistake twice. That is an exceedingly poor strategy." She met his eyes. "Certainly Sigbert is not who I've been waiting to see."

Vitus swallowed a little at that. "Part of me is very sure of that. Part of me might need some additional convincing, at some point. It's not that I don't trust you, it's that I don't - this is new to me too, mostly?"

"Also," Thessaly said, more softly. "Magistra Landry had opinions about people, and I am still trying to sort out what I think about that. Nothing in it adds up tidily, beyond Childeric having been— well. As he was." Then she nodded more decisively. "Right. In that case, shall we pack up the blanket and go inside, and up to my rooms, and— actually, there's something I'd like to show you? Talk about a little, not do anything with, not right away?"

"Now I'm intensely curious." Vitus liked the idea of more time with her, and in more comfortable seating. He pushed himself upright on one hand, then stood, before offering her his hands to help her up. A minute or two later, they had the blanket folded, and he tucked it under one arm. They walked back to the house not talking much. It was dark enough to need to pay attention to where their feet were going, even with a charmlight to help.

Once Thessaly had brought him upstairs, Vitus wasn't sure what to do with himself. "Sit, please." She waved him at the sofa. "Or could you pull that table over, in the middle, so I can put a book or two on it? How long can you stay?"

"I have an early consult tomorrow morning." Vitus said, regretfully. "An hour or so? I can get supper at home. Cook was putting something aside for me. My parents are out."

"This might be a little distracting. Are you sure?" Thessaly flushed, rather prettily.

Vitus watched her, tilting his head. "Now I'm entirely curious. What sort of distracting?"

She brought over two books, with little to show what was in them on the spine or cover, both larger. "The sort of distracting like two weeks ago. And I don't think we have time for too much more experimentation." She sucked in a breath. "Aunt Metaia made it clear to me, when we were talking, not long before she was killed, that she might not have married, but she wasn't an untouched maiden, either. I wondered if she had anything in her more private library, up here, that might..."

"Naughty books?" Vitus blinked. "Oh." He took a deep breath to steady himself, not that it helped. "And you found some?"

"Naughty books. Naughty pictures. They have given me some ideas." Thessaly settled down next to him. He was again suddenly aware of the fact she was not wearing any of the underpinnings beneath her tea gown that were a bit more like armour. He could feel her hip against his, then she leaned forward to open one book. The first pages were more or less innocuous, a man and woman sitting beside each other on a settee, much as he and she were right now.

Vitus said, before he could stop himself, "I have not found I needed a book for ideas. I've dreamt of you.

Waking and sleeping, though I suppose the one is more a fantasy than a dream." He'd permitted himself to indulge that fantasy at most once a day. There was far too little time in his life. And also, he found the idea of taking such things too far without her active encouragement to be a trifle uncomfortable.

"Have you, really?" Her hand moved, settling on his thigh, not entirely indelicate, but certainly tending that way. "I like that idea very much. I certainly have thought a fair bit about you. And the books encouraged me to, what's the word..."

"Explore yourself? Touch yourself?" Vitus could hear his breath catching.

"That." Thessaly said it precisely, though it was not at all prim. "Perhaps we might look and talk a little more about our respective desires, to give more shape, until we can find a proper time to enjoy them? When we can linger, no rushing."

"Please." It came out of him like a groan. The anticipation might well kill him, but it would be such a delightful way to go. As Thessaly slowly turned the pages, it became clear that she was interested in a great deal, much of which he had at least some experience with. She was unsure about anything that might cause discomfort, at least in a sense intended also for pleasure. But she was intrigued by the idea of charms for pleasure and sensation. And Vitus certainly had trained his skills at picking up enchantments cast with the fingers. Thessaly had as well.

The pictures - and the accompanying text - illustrated a range of positions. They seemed more or less agreed on which ones they wanted to try first. They both favoured those that allowed for freely moving hands and mouths and eyes— and those that didn't. There was also an entire category of positions that seemed likely to require flexibility and strength Vitus was not confident he could provide. Thessaly was more optimistic about that set.

"They do say duelling is good for a number of things. Not, of course, that the men discuss that where I can hear, and the women I've duelled don't either. Not while I'm unmarried, anyway. But there are whispers. I could consider that." It would take a lot of strength in her thighs, Vitus thought, to ride him that way.

"I would certainly be delighted to try it, in due course. Once we've done some simpler things." He slipped an arm around her waist, then. "And you were saying you wanted to pick up your duelling drills again."

"I did." Thessaly leaned her head against him, sounding contented. "Shall we save the other book for another time? I rather like just sitting here with you."

Vitus liked that very much as well, the weight of her body against his and the warmth of her. And there was the scent of the perfume or soap or whatever it was that scented her hair and skin. He would, in fact, like to stay here for approximately eternity, except that of course he had obligations. He cleared his throat, and asked what she was up to with the rest of the house, letting her talk about how she was moving things around. She didn't want to put things away, exactly, certainly she didn't want to repaint or put up new wallpaper. It was more a matter of rearranging books and art and other smaller furnishings.

When she walked him back out to the portal, she kissed him once more, taking her time. "We'll find time soon. Promise me?"

"Promise." It was the easiest promise he'd ever made.

5

OCTOBER 17TH AT BRYN GLAS

The next two days passed in a flurry. After Vitus left, Thessaly had found it impossible to sleep. It wasn't just the way she felt after looking at Aunt Metaia's books. She kept being drawn to an anticipation of a future in which she and Vitus would explore more things that intrigued her. New ways of using her body and her magic. Most importantly, doing that with someone she actually cared for.

No, it was everything else. Thessaly had remembered that conversation with Magistra Hereswith and Cousin Owain, what felt like years ago, about how they didn't know what Aunt Metaia had been working on. It wasn't as if Thessaly were going out in public right now. It was no matter to anyone else if she was up into the wee hours, or sleeping until noon. Not other than Collins and the other household staff, and she left them notes making it clear sandwiches or something that would hold well on a tray were just fine.

Two days later, on Thursday afternoon, she was running her hands through her hair when Collins came in.

"Reminding you, Mistress, that Council Member Powell intended to visit. In about an hour, if you want to wash up?"

Washing up was indeed probably a good idea. Her hair was tangling. She'd been into boxes in the storeroom, and was all over dust. Not that she expected to find anything current in them, but she had found some of the early records of Aunt Metaia's investments, and set those aside for later. Thessaly put her head up; she'd been working on the floor. "Oh. Thank you!" She stretched, hearing a crack in her neck. "Bath, yes. And I'll eat something while my hair's drying."

"I'll just come back in half an hour then, to help you put it up. Shall I put out mourning dress or something else?"

Thessaly looked down at the gown she was wearing - worn linen, suitable for storerooms - then back up at Collins. "Something more sedate, but not mourning, I think. One of the medium blue ones?" That did not specify a great deal, given Aunt Metaia's fondness for the colour. "And did I remember to tell you that Vitus will be by when he is done with his work?"

"You did remember that, Mistress. We were planning on supper at seven."

"Thank you." Thessaly divided what she had sorted into one empty box, covered both, and slid them out of the way by the shelves while Collins started the bath running. Five minutes later, she was undressed and in the bath. Twenty minutes later she felt clean and her hair was no longer powdered by dust. Terribly out of fashion these days, powdered hair. She was ready in good time to walk down to the portal with Emeline and meet Cousin Owain. She'd even had enough of a sandwich to hold her until supper. Collins and the other staff were being quite tolerant.

He was prompt, of course, and he nodded approvingly as Thessaly took the now-habitual precautions, showing him through into the library. Tea and biscuits were already waiting. Once they were settled, he looked her up and down. "I suppose I should begin with asking how you are feeling. Now, I have not heard scandal, so I assume you have not gone out like that." Cousin Owain lifted his fingers. "I do not disapprove, but I'm curious about your decisions here. And I do have a particular question."

"I am working privately on projects for my apprenticeship, at least until the new year." Thessaly said. That had been a relief on several levels, actually, and it certainly reduced the need to leave the estate. "The way I put it recently was that going out in public in deepest mourning, pretending I miss Childeric, would be the worst sort of lie. An insult to people who are actually in mourning. Mama, for example. Cyrus Smythe-Clive." She offered the second name deliberately.

Cousin Owain snorted softly. "I heard he spoke to you at the funeral. I hope that was all right?"

Thessaly nodded. "He was kind, I was as truthful as I could be in the circumstances, and— I don't think I hurt his feelings too badly?" Thessaly considered. "When it's been longer, November, perhaps, or early December, he offered an invitation to visit, and I'll likely take him up on it."

"Have you heard from your parents? About potential matches?" Cousin Owain turned his hand over. "It's not a non sequitur."

"Cyrus is now an eminent match, where a month ago, he absolutely wasn't." That was the sort of marriage market maths Thessaly had learned to do by the age of ten. "No, I haven't heard from them since we were at Arundel for the announcement of Sigbert as Heir, four days ago. All Mother said then was that Father was having conversations. I suppose I should see her sometime in private." Not that Thessaly much wanted to do that, and certainly not here, so it would mean sorting out something else. "Not unless Cyrus was utterly willing on the topic. I've no desire to try to fill Tanith's shoes. For one, I'd fail immediately, and besides..." She swallowed. "I liked her too."

Cousin Owain nodded. "And I can scarcely press you to marry without hypocrisy." He leaned back. "I was getting more of his measure yesterday, our regular meeting. And it brought up other topics. That was why I wanted to call."

"Oh?" There were probably a limited number of topics that might be relevant to Thessaly herself.

"The first matter is - you gave Childeric a favour, didn't you? Not that I saw it, but people noticed."

"Yes?" Thessaly said. "It held no enchantment. Tolerably competent embroidery." Something emboldened her enough to add, "A match for the betrothal ring he gave me. Symbols chosen with a particular point, but without investing more effort than the visible show. He did not invest magic in me, I did not in him." Even leaving aside what she'd felt by the point she'd realised she needed to offer some theoretically personal token for his Challenge.

"He did not have it on him when we found him." Cousin Owain's voice was softer, deliberate.

"I do not know what he did with it between when I gave it to him and, well." Thessaly's chin came up. "But if it helps, I will swear under the truth-telling charms that it was simply embroidery. And everyone knows embroidery is not one of my particular gifts, nor charmwork in that mode."

Cousin Owain snorted. "And some of us know you have gifts you don't show." Then he waved a hand. "I had to ask, I will report the answer back. You may hear some gossip about it. If it is bothersome, let me know and I will see about making suitable comments in the right ears."

"I appreciate that." Thessaly did, too. "You had other things to discuss?"

"Largely, what you have been doing with yourself, and what you wish to be doing with yourself. Your plans, such as they are." He shrugged, and while it was reassuring that someone in her family was taking an interest, she knew he was doing it at least partly for reasons of his own. And the Council's. That didn't actually change her answer, though.

"I have been looking, the past few days, for anything more about what Aunt Metaia was working on. I haven't found it yet, but I've only got through about a quarter of the possible places. Whatever it was, it wasn't anywhere entirely obvious, like her desk or the current files in her study."

"It's a house with a surprising number of bookshelves," Cousin Owain agreed. "And more upstairs, yes?"

"More in the sitting room upstairs, the study, a row outside her workroom, tucked against the wall, and there's an entire room for storage above the carriage house." Thessaly gestured back toward the boxes in the corner. "I plan to look in the sitting room more systematically tomorrow."

Cousin Owain nodded slowly, considering. Thessaly waited him out. This was a kind of duelling strategy she knew well. She would not waste her energy. She'd let him make a move and be ready to respond. He took a biscuit, a bit more tea, then spoke, his voice quiet and even. "The question is how much you wish to involve yourself. You have, other than Metaia, no reason to do so, not in whatever Council business this might be."

"And yet, I am involved. Because of Aunt Metaia. Because this is my home now. And even without the issues of the protections, you and every other person on the Council have far too much keeping you busy to go through books and boxes." Thessaly's chin came up. "Not that I'd permit a number of people access, of course."

Cousin Owain snorted at that, amused. "I yield, I yield." He put both hands up in the universal gesture among duellists of surrender of the field. "And no, you should permit no one access. There's also the question of who."

Something in how he said it made Thessaly look at him sharply. "You're exceedingly busy right now, aren't you? And that's not just Aunt Metaia, and Cyrus being new to the Council. It's other things as well."

Cousin Owain went slightly pale, but then he nodded once. "A number of problems with the land magic have become visible over the summer, more the last month or so. Individually, none of them are particularly significant, but taken together, they're quite worrisome. Training someone new in is always time consuming. And Hereswith wishes to do more of that directly, this time, which means finding other people to take on tasks she normally does. Me among them."

"She trusts you," Thessaly said, slowly. "Is that transitive trust, because of Aunt Metaia, or something else?"

"You are sharp." Cousin Owain was approving, if also a bit bemused now. "Both. Metaia and Hereswith were far closer– friends, not just colleagues. And Hereswith leans quite a lot on Oscar for anything requiring good sense and proportionate reaction. But my own preferences for Sympathetic magic make certain kinds of interconnections easier to work with. I'm taking more of that on, looking for links between the places that have problems. Much of it is rather tedious."

"And so you are both busy, and with things that you do not have as much familiarity with?" Thessaly asked, to confirm her understanding.

"Just so. And others on the Council as well. Thus, if we have hopes of finding anything, we must rely on you. What we were talking about in the meeting was what we did and didn't know about it. And I talked to Hereswith, this morning, about what she and I suspect, but didn't bring up."

"Are you going to tell me any specifics, or just gesture mysteriously?" Thessaly said, her voice just as even as his had been a few moments ago. "I assume you have other things to do with the evening. I have some plans of my own."

His eyebrow went up, but then he shifted to take a small notebook out of his inside jacket pocket, flipping it open. "Metaia mentioned that she was curious about something back in the spring. Neither of us could remember exactly when, but Bess pinned it down last week to the first week of April."

"After I was betrothed to Childeric, but before— before anything else." Thessaly thought back. "I was rather caught up in all the social obligations. People kept wanting us to come for supper."

"Did you notice anything around that time that might have suggested a concern?" Cousin Owain leaned to take another biscuit.

"I knew she was worried. And as I said, she talked to me about it directly, on the solstice, as we were getting ready." Thessaly had thought through this dozens of times before now. "Do you know why she changed her will when she did?"

Cousin Owain coughed. "Oh, well. You were her primary heir from the time you finished Schola, for what it's worth, though she rearranged some pieces. And she was already considering how to pass the house to you. As I said at the reading of the will, she argued for the right to name her successor ten years ago. Knowing you would go to Schola."

Thessaly swallowed. "I do love it. I was hating how someone would do something ordinary with it, take down all the wallpaper and the colours." She gestured at the patterns visible around the bookshelves. "I find it cheerful."

Cousin Owain nodded. "You should have as much cheerful as you wish. It is your home." He cleared his throat. "I was closer with Metaia than I think most of the family realised. There were certainly things she didn't tell Sioned."

Thessaly's chin came up sharply, because there was something in his tone. "You don't trust Mother, do you?"

There was a silence, then Cousin Owain's voice was delicate like a rapier. "You don't either."

"No. Not now." Thessaly would not attempt to lie. That was certainly the wrong way, here. She would twist and fall and lose all hope of balance. She carefully reached for her tea, took a sip, and then put the cup down. "And Aunt Metaia didn't."

"Also no. Not about a number of things." Cousin Owain paused for a moment. "It was not. How do I say this? It was not for any large reason. She trusted Sioned to be a good mother. Though I think Metaia had some doubts, the last month or two. But instead, it was a question of priorities. Family status, the proper breeding of the next generation, rather than happiness or a contribution to the greater whole of Albion."

Thessaly looked up at that. "The Council."

"The Council, but also many other roles. The Ministry, the Courts, the Guard and Penelopes, all the specialists who add their knowledge and skill to the world, coming up with new ways to improve things." Cousin Owain spread his hands. "I am curious what you will come up with, given the opportunity. On that point, as you are going through Metaia's notes, you might consider expanding your illusion work to some of what she was doing, protecting spaces. Romulus Heath is handling it for the moment, but we could use another person able to take on some of that. It's an ongoing process, maintaining them and creating new illusions. He would be glad to train you on that side of it once your apprenticeship is complete."

It was not something Thessaly had spoken of, other than briefly with Magistra Landry. "You don't think I should marry some appropriate scion and devote myself to producing children, do you?"

"If you wish to marry, and especially if you choose someone who makes you happy, and children follow, then I wish you whatever blessings in that realm you care for. But you are a clever young woman. You are magically skilled. It would be a shame for your talents to be limited to whatever the current fad is in party decoration or costume. Not that those things aren't lovely, but other skills are needed too."

She considered watching him for a moment. "The Council, you look as if everything is under control, and instead, you're all scrambling a bit, when no one's looking, aren't you?"

Cousin Owain laughed ruefully. "Yes. And the more so right now. When Cyrus settles into things, perhaps a little less. The changes, a new person, that always takes a little to understand, and this one more than most." He let out a breath. "Now, I should leave you to your papers and go home. I have an evening free for the first time in what seems like months, and I have a book I want to read."

Thessaly did not mention she expected another caller. She stood. "I'll walk you out, of course. Perhaps I might come and call sometime soon? I had a bit of embroidery to show Aunt Tegwen, one of the patterns she was curious about."

"We would like that quite a lot." They walked out to the fence and the portal with little further conversation. When he left, Thessaly retreated into the warding, with perhaps half an hour before Vitus was likely to appear. At the earliest.

6

OCTOBER 17TH AT BRYN GLAS

When Vitus came through the portal, Thessaly was there, waiting. He was a hair later than he'd wanted to be. He'd stopped in one of Trellech's bookstores on the way to Portal Square, to pick up two titles he thought she might like. Vitus held them up, tied up in paper and string. "Apologies for being a tad late, but I brought books?"

She came over to him, laughing, then tugged him along into the warding. "I do not need more books, but I am entirely curious."

Vitus did his part by refusing to tell her what they were until they were sitting down. This turned out to be in the library, with a table set up for eating. "If you don't mind eating down here, supper at seven?"

"Of course not. I am your guest. I should get home by, oh, nine? Niobe wanted me to consult on something in the morning, and I'll need my wits." Vitus looked at her, and offered a smile. "A delighted guest. Glad to enjoy whatever you offer." Then he blushed, because he had and hadn't meant that innuendo. He cleared his throat hurriedly. "You are less brightly coloured today?"

"Cousin Owain was here earlier, and I didn't know what he'd think about the more vibrant versions." Thessaly tilted her head. "I'd like to talk that out with you, actually. Do you mind?"

Vitus shook his head. "Of course not." The thing of it was, every time she trusted him like that, he fell in love with her a little more. Or it became a little more certain. It was like cutting a gem, the way tiny gestures, piece by piece, formed facet after facet. He felt falling in love was about working with the stone itself, the way it wanted to cleave and shape, and also about being delicate, not rushing anything. It was an excellent metaphor, and it meant, he hoped, that sometime he'd look and it would be there, blazing away for everyone to see. Undeniable.

Thessaly considered, then nestled in against him, as he moved his arm around her. Today, she wore no bustle, but she had put on a corset. Presumably so as not to scandalise her cousin entirely. It meant she was leaning, more than curled up against him, but they would manage well enough. He listened as she explained what sounded like a fair bit of the conversation.

"It's curious that your cousin said he doesn't trust your mother. Both parts. Not trusting and also telling you about it." Vitus was caught by that one.

"He also said nothing about you, when he might have. I'd not have answered, not right now." She twisted to look up at him. "I feel very private about you at the moment. Does that bother you?"

Vitus wanted to shout from the top of Snowdonia—or in Portal Square, there would be more people to hear there—that he loved Thessaly. But she was right, not just now. She was supposed to be in mourning. They had to behave properly in public. In due course, in five or six months, they could build what they wanted with other people seeing. "I did tell you Mama knows, didn't I?" He thought he had. But the times he'd seen her were still simultaneously precious and detailed in his memory on other nights, and sometimes jumbled.

"You did. That's different." Thessaly let out a soft breath. "You trust your mother. That part is very different." Before he could say anything, she added, "Mother is in a difficult position, and I understand that. But that doesn't mean I'm going to keep doing things for her benefit. I want to help Hermia, when I can, but Hermia doesn't know what she wants yet herself. Apprenticeship, maybe, but it would take the right thing. I'm sure Father is looking to make arrangements for her to marry."

"She could refuse now, yes?" Vitus was not entirely sure how that worked at this point.

"Technically, yes. Certainly, she can refuse particular matches, but—" Thessaly shook her head. "I keep coming back to what Cousin Owain said about using my skills. And what that means. Father's certainly looking for another match for me, even though I can refuse and keep refusing." Then she twisted, squeezing her hand. "Or make my own choice. If that—"

"If that." Vitus felt a lump in his throat. "If that goes how I hope."

She shifted enough to kiss him on the cheek, then leaned her head back. "I was thinking, after Cousin Owain left, about why they asked me. Why they'd think I'd be any help in the first place. The Council. They're scrambling, unsteady, he said as much. I can't imagine that I'll solve anything that all of them couldn't. A fair number of them being creative and intelligent and good at solving problems." Her voice changed. "Even if Aunt

Metaia was excellent at it, everyone said so. The creative part."

"It is curious. I'd have expected them not to say anything to anyone. Though I suppose if there is anything in the house, they'd need your help one way or another. You have found nothing at all?"

"Nothing I didn't already mostly expect? Whatever is here, it's going to be thoroughly hidden." Thessaly sighed, then said, "The other part is that everything that's happened, since, I feel like some of it is connected. But I have no idea what."

"Would it help to talk it out in order?" Vitus asked. "I can do that. We can do that together?" The together part was what he'd like.

"Together."

She said nothing more, so after another few moments, Vitus took a deep breath. "You became betrothed to Childeric in March, at the equinox. Between then and the summer solstice, she became concerned about the betrothal, and the way he treated you. Did she explain why? Did she see anything specific?"

Thessaly shivered, once. "She mentioned nothing specific. But there's the change in her will. There's how she talked about it, at the solstice. Something new happened, or she learned something. She must have."

"Did your Aunt Metaia have concerns about the Fortiers for any other reason besides Childeric? That's the part I can't make fit." Vitus considered. "Something she found out?"

"I suppose it's possible she found something out. That she was paying more attention to them because of the betrothal. And then spotted something else. I don't know what, though."

"And you don't know what— no, wait, we'll come back

to Dagobert in a minute. Then there's the summer solstice, and someone kills your aunt, and there's still no idea who or how. I mean, how they got her outside the warding."

"No. I can only assume it was someone she knew, someone she trusted enough? Or someone who set up an illusion, a cover, but she was cautious. Especially here."

"They'd have had to come through the portal, wouldn't they? And then around the far side, until they could come down by the road to the east?" Vitus had seen enough of the landscape now to fit that into place.

"Mmmhmm. And there's not much on that side, a few cottages. I can't imagine anyone would have come up the road, from the train. That takes ages."

"And she'd changed, so it wasn't something she noticed coming home, through the lawn." Vitus considered what you might hear from the grass. "The barn's in the way."

"The more you lay it out, the odder it is. As if she was meeting someone, but not by the portal, where it would be easy. And she went out of the warding."

Vitus nodded, moving to kiss her hair before turning his head back to keep talking. "And then Philip Landry turned up dead. There's nothing directly connecting the two things, and yet, it's suspicious, the timing."

"It is. But I can't imagine why he'd have wanted to hurt Aunt Metaia. Or why he'd do it like that." Thessaly shivered. She'd seen Aunt Metaia's body, just after they found her. She'd been on her back, as if someone had tended her, but her face had suggested she'd seen her death coming. Some form of magic, Thessaly had been told, but without any obvious signs of exactly what. Philip Landry was the most logical person to be involved, but it didn't answer anything at all.

"All the Fortiers left the Council rites rather suddenly," Vitus said. "Did Philip? I didn't see him after that, but you often didn't, even when he was there." There were plenty of smaller conversations in the side rooms, people making their own arrangements in varying ways. "And it was rather a crush, so many people around. Henut Landry and Alexander were still there when you noticed the Fortiers were gone, but I didn't see Philip. Mama didn't mention him." Vitus thought back to what she'd said. "That's a mystery, then."

"Does this bring us back to them?" Thessaly's voice quavered, and Vitus tucked an arm more securely around her.

"You don't enjoy talking about him, of course." Vitus wasn't at all sure how to weave his way through this. "Can you tell me why?"

"A few bad dreams." She hadn't really moved, but she somehow felt more distant. "About what he'd likely have done once we were married. Why now, I don't know. And just remembering. It wasn't, mostly, anything he said or did, not exactly. It was the look in his eyes. Controlling and expecting. Everything Aunt Metaia was worried about."

"She loved you very much." Vitus felt like it was a silly platitude, but it was also true, and maybe it would help to hear someone say it. "Should I keep going or do you want to stop?"

"We need to keep going. It will not get better, ignoring it." There was the stubbornness, that sounded better. "Childeric got worse. Sigbert stayed more or less reasonable, but he'd not stand up to Childeric. No one told me anything at all, except Laudine. I don't know, maybe that was Lady Chrodechildis's doing? She's still clearly the one directing the family. Only whatever's changed for Dagobert, that includes Laudine."

"And she left with the rest of them," Vitus noted. "What's different about Dagobert and Laudine? That's what I wonder? Other than they have told you some things, they have made overtures, you've said. And the fact Dagobert was hurt, somehow, right around that time."

"You'd said," Thessaly now twisted so she could look at him again, "that he'd been reading about electricity. And that Childeric's body, it had marks like lightning. I forget the name?"

"Lichtenberg marks." Vitus nodded. "Was there anything odd between solstice and Childeric's death? Other than Childeric being worse to you?"

"A lot of worse. There was that odd thing, them keeping me away from that corner of the property. But I didn't see any obvious reason." Thessaly frowned. "Is there a thing like a map of the estate in the Trellech Library, do you think? That would have buildings on it?"

"I suspect the Council has one, if you asked nicely for a copy," Vitus said. "I don't know about the library. I can ask, find a time when it's quiet. Why am I asking? I don't have anything like a good cause."

"You said Laudine was thinking about some talisman work. Could you ask them, I don't know what sounds right, but wanting to understand the geography so you could fit a piece better to that and their home in Essex? Or could you say you were working up a comparative study on the implications of local gemstones? And you wanted to compare several of the oldest and most stable demesne estates?"

Vitus felt his jaw drop. "You just came up with that, right in the moment?"

"Yessss?" It came out as a hiss at the end. "Is that a problem?"

"I have a lot of research I want to do now, but that is not actually a problem." Vitus pulled her closer to kiss her properly, taking a moment for it. "I'll ask something along those lines. And the paper will, I'm sure, be of interest.

Please, any more ideas like that." Then he cleared his throat. "And then the funeral was odd, but I think we're assuming that was the ordinary sort of odd, other people's customs?"

"Well." Thessaly considered. "Were you close enough to see Henut Landry at the funeral?"

Vitus shook his head. "Not as close as you were. What I saw was that she didn't take a bee from the basket, but tossed something in, something she already had in her hand. The Fortiers didn't like that much, but they didn't stop her."

"It was a bee, but it was gold. And yes, she had it in her hand before she came to the grave." Thessaly wriggled closer against him. "I saw a flash of gold. But it's gold for the men, silver for the women of the family, copper for everyone else. Traditionally." She added a sour, "Laudine explained that to me, of course no one else did."

Vitus nodded slowly. "That part, definitely particularly odd. But I do not think it is the sort of thing we could reasonably ask Magistra Landry about. Was that the only unexpected thing, then?"

"I think so? I'll think about it more. It was just all rather awful, and I wasn't sleeping much, and everything sort of blurred." Thessaly let out a huff of breath. "That all is better laid out, but I don't think it gets us any closer to understanding any of it."

"No." Vitus heard the rattle of the door and a knock. "You see what you can find here, and I'll think about the electricity side and the land. Is that supper?"

Thessaly glanced at the clock over the fireplace. "It is. Come in?" She called out, pitching her voice to carry, and moving away a little. "Thank you, Collins. The table would be lovely. It smells wonderful."

Vitus let her, not at all sure how much she was comfortable with the staff seeing, though they must know. After all, he and she had been alone together for several hours now, entirely unchaperoned. Once the table was set, he held her chair. They spent the meal talking about less dire topics. The conversation ranged from some of his recent work with stones to something she'd been reading about stabilising illusions.

7

OCTOBER 19TH AT ARUNDEL

"Thessaly, my dear, will you come walk in the garden with me?" Thessaly turned from where she'd been sipping a cup of tea. She had been invited out to Arundel again, for yet another obligation of mourning.

This marked a month since Childeric's death. Today, the mirrors were uncovered, and the household returned to something like its ordinary function. There had been offerings down at the cemetery, a solemn procession filled with far too many hothouse lilies and more seasonal chrysanthemums. Thessaly had carefully dodged anyone adding wisteria to the flowers she left. That meant purity and true love. She refused to lie like that, even with flowers.

Thessaly had helped clear the previous flowers, and to lay down the fresh ones, however. She wanted to detach herself from the Fortiers as best she could. But she did not see a reason to make enemies if it weren't actually necessary. And whatever she felt about Childeric, his mother had loved him.

Now, Thessaly set the cup down. "Of course, Lady Maylis." She waited for the older woman to precede her, and a minute or three later, they were out on the garden paths. It was getting a little brisk, but not actually cold. Thessaly would far rather be at Bryn Glas, but she should be able to make a polite escape before tea time. There was something still nagging her about why she couldn't find Aunt Metaia's working papers, the notes to whatever she had been worried about.

It was clear to Thessaly that Lady Maylis had something specific in mind. The others of the immediate family were well away. Lord Clovis was talking to his brother-in-law. Laudine and Dagobert were by themselves. Bradamante and her daughters were talking quietly in a corner with her mother. Thessaly did not actually know where Sigbert had gone, or Garin. Though Garin had probably found a place to sit and read a book, or something else that would not attract too much attention.

"Thessaly, my dear." They'd just entered the formal gardens when Lady Maylis spoke. "It has been such a help to have you here, to have you joining us for our customs. I hope they have been of some comfort to you."

Mostly, they had been uncomfortable. Emotionally, physically, usually both at the same time, with a side of decidedly awkward. Thessaly cleared her throat. "They go back a long way. I am glad you have such a respect for them." She was, at this point, wanting some of her own family customs. That would come on All Hallow's in another fortnight. She tucked that thought away for later as well. "If my presence has eased anything for you, I'm glad I came."

"We had such hopes for him. For both of you, for the children you'd have. For his place in the world, I was certain that— well. Whatever childish foibles would have fallen away, like a shed dragon scale." It was a curious metaphor, that, since a lost scale in lore also suggested the place a dragon might be vulnerable. "I know that some of how he went about things was confusing to you."

Upsetting, confusing, those were two possible words. She could think of quite a number of others. Perhaps some night she would work her way through an alphabet, playing a game like the parson's cat. The parson's cat was an aggravating cat. The parson's cat was a belligerent cat. The parson's cat was a conniving cat. Yes, she would be playing some rounds of that in the future.

Unfortunately, it meant she'd missed a reply. She coughed, murmuring a pardon, before she managed, "Very confusing. I always felt at least a step behind, not at all what I wanted." For all sorts of reasons, both her own comfort but also that it was impossible to attempt to match someone who hoarded information like a dragon. The parson's cat was a draconic cat.

"Ah." That single syllable was near impossible to read. The parson's cat was an exasperating cat. "I was wondering if you would consider something. Will you hear me out?"

Thessaly felt she didn't really have a great deal of choice in the matter. Turning and fleeing would be rude, and also a sign of weakness. And on a purely tactical level, she was fairly certain she couldn't get to the portal without someone stopping her. She turned, glimpsing someone who'd been walking along behind the hedge, dividing the formal garden from the alchemical one. By the height and shape, she thought it might be Sigbert, whoever it was moved too freely to be Dagobert.

"Of course, Lady Maylis." Thessaly turned, slightly, to focus on the conversation, and Lady Maylis paused. They were standing near a gap in the hedge behind her and a gate leading into the poison garden.

Lady Maylis gathered herself, rather literally. She

picked up her skirts and rearranged them, the sort of movement every woman of breeding - and bustled skirts - did a hundred times a day. Now, though, it was a point of punctuation. The parson's cat was a fastidious cat. The parson's cat was a guarded cat, the way she gathered her power around her. It put Thessaly entirely on edge.

"Have you given any thought to your future, your plans for your life?" It made Thessaly cautious, even more so than she had been. The parson's cat was a harrowing cat.

"First, to finish my apprenticeship, in due course. I have some projects to work on privately for a few months, likely until the new year. I have not wanted to be out in public, even for that. Anything else is, well. It feels far beyond me."

"I wondered— Clovis and I wondered— if you had considered certain options for your future. Your father has inquired about that, on your behalf." Lady Maylis waited a moment. "Would you consider transferring the marriage agreements to Sigbert? The marriage to happen in due course, a long betrothal, suitable for a proper period of mourning."

Thessaly gaped. She had not expected this. She ought to have expected this. It was exactly the high-handedness she had come to expect. She could feel her heart beating fast and she felt faint. The parson's cat was an indecent cat, the parson's cat was a joyless cat, the parson's cat was a, was a... Her mind stalled before supplying the word 'knavish' as a reasonable option.

She frantically gathered her wits. "I had not considered it, Lady Maylis, not at all." She could still hear her heartbeat thumping. She was about to ask something else, then she saw the figure behind the hedge emerge, looking stunned and flushing beet red. That was definitely Sigbert. It gave Thessaly a direction, at least. "Have you discussed it with Sigbert, Lady Maylis? Or anyone else besides Lord Clovis?"

"Not yet." Lady Maylis sounded utterly autocratic. "It would suit your father."

Sigbert was, as she had recently said, an improvement on Childeric, though she did not know how Sigbert might change if he were actually betrothed. Thessaly took a deep breath, watching Sigbert past his mother's shoulder, then looking back at Lady Maylis before her attention could be drawn there. "I truly had not considered it. My situation has changed in several respects."

First, there was Vitus, and if she could arrange it, she vastly preferred him. "And my understanding, from my trustee, is that any future marriage agreements would need to be written with my current considerations in mind." Not least that she would want to write free access for herself to Bryn Glas into the agreements. Also, a preservation of her rights, property, and obligations to it. "I am not declining, but I am not agreeing, Lady Maylis, if that gives you answer enough for the moment." Turning Sigbert down now seemed too dangerous to risk, honestly.

Lady Maylis pursed her lips. The parson's cat was a lamentable cat. Also limited. Then she nodded her head, just once. "Do check with your, what was the word, trustee, if you would, and determine what would be necessary. We will discuss it again. We would be glad to invite you out again, of course, so you might spend time with Sigbert on the estate." Not in public, of course not, given the state of mourning. "Or you could invite him to Bryn Glas."

"I will be glad to consider whatever invitations you offer." Thessaly swallowed, feeling sick to her stomach. "Please, if you don't mind, I'd like some time to think about what you've said." Now, and ongoing, she hoped that came across, but she was sure Lady Maylis would follow her own sense of time.

"As you wish. I shall go back inside, then, and let you think out here. We will have tea in half an hour. If you see Sigbert, do remind him." She turned, picking up her skirts and walking back down the long path, disappearing into the distance. Sigbert had moved out of the line of sight as they'd finished talking.

Thessaly waited until Lady Maylis was no longer gone, and then commented to the hedge, "I can't see her any longer."

The gate creaked and then clicked closed. Sigbert cleared his throat. "I had no idea." Then he tried again, his voice dropping half an octave, as he tried to sound more in control. "Do you hate the notion, then?"

That put the onus on her to respond. "That's not how I'd put it." She turned to face him, mostly so she could get as much information as possible from his expression. "I am startled that your mother would ask, here and now. I honestly am not sure what I think."

"Childeric did not give you much cause to want to continue with the family." Sigbert's voice was quieter now. "I'd do better."

It would take some effort to do worse, honestly. Thessaly did not say that. She had more sense. It was correct, but saying it would be unkind, especially on these lands. She considered, then said, "It's the sort of thing I'd want to talk out in detail before even considering rewriting the agreements. And I can't imagine doing that for a little while yet." Then she caught something in his expression. "What do you think about it?"

"I knew Maman was going to make a match for me. And there aren't terribly many choices she'll approve of." Sigbert shrugged. "Genevieve Donovan can't marry yet.

Septima Palgrave is betrothed, Winifred Hastings and I wouldn't do at all well together, Maman won't consider Felicia Roberts or Alethea Witham. And there are some concerns about whether Rosanna Hedgeworth is healthy. Idonnea Marchant, maybe, but Maman would see that as marrying down."

Thessaly quite liked Idonnea Marchant, so she wouldn't wish Lady Maylis on her. "And on my end, the other Heirs right now are promised or not ready to marry. Jupiter Delwyn. I know there's been some gossip about how Cyrus Smythe-Clive is more eligible now than he had been."

Sigbert nodded. "We're both in an uncomfortable position that way." Thessaly did not agree with him on that point, but she would not argue about it. He went on with a certain earnestness that seemed sincere. "I know you. I know what to expect. I think we could do well together, if we chose to."

That was an interesting phrasing indeed. Thessaly inclined her head, just slightly. "As I said— you did hear all of it?" Sigbert nodded. "I am not saying no. I am not saying yes. I will consider it. We can talk more about your expectations at some point."

Sigbert nodded, then let out a soft sigh. "I don't entirely know what to do. Maman and Father need me to marry. They'd far rather not have the land magic pass to Uncle Dagobert, or to Garin."

"And your aunt married out, not thinking it might be relevant." She was well and truly tied into the Nevill's magics now, whatever they were.

"Exactly." Sigbert rubbed his nose. "May I be a tad indelicate?"

"Yes." Thessaly steadied herself.

"There is, of course, the obligation to have children, or

at least do our utmost. But I would not prevail upon you beyond that. I would understand if you wanted your own life, your own spaces." He did not come out and say 'other people', but it was hanging there. It made her wonder about his own arrangements, whatever form they took.

Thessaly inclined her head. "I appreciate you stating that."

"I know your agreements with Childeric made allowances. I wouldn't object, as long as it was handled with discretion." He offered that directly, now, and the fact he had made her think a hair better of him.

"Childeric said that, originally." And they both knew how that had gone, at the first hint that Thessaly was considering even a conversation in private with another man. "We can talk. Now, you'd best escort me in to tea. Simplest way to go forward, don't you think?"

She did not give him much choice in the matter, really. Having them come in almost at the same moment would be awkward. He offered his arm, and they walked back in near silence.

8

OCTOBER 24TH AT THE FOUR METALS IN TRELLECH

Vitus had something of a headache, but he'd been determined to make it tonight. He'd hoped to see Thessaly yesterday, but she'd sent a note saying she wasn't feeling well. That, he worried about, far above and beyond his own discomfort. She'd asked if he'd make himself free the evening of the thirty-first. There were family traditions she'd like company for, the sort that took all night. He was hanging onto that.

In between now and then, he was going to be busy. He had appointments with two potential clients tomorrow, both in the afternoon. He had three more the following week, and he'd have to find time to look for specific stones before two of them. And he was working on half a dozen routine pieces. Some were intended for sale from Niobe's workshop, some were to begin to build up stock for himself, examples of the range of his work.

He'd taken time tonight to come out to the Four Metals clubhouse for conversation, though. The lecture from Wednesday night still had Vitus thinking, and he could use some help sorting out what he thought. Now, he let the chat around him flow through his ears, half-listening to see what caught his attention.

"Something to nibble on, Vitus?" Someone nudged a plate of finger food onto the table next to him. He looked up to see Philemon Hollington. He'd got to know Philemon better over the last two and a half months, working together on their exploratory research. It hadn't produced particular results yet, but they'd made some progress. And they'd only had three more meetings in that time, which was not precise enough to solve a complicated problem.

"Thank you, Philemon." Vitus made sure to smile, even though he was still distracted by his thoughts. Philemon claimed the chair next to Vitus, stretching out his legs. Vitus glanced over. "You waiting for someone?"

"Daedalus said he'd be along, and I had a question. Were you at the lecture last night?" Philemon reached out, taking a bit of cheese applied to a cracker.

"I was. I followed maybe half of it." Vitus looked up to see Thirza Remmerton come in, and she took the chair opposite, making a nice little conversation group. "Are we somehow expecting Merryn or Amayas as well? I wasn't thinking to see either of you tonight."

"We must maintain a reputation for unpredictability," Thirza said cheerfully enough. "We suspected you'd be here. You often are on a Thursday."

He had settled into that habit, hadn't he? Wednesday and Friday he went to the lectures and then here or out to a pub to talk about it after. Thursday he was often here, some Saturdays he was doing exploratory work with the five of them. Sundays were at home, so he could see Lucas. Monday or Tuesday was for Thessaly. Though if she asked, he'd make whatever nights she wished available for her. "Not next week, though."

"Plans?" Thirza nodded at one of the staff, who'd brought her a drink and a plate with a sandwich of some kind.

"All Hallows." Vitus hesitated, glancing around to see who else was within earshot. "Thessaly asked if I'd join her for her own remembrance."

"Ah." Thirza let out a soft sigh. "I'm glad to know she's planning on it. Have you told her about the Four Metals, or about our own customs there?"

Vitus shook his head. "Not either. I might well next week. It hasn't been the right moment. I know she's going to the family estate in the afternoon, whatever they do there."

"Metaia told me a little about their customs. Reflective, more than anything else, quiet. Not raucous, but not walling themselves away from the emotion, either. A bonfire's customary, if there's space for one, if that is any help in what you want to bring."

"It is, thank you." Before Vitus could say more, there was the sound of two others coming in. Vitus glanced over his shoulder to find Daedalus Briggs and a woman he didn't know. She was dressed in a plain blue dress, a harder-wearing cotton than Thirza's gown.

"Vitus, I don't think you know Claire Weatherby. She also has an interest in machinery, steam engines in particular, but other applications as well." Daedalus waved a hand and took half the sofa across from them. "What were we discussing?"

"I'm Vitus Deschamps. Talisman maker. Pleased to meet you." Daedalus could not be trusted to do thorough introductions.

Thirza snorted. "And we were waiting for you, for our topic, so there we are." She waited a moment, then went on. "We had a question for you and also Claire, Daedalus thought you might have some thoughts. We've been doing some work on circuits and systems, using magical principles but drawing from some of the work on electricity. Daedalus thought you might be interested?"

Claire shrugged. "Possibly. What sort of thing were you working on?"

There was a pause and Vitus realised they were waiting on him. "The thing I was thinking about yesterday was about the interactions. That bit about a Faraday cage. I've come across it in reading, but I don't quite understand it."

Claire and Daedalus both began talking at once, and Daedalus laughed and gestured. "Guests first."

"Certainly not a lady," Claire said, though in fairly good humour. She added to Vitus and the others, her tone explanatory, not defensive. "I went to Dunwich, my father's a train engineer. That's how I got interested in steam engines. The Four Metals brought me in during my apprenticeship." That explained a fair bit, from the accent to her clothing. "You've been doing some work with the flow of electricity, all right, where I do I start? You understand that electricity flows through wires, or whatever material, but that it also creates fields around it, yes? Actions we can only see by the movement of things in the field."

All of them nodded, though Vitus thought he was one of the more confident about the effect.

Claire went on. "A Faraday cage - named for Michael Faraday - allows you to block those fields. The demonstration last night, of placing an item, with some light metal trailing from it, near a generator, and then repeating the experiment with the cage."

Philemon cleared his throat. "Why would you care about that?"

"Well, for one thing, if you have sensitive materials you

want to protect from those fields, you could keep them in a space that would not be affected by them. You can make them whatever size you can get the materials for. It was the size of a breadbox last night. But if you can get the mesh, you could make an entire room like that. Sometimes it's, oh, half a room, so you have space to generate the fields, but also space where they are blocked. And of course, if they are coming from a generator, you have control over when the fields are in play."

"And you might also not want to be standing in a room generating a field - it'd be like standing outside in a storm," Thirza said.

"Exactly. But if you can set up a switch so you can pull a cord or some such. Then you can turn it on and off. Or you have a generator controlled by someone on the other side of the wall, or— well, there are various setups possible."

Vitus frowned, trying to remember something, and he lost track of the conversation for a sentence or three. Then everything went silent, and he looked up, blinking owlishly.

"Where did we lose you, Vitus?" Thirza didn't sound upset. Rather, she sounded curious.

"I was trying to remember something. Can I run something by you, Claire? From first principles?"

"Certainly." Claire leaned back, then paused to snag some of the food from Daedalus's plate. They were obviously comfortable with each other. He guessed probably not romantically involved, but Vitus wasn't sure, and besides, that was not the question of the moment.

"A while back, I'd have to check my notes at home, but at the end of May, the beginning of June?" He considered. No, he'd seen Thessaly on the first of June at the Temple of Healing garden party. The conversation had been just before. "End of May. I overheard a conversation at the

Stream— Salmon House club." He added the last for Claire's benefit.

"I know people there. I've been inside, even. Very yellow, and those curtains! The paisley is an insult to the eyes." Claire took it in good humour at least. "And?"

"Four people, all a bit older than me, were doing work on a project. I don't think they've published yet. I was keeping an eye out, but I can check. Olivia and Oscar Hemmings, they're twins, and, um." He fumbled for the other two names. "Marius Collins and Aline Holder. A mix of skills, Holder does enchantments, I've talked to her a few more times since. They were working on a device to detect poisons in the water from industrial processes, the kind of thing that damages the land. Terribly useful, if they can get it to work reliably."

The inhale of breath around their circle of chairs made it clear everyone else had figured that out as well. "And?" Philemon was leaning forward, listening intently.

"Their trials had been going smoothly," Vitus said. "But they'd just come back from a day of readings, and they'd had problems. They'd already tested in Sheffield, where there were plenty of factories, in London, on Schola island, so they had data from a range of points."

"And ranges of magic, quite." Thirza was frowning.

"Anyway, I'd have to check where they'd been working." Vitus knew, he remembered, but he didn't want to say it out loud, not without thinking through the consequences. Not without talking to Thessaly about it, either. She might have a number of more thoughts. They'd been out near Arundel, that was the thing. "Anyway, their readings were all over the place. I thought at the time it might be something about the geology, but could a Faraday cage or something like it have caused the same sort of effect?"

"What do you remember about what they said?" Claire was looking entirely thoughtful.

"They said they went haywire. I wondered if it could be a portal opening nearby right as they were testing, but I don't know."

"I suppose it could be something like that," Claire said. "It would be a subsidiary effect, something in a chain. You make the cage around the thing you're protecting, after all, and if they were out on open ground, it couldn't be a cage. But if someone were exploring the concept and were doing things outside the cage to test the effects in the cage? I suppose. Especially if it's magic and not electricity. Electricity wants to find a ground, fundamentally, even if what it chooses is dangerous. Magic will pool and wander and do any number of other things instead."

Vitus nodded. "Should I see about getting in touch with them? The Hemmings, in particular, that kind of problem solving is a lot of what they do, informally or more formally."

"If it's not a bother." Thirza was the eldest of them, most senior, though she and Merryn had been sharing some of the organisational responsibility between them. "I'm curious now. And it's possible the Hemmings or someone they know might have ideas for our project. I'm not opposed to bringing a couple more people in, or at least sharing. Whatever applications we want to take away from it will be individual in our respective fields. We don't need to hoard the understanding."

Vitus considered that. "You think that the individual quality we bring, as crafters, as specialists, makes a monopoly on the basic idea foolish?"

"Just so," Thirza said, pleased. "And after all, the Four Metals want to share how to do more things. And that goes well enough with Salmon House, I would think."

"Does Seal hoard information?" Vitus said, cheerfully, knowing her own house.

"Seal likes our secrets, but we share the ones that it makes sense to share. And this isn't a secret, it's practices we haven't worked out yet." She shrugged. "Vitus, if you'd be willing, gathering more information would be a help. And we can certainly run to treating them to a meal somewhere for a discussion, if that's a lure."

"I'll ask. And check my notes." Vitus said. "It might be a little, what with, well." All Hallows or whatever other obligations people might have, it was one of those fortnights when people were busy or recovering from the strain of it.

"Oh, that's fine. Sometime in November would do, I think, quite nicely." Thirza nodded. "Claire, can we go back to what you were saying about linking engines together?"

That conversation was also of interest to their work, but was much less unsettling to Vitus. He mostly let the others talk, asking a question here or there. By the time they wrapped up, he'd eaten all of his supper. And he had several pages of notes and further references to explore. Mostly, he was still thinking about whether there was anything at Arundel that was acting like a Faraday cage.

9

OCTOBER 31ST ON A WELSH MOUNTAINSIDE

They had been sitting up on the side of a mountain for perhaps thirty minutes. She'd been set up here since she got back from the Powell estate, around four that afternoon. Emeline had gone down to meet Vitus at the portal, and to walk back up with him.

Thessaly had curled up with the stone to her back. Something, despite the cold and chill, had been utterly reassuring. Out here, there were just the elements. Rock and scrubby brush did for earth. There was a bonfire in front of her, for fire. A few of the hollows she could see held little bits of water from the most recent rain. And there was absolutely a good stiff breeze for air. Being here, with all of that, together, helped much more than she'd expected.

And she'd needed the help. She wasn't far from Bryn Glas, though it depended on how she counted the distance. Horizontally, only about three quarters of a mile. Climbing added rather a lot of effort, especially as Thessaly had dressed for warmth. She had on long silk stockings, two layers of ritual robes, and the most encompassing cloak in the house. That had been Aunt Metaia's, kept for occasions like this. It had pockets, and down in the bottom, Thessaly had found a handkerchief - clean - and a note that Thessaly herself had passed to her two years ago.

She hadn't stopped crying since.

Vitus and Emeline had come up the path. Emeline had looked unsure what to do, and Vitus had just sat down, offered his shoulder, and hadn't asked. At least Thessaly had managed to get things set up before completely losing any grip on herself. They were sitting on multiple layers of folded wool blankets, charmed to stay warm through the night. The bonfire was going well; she'd started it right at sunset. And there were half a dozen protective charms around the bit of ground they'd claimed for this.

There likely wasn't too much to be worried about. The local wildlife would either avoid people or could be kept out, at least if she remembered to do the goat-repelling charms, which she had. They weren't so much goat-repelling as encouraging the goats to be attracted elsewhere, and those had been set yesterday and wouldn't wear off for another four days. Maybe five. The mountain ponies would avoid a fire, being more sensible, and the badger sett she knew about was lower on the mountain.

And while the lore held with all sorts of wandering spirits - the tailless black sow, or the white lady without a head - they would stay well away from the fire. That was why this vigil required commitment. Being at home was one thing, being by the bonfire was another, both safe enough as long as everyone stayed put. Travelling from one to the other, however, that could be a problem.

Now, Thessaly sniffled, and rummaged for that handkerchief, since it was easier to get at than the ones she'd put in her bag. "Sorry."

Vitus cleared his throat. "You've nothing to apologise for."

"I didn't even explain." Thessaly hadn't, really, beyond what he ought to wear and bring with him. He deserved better, and she certainly did not want to pick up that abysmal habit from the Fortiers. They'd had to do it by letter, and that made her somehow oddly reticent. She'd like to be the sort of person who wrote long, thoughtful, romantic letters. It turned out that even on a good day, she was the sort of person who remembered to say he wanted warm socks, but who couldn't come up with poetical descriptions of a day, a desire, or her beloved's face. Not in words, anyway. She could do it in images, often enough, that was the illusion work. And perhaps having something in front of her, not purely held in the mind.

She sniffled again, and Vitus shrugged. "You told me enough. That we'd be out here all night, with the bonfire. The rest of it can wait until you want to tell me." He hesitated, then he asked, more carefully, "Was it rough this afternoon, then?"

Thessaly nodded a couple of times. He didn't push more, just turned away to the picnic basket Thessaly and Emeline had brought up that afternoon. He pulled out one of the flasks, charmed to stay warm, and offered it to her. She took it, fumbled opening it, then pulled off her gloves and tried again. That time worked better, and she poured out some tea into the cup that covered the top. Then she curled her hands around it, taking a cautious sip. Once she'd had about half of it, she offered the cup to him, and he took it.

"This afternoon was all formal. It, at least it was about Aunt Metaia, not Childeric? I mean, actually missing her." That made her feel in the pocket again. "Before you got up here, I found a note in the pocket. The cloak was hers. It was something I'd passed her two years ago. Also at All Hallows. And I just—"

"Of course you did." Vitus considered, letting the quiet just be, not speaking for maybe a minute. "My grandmother— Mama's mother— she died about five years ago. And it hurt so much, then, every time I wanted to tell her something. She'd lived with us. I spent a lot of time with her."

Thessaly blinked at him. "Oh." She then added, promptly, "I'm sorry for your loss. What was she like?"

"A bit like Niobe will be in fifty or sixty years? Only not about talismans. She did embroidery and that kind of detailed sewing. Enchantments on cloth. Sometimes it was, I don't know, a blessing for a handkerchief. Sometimes it was protective enchantments, though mostly she collaborated with someone else for that. Can I look at the cloak, the hem of it, for a minute?"

That was not a question Thessaly had expected. "If you like? There's plenty of hem." A rather extravagant amount of it, in fact. She wriggled a little. "Here, there's the bottom corner."

Vitus nodded, and there was plenty to let him pull it up toward him. The fire was bright enough they could see fairly well, or at least Thessaly assumed he could as well. He peered at it, turning it in his hands, then nodded. "See, there? I don't know what all of it does, but those are embroideries. That one is for warmth. That's sensible for a cloak. That one for keeping out the damp. I think all our clothes as children had both."

"Was she the sort that thought you needed to be wrapped up against every possible chill?" Thessaly asked. "Nanny was."

"Yes, like that. But she trusted her own charms, and that was easier, mostly?" Vitus smiled a little. "I was thinking, this week, what she'd think of me. Many things."

"Did she approve of the talisman making? That must have been when you were well into your apprenticeship." Thessaly tried to do the maths in her head, she knew he'd told her.

"Mmhmm. I'd got through the early stages. We were starting to talk about whether I could do a trip to Europe. Seeing where the stones come from matters, as well as meeting all the people who do different work. Niobe's a wonder, but she also thinks it's important to see how people who aren't her do things. If— when, I suppose— I take apprentices, I want to do the same thing."

There were about ten questions Thessaly wanted to ask now, but she made herself focus. "And your grandmother?"

"She left some money. Enough that we could make it work, not a lot in absolute terms? But that's all right. I sort of enjoyed living with whatever family in the trade had a spare room and needed a little extra coin. It was certainly far more interesting than a hotel would be. Learning all about the food." He hesitated, and then added, "Perhaps sometime I can show you some of that."

"I'd like that." It slipped out of her mouth before she could handle it like a Fox should, hedging the question a bit. She would love to travel with Vitus, she would love to do many things with Vitus. Only, the past had a grip on her, and the present was complicated, and who knew what that meant about the future. She swallowed, then said, "What else do you want?"

Vitus gestured at the fire. "We don't need to talk about this now. I don't know if you have customs about that."

"This is about remembering, and that's the past. But it's also a liminal time. A hinge in the year." Thessaly considered. "The Welsh for it is Nos Galan Gaeaf, the night before the first day of winter. A spirit night, that's ysbrydnos."

"So, should I hear voices calling from the dark? Don't go to them." Vitus wasn't flippant, but he said it a little lightly and Thessaly flinched. He took a breath. "Not a thing to tease about, no. And I paid attention in Ritual class and Protective magics, to that kind of thing."

"We've protections. And we're a good way from any of the places that lore worries about. Cemeteries or crossroads. But Gwyn ap Nudd might ride with his hounds, something of the kind." She added, quickly. "Emeline and I did the protections earlier. All the traditional ones, and some other practical ones."

Vitus twisted to take her free hand in his, setting the flask between his knees. "Thessaly, I trust you'll keep me safe. For one thing, you're a much better duellist than I am. For another, this is land you know and I don't."

"That doesn't bother you?" She had so many things she wanted to ask him. Now they had time. They were absolutely not going to be interrupted until dawn, but that particular question was now right there, in front of her.

"No." He rearranged the flask so it was less likely to topple. "Give me a minute to figure out how to put that. Tell me about what we're doing here."

"We're remembering. We're talking. If we see something, like a shape in the distance, or hear something, pay attention to it, but don't go to it. It might be an omen. I'm not skilled at divination, but if you wanted to do some, we could try. I brought nuts. I've learned enough about reading what they do when they're tossed into the fire. It's thinking about those we've lost, recent and not so recent, and what that means for the future. How we go into the winter, I guess. We keep the bonfire going until dawn." She glanced over at him. "I haven't ever done it on my own before, but I know how it goes."

"With your aunt and your mother?" Vitus asked.

"Not Father, no. Different customs there. And with some of the other Powell relatives. We'd go up there, sometimes, though once Aunt Metaia had this house, usually she and Mother and a few of the cousins would be here."

"So this is, it's not just a custom you're keeping. It's in the same place. All right." Vitus considered. "And at least one of us should stay awake, which really means probably both of us."

"It's not very kind to leave one person having to tend the fire, no. If there were a lot of us, it'd be different. We could take turns."

"Well. We'll manage then," Vitus said, a certain note of stubbornness in his voice.

"Also," Thessaly said, "I'd rather not take them, but I brought potions for that, for both of us." She tried to keep the reason out of her voice, but Vitus noticed it. Why wouldn't he? It was rather obvious.

"You haven't been sleeping well? Again, still?" Vitus hesitated. "I could make a better talisman for you, if you like, but is it the sort of thing where you ought to talk to a Healer?"

Thessaly rubbed her face. "I did on Tuesday. It's—some of it is that I just feel all on edge. I want to find what Aunt Metaia was working on, and I can't for the life of me figure out where she'd have hid anything. And if I'm not looking for it, I keep coming back to thinking about who could have wanted to hurt her that much."

"And?" Vitus squeezed her hand. "There's a bit more than that?"

"And." Thessaly looked out at the heart of the bonfire, watching the flicker of the blue of the hottest flames shift to the reds and oranges and yellows. "I keep having dreams about Childeric. Nightmares. The other ones aren't as much? About being asleep, and him opening the door, and coming in, and knowing what he's going to demand. It's ridiculous, of course, because he never actually did anything like that."

"Did he threaten it?" She hadn't told him, not more than brushing past it. She nodded, once. "So it was in your head, just lurking there."

There wasn't anything useful to say to that at all.

IO

LATE THAT EVENING

Vitus wasn't sure what to say. To be fair, there were so many things all tangled together. They were like chains for a pendant that had melded and divided and twisted so many times they couldn't be separated again. He took his time; this was like making the first cut in a stone. Everything could go right or everything could go wrong, and there wasn't much at all in between.

First, he took a breath. Then he turned to see her better. "You realise I'm going to hate him forever for that? There are probably other things to hate him for, but that one is particularly so. He didn't need to terrify you. Not, eh, that terrifying people is necessarily ever needed."

Thessaly was quiet, staring off at the fire, and Vitus didn't want to rush her. He just sat, feeling her lean on his shoulder. Quietly, not looking at him, she said, "Do you mind awfully? That he's going to be lurking there? In the back of my head, in the back of my life, out of the corner of my eye?"

"It's not what I'd choose. But it's certainly a lot better than him being right there physically, isn't it?" Vitus did not bring up the idea that had popped into his head, Childeric as a restless ghost. That certainly was a quick road to nightmares, for both of them. "I'd rather think about going forward."

That got a sharp inhale from Thessaly. "There's another thing." She swallowed. "Lady Maylis raised the question with me, last Sunday, of whether I'd consider transferring the marriage agreements to Sigbert. I didn't want a fight with her, not then— it was the month of remembrance. They have some name for it I didn't catch, a family term? I said I'd think about it."

"Oh." Vitus could feel himself shifting a bit, curling back, and she turned to him, her hand on his cheek.

"I don't want to marry Sigbert. He'd probably be better than Childeric, but I don't know by how much. More importantly, he's not you. And besides, it wouldn't just be transferring agreements. We'd need a whole new one. But Father's going to push about it, I'm almost sure, and probably Mother. Or they're going to push for me to marry Cyrus, and I won't do that."

"Why are they pushing you so much? Do you know?" Vitus had been puzzled by that all along, while knowing perfectly well that the Great Families were like that.

Thessaly let out an exasperated huff. "No. And no one will tell me outright. Cousin Owain probably would if he knew, but he doesn't. Mother won't. Father, well. We're not speaking to each other, and I wouldn't trust what he said if he did say something. Maybe Mother will tell me eventually, if only so I'll do what she wants and stop balking."

Vitus winced, and then moved to get his arm around her more firmly. "All right. So Cyrus is because, what. Now he's eligible and powerful, in all the ways you ought to want?" Vitus felt like all the Foxes he knew were moving entirely too fast, like a cacophony of fireworks going off one after another. "Wait. Can we stop and go back, and you tell me what you think is going on? I feel like I'm missing half of it."

Thessaly hesitated, then she said. "Kiss, first? To make it clear one thing I want?"

He nodded, and a moment later, she was wriggling into his lap. It was awkward. Both their cloaks got in the way, until he got his cloak free and curled around her, encompassing them both in the warmth. Then he cupped her cheek in one hand and kissed her, taking his time.

That was the plan, and it didn't last more than a few seconds. She wriggled to curl around him better, her arms around his shoulders under the cloak, as if she were soaking everything in. When she finally pulled back, her head settled on his shoulder. Vitus liked that a great deal. Then she said, carefully. "Can you reach the bag of nuts near the top? I think I want to try something. Besides seeing if I can explain."

Vitus had to make some odd contortions, but he managed to get a grip on the bag of nuts, handing them to Thessaly. She'd shifted to be sitting more comfortably, now on the folded blankets, her legs over his, sharing the warmth. "Why the— oh." He swallowed. "Divination?"

"It's very traditional." Thessaly considered. "So. Father and Mother want to see me married off properly. By their standards, that means political choices, both more immediate— what happens in, I don't know, the next couple of decades— and longer-term, joining families. Breeding up magic in a particular way. Father's family tends to it, the Fortiers do too. The Powells don't so much, they just aim at competence in its many forms."

"One of those things is less like the others," Vitus agreed. "Do you actually want any of that? It's not like anything I know, not firsthand." He paused. "Mama— and

Papa— would like to see me settled down. It's good for a craftsman, it looks a lot more steady. And I'm sure Mama would like little ones to dote on, and Lucas will be a fantastic uncle. Chaotic, but fantastic."

"I'd like to meet him sometime, if we can," Thessaly said, quietly.

"Mama would like to meet you. When we can arrange it, I don't know, when you don't need to be so obviously in mourning? There are enough other houses nearby. You can't come to us without someone possibly seeing." Vitus made himself keep going. "She knows what I want with you. Enough of it."

Thessaly's thumb brushed against his cheek, and he could feel himself flushing. "I will not ask you that now. That's not kind. Let me finish explaining." Her hand dropped down into his lap, against his thigh, and she continued. "There's a certain kind of family, a group of them. The ones who hold the land magic, most of them, the ones in the Albion Inheritance and whatever other philanthropic society you want to name." She went quiet for a second. "I'm clear that holding the land magic, it's not just power, it's also an obligation. But I think some of them forget that, sometimes. People get caught up in their own particular plots."

"And then there are people angling for the Council, a different kind of power. Or I suppose the top positions in the Ministry, or the Courts, or the Temple of Healing, having authority and influence?" Vitus offered.

"Exactly. Or the most skilled crafters. You know a bit more about that one, but those, and honestly, everything we just said, that takes competence, too. Being made Heir should probably mean a bit of competence?" Thessaly hesitated. "The more I think about it, the more I don't know about Childeric. He did all right in school, but no one was really going to fail him, not on an entire year's work, were they? The professors at Schola are independent, but not that independent."

"Not like apprentice mistresses and masters," Vitus agreed. "Huh. And he completed his apprenticeship, but Incantation is different than some. More subjective."

"Illusion, there's a whole series of practical exercises you have to demonstrate, as well as some pieces you designed yourself. And you told me about yours, how you had to explain your projects and answer questions and have them examined. Alchemy's much the same, I know that." Thessaly shook her head. "Anyway. That's one of the things I started thinking about this week. Why do the Fortiers want me to marry their son so badly? Some of that is practical; there's not another woman of the right age, not already married or promised, who's got demonstrated strength of magic and good breeding. They have money, they don't need an infusion from a dowry. I suppose Cyrus's sister will get more attention now, but Healing's a long apprenticeship, and I don't think her parents are bothering to play any of that game."

"How many people are there who might look for you to marry them? Sigbert, now, but how many others?" Vitus honestly would have to do a lot of research to begin to figure it out, and not the kind he was any good at.

"Mmm. Four, five, maybe? No, Edward Helms got betrothed last month. I saw the notice. Four, that are roughly the right age and station. And when you add in Aunt Metaia's money, I'm suddenly a much more attractive prospect. Even if I can't transfer it to a husband, it could pass down to children." She grimaced. "There are reasons Lady Maylis would ask about me for Sigbert. But I don't know if she has other reasons." She nudged his arm, changing the subject a tad. "The nuts?"

"How do you divine with them?"

"There's one with horse chestnuts, where you put them side by side - if you're a courting couple - and watch how they pop, if they move together or apart. If one hisses, there's steam in between the two, and perhaps not the good way." Thessaly ducked her chin. "I brought a couple up, if you want to try that. The others, we put them in a pan, and see the patterns when they pop and shatter apart. Those are hazelnuts, filberts. I don't know which you call them?"

Vitus considered. "I'm curious about both. You have a pan, then? You seem to have packed thoroughly for tonight."

"Let me get up, and I'll get things out." She kissed him on the nose before managing to wriggle out of the cloak. Once she was standing, Vitus took the chance to stretch and stand up himself. "You could put another log or two on the fire, if you want?" By the time he'd done that, she was holding a cast iron pan, and she had two spiky chestnuts in her hand. "Here, let me put this over the fire and let it heat up. And then we put those… there, that looks steady, on the metal."

He noticed now that there was a large metal pan all under the fire. "You brought that up?"

"Other people did," Thessaly said. "Our footman and stable man, they got it most of the way with a pony cart. But yes. It helps keep the land safer. And the wandering goats and ponies, after." She set the cast iron pan so it balanced, then held out one of the chestnuts to him. "We put them down at the same time and see what happens. Maybe half an inch apart?"

Vitus followed her movements, matching them, both of them setting the nuts at the same time. Then Thessaly considered and said, by way of framing the other question.

"Tell to us, oh nuts of divination, what we should know about what the Fortiers seek." She stepped back. "It will take a bit. Ten minutes, maybe a bit longer, for the filberts. Longer for the chestnuts."

That meant there was plenty of time for him to slip his arm around her. She didn't seem to want to sit down again. "Can I ask, then, what you want from the future? If you could choose anything?"

She let out a huff of breath. "I don't know some of it. I want to have time, space? Both. To figure out what Aunt Metaia was working on, and then to figure out how to do something that matters. Cousin Owain pointed that out. Just using my magic to make things pretty was fine, but there are other things I could do. He offered to let me take on some of what Aunt Metaia was doing, illusions for Silence-kept places, things that need to be hidden. There's someone who could train me on the Council. And..." She glanced up at him. "I like how I feel with you. I don't hate Sigbert, but I don't trust he'll stay kind, and I certainly don't much want to deal with his parents. Dagobert and Laudine are much more, I don't know, willing to say things that involve important information."

Vitus snorted at that. "Not the highest bar, from what you've said. I'm glad you like being with me." He couldn't quite bring himself to ask whether that meant going against her parents, with all the layered expectations. "And living here?"

"I want that. Seeing people when I want to see them, but maybe not the whole Great Families social mess. If I could just see them only when I wanted to, it'd be much better. And maybe I wouldn't want most of the time. Even if I were inclined to Cyrus, it'd involve a lot of social events."

"Is it that you don't like them, or that Childeric ruined

them for you, or something else?" Vitus had different experiences of them, since he had to see them as business, as much as anything else, and that changed the landscape.

"Both. I like them when I can talk to interesting people. And I do like a beautiful gown, now and again. But all the fussing about it, about having the perfect gown for this moment of fashion, of people judging my choices? That, I'm not so fond of." She waved a hand. "We were going to be talking about the wedding gown a fortnight ago, and obviously no one's said anything about that. But it had to be the height of fashion and not too out of step." Then she looked at him. "What do you want?"

"You." It came out of him before he could stop himself. "If that's possible. And then to make talismans. Ones that help people, that make a thing better. I'd not mind doing more work for people with power and influence, but I don't think I'd want to be them." He looked off down the valley, to where he knew the house was. "Your inheritance— I'd like knowing we weren't relying on my income, especially getting started. But I like the idea of you having your own. Building your own things. You choosing to include me. If you did, that's a powerful sort of magic."

"You're not like most people I know, Vitus." She stood on her toes to kiss his cheek again, then leaned against him. They stood in silence for what must have been quite a while, because suddenly, the filberts started to pop. They scattered across the pan, a few pieces flinging themselves out and into the fire. When they'd settled, Thessaly leaned down and blinked. "Does that look like a lightning bolt to you? And then— that's all charred there. How did it get charred?"

It was hard to tell on a cast iron pan, but Vitus could see the change in the texture. "So, if we take that seriously, that's them seeking something that's like lightning. Which we already knew about, a fair bit. And something that's burning? Dangerous? Destructive?"

"I don't like the sounds of that. And it's not very helpful about what either of us do about it."

Thessaly grimaced. He could see her in the firelight. "That wasn't in the question, really. And divination is a complicated art at the best of times." Before she could go on, they heard the chestnuts popping loudly enough it startled something away from the fire, down the hill. It might have been a hare, but it sounded larger, like a goat or a pony. Vitus hoped for something like that, and not something more dangerous.

When they both got a look, the two chestnuts had rolled together, the heat keeping them dancing slightly on the stone, never quite settling. Thessaly nudged him with her shoulder. "I like that. The way they are. The way we can be?"

"Me as well." Vitus considered. "We've got a fair bit of the night to keep. Let's pull out the food, have some of it, and settle down. I'd like to hear some stories about your aunt, if you're willing. And I can tell you more about my grandmother."

Vitus had a lot to think about, and perhaps it was time to step sideways, backwards, to something a bit easier. Honest grief, rather than future mystery, that was a way to put it. Tomorrow would come in due course.

II

NOVEMBER 7TH IN DEVON

Thessaly was decidedly out of sorts by the time a note came from Cyrus Smythe-Clive on the fourth, inviting her to tea on the seventh. She still had utterly failed to find Aunt Metaia's personal notes, the secret ones, and it was driving her up a wall and a tree and also a mountain. Rather literally, in the last case, she'd ended up going off on two long hikes with Emeline, just to work out some of the strain. And they'd duelled every day, which was at least both enjoyable and an enjoyable challenge, though Emeline was complaining it was getting too cold for her bones outside.

Going out meant wearing black, but it was Cyrus, and that felt wrong. And besides, she'd already made that point to him. After some consideration, she asked Collins to pull out a dark purple gown of Aunt Metaia's, suitable for lesser mourning, and not nearly so dire. People did, in fact, sometimes wear purple just because they liked it, and this was also a dark enough shade not to echo the Council purple too closely.

Once she was dressed, with her hair properly put up,

Thessaly made her way through the portal. The Smythe-Clive portal stood directly in front of a large country house, what looked like two wings and the main building. A footman was waiting. "Mistress Lytton-Powell?" She inclined her head, and the man bowed. "If you'd come this way, please. Master and Mistress Smythe-Clive are in the library." The dual name took Thessaly by surprise, and she had to think for a moment before realising it must mean Andie Smythe-Clive was about. The footman led the way to the house, held the front door for her, and then escorted her back to the library on the other side of the house.

Cyrus stood as soon as the door opened, but Andie stayed seated on the sofa where he'd been sitting. He was still wearing black, but Thessaly saw him take in her dress and nod once, before coming over to offer his hand. "Glad you could come. We thought you might want to get out of the house somewhere, ahem, a little friendlier than some places? Though I am presuming on our school days." He nodded at his sister. "Andie has an evening shift tonight, but if you'd rather she not join us, I can banish her upstairs. Or attempt to."

The way he put it - slightly beleaguered, but affectionate - made Thessaly laugh. "No, please stay, Andie. I admit, I'm curious about the proximal cause of the invitation, but it is perhaps a little nice to see different people."

"There, take that chair, or that one, whichever you prefer. And we've tea and biscuits— orange. They're one of our cook's specialties." Cyrus hesitated, as if weighing something. "Hereswith has become quite fond of them already, if that gives you a measure."

That made Thessaly's eyes widen; she didn't try to hide or mute her reaction. "Oh, of course she'd have talked to you."

"Multiple times, in fact. Weekly. But the first time was a

few days after the Challenge, because everything had been, well…" His voice trailed off, cautiously.

"Awful and complicated, and I'm sure she was trying to keep a dozen crumbling magics working, despite the frailties of humankind," Thessaly said. "I'm quite fond of her. And Cousin Owain, too, to put my loyalties out plainly. And they've both been thoughtful with me. Before and since."

Something about how she said it made Cyrus relax minutely. "I'm glad to hear it. I like them both, so far. And Oscar's been a tremendous help, as well. Several of the others." He settled himself again on the sofa. "Gemma's up with her nanny, but if you honestly would like to see her, we can have her come down later."

"You needn't pretend if you're not fond of small children. Or other people's small children," Andie said, waving a hand. "Mind, we are both entirely biassed when it comes to Gemma, but we recognise not everyone is for some odd reason."

Thessaly contemplated, trying to decide what to do with this conversation. "I honestly don't have a wide experience to draw on, outside the more extended family and my own sister. But I liked her quite well when she was small. Admittedly, there is also a bias there." She cleared her throat. "May I ask why the invitation, here and now?" It was blunt, far too blunt for the usual run of Fox House. But she was too tired or too made of nerves or too something she couldn't name to dance around the topic for too long. Too long out of polite society, even if it had only been six and a half weeks since the Challenge.

Brother and sister engaged a look, and then it was Andie who spoke. "First, because from what Cyrus told me after the funeral, it seemed like you could use some kindness. Second, there is some gossip you should know.

And we were…" She gathered herself. "We were not entirely sure anyone else would pass it along. And third, Cyrus would very much like to chat with someone else who knows the Council at least a bit, and who is not entirely intimidated by them. I am not particularly intimidated by them, but I also do not know their personalities."

"Ah, so the first two are a trade for the third. That's manageable, yes."

It made Cyrus chuckle. "That makes you feel more at ease, does it? Have people been giving you a hard time, then? I don't actually know much about where you've been spending your days, actually. Talking to Andie about it after the funeral made it clear. And we weren't close at school, certainly not allies, but— circumstances change."

They did. Thessaly tilted her head. "I still don't think you'll give me much of a challenge, duelling?"

"That has not changed. No, I feel sure. And that's something you've done less of, at the moment?" He offered it a little cautiously, as if concerned some charm would come winging out of the corner to attack him at any moment. It would not be because of Thessaly, not right now. For one thing, she was still feeling out the situation. "I got the impression that you had been rather firmly pulled into the Fortier circles. Only then there was what you said at the funeral, and I am no longer certain how to weigh most of what I know."

"Ah." Thessaly glanced from one to the other. "In confidence, as—" She couldn't quite fill in the next word. Not allies, not friends, not yet, anyway.

Andie offered, "As people with mutual interests and an understanding of grief in various forms. And," she glanced at her brother, "a desire to make our own way in the world, even if our families disapprove."

"Your parents disapprove?" Thessaly said it more to Cyrus than to Andie, but then she blinked at Andie as well.

"Our parents do not understand our desires, no." Cyrus's voice was measured, and Thessaly understood, suddenly, how someone her age could thrive on the Council, given a little encouragement. He had dignity to him, and depth, undeniable gravitas. All the things Childeric had lacked. "And I certainly understand the pressure to marry. Again, in my case. That's one piece of the gossip, though quieter at the moment than it will probably be in the future."

Thessaly winced. "Yes." She glanced down at her hands, considering. Thessaly was not a gifted strategist with people, not like Magistra Hereswith was, or Aunt Metaia had been. She wasn't even as good as Cousin Owain, who admitted himself not at their level. But if Magistra Hereswith had been here, multiple times, that implied things about a network of trust. "Lady Maylis asked, a fortnight ago, if I'd consider transferring the marriage agreements to Sigbert. I did not decline outright. I said I'd think about it." Then she admitted what she hadn't quite managed to say out loud until now. "I did not entirely feel safe declining."

Andie leaned forward a little. "Is it a distaste for Sigbert, or a preference elsewhere, or— both?" Thessaly was not veiled, of course. And as good as she was at keeping her composure, Thessaly supposed there was something in her expression. "Both. You needn't tell us, if you'd rather not."

Cyrus followed up immediately. "If I can offer any protection, I would be glad to discuss that." Not offer it without reservation, but that was a more than generous gift as it was. "Hereswith mentioned that your Aunt had had some concerns about your marriage, when I asked the general state of things. After the funeral."

Thessaly nodded. "I made the agreements with Childeric— well, our families did. I agreed to the terms thinking we'd have a cordial marriage. We'd have the obligatory children. He'd let me have my own life, a lover if I wished and did it with sufficient discretion. It became increasingly clear he didn't intend to keep those agreements, and it got worse after Aunt Metaia's death. He almost struck me once, and he certainly made it clear he'd do his best to destroy anything I cared much about."

She glanced at both of them, then focused on a spot on the sofa between them. "At the same time, I had got to know Vitus Deschamps. A few years ahead of us, Cyrus, Salmon House, newly done with his apprenticeship as a talisman maker." Now she had to avoid looking at them. She would give far too much away. "Childeric took offence, even though we'd not done anything against the agreements. I still haven't, though we have talked about doing some more when we get a proper opportunity. He's very busy."

"Deschamps. I've been hearing some excellent commentary about him. I heard that gossip, too, but I paid it no mind. Whatever else, I know you well enough to know you'd be scrupulous about your actual agreements, and honestly, they're the common set for your sort of family, aren't they? Other than perhaps the financial arrangements?"

Thessaly just nodded, because that was the truth.

"Well. That's not on. Nor is, mmm, an artificial separation from someone you have said you like, and who seems like a decent sort from all I know. I ran into Carrington the other day, in Bourne's." Thessaly was technically a member, but she'd stopped going in her own right around the time of the betrothal. "He was very clear about his praise for Deschamps." Then Cyrus's voice softened. "Besides, these days, I am in favour of people finding love where they can, for as long as they can, even if I can't."

The note in his voice at the end made Thessaly look at him, sharply. She caught just enough of a glimpse of Andie doing the same, suggesting it was something Cyrus hadn't said quite that way before. "Thank you." Thessaly said, as gently as she could. "I don't think there's much anyone can actually do to help. I suppose that brings us to the gossip?"

Cyrus nodded. "There are— well, increasing questions about whether I'll marry again. Or rather, assuming I will. I ran into Odile and Cosmerance, both, the other day, and they were..."

"They were themselves, and all over your prospects. I had tea with them in early September, and it was rather awful." Thessaly wrinkled her nose. "Things have been progressively more awful since, the most overwrought letters." She waved a hand at her dress. "I won't wear mourning for someone I don't actually miss, you understand? Not unless it'd be an insult otherwise. It's a large part of why I'm not leaving Bryn Glas."

Andie considered that. "He did that much to break your willingness?" She lifted her chin. "We talk about that kind of hurt, in our training, though we haven't got into the more delicate bits."

"His mother mourns him. I suspect his father does. I'm not as sure about Sigbert as I thought I'd be." She gestured. "If people aren't thinking I should marry Sigbert, I suspect they're thinking I should set my cap for you, Cyrus." She hurriedly added, "Not that I'm going to. If you wanted to discuss a marriage of convenience, suitable to us both, I'd consider it with you. But you don't want that, of course."

Cyrus's face went through half a dozen expressions. "I'd trust you to set up agreements you were comfortable with. But no. Andie will partner me for the Council dances. We're working on that. If you had no other interest, I don't know. I might have worked around to the idea. But you do, and I won't step in the way of that."

"See, that is why I could make the offer with you." Thessaly was relieved it was tidy. "But if it would be a help to say you and I have discussed the matter, and we are leaving considerations open for the moment?"

It made Cyrus laugh, a warm chuckle. "Giving us both enough space to do what we actually want. Yes, that would be a help right now. And of course I'd not pressure you while you were in mourning. And of course being able to say, legitimately, that you and I had discussed it, that would be a help with Sigbert. Or rather, his parents."

"And my parents." Thessaly winced. "They can't force me to it, but there's a great deal you can do that's uncomfortable that is not force." She leaned back. "Was there other gossip?"

"Nothing I could pin down— and of course, people get cautious around me right now," Cyrus said.

Andie cut in. "They don't have the least idea what to do with Cyrus. I hear that part from near enough every quarter. That he's out, being social. That he's not marrying, that he's holding his own counsel. All of it. If it weren't so tedious, it'd be hilarious, actually."

Cyrus waved his hand. "No one's sure what to make of the Fortiers right now. And that extends to you. Or they're not sure what to make of you, and that extends to the Fortiers. Everyone's unsettled by Childeric's death. I don't know if you, or the family, realise just how much."

Thessaly looked down at her hands again. "How concerned is the Council about it, can you say?"

"Informally, the ones who talk to me? They're very glad it's me and not Childeric. Overall, that the situation was unusual. Not unique. There are deaths from time to time, but this was not like most of the others. It seemed more pointed. You— did you see him after?"

"His clothes soaking wet, and marks on his body like lightning? Yes." Thessaly said. "And Cousin Owain mentioned there was gossip about the favour." Then she said, carefully. "Have you noticed that there are an awful lot of people having more difficulties around our age? Is that anything that you've heard discussed?"

Cyrus grimaced, rubbing his nose once. "A little. Not directly with me, but Hereswith and Oscar both mentioned it had come up. Another reason they're glad it was me. No one apparently has particular concerns about my magic. Dozens of things I ought to learn immediately, but not an inherent frailty. I think that was the term that stuck most. I sat down with the lists last week, and it's hard to tell. I don't know enough beyond the common gossip about people much older or younger, the ones in Schola now."

"It makes it hard to tell if there's a pattern," Thessaly agreed. "Vitus was looking at some of that, with his apprentice mistress. They think the numbers are telling. He actually went through and looked at the apprentice notices, who began and who dropped out."

That made Cyrus's eyes widen. "Is that something he might share with the Council? With credit or without, whichever he prefers. But the actual data would save some time."

"I'll ask," Thessaly agreed. "It explains why some of the marriage-related gossip is especially odd right now. We're getting to the age where matches would happen as people finish apprenticeships. But if they don't finish, or if there's some visible problem. Ugh." She definitely did not know how to sort out what the problem actually was, let alone what to do about it.

"It's a problem that is at least partly the Council's remit. Or at least, people on the Council know who else to talk to," Cyrus said, quietly. "Whatever you can share. And the rest of it…"

"On the rest of it, I suppose there's not much any of us can do about the specific gossip and what it means for us. But if you hear anything more specific, and you're willing to pass it along, I'd appreciate that." That part, Thessaly found simple enough. More information would let her make better choices.

"Good. In exchange, perhaps I might invite you out here to duel at some point? I know I'm not up to your standard, but I could stand to brush up a bit more." Then he heard the clock chime and peered at it. "If you'd like tea with Gemma, it's about time for that. You needn't be polite about it, though, if you'd rather not."

"I think, on the whole, I'd like to see you with your daughter," Thessaly said. "Children, still very much a hypothetical idea, but I suspect any daughter of yours and Tanith's is interesting." Thessaly added a moment later, "I miss her too, though I didn't know her near as well as I wanted."

"Ah. That's a kindness. Perhaps you'll indulge my telling a few stories, then."

"Of course." That said, Andie rearranged things to allow for a small child to be added to the arrangement, tugging a table in easier reach of Thessaly and Cyrus. Five minutes later, Nanny had been summoned, Gemma had been claimed, and Thessaly had been brought into a comfortable chat about the household.

12

NOVEMBER 13TH IN TRELLECH

Vitus was in the Stream, in one of the conversation rooms, but he was trying to ignore all the chatter around him. The lecture that evening had been more scantily attended. Vitus hadn't quite wanted to go home. He hadn't wanted to go find others of the Four Metals. He hadn't quite wanted anything.

It wasn't as if he didn't have things to do. He'd seen Thessaly on Sunday, for several hours in the afternoon. They'd enjoyed each other's company, but it had been more about talking through the past week - and a bit of kissing - than anything more intimate. She hadn't offered any further, and he certainly hadn't pressed. Not that he didn't want more when she was ready. He'd woken from rather demanding dreams on that point twice this week. But it was her choice.

Thessaly had told him about her conversation with Cyrus and Andie Smythe-Clive. Besides the rest of it, she'd been taken by how they were as siblings, how they helped each other. It seemed to have made her decidedly wistful, because she wanted that with Hermia, and their parents had put themselves firmly in the way.

It had made Vitus even more glad to see Lucas, in a way that hadn't come out in language. He and his brother had taken a walk before supper, chatting about Lucas's horses, the cavalry, the other officers. And Lucas, bless him, had understood that Vitus felt a whole host of things he wasn't sure how to talk about. He wished Thessaly could have a bit more of that, but she'd admitted her sister was enough younger it was different. The ages fell in a way that probably wouldn't matter much in a decade, but did now.

Though it was about the same gap as between Thessaly's mother and her aunt. Vitus wondered how much she was thinking about that, and how different the two had been. It was certainly something Vitus thought about, with Lucas wanting a life full of horses and the non-magical cavalry, while Vitus was increasingly embedded in the magical community.

Tonight, he'd been sitting for half an hour, nursing a drink, trying to decide whether to go home. Or whether he'd be better off to go and sleep in his workshop. That was certainly an option, especially if he wanted to be alone and also not have Mama worry over him. It meant he had missed some of the conversation— or perhaps, no, they'd been moving, coming further into the room.

One of the group, it was three people. Vitus blinked a couple of times to get his eyes to focus, then identified Olivia and Oscar Hemmings, along with Aline Holder. He'd last talked to them what, three weeks ago, and they'd shared some info with Thirza and the others.

Aline turned, then said, "Oh, Vitus! You might have some thoughts. Care to join us?" Vitus blinked at her again and she added, "Some of our experiments, and also, wait.

Do you know anyone on the Council who might take a message from us?"

The answer to that, somehow, was in fact yes. Vitus nodded, then pushed himself upright when the other three claimed chairs at the far end of the room, where they could better put up privacy charms. He brought his drink, both because he'd only had about a third of it, and because he suspected the conversation might call for a bit more of it.

Sitting was followed by an increasingly awkward silence. Finally, Vitus cleared his throat. "Where do you want to start? And why were you asking about the Council?"

Olivia and Aline started talking at the same time, before Aline waved a hand and Olivia kept going. "We've kept trying our research, but now we're just confused. We've done readings up near Arundel several times."

Oscar said, "Ten now."

"And eight of them were what we expected, and two aren't. Besides the one we talked to you about, when was it? Back in the summer." Olivia sounded downright peevish and frustrated.

"One of them recent, I assume?" Vitus could at least do the maths on that. One odd reading, even two, could be a number of things. Three definitely seemed like something was going on.

"One last Friday, the other..." Olivia pulled a notebook out of the bag she had with her. "October 7th. A month apart. Though they didn't react quite the same way. The Friday was stronger."

Vitus frowned. "And you were wondering if I had someone on the Council who would take a message seriously why?"

"Because it seems like the sort of thing someone ought to look into properly. And we certainly can't get permission to go tromping around actually on the estate."

"I certainly can't either," Vitus pointed out. "Given everything. I was there for the funeral, on the twenty-seventh of September, but I'm decidedly not on their invitation list for anything else." Thessaly was, though. Now he'd thought that, he was caught by it. Not that she had free access to the estate either, but she'd mentioned specific spaces she was supposed to avoid.

Olivia, at least, looked somewhat abashed. "Oh. I just meant, I mean, we've never been. Not the sorts who'd get invited at all."

"Give me a moment. Let me think through the parts of it." Vitus mostly didn't want to speak too quickly. Certainly, he thought that Council Head Rowan would consider a note from him, given the previous conversations. And Thessaly could certainly pass on a message to her cousin, or to Cyrus, beyond that. "I probably can. But can you tell me more about what you got from the readings? Or didn't get from the readings?"

Olivia launched into an explanation, though at least she was willing to pause when Vitus looked puzzled. A good half of it involved sympathetic magic and materia well outside his usual run of things, and about a quarter involved locational magics that definitely weren't his usual work. "So, you're looking for, erm. Connections between what's in the water, and the land, and things that are known to be a problem. Soot and gasses and such from factories."

"Sewage, we didn't expect much of that in the Arun, of course, but we did in London. No, there's quite a lot of natural variation, of course. Some of what we're measuring, it depends on the direction of the wind or the speed of the river. Spring is likely going to be different from autumn. We'll need to keep doing testing in all seasons until we've got a complete run. But we've done enough now to have a good sense of the usual range."

"Right. And this was different. Two times." Vitus had grasped that much. "I suppose you're keeping excellent records about anything that might be a variable?"

"We are. And we'd borrowed horses for that one. We covered twenty miles or so. A fair distance, but not so far that the weather was dramatically different. We tested five times along that run, and the other four, all except the one nearest Arundel, they were what we'd expect. There was variation, but entirely within the expected parameters." Aline rummaged in her notes and held them out for Vitus to look at.

Set out in pencil, the contrast was striking. "And what's this measuring, exactly?" Vitus ran his fingers down.

"We don't have a good name for it, exactly. The magical potency of the area. We expected a shift near a demesne estate, you can see the readings for a couple of others if you flip back. We were up by Baddock Hall last week, and Willow Hall, out by Canterbury, the fortnight before that. But this is, I don't know, an abyss, where those are a peak. Sometimes it's gentle, like a hill. Sometimes it's a mountain. Definitely not a valley."

"And it's not doing that all the time." Vitus stared at it, taking a moment to look back through and at least get a sense of the ranges. Though of course, this kind of quick reading didn't really let you do any analysis. He cleared his throat. "I do know someone who might be there visiting again." He knew more than one, actually, but he wasn't sure when Florent Montague might visit, and it certainly wasn't something he could ask. "Is there something that person could do, a sample of soil or plants, or a charm or something?"

That got a quick flurry of conversation Vitus didn't follow between the three. Oscar took the lead on it. It was obvious from the interactions that he was the incantation and enchantment specialist in the mix. After a couple of minutes, Oscar turned back to him. "Someone who'd need an explanation?"

"Someone who'd probably do it for my asking, so long as I could give a brief summary and details on any risks. It couldn't be anything that'd trigger their warding, but something more passive? Maybe. Probably."

"I can put some things together for you, um. By Friday. Maybe tomorrow. I don't know if I have enough kermes in stock."

"Poddington and Groves just got more in." Aline chipped in, that was one of the better materia shops in Trellech.

"Right. If you can ask, it'd be something in a locket or something of the kind. Watch fob. Or a compact in a pocket, just somewhere on their person. It'll have some strips of charmed paper on it. They'd need to keep note of how long they were there, and if there were, what do we call them?"

"Direct and intensive magical events. Direct work on the warding or protections, duelling, that sort of thing. Ordinary cosmetic enchantments or talismanic effects..." Olivia gestured at Vitus. "Shouldn't cause a problem, but a list of worn talismans would be handy, just to filter out any overlapping effects. And we might have a stone or something to carry."

"I can ask about that, certainly," Vitus said. "I'll send a

note before I go home, chances are she won't get it before tomorrow morning."

"No, you've given us a way to go forward. And without, um, making undue demands." Aline leaned back, looking a little less intense. "Why is that?"

"Well, I'm not fond of the idea of gasses and what have you fouling the land and the water and the air," Vitus said. "I'd have thought that was self-preservation in part." He couldn't say the other piece of it, that there was something odd about the Fortiers and Arundel, and maybe this would help. He knew Council Head Rowan was still curious, and Thessaly. And Vitus certainly was in his own right, not just because of them.

"And?" Olivia leaned forward.

"The rest of it, perhaps you'll owe me a favour down the road. Testing something, perhaps trading enchantment or consulting or something of the kind. I'm still establishing myself. I don't know what I'll need. Having a connection with creative people who solve problems, that seems to be an advantage worth having, doesn't it?"

It made the other three laugh. "Fair. A reasonable favour, we can trade for that. Proportionate. Besides, we're all of Salmon House. We know you won't be trading solely for your own advantage, like a Fox."

Vitus wanted to protest; he was quite sure that wasn't how Thessaly went at the world. But it would definitely be a sign of protesting too much and too specifically to avoid comment and teasing. Instead, he just shrugged. "As you say. Oh, does anyone need another drink?" One of the club's staff was coming around, checking for orders.

Once that was tended, the conversation settled into something broader, a mix of points from other recent lectures, something Aline had been looking up, one of the talismans Vitus was designing. By the time he took his leave around eleven, he felt like it had been a good evening. He paused just long enough to slip the note he'd written for Thessaly during the latter part of the evening into the mail drop at the Scali Bank and went home to get what sleep he could.

13

NOVEMBER 16TH IN ARUNDEL

The problem with visiting Arundel in November was that there was a dearth of places to be out of the weather that were both decorously public enough and not near Lady Maylis, Lord Clovis, or the Dowager Lady Chrodechildis. After a bit of awkward consideration, Sigbert had offered the orangerie along the far edge of the garden. It was a pleasant place to sit, with white wicker benches and chairs tucked under one area of trees. The temperature was comfortable, too, enough that Thessaly took off her cloak.

She tried not to think too often of the charmed locket attached to her watch chain. And she was careful not to draw attention to the small charmed stone tucked into the depths of the single pocket on her skirt. For one thing, touching them too often might affect the delicate enchantments. Second, she absolutely didn't want Sigbert or any of the others to notice.

Sigbert was, she thought, nervous. That was very curious. They had been sitting for a minute or two. He had just utterly run out of commentary about the decorative ironwork and the varieties of oranges and lemons in the orangerie. He turned to her, opened his mouth, then swallowed. "Pardon, Thessaly, may I speak perhaps a little plainly? The sort of conversation I want to have in private, without Maman or Father overhearing?"

"Of course." She couldn't quite resist. "I think they're hoping for that, or your mother would not have encouraged us to go off and talk like this."

His nose wrinkled up. "Maman does have ideas. She's very set on you transferring the marriage agreements. It would make things, erm. Tidy?"

"Momentary tidiness is not the best reason for a marriage I've ever heard," Thessaly said, though she managed a smile at the end to ease some of the sting. "And it's more complicated than just transferring them. My situation has changed."

"Maman was furious about that. And Father." Sigbert met her eyes, then considered. "May I ask about your parents?"

"Oh, also furious. Mother and Father are pressing me to consider suitable arrangements as promptly as possible." Mother directly, when they'd had tea at Cousin Owain's on Wednesday. And Father, indirectly, though Mother had conveyed his arguments both in conversation and by letter. Father's line of persuasion had to do with benefits to the family, with no consideration of Thessaly at all beyond being a pawn in a decades-long game of chess. Mother had, at least, talked about who might suit, as if there were choices. "You do have some potential competition. But I told Mother and Father the same thing I told your mother, that it is too early for that, even for negotiations."

"Who else?" Sigbert tilted his head. "If I may ask."

"Cyrus Smythe-Clive. He and I have discussed the matter, even." It was so pleasant to tell the absolute truth there. "And Mother floated a few other names to consider. Some years older."

"Interested in a child, then. A second marriage?" Sigbert was at least deft enough with that part. Then, earnestly, he said, "May I take your hand, Thessaly?"

The fact he was asking was a pleasant difference from his brother. Her hands were gloved against the November chill as well as for propriety, so she nodded, and felt him take her right hand in his.

"Childeric mistreated you. I would not do so." Now, that was an interesting move in this duel, as it was unfurling.

Thessaly made a deliberate choice, blinking several times. "I think that pair of sentences needs more explanation and context, please." It was not for her to give more away.

Sigbert dropped her hand, standing up, apparently so he could pace a little, from one side of the seating area to the other. "I loved my brother. Of course I loved him." It sounded like he might be protesting a hair too much, actually, but Thessaly would not call him on that, not in this moment. Instead, she just nodded once, hoping it would encourage him.

"But we were different. He was always the favoured one, the golden child. He did everything first." That was true, and it was a certain undeniable aspect of their respective ages.

Thessaly considered. "And better?"

Sigbert snorted. "That's the thing." He paused, standing right in front of her, rather than a step or three to either side. "He did well enough in school, but there are several reasons he wouldn't duel you."

"He didn't like losing. I thought that was obvious enough." Thessaly folded her hands in her lap.

"That was true, but it was one part of it. He wasn't actually that good, I think. It didn't really strike me until he was working with Master Fulton, preparing, actually. I hadn't seen him duel much, and he wouldn't duel me, either." Sigbert spread his hands, as if measuring, then went back to pacing back and forth.

"Did he let you watch?" Thessaly was intrigued now, beyond wanting to see where Sigbert was going with this conversation.

"Several times. So long as I praised, not any other commentary. Fulton was— mmm. He did what was safe, not what he'd been hired for. Childeric didn't fall over his own feet, but he wasn't quick magically. Not the way he bragged about, made everyone assume he was." Sigbert stopped again. "I'm not like that."

"Would you duel me?" Thessaly put it out as a challenge. "Not today. I'm not dressed for it."

"If it would help you consider marrying me, certainly. Suitors have been set worse challenges, by far," Sigbert said. "I want to do the thing properly. You seem reasonable, if treated reasonably. We could have a good life of it. Make both sets of parents happy."

"You realise your parents have not, shall we say, endeared themselves to me as relatives by marriage. Not recently. Even allowing for their grief and the upset and all that. They also kept me in the dark about what was planned, plans that very much affect me, and they certainly did not discourage Childeric in any of his actions."

"No. That is a problem, isn't it?" Sigbert stopped again, before going back to pacing, more slowly this time, with his hands tucked behind his back. "I can only move them so far, though. It isn't as if I became the golden child. It's just that there isn't a golden child right here to compare me to. Just his memory." That went sharper and sour.

"And he is even more perfect in memory than in life," Thessaly said, slowly. "He was really rather awful to me. What will you do if I tell you?"

"I'll make oath on not telling, if that would be of help." Sigbert offered it remarkably promptly. "Not to anyone without your permission. Whatever is discussed in the rest of this conversation?"

Thessaly inclined her head, and she listened to him. He used one of the standard forms. This was an oath that anyone who went through Schola learned well enough, because it was handy in such cases. She could see him wince as the Silence magic twisted around him for just an instant. Once that was done, he came and sat again, as if listening would take all his attention. "I would like to know what you will share."

It took her several moments to consider how to put this. "I expected him to honour the agreements. But even at the betrothal, he was making a show of it, in public, where others could see, and he was beginning to ignore me, in private. He went off to play cards the afternoon before the party. For example. He cared about his pleasure, and whether I could keep up, not my comfort."

Sigbert opened his mouth, then closed it, before trying again. "And later?"

"You've read the agreements?" Sigbert nodded, so Thessaly went on. "Nothing I did with Vitus Deschamps went against our agreements. And yet, he was furious. The gossip was, all right, discomforting. But he didn't even ask me the truth of it. He threatened me. He threatened Vitus. And all while I'm sure he had a mistress. I hope she's doing all right, since?"

Sigbert gaped. "You knew?"

"Gossip finds a way," Thessaly said. "It's like water. Even if it weren't the sensible wager, were I a betting woman. I don't know much about the details, but that he had a mistress, yes. Someone in Trellech, I gathered."

"He did." Sigbert looked down, as if tracing a line through the paving stones of the floor. "A widow, her husband had been one of the better up-and-coming tailors. He died suddenly. Childeric helped pay for her flat. Some of the inheritance from Grand-père. He'd see her once or twice a week, on his schedule. Sometimes we'd be at some private party. Nothing unseemly in public, of course. Maman would have been furious at that."

"And your father?" Thessaly leaned forward a little. She didn't know if she wanted to ask if Sigbert had a mistress or dalliances. She wondered if he'd say anything if she didn't press the point, and that was perhaps more useful information.

"Oh, Father was the one who encouraged us. And he arranged some more substantial token for Mathilde, not long after Childeric's funeral. Enough to see her set up in her own shop." Sigbert looked up sharply, caught out, apparently, in honesty. "I also have a mistress. I wouldn't impose on you for that sort of thing, not unless we were trying for a child, or unless you asked. That's our custom." Then he tilted his head. "I don't think Uncle Dagobert does. Not for a while, actually. I think that's part of why Father disapproves of him."

Thessaly thought it a rather odd custom, and also potentially rather tedious for whoever the mistress was, to be at someone else's beck and call, and with only dubious security. "And what do you think about my seeing other men in private? Well, likely only one."

Sigbert shrugged. "It is not how we've done things. And gossip would, of course, be unacceptable. Maman and Tante Bradamante would disapprove. And Grand-mère. But in private? I would not be bothered by it. With all the appropriate precautions against a child, of course. There is the bloodline to think of." It was a more direct answer than she'd got from Childeric, at least. Sigbert added, "And you have your own property. It has a portal, yes?"

"It does." Thessaly inclined her head.

"There. You could easily ensure discretion." Sigbert took a breath, as if he were deciding whether to say something. Thessaly applied all the patience she'd learned, duelling, about waiting for the necessary time, for the right moment. "Childeric hurt me. Bullied me, hit me a few times. Forced me into doing what he wanted, much more often than that."

"Threatening to tell your parents, something like that?" Thessaly needed the shape of it. Sigbert nodded, once. He obviously wasn't inclined to go into the topic or topics.

"I miss how he was, when he was in a good mood. I miss having a big brother who went ahead of me in the world. But I don't miss that, the way he was when he got spiteful." Now, Sigbert was definitely talking to the ground, unable to look up. Thessaly hesitated, then reached out to touch his hand. Not to hold it, not to do any of that. "And now, there's none of him."

Thessaly let out a breath. "No." She cleared her throat. "I'm not saying I'll agree to marry you. Your parents are still, shall we say, a cautionary tale. But if it would help you to tell them you'd talked to me about it, you may. And that I appreciated the clarity of your position, however you wish to put that. You may say that."

"That would be a help." Sigbert glanced out the glass. "I suppose we should walk back up. Or would you like to stretch your legs a little more, a circuit of the gardens?"

A circuit of the gardens would give the charms she carried a little more chance to work, and perhaps a chance for her to get a bit of dirt. She could pretend to lose one of the decorative buckles from her shoe. She had set that up as a possibility this morning. "The gardens, please. I could use a little fresh air before tea." He stood, offering to help her arrange her cloak, and then they walked, side by side, not arm in arm, on a tour of the sleeping gardens.

She got a chance to sneak a little dirt from the furthest edge nearest the Arun, and slip it into the tiny snuff box she'd brought for the purpose.

14

NOVEMBER 19TH AT BRYN GLAS

By Tuesday night, Vitus was very glad that Thessaly had made it clear he should come by. She'd put him off on both Saturday and Sunday— Saturday, because she was going to be at Arundel, and Sunday for reasons she hadn't explained. She didn't owe him an explanation, and there was a decent chance it was something to do with her parents or her family.

But then he'd caught several bits of gossip, some on Sunday, some yesterday, about her. Their parents had been out, so he'd gone with Lucas for supper in Trellech. They'd ended up at The Boar's Head, then gone on for a drink with a group of people at Wishton's, which was rather more upper class than Vitus usually ran. The conversation had been pleasant, but more superficial, so Vitus had been quieter, listening to the comments around him.

Lucas had asked - Vitus was fairly sure it was a deliberate strategy - about something related to the Challenge. It had been rather easy to get related topics going from there. Including Thessaly. Some of the gossip was that she was going mad with grief, or perhaps somewhat feral. No one had seen her since the funeral, at least no one who was doing any of the gossiping. One source had talked to someone at Hermia's finishing school, or said she had. Vitus thought it might be a lie. That woman had said Thessaly's family was terribly worried for her, but sensible people had wondered if she was cursed.

Implying, of course, that she'd had a part in Childeric's death, directly or indirectly. Vitus had had to leave the room after that one. His coming to her defence wouldn't help anything at all. He'd tell her when there was a chance.

The other gossip had been along those lines, if less personal. That she was running out into the woods, barely dressed, like something out of a Gothic novel. Another had it that she was stalking the halls of 'that house in Wales' wearing all black, her hair tumbled and wild. For one thing, the halls at Bryn Glas were mostly rather short, not at all designed for proper ghostly haunting of that kind. And for the second, Vitus was entirely sure Thessaly was wearing as little black as possible.

It meant that he turned up on Tuesday, unsure what to expect. Thessaly met him at the gate. Then she stopped, one hand on it. "I was wondering, would you like it if I attuned you to the wards?"

Vitus halted, halfway through the gate. "I thought you'd been advised to wait?"

"It's not that I can't add people. It's that while things are settling, it's tricky. And also, if I'm not adding people, Mother and Father can't fuss about them not being added. I am not suggesting it to them. I am suggesting it to you."

Vitus wanted to dance, to swing her around in his arms, to take her to bed. He managed to swallow most of that down. "It means a lot that you trust me like that. I'd like it very much."

"Well, then. Hand here, if you don't mind, and I'll

manage the charm." The attunement took a minute or so, and caused a rather intense buzzing feeling through his hand. "I'll have to do the house, too. They're different. Come on!"

Certainly, this wasn't the Thessaly anyone was gossiping about. She was bright-eyed, her hair was simply put up, but smooth and glossy. And she certainly wasn't wearing black. This was a sea-green overdress over a pale yellow undergown, like the shade of a white wine or mead. Now, she held out her hand again, after she closed the gate behind them, and tugged him along to the house, repeating the process there.

"Now you can come visit whenever you want." She tugged him upstairs again, and Vitus followed. Of course he followed.

"Did something make you decide this all of a sudden?" He wasn't at all sure how to ask, even once she'd nudged him to sit down on the sofa and settled herself right next to him. Distractingly close to him, but that— well, at the moment, distractingly close probably did include the far side of the room, at the very least.

"It feels right." Thessaly shrugged. "How have you been? And I'm sorry about Saturday. And Sunday. I learned some interesting things, though? And I have the charmed pieces to give back to you. Don't let me forget."

"What sort of things?" Vitus considered, then shifted his arm to rest along the top of the sofa, encouraging her closer. She immediately shifted to lean against him, which was even more disruptive to anything like a coherent train of thought.

"Sigbert had a very earnest conversation with me about how he's not like his brother. He'd treat me much better." Thessaly wrinkled up her nose. "I think he was telling the truth, honestly. But I was just as honest that his parents are actually rather a lot of the challenge there. Besides the part I wasn't telling him about preferring you."

"I am glad to hear you still do." It came out awkwardly, and a little hollow, and Vitus didn't like that at all. "I mean."

"There's something wrong there. I don't know what sort of wrong it is, but someone needs to find out. It's not as if Magistra Hereswith can just stroll in and look around. I could. I mean, if we decided it was worth doing." Thessaly paused. "And it's not like we can just ask Laudine and Dagobert, though I suspect they know. Some of it, at least, maybe all of it? And even if Magistra Landry knew, I'm sure she wouldn't tell us."

"We?" Vitus swallowed harder at that. "Talk, um. More about that? Please?" Though she was, he thought, right on both counts about people who might know more and who wouldn't say.

She twisted so she could see him, and that meant he could see her face. "I'd much rather make a future with you than with Sigbert. I don't know what that looks like, and my parents— well, that was Sunday. Mother, directly, and Father indirectly. Again." She grimaced. "You'd think when the previous tactics didn't work, they'd at least try something new."

"Your parents are, erm, not up to your standards in a duel?" Vitus offered it a little uncertainly. But Thessaly lit up, smiling.

"Just like that." She rearranged herself again, leaning against him. "There's a short list of people they'd like me to consider. I am firmly refusing to consider anyone, beyond the conversations I'm already having with Sigbert, until at least January. Past the holiday chaos and obligations, not that I'm planning on going to any of that this year."

"There was some gossip about you hiding away." Vitus considered, then added. "You don't look like the gossip suggested. You're not haunting the place, or tearing your hair out, tear-stained, or whatever."

She turned back. "Really? That's what people are saying?"

"Some of them. It wasn't the kind of thing where my pointing out the problems in their logic was going to help. Wishton's."

"Oh, well. I suppose Bourne's would be worse, even. Sigbert and Childeric were there quite a lot. Sigbert still is, probably." She waved a hand. "He doesn't have the luxury of being in deep mourning, even if he wanted to be. Mind, I'm not sure he wants to be, exactly. More like he misses the brother he wishes he had, not the one he actually did."

Vitus shivered at that. "I keep thinking about Lucas, honestly. What it would be like if we were like that? And I hate the idea."

"The way you talk about him, it's always so fond. Sometimes confused, he likes such different things from you? Goes about things differently, too?" The last one was definitely a question.

"He does. I suppose that's partly the different houses. A lot of the Boar House magics, I gather, are about focus and aim. In a military context, particularly, but it applies to other things too."

"And Salmon is solving problems?" Thessaly offered it a little uncertainly.

"That. And sometimes they're the same problems Lucas is tackling, and sometimes not. I do think it's an advantage to the talisman work, especially if you're anchoring it in the personal rather than the theoretical." Vitus hadn't really ever talked with anyone about that.

"What does Magistra Hall do?" Thessaly asked. "Or what house is she, actually?"

"Horse." Vitus said, amused. "Which, now you ask, explains some things about her preferred approach. And why certain people won't come to her. She is not terribly fond of individual ambition in the less pleasant senses."

"And you?" Thessaly's voice quivered for a second.

"I am in favour of ambition, but clear-sighted ambition. And ideally with some larger goal in mind. I want to make excellent talismans so that people can do the best they can, at what they care about. I wouldn't take a commission for the more manipulative ones. That's both because I disapprove, and that would show in the work, and also because that is not my best skill set. You, Thessaly, are of Fox House, but your ambitions seem to me to be mostly about learning more, and figuring out what might be useful." He tilted his head. "Did you ever consider challenging for the Council, perhaps in the future?"

She shook her head, rather violently, several wisps of hair coming out. "No. I'm not. That's not the shape I have?" She was fumbling with the words, and then she sat bolt upright. "Wait."

"Wait?" Vitus was startled as she got up, turning around, as if trying to spot something she'd forgotten, a book put down on a table, or something of the kind. Before he could say anything more - before she answered - she went striding off into the bedroom, her gown billowing behind her, and then seconds later, she was coming back. "Do you know how to do the charm, the sympathetic magic one, like calls unto like, any of the variations of it?"

It was a common enough one, if advanced, and Vitus did in fact know it. "Yes?" It came out weakly. "Why?"

"Use this." She ran her hand through her hair, which only pulled more wisps out, then she grimaced and pulled the hairpins out, letting it tumble down over her shoulders. Vitus tried very hard not to be distracted by that. "Please?"

Thessaly was holding out a garnet pendant on a chain, talismanic work. He could tell that even without holding it. "That?"

"Aunt Metaia gave it to me. It's not, I have the rest of the necklace set? But I'm suddenly wondering if she put earrings or something from the set with the papers. Or—mostly, I can try things to break an illusion, but I don't know where to start."

"Right." Vitus rubbed his nose, then reached out to take the pendant hanging off the chain. He mentally ran through the variations he knew. "Do you think it's most likely up here, rather than, I don't know, the library or her study or something?"

"I think it's likely one of those three places. I'd guess here or the study before the library, though."

Vitus tried the charm after taking a moment or six for preparation. At first, he thought it hadn't worked, and then there was a tug toward the bottom of the bookshelves, what looked like a plain wooden panel. Thessaly moved, going over to kneel in front of it. She tapped it, knocking it with her hand. The panel next to it made a solid sound, but the one the pendant had most likely aimed at sounded different, lighter and more hollow.

Thessaly stared at it, feeling around the edges to see if there was some latch. Then she blew a breath out, making all her loose hair shiver around her face, and called magic to her fingers. Vitus could see it glowing softly, a golden warm colour. She blew on it, and it drifted, and suddenly the entire panel changed colour, from a paler wood to a darker one, and a latch appeared on one side.

Thessaly reached to open it, revealing two flat shelves, both stacked with papers. She looked up from where she was sitting on the floor. "Thank you." That was all she said.

Vitus shifted from foot to foot, then came over, bending down to offer her the pendant back. Thessaly fastened it around her neck, still looking at the papers. "Should I leave you with them?" He wasn't at all sure what she might find.

She hesitated, then nodded just once. "We'll talk soon?" She looked back at the papers, almost like they drew her in with some sort of compulsion. "When I have a chance to figure them out?"

Vitus shifted just enough to kiss the top of her head. "At least I can now let myself out. Send me a note if I can help, all right?" He wasn't sure what he felt about her mood shifting so quickly, but on the other hand, it wasn't as if he didn't know and understand her priorities. He certainly could give her space to figure out what she could, about this mystery that twined through every part of her life.

15

DECEMBER 5TH IN ESSEX

To be honest, Thessaly rather lost track of the next days. The next fortnight. She spent them poring over the papers Aunt Metaia had left, reading through them in detail. She'd stay up until all hours, deep in the night, fall asleep, and go right back to it as soon as she woke. Had anyone actually seen her, they would have thought all the gossip entirely accurate.

She paused for food, of course, and to bathe, but she didn't bother getting dressed beyond a wrapper, her hair in a long braid hanging down her back. Part of it was that there were a lot of papers, piles of them. Once she'd figured out the trick of how they were hidden, she found two other sets, one in Aunt Metaia's study, another in the library, one with an earring, one with a brooch of the same style of garnets. It made her wonder, yet again, about why Aunt Metaia had insisted on the gift on solstice night. She'd thought, at the time, that it was solely about Childeric. But the earrings made her sure that Aunt Metaia had been taking precautions in half a dozen directions.

Many of them were simply private notes, but the stacks also held specific projects, bounded by a length of folded cardstock. And the one that she'd been working on in June, in May, the months right before her death, those were scattered over five or six folders and bundles. Thessaly had thought about taking all of it to Cousin Owain and Magistra Hereswith, but everything was tumbled together. They certainly didn't have time to work through all of it, and Thessaly had nothing but time.

Besides, some of it was about the house, and some about Aunt Metaia's investments. There were two ships likely returning soon that she had also invested in, carrying rather arcane materia. It would be interesting to see what happened with that, but that was something to come back to early in the new year, when they'd arrived.

She also remembered to write a note or three to Vitus, but figuring out when to see him baffled her. He wrote back, and he seemed to accept her explanations, as confusing as they probably were. Thessaly promised herself, and then him, in writing, that once she got things sorted, she would figure out more time with him, without having to rush.

Finally, though, she decided. She wrote on the third, asking if Laudine might be at home for the visit she'd mentioned some time earlier, and got a rather prompt reply, offering the fifth. That meant giving over the afternoon and evening of the fourth to Collins and her ministrations. Her hair was tamed, various cosmetic charms, enchantments, and lotions applied, all the details she'd been neglecting for the fortnight beyond the barest basics.

On Thursday afternoon, she found herself walking through the portal into an estate she did not know. It was a Tudor manor, all brick and stonework, the house clearly added to at various points over the years. One of the maids met her at the portal, escorting her through the entrance hall, then right, into what turned out to be a drawing room looking out on a lawn and trees.

Laudine stood. "Thessaly, so glad you felt you could accept our invitation. Please, sit. Shall I pour?" Tea was already set out, and a porcelain tea set. One could tell a great deal about someone by their tea sets, Thessaly had always thought. Here, she had expected something involving profuse flowers and perhaps bright colours. Or perhaps something with stronger colours that evoked the alchemical work Dagobert favoured.

Instead, she found a set of striking blue jasperware, deeper than the classic Wedgewood blue. She recognised the shade immediately as being from the Athelstan potteries. He'd trained with Wedgewood back around the turn of the century, before expanding and developing magical processes. The blue fairly glowed, picking up the golds of the panelling in the drawing room and the soft charmlights above and the winter sunlight outside. She managed to nod before taking her own place at the table.

The business of pouring the tea and being offered the biscuits and other treats took a few moments. Thessaly wondered if Laudine found that as soothing, the rhythm and structure of it. Once everything was sorted, Laudine fell silent just the right amount of time. "I understand from Maylis that she hopes you will make arrangements with Sigbert. May I ask how you feel about that, and whether I might offer any information to help in your decision?"

Laudine had, in all honesty, made an offer of assistance before. At least twice, though it depended on how one counted. Thessaly wasn't foolish enough to assume any conversation would be in confidence, but she had come because she hoped Laudine might share something more. "I hoped for that, yes. I am conflicted, I suppose is the best way to put it, by several things. As well as not wishing to rush a decision." Thessaly was, of course, in proper black, as was Laudine. That was perhaps what was making the other shades and colours in the room stand out to the eye. "May I ask first how you are doing? And Dagobert and Garin, of course."

"You are always so kind, to ask after him. Few do." Laudine gave her a warm smile. "If, perhaps in January, when it's been three months, you'd be willing to come show Garin a bit more in our duelling salle, I am sure he would be delighted. As a favour, of course. None of us here could give you a proper match. It is not one of my gifts, and I believe even Dagobert was not really to your standard, before." She went on almost immediately, "He is continuing to recover. He is in London on a matter of business through supper tonight. And I am doing well enough, though I fear I am not one of those women who glows while enceinte."

Thessaly considered that information, picking up her cup and contemplating the design. It was only then that she realised the scenes were not the ordinary sort of thing, the Neoclassical myths and tales that were common on such cups. Instead, these had what were obviously tales from French lore, what Thessaly thought might be from the trouvère songs, or perhaps the Lais of Marie de France. One certainly seemed to be Bisclavret, a wolf among a pack of hunting dogs. Then the king and his court were bending to investigate the gentle wolf. "The set was my grandmother's. I thought you'd appreciate the shading and the designs, but it's also the one I prefer when with friends." Laudine sounded amused, and looked it, when Thessaly glanced up.

"It's lovely." Thessaly sorted through her possible approaches. What she had found in Aunt Metaia's papers had a lot to do with the Fortiers, but it was not actual evidence. She did not expect that Laudine would confess to whatever the matter was, for all sorts of reasons. For one, it was likely there were magical oaths in play about that information. But she wondered if she could get a little more. "The questions I have are delicate, but you had indicated...."

"I will not be telling Maylis what we discuss. Nor Clovis nor Chrodechildis. I may discuss it with Dagobert. We rarely keep secrets from each other." That was also far more blunt than Thessaly had expected. "I do not promise to answer all your questions, of course. But I know what it's like to marry into the family, and the, what shall we call it, the thorns that can present."

Thessaly nodded, then took a breath. "Would I be correct in understanding that there is more distance between you and your husband and the rest of the family? I've seen a little of it myself, but I am trying to understand the scope and the implications." Then, she took the risk and added, "Around the time of your husband's misfortune."

Laudine did not move for a second. Her control was excellent. Then she cleared her throat. "As all families like ours tend to, the Fortiers have particular projects and secrets."

"That is no surprise, of course. I presumed they existed, though, well, Childeric did not communicate well about even those things he might reasonably have shared. But I could see some of the shadows of them, even if they made no sense."

"Just so." Her tone was prim and precise, but Laudine offered a half-smile, clarifying that whatever disapproval she felt, it was not about Thessaly. "My husband disagreed with certain actions, and was cursed for his disagreement.

By two people at the same time, hence the lingering impact, or so our Healer thinks. An unanticipated combination."

Thessaly forgot to breathe for several long moments. "Oh." Time for another risk, then. "By others in the family."

"Yes. Though I won't name who." Laudine considered. "I knew nothing of the plan at the time, and I do not know most of the details now, just the outline. But when Dagobert began to recover, to talk about any of it - he is hedged round with oaths, of course, which makes talking about details complex - we made our decisions. I am committed to the wellbeing of my husband and sons." That plural made Thessaly's eyebrows go up. Laudine smiled more broadly this time. "We're fairly certain. I had my midwife's visit yesterday. We won't be telling the family for another few weeks, just to be sure."

"They would have different opinions about a son than a daughter, yes," Thessaly said. That made her consider. "Bradamante wasn't involved in whatever it was, was she? The way Yves has been making more of his own pursuits."

"Ah, you spotted that, of course. They have not been as subtle as they might be, for those paying attention. No, she was not, though I believe she has some general understanding of the project." Laudine shrugged slightly.

It made Thessaly confront the next question. "Childeric and Sigbert?"

Laudine gave a very slight nod, the sort of thing an observer had to be focused on to notice. Which meant Thessaly could not usefully press the point. "And others on the estate? Magistra Landry has been— erm, especially pointed about a few things?"

"With us, as well. May I ask if there was a direction to her advice?"

"She..." Thessaly did not want to get Magistra Landry in difficulty, for several reasons, starting with Thessaly's desire for her own wellbeing. "She bid me be cautious of Sigbert." It was perhaps time to admit to something. "Childeric was increasingly difficult, in private. He did not bother to tell me things that I should have been told. Childeric was acting against the scope of the betrothal and marriage agreements. He almost struck me at one point. Sigbert has promised he would not do that, but I do not know how far I might actually trust him."

"Ah." Laudine stood then, to go look out the windows on the lawn. "I wish I could say that my nephews - those nephews - are the sort of men I wish they were. Let me say that I am not surprised either by Childeric's actions or by Sigbert swearing he will not do the same. I do think Sigbert wishes to be different, but I do not know if he will manage it. I think Maylis is pressuring him in ways that cannot end well, for one thing. Not for him, and not for you, if you agree to marry him."

"And your sister-in-law, and her husband, are very present. As is the Dowager Lady Chrodechildis." Thessaly could spell that out without further trouble.

"Just so. And so, I cannot advise you on what decisions to make. You have a better sense of the landscape, of the pressures you face. And I am aware, even if Maylis is not giving credence to it, that you certainly have other options, depending on your preferences and priorities." There, she turned around. "Dagobert has enjoyed his conversations with Vitus Deschamps quite a lot. So has my father, who is perhaps the more challenging to win over. You need not protest your innocence, you are not promised to anyone right now, you have standing in your own right. I, myself, would welcome you to the family if you married Sigbert, but you should not decide on that account, certainly. And my enjoyment of your company is not predicated on a family connection."

It was, all in all, a frank assessment. "I shall take more time to consider my options then. And perhaps visit, again? This is certainly a beautiful estate. A much larger home than Bryn Glas. of course."

"I would be delighted to take you through, if you like. The gardens aren't much, it is December, but the house itself is rather lovely. A bit big for just the three of us and the staff, but plenty of space for Dagobert's lab and a library and such. He's considering acquiring an apprentice or assistant in the new year, as well. I shan't rush your tea, of course."

From there, the conversation went along to the history of the house - early Tudor, as Thessaly had guessed. Laudine was clearly fond of the house and its history. She shared little details of additions and enhancements, making it clear she found many of the older features charming. Even the ones that were distinctly unfashionable.

16

DECEMBER 10TH IN TRELLECH

"Thank you, yes, there. Now the deposit is properly registered. I'll be in touch with more details about the timing once I've had a chance to work out the proper calculations. Sometime around January second or third for the working, and then some additional time for the setting."

"And you're certain you can't do it sooner?" The woman in front of him wasn't being presumptuous or demanding, instead she was something more like plaintive. Mistress Fellowes was yet another referral from the Carringtons.

"I'm afraid not. For the best potency, we really do want the moon moving through the constellation of Perseus. The sun might be better still, but I'm certain you don't want to wait for April or May."

"No, no, not that. If you say early January, then, well, I suppose I'll continue being cautious about going out in the rain." The woman twisted her hands slightly. "And you'll let me know the costs?"

"Of course. I'll be going to London to select coral for

the work later this week. And I've noted your preference for white coral, but also your agreement for the best piece for the purpose." Vitus had, in fact, made quite a few notes, well beyond his usual form for a consultation.

"The red pink is lovely, but it's so hard to match to anything to wear, isn't it? Though, of course, I want it for what it does, not what it looks like." She stood, rather abruptly, and Vitus stood as well, moving to pull the chair she'd been sitting in back. "I should let you do your calculations, shouldn't I?"

"Let me walk you out, of course. Here, this way. The cafe across the street does some lovely baking, if you'd like to sit for a moment and gather yourself." They tended to let him buy what hadn't sold at a discount, and he cheerfully mentioned them to his clients. That was a delightful and often tasty symbiosis.

Once she was making her way across the street—indeed, to the cafe— Vitus retreated back upstairs to his workspace. That was the third consultation this week wanting protection against lightning, and it was only Tuesday. He'd have to consider, rather carefully, how many talismans he might make during the proper hours. Ideally, he'd get out away from the bustle of the city for it. Perhaps Thessaly would allow him to do the work up at Bryn Glas. The enchantment of the stones didn't need any particular tools or space, though the carving and setting would. He didn't much fancy being outside in very early January with bare hands, but needs must. And all three clients so far had been very willing to pay well, not even questioning the deposit or summaries of the cost.

It was all rather baffling. He'd inquired, each time, if there was some particular reason for the desire. Each time, they'd said they'd had horrible dreams of a lightning storm. Vitus couldn't see a pattern in them. Two had come via referrals from the Carringtons, the other entirely independently, he'd been at some of the electricity lectures. They lived in different parts of Albion; they did not have any obvious shared family connections. Thessaly would probably know, if he got a chance to ask her.

That side of things had been— well, worrisome and also complicated. For a fortnight, he'd only a handful of notes from her. Then she'd written about visiting Laudine, but he'd been so busy they'd not talked about it. Besides the requests for stones related to lightning, there had been several requests for talismans against nightmares. He had jasper for those, and he could come up with something less anchored to the constellations or fixed stars for that, thankfully.

He was hoping he might have a chance to talk to her properly soon. She'd indicated it was possible. But of course, her family had its own customs for the holidays. She had to turn up for at least some of them, even if her mother was still in formal mourning for her aunt. And Thessaly was, at least so far as other people knew, in mourning for Childeric.

The problem of Albion, Vitus decided, was that it wasn't as if they could just ignore all of that. Whatever choices Thessaly made, or whatever choices Vitus made, for that matter, people knew them. Other people knew their families, they'd make decisions based on what they saw or thought they saw. Whatever interpretation they put on a choice, certainly. There were times Vitus found that a little reassuring, in having an idea of what might be good for business. And there were times it was utterly infuriating.

Now, he sighed, and went to gather up something for his luncheon from the keep-cold box in the kitchen, reheating soup and putting together some bread and butter. The woman in the next building who did his cleaning kept him stocked with that sort of thing, and Vitus appreciated not having to think about it much. The restaurant where she bought the food was quite good, or possibly she got it from more than one. He hadn't expected to feel run off his feet this quickly, establishing himself. Vitus couldn't complain about it - his personal accounts definitely were more reassuring than they had been. And it would be even better in January, when he got payment for final pieces rather than just the deposits for the work.

Once he was done eating his soup and bread, he washed out the dishes. Back by the front door, he touched the panel that would change the sign downstairs, at street level, to show that he was at home to callers. He had no other appointments this afternoon, and he didn't intend to start anything that couldn't be interrupted. There was plenty of research to do, and the list to finalise for his visit to the gem merchants in London.

It was perhaps three in the afternoon when he heard the bell ring, indicating someone was downstairs and seeking him. Vitus closed the notes he'd been working on, with bookmarks in place, tidied his jacket, and went downstairs. He was startled to see Cyrus Smythe-Clive there, waiting in the vestibule.

"Good afternoon, Council Member."

"I was in Trellech, having a visit with my sister, and a look at something in the library, and I thought you might help with a question. A consultation, of course, at your usual rates. Half an hour to an hour, most likely, but let me know if you have another obligation?"

Vitus certainly would not turn that down. "Of course. And no, that timing should be fine. Please come upstairs." He led the way; he had to open the warding on the door, of course, and Smythe-Clive didn't jostle his elbow. Vitus showed him through into the consulting room, which was showing to good effect in the afternoon sun. "Either the table or the chairs, depending on if you think we might need reference materials out. And may I offer you tea?"

"Oh, the chairs, I think. Though if you take on the request, I suspect you'll want the books." Smythe-Clive settled in what looked like a remarkable degree of confidence. "And thank you, no tea is required."

Vitus took his cue from that, gathering his working notebook and fountain pen from the desk before settling in his own chair and opening the notebook. "Please begin."

"I am here both at my own behest, and the Council's. Hereswith— Council Head Rowan— was curious if you had seen any tendencies in your consultations. We are not, of course, asking for any confidential information, specific names, but, as she put it, the pulse of the inquiries."

Vitus twitched once. "I was just thinking about that, actually. I've had an outsize number of requests for protective talismans of various sources. Some more general, half a dozen of those since I set up properly. That's about what I'd expect. But then some specifically against lightning this week, and some against nightmares. Several others where the focus we settled on was not primarily protective, but where those considerations were in play."

Smythe-Clive nodded slowly. "That's exceedingly intriguing, yes. And we appreciate that information, formally and informally. If there's anything else you feel you can share, now or later, Hereswith would be pleased to hear it. She mentioned you'd offered some information previously, as well as some talismans for the general workings at the most recent— erm, my— challenge?"

"I did, in collaboration with Magistra Hall. I'd be glad to consider similar requests in the future, of course." That was the simple answer. Honestly, he'd be a fool to turn down that kind of work. Not only was it financially practical, he'd enjoyed the challenge and the quality expectations.

"Oh, I'm fairly confident Hereswith will have some ongoing requests for you, then. I'm likely to play messenger. I'm a tad less busy yet than the rest of them." Smythe-Clive tapped his fingers, but of course he didn't explain what was keeping the Council so busy. Vitus did have the sense, at least, that it was uncommonly busy. Instead he changed the subject. "The other aspect, as I said, is more personal. One part is information, another is a request."

"Yes? Go on." Vitus tilted his head, showing his focus.

"My sister Andie, and I were pleased to host Thessaly Lytton-Powell for tea, last week. I don't know if she's had a chance to mention it to you?" Now, the other man's voice was completely smooth. Absolutely of Fox House, Vitus was certain it was something they trained in. Vitus did not know how to respond to that, what answer might remotely be safe. Sensibly, he stayed silent, just nodded once.

Smythe-Clive went on, as if there were no awkwardness. "She mentioned that Childeric Fortier did not respect the agreements in place, including about her choice of association with others. That's not on. And I have appreciated her skills since we were in school, though it was more commonly partnering in Alchemy or Materia than anything less academic."

Vitus let out a breath. "Not a duellist, then?"

It made Smythe-Clive chuckle. "Not at her level, though on one of my better days, I could give her a bit of practice. Have you had a chance to see her duel? I suspect not."

"No." Vitus would like the chance, but he absolutely could not think of a way to ask. A duel required an opponent, an opponent of proper skill. And it would need to be someone who would not be difficult about Vitus's presence.

Perhaps if Alexander Landry had been in the country, he might have done on both counts. "I suspect it would be good for her to do more of it, but it's not the sort of thing I could casually suggest."

Smythe-Clive looked thoughtful. "I will see if I can encourage her again. Perhaps after solstice, when it would be a bit more acceptable. I certainly know a few people who would be glad to."

Vitus let out a slow breath. "I appreciate that. I want the best for her." That was all he said, but suddenly Smythe-Clive was leaning forward.

"Oh, you have fallen hard, haven't you? I remember how that feels. I wish Thessaly well, and you as well. She and I plotted a touch, putting around the comment that she and I discussed the matter of making a match, as I am suddenly vastly more eligible. I said I would not consider a marriage of convenience when there was someone she truly cared for, but we are both glad to use the conversation to defer pressure. I give you my word, and I'd give you my oath, if you wished, that is all we agreed on."

"I do not need your oath, Council Member." Vitus felt himself retreating into the formality like a shield. "I understand she's under a great deal of pressure and expectations."

"I hope, in the circumstances, that I might ask you to call me Cyrus. But I thought you should know how the landscape looked, from my end." He paused for just a moment to signal the change of subject. "The last query I have will, I think, be easier. I would like to have you craft a talisman for my sister. We do not have a tidy gift-giving occasion just yet - she has a September birthday - but that's no matter. Something that would be of help in her healing work, whatever that might mean. I have an idea of a budget, of course, but I am interested more in the right thing."

"To be a secret from her, or with her cooperation?" Vitus was up for the former, but he added, after a moment, "With her cooperation would likely produce something more effective."

"Indeed." Smythe-Clive— Cyrus, the enthusiasm for his sister made that a little easier to manage— tapped his fingers together. "Could we discuss some options, then have her visit, without you detailing the full plans? Get whatever information from her that would be a help, and then the final choices could still be a surprise?"

"That would be quite satisfactory on my end. Now, did you want something to match with Healer's red, then? A ruby or garnet or spinel, they all have different properties."

"Do, please, instruct me." Cyrus settled back, posed to listen. Vitus had to smile.

"Let me talk through some options, and then if you can wait a few minutes, I can bring out a few specific examples. I gather you don't have more than the ordinary understanding of different stones."

"I have some idea what I like, but no, you may consider me entirely untutored in anything that doesn't have a strong association with ritual, especially the more elemental forms. Do please assume you should explain from the basics?"

This might, in fact, be a delight. Vitus nodded. "In that case, let me begin with colour as one aspect." He settled into his lecture amiably, half his mind running through his current stock and what he might bring out by way of demonstration. Vitus only had the one small ruby right now, but he was seeing the gem merchants tomorrow. He could at least explore their stock. And he had a number of garnets and spinels in his storage cases.

17

DECEMBER 20TH AT BRYN GLAS

"Will you stay? I don't want to be alone." Thessaly's voice was steady until the last word, then it cracked and she turned away, toward the fireplace in the library. The house was decked out for the solstice, though they, of course, weren't entertaining guests. Or not besides Vitus and possibly Cousin Owain. But it was the solstice eve. Cousin Owain was busy at the Council Keep, and would be all night.

Vitus had taken a step back, rocking on his heels, visibly surprised. "Stay?" It was only a tiny consolation that he sounded as uneven as she felt. "I hadn't planned on it, but I could. You'd like me to."

She swallowed. "I mean, not just in the guest bedroom. If you'd like that?"

"That's sudden." He rubbed his face, then immediately said, "It's not that I don't want. It's just we hadn't been talking about it, hadn't been doing, erm, more than we had? That's a leap."

"I don't want anyone else deciding for me." Thessaly turned back to him. Mother had made it clear the day before that Father was looking to sell her virginity, and she was having none of that, for several reasons. Now she pulled her wrapper closer to her. It was a reasonably festive design, a medium green embroidered along the edges with holly and mistletoe, the red and white dancing among the darker green of evergreen boughs. "And I don't want to be alone."

Vitus took a step closer to her. "The first one's a good reason. The second one's a— that's not the best choice for doing something like this." She flushed, shivering, and he took another step, a hand cupping her shoulder. "I'm not angry, but it's the sort of thing we should talk about."

"All right." She turned to face him. Thessaly could be brave, even if it felt like she'd lost the knack of it the last six months. Childeric had torn it away and ground all the roots of her courage into dust. She watched his expression, and before he could say anything else, she went on, the words tumbling out in a heap. "I don't want to be alone, I want to be with you, I want to be like we were at All Hallows. Us in the dark and the quiet and all of it good. Only, maybe, with some new kinds of good."

His mouth opened and closed twice before he managed to reply. "It may not be delightful. Something that new to your body. Did duelling feel good the first time?"

That made her grin, the sort of savage grin that her mother had trained out of her— well, as it happened, not long after her first duelling lessons. "Actually, it did. But I'm old enough to know that the first of something doesn't limit the last of it. Or the later. Will you?"

There was a long pause, his face still. But there was a burning in his eyes, to match the fire in the fireplace, and she knew what his answer would be when he worked around to saying it. "I've not told you a tenth of the dreams I've had about being with you." Then he let out a puff of breath and stopped.

Thessaly touched his cheek. "I am sensible. I've got a potion. I can take it now." Aunt Metaia had taught her the charm against pregnancy, but she'd not practised it for a good while, and she wasn't entirely sure she trusted it. And while she could ask Collins or Emeline, that was not a conversation to have on no notice. The potion would do nicely.

It also seemed to answer some of his concerns. Vitus rubbed his face. "Look, if I'm going to stay, I should let Mama know at home and gather up a few things. Especially since I was planning on going to the Council rites tomorrow. I know you can't, not with a lot of fuss."

"But you can. And then you can tell me what the news is." Her mouth twitched a little more. "And the gossip."

"All right, I'll— I'll be back in a few minutes. Twenty, thirty? Where should I come find you?"

"The bedroom. Begin as we mean to go on, yes? There's food waiting in the sitting room, but I find I'm not hungry for it right now. And Collins and Emeline and the staff, they have their own celebration tonight." She wished them well, but that wasn't for her. There were lines of class and expectation that couldn't be crossed.

Vitus took a step back. "I'm going to ask you again, several times, what you want. So you might think about that some more." It came out a little harsh. Not that she blamed him. This was sudden. But then he leaned in to kiss her, rather tenderly. When he pulled back, he was gathering up his cloak and headed out the door. Thessaly watched out the window to see him cross the garden, even more pleased she'd added him to the wards.

It was more like forty minutes before he came back, long enough that she was restless. She'd made her way upstairs and checked the fire in both the bedroom and the sitting room. She'd peered at the food, she'd changed the lighting at least three times. And, because she knew when to admit what she was up to, she'd summoned Collins while her housekeeper was still expecting it. She'd let Collins know Vitus would likely be staying. It would do no one any good to be surprised in the morning.

Collins set about laying out clean towels and producing a man's dressing gown from a cabinet cunningly set into the wall that Thessaly had never taken much notice of, other than it had not held papers. Then Collins put out various small items in the bath. All without any comment at all. At least there was also no disapproval, but honestly, Thessaly wondered what Collins and Emeline, in specific, thought of the situation. They arranged Thessaly would ring in the morning when she was ready.

When Vitus reappeared, Thessaly had been sitting on the bed, her legs hanging off the side, thinking. He knocked, first at the sitting room, then at the bedroom, and she held out her hand. "You came back."

It sounded ridiculous, and she blushed. Vitus came over, taking her hand, then bringing it to his lips to kiss the palm as he bent over. "I wouldn't leave you like that. May I leave my things— erm..." He glanced around.

"The bench there, or if you'd like to hang things up, Collins told me apparently that cabinet is for the purpose? Things I had not known about my aunt." She then held up the potion. "And let me take this."

"Ah, well, if you're taking after her, I suppose that might be a little easier on the household." Vitus glanced around, taking the bottle from her hand and setting it aside as soon as she'd drunk it. "May I?"

"Please." Now, Thessaly was suddenly shy. "I— I want to do this. If you're willing. I mean, I should have said something sooner. Only there wasn't a really good time. We were both busy."

Vitus considered, then sat next to her on the end of the bed. His feet touched the floor for a moment before he worked on removing his shoes, then his jacket. "We have been. I'm still busy, but everyone else is busy for solstice. And besides, I can't possibly fit any additional lightning talismans into January at this point."

"You'd still like to do them here? I mean. Whatever tonight's like, you can do that." Thessaly felt insistent about that. "Not the grove, but anywhere else is fine."

"I don't really know what the effect would be in that grove, so no, let's not add ancient unspecified magic to the problem. Especially when we're dealing with lightning." Vitus was now in shirtsleeves, and Thessaly found that decidedly distracting. She'd almost never seen another man that way, not since her school years. Not even Father. He tilted his head. "Look, are you nervous?"

"Yes?" Her voice squeaked. "I want— whatever it is we do. I just, I don't know how to get from here to there. And I want you to enjoy it."

"It is a bit of a surprise, yes. But I've now had, what, forty-five minutes of anticipation. I, for my part, am nervous about making it excellent for you, but I don't think my enjoyment is at all in question." He took a breath, reaching to touch her shoulder. "Eventually, we'll want more of our clothes off, but we don't need to start there. May I kiss you?"

Thessaly nodded, and then he was leaning in, kissing her, one strong hand coming up on her back, spread so she could feel each of his fingers. They didn't dig in, they just were solid and there. It had been a long time, she realised, since she'd been able to lean into a touch and trust it. Well, except for Vitus, and they were still so new to what they were doing together that leaning in felt different.

When he pulled back, he let his hand come up and cup her cheek. "How is the rest of it going? Are you still trying to make sense of the papers?"

Thessaly nodded. "I left them in the order she had them. Surely that means something? Or it's relevant in some way. But I still can't make sense of it. I've made copies onto other sheets, so I can rearrange them, see if there are patterns, but I'm missing something. I let Cousin Owain know, but there's nothing obvious there. It's all coded. And they've all been frantically busy."

Vitus considered. "Let me think about it. And maybe, if we have time, have a look tomorrow? Or sometime. If you're willing. You could decide you don't want to trust me that far."

She blinked at him. "I think trusting you here and now is— well, it's a sign of how I trust you, yes?"

"Did your aunt trust everyone she took to bed, do you think?" Vitus asked it, half teasing and half something else. Thessaly looked at him, frowning, because now she was thinking.

"She never wanted something lasting, I think. Not someone having control over her. I have to say, I understand that. I just don't know how she did it, especially earlier. Once she was on the Council, once she had her own money, I suppose it was easier. But that wasn't the original, um. Set of materia to draw from."

Vitus ducked his chin. "Money changes things." Before Thessaly could say anything, he went on. "I'm glad you have more freedom. Or will, when everything settles, I suppose. Do you get a pause in it for the holidays?"

"More or less. I'm sure the Fortiers will have me out to Arundel again. But Cyrus and Andie were hosting something small, just before New Year's, and he offered an invitation to that, if I'd like. Council and various other connections. I can't ask if you'll come with me. It would be too obvious, but..."

"That sounds like a good thing to go to." Vitus hesitated. "And you're fine with him taking an interest in me, my work?"

"Oh, absolutely. Better you than other people." Thessaly looked away. "I— you don't mind, my continuing to not tell the Fortiers no?"

She watched Vitus closely now. He took a breath. "I don't like it. But you're right, there's something odd there. And I don't think anyone's going to figure it out who isn't there, on the estate, sometimes. I can't do that. Cyrus or anyone else on the Council can't do that. You can."

"And whatever Laudine knows, or her husband, they're not likely to tell me much more." Thessaly let out a long breath. "All right. I'll think about it." She added, after a moment's consideration. "And Cyrus has nudged someone he knows for an afternoon of duelling. Half a dozen of us, likely."

"That will be good for you." Vitus sounded absolutely certain of that. Thessaly wished she felt the same. It had been months— well, just about six and a week— since she'd had a proper duel that was any challenge other than with Emeline. Who was quite good, but who was also unwilling to risk injuring the person she was hired and oathsworn to protect. It made for somewhat limited scope.

Before she could get too snared in that, he moved, kissing her again lightly, and then he whispered in her ear, "Perhaps we might remove some of our clothing, both of us?" She shivered, feeling it run up her back. She let him guide her, loosening the wrap, then the buttons, tiny ivory ones, on her nightgown, as her fingers fumbled at undoing his shirt.

Once the gown was falling off one shoulder, exposing a broad triangle of her skin, it felt scandalous. He paused. "Do you like being seen?" Thessaly blinked, not sure what to make of the question. Vitus kissed the bare skin of her shoulder. "You dress, in public, for the face you want to show. You've been dressing here, at Bryn Glas, for your own pleasure and comfort. This is something different. Do you want to be seen?"

"By you." It caught in her throat. "What do you see when you're looking at a gem you might carve?"

Something in that brought him to a low chuckle, a rolling purr of one, as if she'd asked the perfect question. "I see the potential of what could be there. Several ways to get to that potential, usually. May I move your hand?" She nodded once, though she wasn't sure what he had in mind. A moment later, he was guiding her fingers, her palm, into his lap, into a swelling hardness there. He rocked into the touch, once he could, letting the fact he got pleasure from it show. "In a little, if you permit, that's the part of me that will slide into you. You did pay attention to your aunt's books, in all the particulars?"

Something in the way he put it, certain that she'd been attentive, made her moan with it. He took advantage to press her back on the bed; the wrapper discarded now, his shirt on top of it. His hands were roaming over her skin now, as he could, from the neck, from under the hem. She had no idea what to do with hers, until he paused, and encouraged her to undo more of his clothing.

Within a few minutes, they were in a tangle on the bed. Her hair was coming down out of its braid, and her nightgown was mostly up around her hips. "More?" Vitus lifted his head. "Or just this?"

If she stopped now, she might never talk herself into more again. Or she'd let herself be pushed into a marriage she didn't want, with someone who wouldn't have nearly the care for her Vitus did. His eyes were shining, bright like gemstones she didn't know how to name, pink on his cheeks from a flush of pleasure. "Show me more. Please." She stumbled over the words, but she'd got her point across.

A moment or three later, he'd encouraged her to lift up enough that he could draw her nightgown off. One of her hands got stuck in the billowing fabric for a second. Then he was pushing his trousers and the rest of his clothing off, until they were both on the bed, skin bare. The fireplace and the charms meant she wasn't cold, not exactly, but she was suddenly entirely aware of her skin, and she didn't know how to go on.

"Here, focus on what I'm doing. Or kiss me. Kissing is also excellent." Vitus stretched out beside her, one of his hands stroking down her hip, her thigh, before moving between her legs. As his fingers came closer to there, the spot that was beginning to ache, he kissed her. It was not a polite kiss, it was an eager one, tumbling over in delight, like a puppy. Only, much more adult than a puppy, because his fingers were deft, his other hand was, he knew exactly what he was doing.

Sometime, perhaps, she'd be brave enough to ask him where he'd learned his skill, so she could thank whoever it was, if only in her thoughts, for the gift. That got pushed out of her mind, though, as his hand became more active, urgent. She whimpered at a sensitivity that wasn't like anything she'd managed on her own. She knew where she liked to be touched, but it was predictable. She knew where her hand was and where she was telling it to be.

This was like a duel, gloriously like a duel. There were

a set of likely things that might happen, some of which she understood better than others. But she had no idea which she would find now, or next, or in a few minutes. His fingertips teased. As soon as she thought she understood that, they were stroking. Then there was a long finger sliding into her, pressing inside her, that made her hips twitch and arch, trying to make sense of it.

"There we go. Just like that. Does that feel good, my sweet?" It was an endearment he hadn't used before, and Thessaly liked it. She opened her mouth, he did something slightly different, and she moaned, her head back. "Oh, yes, more like that. You needn't find words, that was clear." His fingers did it again. Then there was a second finger inside her and she arched more.

"Can you work a hand down between us— gentle, though?" Thessaly managed it, though she had no idea how. She felt like she was fumbling every time she moved. But then her hand grasped around something hard and hot and swollen, and it was Vitus who was moaning, pushing into her hand. He managed to suck in a breath, focusing on her so intently it almost hurt. "Last chance, my love. Do you want this? Nod if you do."

Thessaly managed the nod. Almost instantly, he was shifting, moving as nimbly as any master of the duelling salle, to settle between her legs, his hands braced on either side of her shoulders. Then he moved one, arranging himself. "This might pinch. You let me know when I can move."

What she felt wasn't a pinch, not exactly. Oh, there was a stretch. There were new feelings she didn't have names for. But it was the heat, the solidness, the presence that got to her. She whimpered, not sure how to express what she was feeling at all, before just staring at him, meeting his eyes, and nodding.

Vitus began to move inside her, slowly at first, walking her through the dance of it at half-speed. That didn't last long, though, because her hips kept insisting on rising to meet him, like responding in the moment to the mazurka. She wanted the speed and the rush, everything slipping together into perfection.

Whatever it was he saw, it lit him up. He was grinning like a fool, then he put his right hand back beside her shoulder and began thrusting in earnest. He put his hips into it, the weight and leverage of his body, over and over again, and she let herself delight in the feelings. One of her legs came up, curling around to try to pull him closer.

Then, without warning, he did something else. Vitus flipped them around so he was on his back, her thighs were on either side of his hips. He was even deeper inside her. Vitus's hands came up to guide her, moving like on a horse, though astride, something she hadn't done since childhood. He arched beneath her. Then once she had the feel of it, it meant his hands could tease and stroke her body. He seemed to touch everywhere, now her breast, now teasing that place that brought so much pleasure, now cupping around her hip. She drove on and on, her back arching, then her thighs lifting her.

It couldn't last. Humans were frail. She could feel herself dripping with sweat, like the aftermath of the best bout in the salle. Thessaly could feel her thighs becoming exhausted. She felt herself rising to the pleasure, over and over again.

In the end, he decided for them. He flipped them once more, so she was on her back again. His hand darted between them to tease, as he began to thrust even harder and faster. Everything was urgent. Each movement shoved her breath out of her, until she was gasping with it. She hovered on the edge for a few final strokes before he was begging her in an undertone to please, please, that, please.

She finally understood what the books were on about. Everything came down to a surge of pleasure that made everything fade out of existence except Vitus and her joy in having him. Thessaly felt her body clench on him, hard, over and over again, far stronger than she'd found with her own fingers. He grunted, and then, just as her pleasure was easing a hair, she felt him deep inside her, and a sudden heat and liquid. He managed a few more rolling thrusts before lowering himself to his elbows and nuzzling at her breasts and her neck. She got a hand up into his hair, stroking, but that was all she could bring herself to do.

It took a few minutes until he slipped out of her and nestled beside her. By then, she didn't want to move. She wanted to linger in well-earned satiation and exhaustion for as long as she could. He arranged them so there was a blanket over them, pillows under their heads, and she curled into his arms. Everything else in the world could wait.

18

THE MIDDLE OF THE NIGHT

The first Vitus knew of anything wrong was getting kicked in the shin. It woke him enough to realise that he was not in his own bed. He was not in his working rooms. He was in Thessaly's bed, and she was having a dream. Nightmare, more likely, the way she was reacting. The sun had not yet risen, but at this time of year and this far north, that only meant it was sometime before eight in the morning. It was still oppressively dark out, not a glimmer of light.

Thessaly twisted, still in the dream's grip, and Vitus wondered about waking her. He'd heard it was dangerous to wake someone in the middle of a nightmare, especially if there was any chance of a premonition. He had not in fact discussed that with her. He hadn't thought to be sharing her bed yet, and it had not been a priority to this point. Besides, plenty of people wouldn't admit to it, even if they had a hint of truth in their dreams. He pushed up on one elbow and waited.

Perhaps thirty seconds later, she blinked several times,

her hand reaching out. "I, wait, oh...." That was not much for sense, but she had only just woken up.

Vitus cleared his throat. "A dream? A bad one?" She startled at the sound, but then reached for his hand and squeezed it.

"Yes." She rubbed her eyes. "What time is it? There's a clock there, on the table." She gestured vaguely with her elbow at the table.

Vitus called a small charmlight to his hand. "Midnight. A few minutes past."

"Oh." Thessaly let out a huff of breath. "I don't really know what to make of it. Or why it was upsetting?" She frowned, her forehead furrowing. "There was something satisfied, and something hollow, and something, I don't know. About time? I'm not making any sense at all."

"How about you write down whatever you remember and— you said there was food on the cart that would keep? You could use a little. I could, too." Vitus could at least take care of her that way. She nodded, and he rummaged for the dressing gown. It was a shimmering grey silk, flowing, abundant in a way his dressing gown at home wasn't. That done, he padded off to the sitting room to investigate the food. There was a stew, lamb, held under magic for the winter, and vegetables, Welsh cakes, hearty bread and smooth butter. And some wine, which was somehow not what he'd expected.

Thessaly was a few minutes, and she came out rubbing her nose and tugging the wrapper around her, since the fire had died down to coals and ashes. "It doesn't make a lot of sense. Why would I be dreaming of Philip Landry? And there was lightning, but it, I don't know, I wasn't scared of it? It was strange. I was inside, so I don't know why there should have been lightning, anyway."

Vitus wasn't sure either, though he also didn't want to

put ideas in her head. "Have you been talking about either recently? The last few days? And here, there's stew? I don't know what kind."

"That's lapsgóws." Thessaly said, cheerfully. "The northern version of cawl. Lamb, leeks, carrots, potatoes, broth. Oh, and Collins brought up the wine. Grand. It's Welsh. Someone got it into his head to make a vineyard like the mediaeval ones, but I rather like it? The idea he's trying to rebuild history, as much as the wine, but the wine's quite drinkable." Whatever uneasiness the dream had brought, the food seemed to have banished.

Vitus pulled together bowls for both of them, a heartier pottery than he'd expected from this sort of house. But it was entirely in keeping with the Arts and Crafts feel of all the spaces he'd seen. There was something satisfying about them, not only to hold, but the way they were meant for use. They were a sturdy beauty rather than distant perfection and the fear of crushing a delicate bit of porcelain in the hand.

The food was also excellent. He'd expected that, from his previous visits, though those had been tea or biscuits or such rather than a full meal. If Thessaly were eating like this regularly, he might stop worrying about her well-being quite as much as he had been. They were both quiet while eating, other than the sounds of the spoons and the glasses, but when they'd put their bowls back on the cart, Thessaly leaned against him. "Back to bed?"

He nodded. She disappeared into the bathing room for a few moments, and when she came out, he did the same, washing up and making use of the facilities. By the time he came out, she was in bed with the covers pulled back on his side, making it clear she'd stripped out of everything she'd been wearing. "Is that a hint? How do you feel, then?"

"Grand. Like I want more, if you're willing." Thessaly was lying on her side, facing him, one arm stretched out. He wondered, suddenly, if he'd ever be able to carve her into a piece, the way she was both languid and ready to move, like a great cat considering pouncing.

Vitus felt himself smiling. "Willing is not the problem. You're not sore? Too sore, I mean?"

She shook her head again, and stretched, a very physical stretch that made it clear how well she knew her body. "Much less than after some duels. More, please?"

"Something a little quieter. If you turn the other way, I could nestle behind you. You'd like my hands, I suspect, and then I'd rock into you." The idea hit her as both novel and interesting. He could see the expressions across her face, just before she obligingly twisted, her other hip now against the bed, then her shoulder. He shrugged off the dressing gown, slipped his feet under the covers, and then pressed up close to her. It would take him a little while to be more active about her desires. He suspected, from the way he was rising to the moment already, that it would not be frustratingly long. In the meantime, this let him make the best use of his right hand, his left coming under her to stroke her skin and cup her breast.

It was absolutely the right choice, something that was about closeness and touch. Vitus had expected it to be quiet, but it turned out he wanted to whisper a lot into her ear or her shoulder or her hair. About how she felt against him, about how he was enjoying this, about how he wanted all of this to delight her. And then, once he was more active, about what he was going to do, how he would slide into her, fill her again.

The words were nearly as provocative as the touches. By the time he pushed inside her, she was quivering with desire. He could take his time with it, though. The earlier bout had taken the sharper edge off. That meant they could rock and move and tangle for quite a while before he finally shifted how he was using his fingers. Those touches teased her to her climax and brought his. He fell asleep with his face buried in her hair, and he'd never been happier.

When he woke again, it was sunny out, through the window, a clear winter sunlight. Thessaly was no longer in the bed, and he looked around, blinking. The door to the sitting room was open, and he could hear quiet noises out there. He got up, using the facilities again and washing his face, before tentatively emerging. Thessaly was sitting on the floor, wearing a flowing gown in a deep green that was pooling around her, several piles of paper out. "Good morning!" She sounded bright and cheerful.

He smiled at her, gesturing. "May I?" She patted the floor near her, and he sat down, careful not to kick any of the papers or make them move. "I thought about a dozen Solstice gifts for you, but I thought, in the end, you might like a say in it. I brought some stones and some sketches. It doesn't make something pretty to unwrap, but— "

Before he could finish, her arms were around his neck, and she was kissing his cheek. "I'd like that very much. I have one for you, but Collins can arrange for someone to deliver it to your workroom." That made him curious, and she slid a rather large and solid package over to him with a bit of effort. He unwrapped it to find a desk set, the sort intended for magical researchers. There was a stand for a book that would keep pages open, or, he found when he read the attached information, turn them with a word. The inkstand was charmed against spills and stains. There were little boxes for small items, a tray to contain things, and she'd added a shallow tray with different hollows. "I thought one might work for stones better than most things."

"It is splendid. I would think of you often anyway, but this just means I will think of you even more so. I'll be back at work for at least part of the day come the twenty-seventh." There were other obligations between now and then.

From there, the conversation devolved into a pleasant discussion about the stones he'd brought, their particular properties, and his ideas for what could be done with them. He'd brought a larger piece of obsidian, good against nightmares and protective, and then three smaller stones. The garnet would match the pendant she had from her aunt, and while he wished her all the protection and joy, that maybe wasn't the right stone for this. Niobe had a piece of lapis lazuli, a little oddly shaped and small, but her fingers lingered on that one. It had particularly vivid veining, the kind they'd been discussing from the start. And there was a small topaz, with an inclusion, but the sunny golden light of it brought joy and peace and all the blessings of the sun.

Of course, he also thought about the emerald, tucked away in Niobe's protective storage. It was still there. He had visited it every week or two, when doing other work in the shelving. But equally, he could not offer it to Thessaly, not until they were more settled about what they were doing. Until she could be clear she was promised elsewhere. He managed, in the course of the conversation, to determine she liked them as a stone, though they weren't one favoured in her family overall.

She did not decide immediately, and he could tell that the choice was about whether she was going to make whatever she selected public or not. That affected both design and purpose, naturally. He left the notes with her, or rather, he'd made copies for the purpose. By the time he set off for the Council rites a bit after noon, he felt like he was on top of the world.

The rites themselves were, well, the same and also different. There was no Metaia, dancing with Owain Powell. He was partnered by his sister, or at least Vitus was fairly sure that was his sister. They certainly looked closely related, the length of their faces and the shape of their eyes and their noses.

Council Head Rowan seemed to be everywhere at once, even more so than usual. Cyrus Smythe-Clive was a tad solemn for a festive occasion, paired in the formal dances by his own sister. Vitus circulated, chatting here and there with various people. Some of them wished to arrange a consultation early in the new year. Two of those who'd commissioned talismans against lightning wanted to check all was still well. The fact that lightning, in specific, kept coming up made him think of Thessaly's dream, and he wondered again why Philip Landry might be relevant. He'd have thought that lightning would be about Childeric, if anyone, and Childeric was firmly dead and buried. Of course, so was Philip.

He saw Lord Clovis and Sigbert. They'd come in a hair late, looking flustered, before taking up their places in line to make their offerings. Later, he saw them amongst the guests, along with Lady Maylis and the Dowager Lady Chrodechildis. There was no sign of Laudine or Dagobert, and Vitus would not have approached them here. It was too public. Vitus was getting punch from the refreshments table when he heard what he was fairly sure was Sigbert's voice, behind him, a few feet away.

"So curious, but that's why we were late. We got the news just as we were leaving. Her maid found her dead when she went to bring the luncheon in. Of course, she wasn't coming today." The antecedent wasn't clear to Vitus, until the person Sigbert was talking to mentioned the name. Magistra Landry.

That was a shock. Vitus thought back to when he'd last seen her. Shaken, of course, by Philip's death, as any reasonable person would expect. And then at Childeric's funeral, she'd been veiled, which obscured a lot. But she had not seemed feeble or in ill health in other ways. Certainly, she'd seemed more robust than either Dagobert or Laudine that day. Entirely in control of herself, her magic, and her place in the world, that was the way to put it.

It wasn't as if he could ask, of course. He stayed where he was for another minute, appearing very indecisive about whether to select the shrimp paste or the cheese, and then dithering over which wine. He only made his choices once he could hear that the people behind him had moved away. Fortunately, the footman tending the table was used to that sort of oddity from guests here, and certainly well-trained enough not to comment, even by a shift of his expression.

Vitus retreated with his refreshments to a quiet corner to contemplate, and to see who else might be interested in a conversation in due course.

19

December 23rd

Thessaly had been making the best of the event. They were in the liminal space between Solstice and Christmas. She knew the Fortier tradition had a great bit of feasting on Christmas Eve, various expected events on the day, and the extended family gathering on Boxing Day. Those weren't the rituals that mattered in the magical sense, but they had become custom long ago, and custom they remained.

She had not been invited last year. She was not yet betrothed. And she was not invited this year, as she was not betrothed again. She gathered the festive part was smaller, understandably, since this was still a house with parents in mourning, a brother, aunts and uncles and cousins. But she had been invited today, on the twenty-third, when there was no standing custom, encouraged to spend the afternoon.

Thessaly had, of course, permitted Sigbert to escort her to the orangerie again. He'd kept up his end of the conversation, congenial and pleasant, even focusing more on her interests than his own. However, he mentioned something he needed to check on, elsewhere on the estate, and so he'd gone off to do that, leaving her sitting on her own. She'd rather be in the orangerie than inside the house, with the repressive expectations of Lady Maylis and the Dowager Lady Chrodechildis.

She startled when she heard the doors to her right creak, and then the sound of footsteps. No, footsteps and a cane. There was a murmur and a set of footsteps going in the other direction, the others coming toward her. Thessaly figured out who it was by outline, the sun was behind them, before she could see them well. "Laudine, Dagobert." She considered for a moment. "And Garin, off to play at the far end."

"To read, probably, but yes. We needed a brief break from the rest of the house. May we join you? Did Sigbert leave you on your own?"

"He said he had something he needed to check on before tea. His father had asked. I've no idea what. He was very polite about it." Thessaly gestured. "Please sit." She and Sigbert had been sitting on the wicker bench. There was a separate chair. Laudine claimed the other seat on the bench, and Dagobert the chair, settling down with a soft grunt.

There was a silence, an increasingly awkward one. Thessaly was certain they were here with some purpose, but she wasn't sure what it was. They were careful not to leave their son in the house, even, presumably, up in the nursery or their own rooms, and that was telling, actually, in a dozen ways. But it wasn't anything she could ask about.

After perhaps a minute, Dagobert cleared his throat. "I beg pardon, I must ask something delicate. Well, more than one thing. First, I do not know if you had heard the news, but someone should make sure you knew. Henut Landry died sometime over the night of the twentieth, or early on Solstice day."

Vitus had told her by note, but since he'd overheard it from Sigbert, she didn't feel she could entirely admit to that source. "Oh, no. Alexander will be heartbroken, I'm sure. Was it an illness of some kind?"

Dagobert had the good grace to look embarrassed. "We're not sure. We called for the undertaker; her man of business had all the necessary documents, since Alexander is abroad. But once her body was removed, the gatehouse wards sealed behind her, and we can't get in. No investigation."

That was— well, that was the sort of problem that estates like this didn't admit to. Thessaly considered her options, then raised one eyebrow inquiringly. "I hope you might let me know when the funeral is?"

The two looked at each other, but it was Laudine who spoke. "I beg pardon, were you closer than I thought?" Was it a personal grief, to add to the others, or was it something else? That was what she meant.

"Not close, no. But she was kind to me, after Childeric, and she gave me some thoughtful advice. And I know her people feel strongly about the proper rites after someone is dead. Alexander isn't here, but perhaps in due course, I could tell him about it."

"Ah, you would think of Alexander, I suppose. We have sent him a letter. Clovis did, and I added another to the packet. It will be—" Dagobert shook his head. "He is in Egypt right now, with some of his mother's family. At least they will be some comfort."

Thessaly was not entirely sure about that. They were family Alexander had not met previously. She didn't know the details of his itinerary, but she thought he might only have been there for a month or so. That wasn't enough time for trust, for being able to rely on them. Especially not for someone like Alexander, who knew a show of emotion as a weakness. "I hope he is well, and that his mother's family is all that might be hoped."

Now, Thessaly thought back to that conversation, what felt like years ago, instead of months. "I was in the cemetery the day Sigbert was announced as Heir. She was tending Philip's grave. She told me a little of their customs." Then she took the risk, because she could see a way forward. "She said, Dagobert, that— I do not have context for this— that you had had correction for your past choices. And that you were listening to Laudine more, and that was good. I don't know if that means anything to you." She would carefully dance around what Laudine had confirmed for her, that Dagobert's curse had come from family.

It did. She could see it in their eyes, though not what the context was. Laudine cleared her throat. "Thank you for sharing that. A particular choice, and we respect and thank you for that."

"You have been more generous with information that I might find helpful, it seemed proper to do the same in return." Thessaly turned her palms over. "May I ask about the rest of the family, if there are any particular considerations I might want to know about?"

It made Dagobert almost laugh, the sort of sound that was frustration and amusement tangled together. "Clovis is furious, but of course, there is no one he can reasonably be furious at. Father, perhaps, he was the one who made the original oaths with Henut, and who approved her warding and all. They had quite a negotiation, as I understood it from him, though he thought we did well out of the arrangement." He tilted his head. "Would it help to hear the summary?"

Thessaly felt that information generally helped, so she nodded. "I've heard a bit over the years, but it occurs to me I am likely missing something. Nothing personal, of course, but..." She let her voice trail off.

"I was still fairly young at the time, just twenty-five, and it was near a decade before Laudine and I would marry." Thessaly had not considered their respective ages, and Dagobert's mouth twisted up slightly. "She's eight years younger. I was finishing my apprenticeship that year. There was a family connection. That was why Henut came to us, of all the places in Albion. Her husband had been killed in fighting in the siege of Paris in the Franco-Prussian War. A miserable mess, and the worse because of the number of French magicians who died in it. She and Philip, who was, what, twelve, had been in Paris, taking shelter near the Grand Salle des Portes, and she managed to get through."

"A siege would not take the portals into account, no," Thessaly said. "And you said a family connection? Via her husband?"

"Just so. Gaultier Landry was from an old French family. He was a cousin to my father." Dagobert paused, as if trying to count the relations.

"Distant cousins. Third cousins, once removed." Laudine said it primly and crisply, and Dagobert smiled at her. Childeric would have resented Thessaly speaking up in that sort of situation, and she was fairly sure Sigbert wouldn't care for it either, though not as harshly. It made her think better of them, beyond what Henut had said. "They shared a passion for history, as I understand it. They didn't meet often— Gaultier spent much of his early adulthood in Egypt, and then they were in France. But they wrote letters. I've seen a number of them."

That was also interesting, that the letters had been kept for some period of time. And that Laudine had been that much in Lord Vauquelin's confidence, though perhaps the letters did not have many secrets in them. "And she came a few months before Alexander was born. I remember hearing that."

"Just so. Mid-September, and Alexander was born in November. There were private negotiations. Just Father and Henut, the sort that were entirely civil on the surface. It was clear to me he wasn't sure how it was going to go, and he took precautions. Sending Philip to play with Bradamante's daughters, for example, and I'm sure Maman had a part in managing things." Dagobert shrugged. "They were given the gatehouse, and there were expectations on her side, once she was recovered. Aiding the family, that sort of thing. She did all the protective charms for bare skin, as for your betrothal. Also a fair bit of the household warding, and a number of the more complex rituals. Especially as Father got older."

"Did they, I mean, obviously, they were around a fair bit. But separate?"

"She had her own maid. Another would help with the heavy cleaning every week. Her meals were brought over from the kitchens, and every so often, she and her sons would join us for a meal. Once a week, once a fortnight, it depended on what else was going on. She was never, mmm. Henut could charm if she wanted to exert herself, but she rarely bothered with anyone in the family. She saved her attention for Philip and Alexander, and for her work. She certainly did not flatter, even when it would have smoothed the way."

It gave Thessaly a good idea. "And she was mourning Philip's death, right up to the end." She considered. "Do you know any more about how Alexander is doing? I thought it a little odd that he went away so soon after Philip."

"Some of the arrangements couldn't be altered easily. Time with his father's family, and they have been touchy about the whole thing. They did not approve of Henut. And then other arrangements, from there. But I rather got the sense Henut preferred him to be well away from Albion. It is not as though she explained her reasoning to me. Or that I was in any fit state to notice much at the time." He cleared his throat. "I gather Philip's funeral was rather a production?"

Thessaly nodded. "There were other people there. I gather there are people in Albion who know the proper rites, as she would have put it. Is she to be buried here, or ..." There weren't a lot of other options, beyond the Trellech cemetery.

"I believe that's what her will says, part of the agreements with Father. Maman is trying to find a way around them. But Clovis has argued that her son is buried here. And that Alexander will be returning in due course, and it is the only home, that and their townhome in Trellech, he's ever known. Maman admits that is true. But she will not be buried for some time. I gather there are extensive preparations after the ritual itself."

Thessaly thought back to a previous visit to the cemetery, and yes, she remembered something about seventy days, though she didn't know when that was counted from. "I'm glad she'll be by Philip. I suppose it's silly, really, but it brings me a little comfort to think of it. Only, I wish she'd had a happier year of it, before— before whatever..."

Laudine blinked at her several times, as if Thessaly had said something unexpected. Then she changed the subject, "Chrodechildis is being a tad difficult about other matters. I'm assuming you still do not wish to give an answer regarding Sigbert. May we assist you with changing the subject at tea?"

"I am fairly sure Sigbert will also assist. He's worked up a fairly good line in saying I should have time to decide without pressure. I do appreciate that. Even if I suspect it's at least half because he thinks that the best strategy to my agreeing to what his mother wants." She glanced at the sky, measuring the sun. "We should probably get back, actually, I don't know what the time is."

"I will go fetch Garin." Laudine stood, brushing her skirts into place, while Dagobert was slower to rise and prepare to move. He looked, Thessaly thought, more recovered, but still not actually all that well. He was lacking vitality in some fundamental way that flavoured the colour of his skin, the ease of his movements, but wasn't just about those things. She'd have to think about that more. It had not escaped her notice that while he'd spoken fairly about his family, he had not chosen to protect their reputations in several places.

20

DECEMBER 27TH AT BRYN GLAS

"I don't understand why you're feeling this is yours to solve." Vitus stopped, then waved his hand. "Let me try that again, please."

He stopped to better gather his thoughts and come out with something that sounded less accusatory. He'd come out to Bryn Glas on the Friday, after spending a few hours in his workroom. Mama and Papa had gifted him a few new books for his library. Lucas had somehow hunted up a perfect tea set, each piece echoing a different gemstone, but otherwise in the same pattern.

It made a pleasing effect lined up on the sideboard in his flat. And of course, he'd wanted to set up Thessaly's present in pride of place on the desk. He'd discovered it fit well, with room to spare. He'd also made a start on the sketches for the piece for her, though, of course, those depended on her actual choices.

"Father was odd. I went to supper on Christmas. I couldn't disappoint Hermia. On the condition that Emeline could come with me, and stay in the room." Thessaly turned away to stare at the fireplace. They'd settled on the sofa when Vitus had come in.

He considered both the tone in her voice and the way she was sitting. "I don't want to press you. I want to understand. Before we get into that, though, may I ask something of particular personal interest?"

It got her turning back to him, raising one eyebrow and cocking her head. He rather liked what she was wearing today, particularly. It was, he suspected, another gown out of her aunt's closet, this one a flowing plush velvet in a blue-purple he hadn't seen her in yet. It had tiny seed pearls sewn along the edges, and each time Thessaly moved, they shifted and caught the light. But they did it subtly, as pearls did, not as a cut gem would, and he kept considering the difference. "Yes?"

"You're beautiful." It came out before he could think of it, and then he flushed. "I mean. The gown, your hair, the way you look in the firelight. All of it."

It made her tilt her head further. "Thank you." She made it something gentle, though there were layers he didn't understand to how she said it. Then, a second later, she added, "That wasn't a question, though. Definitely not an interrogative form."

Vitus laughed. "No. I wanted to ask how you felt about solstice eve. About what we shared, what— oh, I'm saying this badly too."

However badly he was stammering like a schoolboy, she didn't turn away. She reached for his hand, curling her fingers through it. "Can you stay tonight? And if you can, would you?"

It was precise, like she was a mistress of ritual arts as well as duelling. Though perhaps in this, they weren't so far apart. "Can, and I would be delighted to." He'd packed spare clothes in his satchel. The sheer memory of a few nights ago, the prospect of being in her bed again, both made him react. She didn't miss that, and that got even more of a rise out of him.

"You are the experienced one, of the two of us. You made that clear. Why on earth are you shy now?" Thessaly lifted her fingers of the hand that wasn't holding his, her left. "I'm not asking about your before. Or rather, I'd like to know, but only if you're comfortable telling me. It's not the sort of thing that should be a demand, surely?"

"Some people would make it one." Vitus let out a breath, and now he was the one looking at the fireplace. "Three other women, and all rather unlike you in specific ways. The second year of my apprenticeship, I became close with one of the colourmen's daughters. She was apprenticing with her father. We both use stones, of course, though they take the leavings of the cutting and stones that can't be polished, and all that. And they don't need the gemstones, most of them."

"But sometimes, for a magical pigment, you want just a touch of something - emerald, sapphire, ruby. Above and beyond things like lapis lazuli for the blue." Thessaly saw the point immediately. He'd forgotten again that she knew this well enough from her own work. Illusion relied on the real to anchor it. She raised an eyebrow at his expression of apology, then added, "It's not as if we've talked much about that side of things recently."

"Just so. You— do you know the Masons? Two brothers, two sisters, one of their husbands, and then two sons and two daughters in the next generation. Definitely a family business, various people taking on different aspects of the thing. I go by there every month or so to restock my inks." Vitus smiled a little. Last time Alice had been in the shop, she'd teased him up and down about the gossip, and the way she'd done it hadn't hurt. She'd been careful to make sure they were private, too.

"Is that where you get your lovely inks, the ones I've been admiring on your notes? The colour quality is excellent. And no, I know the name, but I don't think I've ever been in. Mother and Father considered them a little, um. What's the word? Below the salt. Mother's always favoured Allbright and Echo, and Magistra North only ever goes to Petrus and Sons."

"It is. I particularly like that verdigris shade they manage. Or their copper. It's striking, especially when used as an accent on a piece. And their black is as dark as anything I've found anywhere. Anyway, Alice and I had a grand time together, but we knew it wouldn't last. She wanted to go into the business. That likely meant marrying someone else in colour work. It's one of the few ways recipes get shared. And oh, Alice is desperately ambitious in a particular way."

It made Thessaly laugh, and then wriggle closer to him. Vitus took the hint and rearranged, so she could settle against his shoulder. "She has your love of colour, your eye for it. But she is short, plump, and given the opportunity, she strongly prefers a sofa, a fire, and a good book over physical activity. Which suits her, mind."

"And I do enjoy a ramble up a mountain from time to time. As well as the duelling. Though not generally in the winter. If you'd like to join me in spring or summer, however, you'd be welcome to." Thessaly considered that. "In bed?"

"Ah, you're similar enough there. Generous, curious, a great deal of pleasure. Not that I've been with her since we parted, and now she's married. Though I still enjoy speaking with her, when she's in the shop when I am. She and her husband do a fair bit of the traveling to find sources." Vitus thought that was about the right amount of detail. "The other two are a little less interesting a tale, and you're not likely to run into them."

"Oh?" Thessaly peered at him, twisting to do so. "Do go on?"

"Marianne was not so well-born as you, but more that sort of thing. Privately educated, went to a finishing school on the Continent, in Switzerland, and she was having a bit of a rebellious streak when she came back. Whatever you are, rebellious is not exactly the word, before you argue." Vitus squeezed her with his arm, just the once.

"It is certainly not what my parents would wish," Thessaly pointed out. "On nearly any point, except perhaps my apprenticeship."

"Regardless, Marianne had, shall we say, a variety of experience before she and I ended up at a gathering at the Stream. She was there as a guest, of course. And we took an interest in each other. It was a delightful summer, but I could tell she was getting bored by the end of it. Then she married someone who spends much of his time in Paris, sometimes elsewhere on the Continent. She very much enjoys being feted in fashionable cities."

"And you would not provide that, even when you are established. Your work is likely to keep you home," Thessaly said.

"Just so. The warding needs regular renewal. Not that travel is impossible, but not extensively." Vitus considered. "And then there was a woman while I was in Austria, Magdalena. She was a tremendous cook, she'd been tending to her mother. Some years older than me, a widow, and we passed a pleasant few months together before I had to move on."

Thessaly leaned her head back on him more securely. "I am no cook. I will grant you that. I've never really had the chance to learn, other than over a fire, for special occasions. The kitchen at home was Cook's realm, and here as well." She considered. "Do you miss them?"

"I do. I like to think when we are intimate, that kind of intimate, it ought to change us a bit. We ought to think about what we've left of ourselves with that person. I'm pleased with my choices. I don't hear from Marianne much, though a holiday card, now and again. Sometimes I see Alice, as I said, and Magda writes." He grinned, suddenly. "I told her about you, my last letter, and she wrote back for the holidays, reminding me of all the ways to be decent to you."

"That's certainly kind of her." Thessaly worked her fingers into his. "Huh. I— well, you know I haven't been with anyone. I knew, when I was in school that I'd be matched off, and some of them would care. Though I keep coming back to why Childeric didn't even try. Besides the agreements, the desire for family magics that have to do with virginity." She shook her head. He could feel the tenseness back.

"Did you want to?" The question came out of him before he could properly consider it.

Thessaly thought about it. The silence grew long enough Vitus was worried she was upset. But then she squeezed his hand before finally speaking. "I liked the idea of it, but I didn't see anyone I liked enough to, to be worth thinking about specifics." Then she ran her thumb against his hand. "You, I, um. I was wondering about it from when we met in the library. The first time. Aunt Metaia had told me a bit more about her own pleasures, about the fact she had them at all, I mean, with someone else. And I wondered about what it'd be like with you."

"Did you?" He could feel himself flushing now, with

pleasure and hope and anticipation. "I hope the reality didn't spoil the fantasy."

"Oh, you." She leaned to kiss his nose. "Rather more detailed fantasies now. I've more specifics to work with. But also rather more of them, actually. Distractingly often." Thessaly tilted her head. "On that level, I can sort of see why people make such a fuss about waiting. All that desire brings magic with it, and potency and all that."

"How do you feel about that, then? Foiling that particular line?" Vitus felt again like he was intruding on something, but he wasn't sure what. He was sure Thessaly would tell him or indicate if he'd gone too far.

"I think it's a ridiculous magical theory, honestly. People can get passionate about all sorts of things, and plenty of people do. If the bits about virginity were honest, it'd apply to men, as well as women. Yes? I do realise the, I don't know, physical forms are different, but it's still unfair. And I don't intend for things to get far enough with Sigbert that it would matter. Though."

Vitus coughed. "Though?"

"Father was being rather specific at supper. About pushing me to commit to the arrangements. I pointed out that it's only barely been three months, it's Sigbert's brother, and Lady Maylis is committed to mourning for at least a year. Anything less would be a scandal, and a visible insult to Childeric. Also Sigbert, honestly. If they want a formal wedding, the kind of show they had in mind with Childeric, she needs to wait. At least to the nine-month mark to make it public."

"Did you hear anything else about Magistra Landry?" Vitus had been wondering that. Her note after the twenty-third had been informative and also not. He'd read through the conversation with Dagobert and Laudine, and then her comments on tea and supper. "I got the sense there's rather more there, but I can't get a grip on what it might be."

"I suppose it depends a great deal on the manner and cause of her death. She was not particularly elderly, nor was she infirm. Not that I think she'd have admitted to it while alive. But I never saw any hint of it in her." Thessaly turned, so he could see her face better. "I think Philip or Alexander would have acted differently if she'd had some illness they knew about, or some weakness. Don't you?"

"I didn't see them nearly as much. And I'm not as skilled in that." Vitus thought about the way they had been, the last time he'd seen all three together. "But no, you're right. I keep wondering about the arrangement for the flat. I thought at the time that it seemed she was tidying up loose ends. Not wanting to have to deal with things."

"But surely, if there were some magical working—what was she doing? And why Solstice? And it doesn't seem to have done much, which. Well. I would expect anything she did to be effective, wouldn't you?"

"If her reputation was even a seventh of the truth, oh, yes," Vitus said, wholeheartedly. "I suspect we're never going to have an answer to that mystery, yay or nay." He moved to kiss her temple. "Do you think your father is going to be, erm. Especially difficult."

"He can try. He will try, I'm sure. But he can't get in here, and he can't choose my trustees. There was half an hour of him trying to talk me round to letting him doing so. And there was a thread through it I don't understand. Mother might find out more, but I don't know if she'd tell me. And I don't think Hermia spotted most of it, except that Father was being difficult." She sighed. "Father wants power. And he thinks the Fortiers are the best route to it. He's not wrong, but he is also not right." Then she pulled away. "Will you come to bed? I want a better taste to the conversation."

"Taste, is it?" Vitus gave her a moment to stand. "We could do something about taste, I suspect. And a great deal of touch, and likely also some sounds. I have not yet begun to demonstrate the range of possibilities." He certainly had some ideas about what he might try. His mouth on her, to see what she thought of that, perhaps encouraging her to try the same, the other way round. He certainly hoped to draw out some cries of pleasure, and perhaps also the murmurs of contentment that she ought to have in her day. "Do I need to help tidy anything in here?"

"Oh, no. I told Collins we'd ring in the morning. She quite approves of you. For the record, she made sure to ask what you'd like for breakfast." At that, Thessaly considered, and then she leapt forward. The velvet hung the air for a second before it was tugged along behind her, as she dashed for the bedroom as quickly as trailing skirts would allow. In her hands, that was remarkably rapid, and Vitus laughed and gave chase.

21

JANUARY 7TH IN TRELLECH

Thessaly was a tad unsatisfied with the day, though at least the late afternoon promised improvement. She had returned to her apprenticeship this morning. Magistra North could not, actually, complain about properly observing mourning. Her apprentice mistress would go up in a puff of hypocrisy, given how long she'd lectured Thessaly over the apprenticeship about attention to details and societal expectations.

On the other hand, she'd made her displeasure at the disruption very obvious. Thessaly had not been available to take on any of the burden of holiday decorations. Nor had she helped with the myriad adjustments to children's toys. Nor any of the other tasks that were beneath a full mistress of the illusion arts, but common fare for apprentices. It did make the dolls better, mind.

Thessaly could still remember when she'd got her first delicate doll. Clara had a porcelain head and shining hair. Aunt Metaia had changed the hair and eyes to match Thessaly's perfectly. Then she'd added a little dragon embroidered on the hem of the cunning little coat, as an extra treat.

That doll had gone to Hermia, in due course, and now reigned over the nursery shelves. Thessaly hadn't begrudged that. A doll should be played with. Aunt Metaia had made the changes, bar handing Thessaly the coat to keep. Though now Thessaly thought about it, there was a particular social marker there, wasn't there? That Hermia didn't get her own doll.

She wondered suddenly how delicate the family finances had been then, or were now, or whether Aunt Metaia had offered to buy Hermia her own and their parents had refused. Or, as a third option, whether her parents just hadn't cared that much. She added it to the little notebook she kept for questions for Amadeo Scali. Though she did not know whether it was something he could find out or whether he'd tell her if he did.

At any rate, Magistra North had only been able to disapprove so far with where Thessaly's learning was. Thessaly had spent the morning sharing her notes and projects while she'd been at home, and they had all received a passing approval. And Magistra North had admitted that Thessaly could likely develop the skills to take on some of the work Aunt Metaia had been doing. Useful work, that was the thing Thessaly kept coming back to.

But Magistra North had been, even during the moments of agreement, disapproving. Thessaly had obviously failed to thread the needle between obligation and apprenticeship and grief or whatever one called dealing with Childeric's death. At least that was done with until tomorrow, and it was a short week to return, since there had been Twelfth Night celebrations on the sixth.

Now, however, Thessaly had something to look forward

to. Cyrus had been kind enough to set up a duelling engagement - four or five people, including the two of them - at one of the private salles in Trellech. He'd promised at least one other woman. When Thessaly had inquired of Emeline, Emeline had declined joining in. She preferred to keep her skill more private. But she'd promised to talk through what Thessaly might want to work on, after playing chaperone.

The salle was not difficult to get to, tucked into the far corner of Club Row. Emeline went first, moving to one side as Thessaly entered. Cyrus was already there, chatting with a man Thessaly knew, and a woman Thessaly did not know by name, though she'd seen her here and there. Cyrus immediately turned. "There's a changing room there, and your companion is welcome to sit in the viewing area. And to check the salle's warding. This is Magister FitzAlan, one of my colleagues, and this is Mistress Helena Audley, who I suspect you've heard of."

"Oh, my." Thessaly was delighted. "I saw the duel you had, the demonstration one, of course, with all its limitations, what, four years ago now? A delight. Oh, I am looking forward to this." Mistress Audley was a good eight or nine years older. She must have been at Schola around the same time as Laudine, and Thessaly had not had a close view of that bout.

"I was a tad enticed myself. Do, please, call me Helena." There was a murmur of agreements on first names all round, which also boded well. Cyrus had hopes that if this went well, it might become a regular circle of duellists. Thessaly hadn't expected FitzAlan— he'd mentioned just preferring the surname, no title. But it made sense that Cyrus might also use the occasion to deepen a tie with his new colleagues.

With that, Thessaly went off to change, with Emeline

coming along to assist with getting her out of the corset and bustle. If she were going to be significantly active, Thessaly wanted full freedom of movement. She had a set of rationals made up in a deep grey, suitable for exertion and a nod to mourning dress. More practically, they wouldn't show dirt as easily. The billowing bloomers fastened in cuffs at the ankles, just at her boots. Over it, there was a dress that came down to about knee level. Still rather a lot of fabric, but much lighter than her day dress had been.

She checked her laces were still suitably tight since she had made a point of wearing her duelling boots for the day. Not that anyone saw much of the detail under her skirts. But the soles, the charmwork, and the way the buttons ran on the outside of her ankles all made them more supportive and sturdy for duelling.

By the time she emerged, the other two expected were there. Albert Horning had been a few years ahead of Thessaly and Cyrus at Schola, and Ismene Warden had been a bit of a legend by the time they started school. Ismene and Albert went to change, while Emeline made a proper circuit of the salle, confirming that all the protections were in order before she took her seat.

Cyrus, who knew at this point that Emeline was bodyguard as well as companion, just smiled at it. Thessaly took the opportunity to stretch. When everyone was assembled, she cleared her throat. "I'm afraid I'm rather out of practice several ways round right now, but I appreciate Cyrus setting this up so I can remedy that."

"It is rather difficult to keep up the skills when one can't be out in society. Have you considered building a salle? Cyrus mentioned you're living up in northern Wales now?" FitzAlan was stretching as well, taking his time with it.

"There's land, and I am considering it, but it will be spring, at least, before we could begin. We weren't able to sort out optimal site choices before the winter. And then, of course, there's the challenge of getting people to come. Or getting the right people to come." Thessaly shrugged a little. The thing of it was, having a salle for her own benefit was one thing, but it would be lonely if no one joined her.

That got a laugh out of everyone. "Oh, yes. Once you have your own salle, people flock. But it's not as if taking the portal is a tremendous burden. I'd certainly consider it on a regular schedule." Ismene said it smoothly, as if she were sure there'd be cause. The others echoed that, and of course Cyrus and FitzAlan were already likely to be somewhere with a portal and not a great deal of traffic waiting for it.

They started out with Cyrus and FitzAlan, partly to give the other four a chance to work out a rota of matches. Ismene offered to take on Thessaly first, with Albert to fight Helena. Then they'd see about another round of bouts. Everyone expected to get three or four, maybe five bouts in, which gave Thessaly a good idea about the level of skill, given they'd booked the salle for two hours. That meant things would go fast.

Watching Cyrus was interesting, actually. He was still not a naturally brilliant duellist, but since she'd last seen him, admittedly, several years ago now, he'd improved. He had a much more sure sense of where he was in the salle, and how to use all his resources. His charmwork had definitely improved, especially whenever he leaned into the more elemental forms. A gust of air almost knocked FitzAlan off his feet at one point. Then there was a rolling movement of the earth that turned into a boggy swamp under FitzAlan's feet.

The older man— he was a little less than twenty years

older, so secure in his position and skills— laughed, several times, apparently delighted by the challenge. They went back and forth, one gaining the upper hand than the other. All of a sudden, FitzAlan pulled out several unexpected twists in quick succession, bringing Cyrus down on his back in a cloud of dust. He reached down to help Cyrus up, and Cyrus was grinning.

"You've got better," Thessaly called out, agreeably. "But there's still room to grow." That earned her a laugh, and she suddenly wondered how long it had been since he'd laughed like that. He'd said he was arranging this for her, but clearly he'd needed something like this himself, perhaps tremendously.

He and FitzAlan bowed Ismene and Thessaly into the salle, with FitzAlan lingering to oversee the match and get them started. Ismene declared, cheerfully, "I know you want to get a sense of how things are for you. I'll match you for a little. Not forever, though."

"I wouldn't think of asking." Thessaly took her position.

FitzAlan counted the opening, stepping back, and Thessaly threw herself into it. There was nothing in the world for her but the magic, her feet on the ground under her, and her own wits. The world had changed for her as well, if perhaps less dramatically than it had for Cyrus. Or at least less visibly. She was slower than she wanted to be. That was lack of practice. Despite all her efforts, she'd lost conditioning. Thessaly was in no shape for a lengthy bout right now. She'd have to work on that with Emeline. She managed to get Ismene off-balance once, then again, but then Ismene stepped up her protections and Thessaly had to work to find any opening.

What she managed was, naturally enough once she thought of it, illusion. Casting any complicated image on the fly was a tremendous challenge, of course. But she managed to call up two images of herself, then shift them around so it was near impossible to tell which was real and which were illusion. It gave her just enough of an edge that she got a touch on Ismene, a solid enough one that Ismene yielded the match.

"I'd say that's cheating, but of course it's not." Ismene held out her hand.

"Use every skill you have," Thessaly agreed. "At least that's within bounds. But I know I'm weak a dozen places, including in the knees at the moment. And my footwork is horrendous."

"I noticed you keep your left elbow raised a bit more than the usual. Any reason why?" That chatter occupied them amiably as Albert and Helena set up and went into their own dazzlingly rapid bout. They were going so fierce and so fast that it was difficult even for the skilled duellists watching to follow all of it. FitzAlan joined the rest of them in the viewing area, and all five of them, Emeline very much included, were passing comments back and forth. The match lasted, too, a good five minutes. Finally Helena managed an elegant combination of charms that shattered one of Albert's protections and then made good on the thread of possibility. He went down, head over heels, before pushing himself upright and laughing.

From there, they explored the variations. FitzAlan was sturdy in a way that Thessaly found interesting to duel, and he seemed to have an endless library of charms and feints and strategies at his disposal. Cyrus, oh, she wanted to figure out a lot more about what he was doing, and she suspected he'd tell her at least some of it in due course. Albert had a sharp knack, the kind of tricksiness that made Thessaly think of Aunt Metaia. He went at problems from an angle, and rarely the one most logical to pick. He was tremendously successful with it.

And Helena had not flattered her, Thessaly did not want praise she had not earned. But she had agreed that with some regular time in the salle, Thessaly had an excellent chance of excelling. Certainly, Thessaly wanted to give Helena a challenge in due course, but Helena had won their bout handily ninety seconds in, purely on speed and dexterity.

It meant each of them had a chance against each of the others, too. By the time their slot was over, everyone had had a go, and they rapidly made plans for the next Tuesday. Helena promised to send along some recommendations for Thessaly, places to start with improving. But she hadn't lost so much skill she'd embarrassed herself.

Thessaly changed again, a necessity given the distance to the portals, and Emeline was quiet until they'd gone through to Bryn Glas. "Not that I'm saying that you should do away with my services. But it was a pleasure to see your level of skill, tried by people who know what they're about."

Thessaly let out a long sigh. "It felt so good, too. I'd missed it. I think I hadn't allowed myself to miss it. It hurt too much? Can we do some more footwork drills tomorrow evening? In the bottom of the carriage house, or clear out the entry hall or something?"

"I'll talk it through with Collins." Thessaly beamed, and went off to go and change into something comfortable and full of colour. Then she flung herself back on the pile of research that awaited her.

22

JANUARY 9TH IN TRELLECH

"I beg pardon, what?" Vitus felt he had not handled that at all smoothly, but he couldn't think of anything better to say. Florent Montague had asked to speak to him, a consultation for other work. Fortunately, they were in Vitus's consulting room, behind his own warding, rather than at one of the clubs.

"Are you available to help with a somewhat urgent question? I don't have all the necessary skills for it. For the Fortiers. Or, these days, the steadiness of hand I'd prefer."

"Lord Clovis and Sigbert Fortier," Vitus said. "Did you mention you were asking me?"

"I said that you taking it on was my requirement for my part of it." Florent settled back, unreadable other than the surface politeness he made visible. Vitus had, in fact, followed up on the invitation he'd made after Vitus had finished his apprenticeship. He'd had drinks a couple of times with Florent and Dagobert in various combinations, but this was different.

Now Vitus took a breath. "What is the project, then?"

"There will be oaths required on it when we get to that

stage. They have a long-term project in play, one where the next step involves stabilising certain energies and magics. A different range than the pieces you did for the Council, for the challenge, but somewhat similar. The other aspect involves figuring out what stones might work, to be done from samples and sympathetic resonances. I certainly have some expertise in that, but I think it needs your eye as well."

"And they know you're asking me. In specific. I would not have thought that would be acceptable." Vitus said it outright.

"I am doing them the favour. I gather they were not sure who else to ask, and my being open to the request is of help to my daughter and her husband. For my part, I said I needed your touch with several aspects. Clovis is not precisely pleased but accepted my terms. Sigbert was agreeable. I do not expect Maylis will invite you to stay to tea."

That was the sort of mess that Vitus very much wanted to discuss with Thessaly. "And the scope of the project, in terms of the work, time involved, and contractual considerations?"

"If you're willing, a visit to Arundel this afternoon to see the space. It is outside their estate wards, but not far from the portal, on the Arun. I'd like you to consider what the land tells you. At a suitable time, we could meet to select specific stones and approaches to try. Next week, perhaps." Florent looked amused. "The other condition I made is that they pay well." He laid out the amounts - for the planning, for the creation of the talismans, for the setting of them, then added. "That's per person divided evenly. If you'd like, I'd be glad to defer most of the creation to you and handle that portion proportionately. You have more freedom in your schedule."

Vitus did some rapid calculations. He had done the enchantments for the stones against lightning. He was working on setting them, in sequence of when the order had been made. Vitus had plans to see Thessaly that evening, and his brother on Sunday. Other than that, he could work straight through Friday and Saturday and much of Sunday, as long as his magic and focus would hold. And if so, he could get more time clear next week.

"I've a number of projects at the setting stage, but yes, after that, I will have more time, likely by the middle of next week at the latest," Vitus said. "Those are acceptable terms." Then he took a bit of a risk and met Florent's eyes. "If you think they'll keep their end of it. Sufficient information to do the work, a review by a trained ritualist on the oath, and filing as a contract."

"I would expect no less. I know Niobe has taught you that side of the field just as thoroughly. Would one of the Scali do, on the contract and the language of the oath?"

"Yes." Vitus said. "And they pay the fee, naturally."

Florent's eyes were dancing, as if he were looking forward to being difficult to the Fortiers in ways they couldn't argue with. "Naturally. Shall we go out and have a look then? Sigbert agreed to make himself available, and Clovis might be there, he wasn't sure."

"That would make sense, yes. I can't really begin to scope the work without it. Just give me a moment to pack up what I need, if you would?"

Florent amiably withdrew to near the door, looking over some of the prints Vitus's mother had selected for the wall. They were inexpensive watercolour pieces, each themed around a particular gemstone, but including flowers, birds, trees, whatever seemed relevant. He found them rather charming, as well as suggestive of associations worth pursuing. Vitus packed up his satchel, making sure he had a working notebook, his various measures, tools for measuring the magical energies.

They did not have to wait at Portal Square. Florent paid the fee for immediate access, but it was not terribly busy. They came out at the other end, and Florent set the waiting footman off to let Sigbert know they were there. He joined them only a few minutes later, just long enough for the message to be passed along.

"Father will join us out there. It may be a few minutes." He offered his hand to Vitus and Vitus shook it, the proper firm and brief handshake for the circumstance. "You're Deschamps, of course." It was not exactly a warm greeting, but it wasn't a chilly one either. "This way, we'll go around the edge of the warding. It's not terribly far." Sigbert set off briskly, through a series of paths that went west to the Arun, then followed the river down to an old mill. The wheel was engaged, but it wasn't clear what the mill produced. He remembered Thessaly talking about an old barn that had been damaged; the mill looked shabby, but in one piece.

"We can't permit you to see inside the building, not until the oaths are made. And the contract, yes." Sigbert added that before Florent could do more than open his mouth. "But I gather you need to have a look at the outside. We are looking for talismanic pieces to stabilise the shifts between the interior of the building and the exterior, when engaged in complex magical work."

Vitus considered that. "So, you want me— us— to come up with a plan with only half the information?" He then coughed. "Pardon. Would it be possible for you to do whatever you are doing inside the building without us seeing? So we could see the measurements needed, get a start on taking them? I gather that this is an unusual project, so we can't use any of the usual models as a starting place."

Vitus saw a flash of something in Sigbert's eyes, too fast to interpret accurately. Again, he wished for Thessaly. Sigbert opened his mouth, closed it, and then said, a little tightly, "I'll need to ask Father when he gets here." By that, Vitus diagnosed that the information might be too revealing.

"Let me start by doing the ordinary physical measurements, then, for the space to be encompassed." That sort of thing was routine and simple. Vitus had brought his various measuring tools, physical and magical, and he went off with Florent. As the junior present, of course, he did more of the moving around and adjusting, including clambering on the railing on the river side of the building. Florent, however, made a point of treating Vitus as an equal, conferring on specific details. He asked whether Vitus preferred the Athol method or the Resonance model, with an amiable discussion of the benefits and challenges of the lot.

Vitus took advantage of the opening with gratitude. It gave him a chance to bring up something he'd discussed with Herr Becker in Berlin. That was about the question of stabilising long-term effects, the advantages of certain kinds of inclusions in the stone, and designing the cut to fit the area involved. Florent had obviously set that up, and Vitus could tell the details were well over Sigbert's head. On the other hand, it was making it clear that Vitus knew his work, and that Florent acknowledged his expertise.

That took them a good half hour, and by the time they finished that up, Vitus could see another figure coming down the path, which resolved into Lord Clovis. He nodded once sharply, offering no formal greeting to his lands, which they were apparently not on. Or not the magical estate proper. "Florent. Deschamps, I gather."

"Vitus Deschamps," Vitus said, offering his hand.

Florent stepped in smoothly. "I knew Vitus was the right help for this. He's made several suggestions that will allow for a bit more elegance in the work, and also more—what was the word you used?"

Vitus recognised a power play when he heard one. He was trained for that part in this context. Not on Florent's part, but by Florent on Vitus's own behalf. Now he was really curious about what Florent had discussed with Laudine and Dagobert about Vitus himself. He cleared his throat. "There are methods of managing fluxes and shifts in magical vitality or movement that are more and less flexible. Without knowing more specifics of the project, it's hard to suggest the optimal approach just yet, but I thought something that had more potential for expansion and contraction might serve."

Then Vitus pushed himself to courage. "I understand, of course that you won't want to share details until the contracts and oaths are settled. But it would be a help for our proposal if you could activate what is done inside the building, so we could take readings from out here. Otherwise, the work will take rather longer in the next phase."

Florent smiled but just nodded when Lord Clovis looked at him. Lord Clovis sucked in a breath. "Let me talk it through with Sigbert, if you'd give us a few moments." Vitus smiled pleasantly, and the two withdrew to the far side of the mill building.

Once they were well away, Florent said, "You handled that well. Clovis would like to be high-handed. It is what he prefers in general, but he needs us. Both of us. And he wants this done fast, from everything I gathered. Now, if they do agree, the same sets of readings, but what else?"

"I was thinking Argentium's Fourth and Seventh, and then possibly Gwent's First?" Vitus suggested. "One thing I'm not sure about is the interaction between the demesne estate proper and whatever they're doing here."

"Ah. Yes, that is a factor. And you've not done much on any demesne estate, or any of those sets of magic, other than the Council work?" Vitus shook his head, and Florent settled into a pleasant discussion and explanation of the usual run of things to expect.

After perhaps five or seven minutes, Sigbert turned and headed into the building, and Lord Clovis came back. "It will take a few minutes to put everything in motion, but I will tell you when you may take your readings. I'd be available for the contract and oaths tomorrow, if the terms are otherwise agreeable."

Vitus nodded. "I would not be here if they were not suitable." Well, he might have. He was deeply curious about what the Fortiers were up to. And he was certain Thessaly both wanted and needed to know. But that was not how one handled business negotiations. Certainly, one didn't tell someone you wanted access to their estate. Vitus might not be of Fox House, but that was rudimentary plotting.

They waited in silence— Lord Clovis rather repressed any desire of either Vitus or Florent to continue theoretical discussions— until there was a hand waved out the window.

"A minute from now." Lord Clovis took several steps back.

Vitus pulled out his pocket watch and marked the second hand, waiting until it had swept the dial. Then he and Florent settled into taking the measurements, pausing each time for both men to write them down. Before they'd finished the first step, the repetition of the previous ones,

Vitus had a strong suspicion. By the time they'd run the Argentium and Gwent series, he was certain.

They finished, and Lord Clovis went and waved his handkerchief where someone inside might see it better than a hand. Vitus buried his nose in his notebook, flipping back to where he'd been talking about the readings the Hennings had shared. No, that was the same.

"May I ask how often you do whatever it is you're doing?" Vitus said, feeling like the last half of that sentence had not been ideal.

"We would like to activate it more frequently. Intermittently, the past few months, at least once a fortnight, often more like weekly."

That wasn't absolute, but it was suggestive, and especially if whatever they were doing had a lingering effect. Vitus nodded, then said, "I have the readings I need. I should be able to offer at least a partial proposal tomorrow, once the contract and oaths are done, for the work involved. Tomorrow afternoon?"

"One at the Scali Bank, then." Lord Clovis nodded once more, as Sigbert emerged, with his cheeks flushed like he'd been exerting himself. "I'll leave Sigbert to walk you back. The contract will allow for access through the path indicated, which skirts the estate, at any time, and the portal as well."

"Much appreciated. We may want to do some night-time alignments. The angle and strength of the sun can affect a number of factors," Vitus said.

That seemed to settle the business. Lord Clovis shook their hands and disappeared. Five minutes later, when Florent and Vitus had confirmed they'd got all the same measurements written down, Sigbert walked them back to the portal.

Back in Trellech, once they'd stepped away to the edge

of Portal Square, Florent turned. "Tomorrow, then. I am glad for your help with this. It eases my heart about— ah, well. Family. Never entirely simple, is it?"

There were many things Vitus would like to ask, and none of them were worth risking in this case. "Sir, no, I suppose not. I'll be in my consulting rooms until evening, and back by nine in the morning, if you have any further questions. Otherwise, I'll see you at the Scali."

"Likely then. Do have a good evening."

Vitus was seeing Thessaly, so that seemed plausible, though he had no idea what she'd make of what he'd been doing.

23

JANUARY 9TH AT BRYN GLAS

As soon as Vitus came through the portal, she could tell that he was upset. Or no, that wasn't quite it. Agitated, or tangled up about something, possibly both. Thessaly had been waiting for him in the library, because it was rather chilly out, with the fireplace going. Collins showed him right inside, though he paused in the entry hall to take off his cloak and gloves and hat.

"Should I bring tea shortly, mistress, or wait?"

"Give us a few minutes, please? I'll ring when we're ready." Thessaly said it without consulting Vitus. "Unless, hm. Could you bring some of the mulled wine out? A glass each?"

"Yes, of course." Collins was back with the glasses before Vitus had finished removing all of his various outer-most layers. She left the glasses ready on the table. She closed the door behind her as she went out, leaving them alone.

Thessaly held her hand out to him. "What's the matter? Or what's happened? I don't quite know what the proper question is here."

Vitus took it, turning her hand palm up and kissing it, which was also confusing. Pleasant, but decidedly uninformative. He sat, hesitantly. "Florent Montague asked me to help with a project today. He agreed to take it on only if I was brought in."

She blinked. "A project? An interesting project, a beneficial project, a worrying project?" She was back to something of a game of parson's cat in her head, her mind wanting to tidy the adjectives and put them in better order. That was also not getting her closer to answers of any kind.

"For the Fortiers." Vitus swallowed hard, reached for the mulled wine with his free hand, and took a long sip. He closed his eyes, set the glass back down, and added, "That was the perfect thing. Perhaps some soup or something, if there's any ready?"

"That was part of the plan for supper. We can, I suspect, have supper early, when you're ready." She glanced over at the clock. "Not actually very early, you were— were you busy the whole afternoon?"

Vitus nodded. "Florent came for his appointment, he explained the broad outline, and then we went out to the Arundel portal." He stopped. "Didn't you say there was something Childeric and Sigbert steered you away from? Near the Arun, maybe on it?"

"There was. I didn't see much of it. A tithe barn. It looked like there had been a fire, maybe struck by lightning?" Her hand came up to her mouth. "Lightning."

"Lightning." Vitus echoed it carefully. "What are you thinking, then?"

"I suppose that's the thing with lightning strikes, we think they're all individual moments. But what if some of these are connected? You said a lot of people have had dreams of it, unusual fears. And then there's Childeric, and I had that dream about Philip. And the barn. What if there's some reason lightning is, what's the word, prominent in the general psyche?" Thessaly took a deep breath, obviously aiming to keep calm. "Have you seen the tithe barn?"

"No, that wasn't where I was. There's a watermill, with a building attached along the Arun, the southwest corner of the estate but not within the estate wards. They were very careful about mentioning that." Vitus let out another huff, his own mind swirling.

"What did they ask for? What did you do? Do you want soup before I ask you many more questions?" Thessaly felt everything was tumbling out, all sorts of chaos that wasn't getting anywhere near an answer.

"Let me explain." Vitus laid it out, remarkably smoothly, considering the number of twists and turns. She was struck by the scope of the question, as he got to the measurements and what they implied. It wasn't one she felt she understood at all, even the size of the problem. He finished with, "I need someone who can help me make sense of it, and whether I should go ahead, and what on earth they want."

Thessaly leaned forward to kiss him. "Let me see if Collins can bring us supper. This is the kind of thinking that goes badly on an empty stomach." She rang for Collins, had a brief conversation with her at the door, and five minutes later, a simple supper was laid out. Thick soup, rather than stew, bread and cheese. Vitus waited for her to begin, and then tucked in, swallowing half of it almost before she could have a few bites. Then he looked up, embarrassed.

"Did you not eat lunch?" Thessaly wasn't sure how to ask this. Vitus considered, then shook his head no. Thessaly swallowed. "Problem of time, money, or nerves?"

The way she put it worked well enough, though it made him almost inhale some of his soup. She waited, her hands folded in her lap, using all the signs of decorum to make her point. He then smiled. "Time and nerves. The money's going well enough, and it'll be a lot better when I can finish setting the last of the lightning talismans. If all goes well, I'll have them ready for delivery by Monday or Tuesday."

"That part is excellent. If it's forgetting to eat, I can get Collins to make up some packages of food for you, easy to pull out. I know you said you get things from the woman next door, but..." She waved a hand at the half-eaten soup as Vitus went back to it, at a more moderate pace.

"I'll let you know. How's that?" Vitus offered. "The nerves, more than the time, really. I wasn't sure what Florent would ask, and then finding out what it was."

That at least let them get back to the topic. "What did you think, in both cases? Or feel? Nervous, excited, uncertain, all of the above?"

"Definitely all of the above." He took a few more spoonfuls while he was thinking. "Flattered, that Florent had come to me initially. All nerves once we got to Arundel. And now, after seeing the readings, I desperately want to talk to the Hennings and the others."

"You're not under oath yet," Thessaly pointed out.

Vitus blinked at her several times, then he twisted and kissed her. He tasted a bit like potatoes and leeks, and that was absolutely not a problem, but when he pulled back, she tilted her head. "What was that for in particular?"

"Because I was trying to figure out what to do. What do we do with that? I mean, if you want it to include you." He looked down, suddenly shy, or at least she thought shy was a reasonable word.

This was far beyond anything Thessaly had sorted out

before, but she took a breath. Aunt Metaia had dealt with big and complicated things that went far beyond her personal interests. Cousin Owain had and still did. Magistra Hereswith did. That also gave her something of an answer. "Do you think this is something where the Council has a legitimate interest? That's the first question. Whose, um. What's the word I want?"

"Jurisdiction?" Vitus offered. "Papa talks about that. Because it depends on who has the right of law, or custom, or power to do something."

"That." Thessaly nodded. "What, um. You might not be able to answer this, but it's a good place to start. What do those odd measurements mean? Distinct from the fact that they changed, and that they're similar to the project the Hennings were working on."

Vitus leaned back, frowning and deep in thought. He took a couple of minutes at it, and Thessaly got up to stare at bookshelves, more to give herself something to do than because it might help. Eventually, she heard his voice speaking slowly. "It's changing something about the magic in a particular area. I don't know if that's land magic or not, the way the demesne estates mean. But it's right next to a demesne estate."

"And possibly affecting it too, but we can't tell. It's not like they'd let you do tests inside the wards. And if they're guarding whatever it is, I probably couldn't observe." Thessaly pointed out.

"No, it's more than that. One of the things I was trying to figure out is, the readings the Hennings are getting, they got some ordinary ones, the range they'd expect, and then they got others they didn't. So sometimes it's, what's the word I want here. Not ordinary." Vitus was gesturing with his hands now, his fingers moving in little shapes that Thessaly found unreasonably distracting, because she suspected he meant things by them, emphasis or interrelationships.

"Sometimes it's as expected. And sometimes it wasn't. You mentioned the variation, didn't you?"

"The Hennings and all said every couple of weeks, maybe one or two tests in ten. Enough to be noticeable, but not most of them," Vitus said.

"And how often they're doing whatever they're doing?" Thessaly said. "About the same?"

"I asked that." Vitus swallowed. "Every fortnight, getting to more like every week. So that might fit, too, if the other readings were at the time or perhaps shortly after."

"Is there a chance? No, probably not. If you could take readings tomorrow, when you knew it had been active today. Something like that. But probably not tomorrow."

Vitus shook his head. "I think I'd need a better excuse, to be sworn to the project, and all that. Not right away." He looked at her, now more serious. "You think I should talk to someone about it?"

Thessaly nodded. "Look." She gestured at the pile of papers, metaphorically, since she was keeping them in Aunt Metaia's safe now. That was in the study, built into the core of the house. "Aunt Metaia was worried the Fortiers were up to something. Whether this is what she found out about, or whether this is coincidence, or what, it certainly seems worth investigating. And Magistra Hereswith and Cousin Owain asked me to let them know if I found anything that suggested whatever it was. I think we should tell them, at least one of them, and see what they say. If we ought to tell the Guard or the Courts, they know who to talk to, or could help us find the right person."

"Not Cyrus?" Vitus offered it lightly, or tried to, but it fell flat.

"Cyrus is still very new to what he's doing, and— well, he doesn't know about most of this part, just that Aunt Metaia might have found something." Thessaly swallowed. "And I sort of want to talk to them about the dangers. They know more about handling that. Before you make the oaths."

"Would they ask if I'd talked to anyone about it when they anchor the oaths, do you think?" Vitus said, suddenly.

"You have now talked to me. But you also don't actually know that much, do you? Two sets of observational and measured data, but you don't know what that means. You don't know the unaltered norms of the space on an average Tuesday or whatever day you want to pick. You don't know the seasonal variations. Both sets might be within the expected range. Maybe something about having Sigbert, as the Heir, doing whatever magic is being done? It might come out differently if it were someone else. I can think of all sorts of aspects that might have an effect."

"Think of it like a talisman, then. All the facets coming together, but we don't yet know what stone, how it's best cut, what might ruin it." Vitus let out a sigh.

"Or an illusion. A long-lasting illusion, you have to think about all of that. What spring light is like, or summer, or winter, or as the sun moves in the sky. Either that has to be accounted for, or left out, or, well, both. It's often both." She looked up to find Vitus blinking at her. "I might have been reading some of Aunt Metaia's books on that, about making lasting ones?"

"Tell me about it sometime, perhaps?" Vitus looked almost sheepish. "Pardon, I didn't even ask you about your day. Week. Tuesday."

Thessaly smiled broadly. "The duelling was wonderful.

We're planning to do it again next Tuesday. And I feel.... I feel, I don't know, more connected now. To people in general, not just a few specific people? Maybe that's why I'm thinking it's worth talking to Cousin Owain and Magistra Hereswith." She thought through the practicalities. "Look, it's not very late yet. Let me write a note to them - two notes - and get Emeline to take them to the Keep or perhaps Cousin Owain's. With a note that it's timely, you've an appointment when?"

"One. So tomorrow morning would do. I had plans to work in Trellech."

"So we will see if they can get us a time tonight. Are you staying?" Thessaly leaned forward. "Say you'll stay? As someone I especially want to be connected to."

"Is that what we're calling it now, when we're in bed? Being connected?" Vitus looked a little more relaxed, which had been her goal.

"It's certainly true, at particular points in the process." She waved a hand. "Let's finish eating, and then we can lay out what you want to present to them. Together, of course. And then we can reward ourselves for a good evening's work."

"You make it sound so simple." Vitus did laugh, then. "Though that's an incentive to do the work, isn't it? All right. I'll finish eating, you go write the notes."

Thessaly stood, pausing to kiss him, and then she went off to the study for the good notepaper, stopping at the kitchen door to let Emeline know she'd have an errand in a few minutes. It was not exactly comfortable to think about what they'd need to discuss, but at the same time, she very much liked the idea of doing it with Vitus, and not, she very much hoped, entirely by themselves.

24

JANUARY 10TH AT DINAS EMRYS

"And you're meeting with the Fortiers this afternoon." Council Head Rowan leaned back. Vitus could feel the sticky dampness of nervous sweat under his clothes. He'd have to find time for a cleaning charm or to go by his rooms and change before the meeting at the Scali Bank. He and Thessaly had just finished explaining what they'd learned and their concerns.

"At one. I'm afraid I can't put it off without being obvious. And I rather got the impression the Fortiers want this done as soon as possible."

"They didn't say why?" That was Council Member Owain Powell, Thessaly's cousin. He tapped his fingers on the notes he'd been taking.

"I could not ask. Florent Montague asked about the timing before speaking with me and they wouldn't explain to him, either. I don't know if they're hoping for some particular event or date. I looked ahead at the astrological charts, but I saw nothing terribly obvious in the next month or two. Mercury is retrograde beginning on the twentieth, I suspect that's why they'd like the agreements in place and the work begun this coming week. There are some interesting alignments as Mercury stations direct on February tenth, but the rest of the charts are, well, the sort of thing that would depend more on interpretation."

"Do you have the charts handy?" Owain Powell asked, clearing his throat. "We can have someone else look at them as well. Given the range of possible interpretations." It was not, in fact, an insult to Vitus's skills. His work relied strongly on both knowledge and practice of astrological alignments and timing, but every practitioner in that art had their own particular preferences when it came to technique and evaluating a chart for purpose. And of course, while Vitus knew the theory for other uses, he'd mostly focused on the implications for talismans.

He reached into his satchel, pulling out the copies he'd made. He hadn't assumed the Council would take this seriously at all, but it had been easy enough to make a copy for them, and one for Thessaly.

Council Head Rowan turned her attention on Thessaly. "And you, you've not found anything more definitive in Metaia's notes?"

"No, Magistra." Thessaly looked up and met her eyes. Vitus continued to think Thessaly was braver than he was. "There are a number of references, related to illusion magic. But they're in her shorthand and, I don't know, what looks like the initials of a title. I haven't figured out all of the abbreviations yet."

"Will you turn over the papers to us, then?" Council Head Rowan leaned forward.

Vitus expected her to say yes. He knew Thessaly had gone through them over again and again. Instead, Thessaly's back went straight, her shoulders down, as if she were taking a duelling stance while sitting, utterly clear on her purpose. "No, Magistra, I will not." It was entirely polite, and it utterly startled and confounded both the Council members. It also startled Vitus, though he did his best to not let it show.

"Why not, Thessaly?" Council Head Rowan's chin came up, followed by a steady and quelling look. "This isn't your problem to solve."

"If Aunt Metaia had thought you should know, with the information she had, she would have told you. She did not. Until I understand more about that reason, I want to keep working on it." Thessaly's chin came up. She then added, "Also, I know you're all terribly busy. This isn't something that can get handed to someone else, and I have time."

Council Head Rowan glanced at him, and Vitus was utterly unsure how to respond. He did the sensible thing and kept his mouth closed, keeping his silence. If they had a question, they could ask him. He didn't need to volunteer information. Owain Powell focused on his cousin again. "Thessaly." His voice trailed off when she raised one eyebrow and kept silent herself.

"Would you give us a few moments to confer?" Council Head Rowan stood. "We'll be just upstairs. One of the staff can ring if we're needed. Five minutes, perhaps ten." She didn't wait for more than a nod of response before sailing out of the room, Powell close behind her.

Thessaly watched them go, then turned in her chair to face Vitus. "Don't say anything. They've gone up to Magistra Hereswith's office, I expect." Vitus opened his mouth, closed it, and kept it closed. She smiled at him, though it was a distracted sort of smile. "Good." Vitus wasn't at all sure what he was being praised for, but he offered a fainter smile back, and waited.

After a minute, Thessaly drew a small notebook out of her reticule. She was rather properly dressed for this, as she'd be going off to her apprenticeship after. She was wearing a deep lavender gown, tailored to be up to the latest fashion in other respects, with details in black and pearl. The room they were in suited the outfit. It was clearly some sort of small parlour for meetings with three or four people, with a fireplace and two small sofas facing each other, with two chairs between them at the end. Vitus had taken the sofa across from Thessaly, because he was sure sitting next to her would give too much away.

Vitus still felt unprepared for this conversation, wherever it went from here. Thessaly seemed serene. She was making notes, but as if they were some minor list, shopping, presents for an upcoming occasion, nothing more. He could only settle there and watch her, and hope that he'd get enough notice when the Council members came back, it wouldn't be too obvious.

They took their time. The clock on the mantel ticked over. Five minutes, ten, almost to fifteen, before there was a slight rap on the door just before it opened. Vitus straightened. Thessaly just looked up and waited.

"We could insist, Thessaly." That was her cousin. Both of them had not yet sat down. They were standing by the chairs.

"I owe you a great deal for the help you've given me, Cousin. And I owe the Council due consideration, in those areas that are within your remit," Thessaly said. "But I do not owe you obedience. It is likely the Council has some say here, but we do not yet know that for certain. That is, in fact, a great deal of the problem. There is insufficient information. A great deal of suggestion, but little that's solid, little that can be held."

Vitus suddenly bit his tongue, because that, of all things, had triggered something in his mind. He thought back to what he knew, what he'd seen, how he'd seen it.

Thessaly caught it, he was almost sure of it. One of her fingers moved just a hair.

"We can't ask you to take the risk. Master Deschamps, you must be aware of the degree of it."

That, on the other hand, startled Vitus into a response and something that he hoped matched Thessaly's resolve. "I beg pardon. I was offering. You can't stop me from taking the commission, can you?"

Before either of the Council members could answer, Thessaly's voice cut across the room. "They can't. If they could, they'd be insisting already, not asking." She tilted her head, and now she honestly looked amused. "Aunt Metaia didn't talk details with me, but she talked about personalities. And about scope. What is within reach of which magic, and what is not." Now, she folded her hands in her lap, as prim and decorous as any proper Victorian woman. "I am willing to consider a conversation of interested parties, however."

Council Head Rowan looked amused, rather than angry, but she let out a little sigh. "Owain, would you let Cyrus know that I'd like a word in a few minutes?"

Council Member Powell sighed, looking a little resigned, but he nodded, going off and out through the door. Now, Council Head Rowan sat, taking a moment to smooth her skirts out. "I do not like the idea of you taking this risk. Metaia is dead, almost certainly because she either found something or someone thought she had."

"And I am staying within the wards or accompanied. Emeline's out in the main hall, you know that," Thessaly said. "I have picked up my own duelling again, and Emeline agrees I am a little out of practice, but skilled enough to handle any concern I can see coming. I will meet no one at the gate I do not expect. I will check to see it is the person I anticipated."

Council Head Rowan opened her mouth, then closed it. "Check?"

"I am training in illusions." Again, Thessaly folded her hands, entirely prim and tidy. "Near enough my journeyrank. Of course I know the ways to dispel them or at least know they're there."

"I'm not going to convince you, am I?" Now that steady and rather heavy gaze fell on Vitus. "Or you, Master Deschamps."

"No." He said it cautiously, but as firmly as he could. "How do we go forward, then?"

"What did you have in mind for this afternoon? And you had a thought earlier. May I hear it? Especially if you think it is relevant." Council Head Rowan spoke clearly and evenly, but this, at least, didn't feel like a command.

"The thought was that a watermill can do a great many things. I was talking with friends, oh, months ago now. November, perhaps? I could check my notes. We were talking about ideas such as a Faraday cage, which generates fields that affect the world around them or within their confines. It occurs to me that what information we know suggests such a field, though the means by which it's generated or the reason are obviously mysteries." He took a breath. "I can probably find out. At least enough to do a more thorough investigation."

"You're going to do it whether or not you have permission." Council Head Rowan sighed. "You're right, I can't stop you. And you have access we do not, not without an act of the Courts or the Guard. Thessaly, will you please make arrangements with Cyrus to share information with him regularly? It would be much less obvious if you pass along something after duelling or find some excuse on a Friday or so."

Vitus said, "I'm working on a commission for him, for

his sister. Between us, Thessaly and I have enough reason to be in touch that has little to do with anything obviously of Council interest."

Council Head Rowan turned her palms upright. "All right. Don't get hurt, please. If there's anything that looks like an actual threat, anything we can act on, anything that can go to the Guard or the Penelopes, you are to bring it to us. Whatever the hour. I'll let the staff know that any message from you is to be sent along to me immediately if you mark it urgent."

Thessaly inclined her head. "Agreed." She then stood. "Do give Cousin Owain my good wishes. I really ought to get to Trellech, Magistra North will be waiting. Vitus?" She inclined her body, and he immediately offered his arm, murmuring his own farewells briefly. Mama would scold.

He waited until they were outside in the courtyard before clearing his throat. Thessaly looked up at him, arching one eyebrow inquisitively. "You were going to say something in there?"

"Oh." Vitus swallowed, recalling what he'd been thinking. "About the problem not being solid. It seems to me that there's no small part of an illusion here, or at least a distraction. Guiding the eye to one place, so you ignore what else is going on. The question is which part is real, and which is a feint, yes? Putting it in duelling terms."

"Mmm." Thessaly made a contented sound. "Yes. And that's a fine thought. We'll discuss more, when we get a chance? I really do need to get back to Trellech."

"Of course." Before she could turn to go through the portal, he pushed himself to a bit more bravery. "May I come see you duel sometime? When we can arrange it. I believe I would enjoy watching your skill— again— very much indeed."

Thessaly laughed. She didn't embrace him, anyone

might see, or kiss him. But she was glowing with the compliment. He had made it just right. Vitus felt the satisfaction of that, and he knew she'd arrange it at some point, when she could. Whatever else there was, she understood what he'd said.

25

JANUARY 17TH AT BRYN GLAS

A week later, they had their chance. That was how Thessaly saw it. Now she had to convince Vitus of it. "They'll all be away tomorrow. From mid-afternoon until late evening."

Vitus was leaning against the arm of the sofa. He looked exhausted, like he had slept little that week. "How do you know that?"

"It's Bradamante Nevill's birthday. There's a gathering, family only, but all the family, at the Nevill estate. The Fortiers are all going, but Sigbert made a point of apologising for the fact I wasn't invited."

Vitus lifted his head, peered at her, and then leaned it on the back of the sofa again. "So at least someone is being slightly informative."

It made her smile. "Yes. And I think we can trust the information."

"There was reason not to?" This time, he lifted his head and kept peering at her.

"This is how we are certain that I was in Fox House and you were not. Or that I learned something from

Mother and Father. Probably both." She gestured at the book open on the desk. "That's the Gold Book."

"Which lists.... oh." Vitus looked bemused now. "It lists the births and marriages and deaths and education and such of everyone in the Great Families. Which includes Bradamante."

"Exactly. So I can confirm that yes, her birthday is tomorrow. And she's turning fifty, so a good year for a bit more fuss, even if the family is still in mourning. Hence the family only. And not being currently betrothed to Sigbert, I do not count as family for these purposes."

Vitus grimaced, pushing himself upright, standing to go pour himself some more tea. "Not for any purposes, I hope." There was a note in his voice she wasn't sure of. Thessaly could manage that sort of basic strategy, so she waited until he came back, patting the sofa beside her.

He blinked, stopping a foot away. "Unless you'd rather the bedroom?" She arched one eyebrow, hoping for something more provocative than ridiculous.

"You're distracting me. Deliberately." Vitus didn't move, though, just peered at her.

"Illusionist," Thessaly pointed out. "Not distracting, not exactly, this time. But I'd like to understand, and if you'd find it easier to talk about whatever— whatever that was?" She gestured a little incoherently at the other end of the sofa. "Or whatever else we should discuss. We could then have something to look forward to after we finished the discussion."

"For someone who was assiduously careful with her person less than a month ago, you have taken to the idea of bed play rather thoroughly." Vitus smiled, though, the slow smile that was him unbending a bit.

"I had something I'd like to try, if you're inclined." She did, too. She'd bookmarked three possibilities in one of

Aunt Metaia's books, though she suspected it might be the second. That would let her take on more of the physical effort. Besides, they hadn't tried it yet. "Bedroom?"

He let out a little sigh, amused, and held out his free hand. It took a couple of minutes for her to change into a nightgown and wrapper. Vitus put on a dressing gown and loose pyjamas rather than the suit he'd been wearing. It made Thessaly pleased, in a satisfied way she didn't have words for, that he left things in the wardrobe now. There was a spare shirt, a different set of cufflinks, a tie, handkerchiefs. She hoped soon, he'd leave a little more, the things she could look at on the long nights when he wasn't there.

Now, he moved to sit on the bed, one foot pulled up under his other knee. She settled with her back against the pillows at the head, upright, but comfortably relaxed. "What do you have in mind, Thessaly?"

"That depends. I need more information to have a plan." Thessaly gathered her wits. "Can you tell me the overview of the warding, what you have access to?"

"They added me to the warding on the building yesterday, but I have not yet been inside. Nor has Florent— the family obligations, today. I said I might go have a look in the next few days."

"And you think you can get into the building." Thessaly said, probing for that.

"Yes. Whether I can do anything inside the building beyond observe and take measurements, I don't know. I don't know if there are charms against interfering with what's in there." Vitus swallowed abruptly. "The oaths mean I can't pass along what they told me. On the other hand, that was precious little that's specific. I assume there's more of that coming later."

"And if I already know it, you're not the one telling me, are you?" Thessaly pointed out.

It made him look at least a little amused. "You needn't apply all your rhetoric to me. The oaths were thorough enough, but they didn't go so far as that. The Scali disapproved. Not without additional financial considerations to compensate for the additional bindings."

"Ah, so the Fortiers have some other motivations. They thought it safe enough, without spending— what, rather a lot?"

Vitus nodded. "The same over again, was what was suggested."

She let out an indistinct sound, because that was indeed rather pointed. "All right. So you can open the door. I can possibly get in. Are there talismans that might help? Illusions? How do we do this sensibly?"

"They usually have a footman at the portal, don't they? Or at least, they have all the times I've been there."

"If there's any expectation of strangers arriving, yes. It's outside the warding. Someone has to let guests into the estate wards." Thessaly shrugged. "But I can get to the estate on my own, and you can now, too. Though I don't know if they'd know. Better to go around."

"In that case, I can make the excuse of coming out to investigate when I can take my time. Can you— can you hide yourself well enough? We'd come through the portal together, so it would only open once."

Thessaly considered. "I can't manage anything like invisibility. It's an interesting technical challenge, but not a solved one." She considered. "But there's no snow on the ground. It's hard enough not to show footprints unless there's frost or something of the kind overnight. Do you have a nice billowing cloak? You look like the sort of person who should, if you don't."

That broke the tension in the room nicely. Vitus shifted to kiss her - first on the lips, then on the tip of her nose -

before he leaned back to answer. "I do. You think just blending in with the cloak, then, and then keeping to the other side of me?"

"That should do, yes." Thessaly knew it was a risk; Emeline would be upset, but Emeline couldn't come. For one thing, it was outside the terms of the contract, even if this were arguably Council business. Second, Thessaly could likely hide herself, but not two people. And third, well, it was something she wanted to do with Vitus, and just with Vitus.

It was and wasn't the same as being in bed. A plot was, perhaps, another and similar kind of intimacy. Vitus took a breath. "And when we get there?"

"You have tools for investigating, yes? Lingering magic, effects that don't just start and stop?"

Cautiously, he nodded.

"Bring what you need for that. I'll look for illusions. And not just the ordinary sort, but there's a number of charms that might make something easier to use, like a light shining on it. And we'll see what else we figure out."

"And we're not going anywhere near the manor or the other buildings." Vitus's chin came up. "That's a much bigger risk. I can probably talk myself out of trouble, if you can hide, but not anywhere else."

"I won't risk that. Besides, just being pragmatic, if they have things in the manor, it's almost certainly well hidden, the kind of hidden that would take hours and hours to search. They've a wine cellar, an extensive materia storage, the library— two libraries, I've never even been in the family one, dozens of rooms."

Vitus let out a sigh. "And you're sure this is a good idea."

"I'm certain someone needs to do it, we have the correct position for it, and I think we can do it." Thessaly could feel the threads of it, like preparing to begin a duel. "It's possible. I can't swear we'll be successful, but it feels, it feels right to try." She glanced up to one side, to where Aunt Metaia's portrait stood on the shelves right outside the bedroom. "And I need to know what, what to worry about. With Sigbert."

"Sigbert." Vitus grunted. "Has he, this week, I mean, has he pressured you more?"

"He insisted on taking me to lunch on Wednesday. It was a tad awkward. I've bruises up my arm from duelling." She held up her arm. "Or I did then. The salve's done wonders."

"Lucas recommends that one, and he should know. He ends up bruised all the time. Horses being as they are, and cavalry officers, even more so, I gather." Something in that made Vitus smile. She'd noticed that, in how fondly he spoke about his brother.

"Please tell him thank you, then, when you get a chance. If you would." Thessaly let out a slow breath. "You bring what you need for your work. I'll be prepared to explore and see what I can figure out. At least we might make some notes? Bring some information back?"

"I'm not going to talk you out of this, am I?" Vitus asked.

"No." Thessaly felt it was essential to be clear on this.

"And if I don't go with you, you'll lurk around the outside, even if you can't get in."

"Yes." She tilted her head. "I might try talking Sigbert into showing me. I'd really rather not, though. I'm not at all sure what that would involve."

"Perish the thought." He stretched, and Thessaly was very much distracted in the arch of his body. He was not a physically impressive sort, not like some duellists she knew were. But there was something elegant about him, and especially when he relaxed like this, letting her see things no one else got to watch. "I've a talisman for light, one for privacy that will mute sound. I'll see what else I can gather."

"I'll bring what seems sensible from the household stocks of potions. And I did find Aunt Metaia's kit. There are some useful things in there. I even know how to use most of them."

Something in her comment made Vitus smile suddenly. "Well. If it's most of them." He reached for her hand. "I'm still nervous. I'm not going to tell you to run if it's dangerous. After all, I know you're more capable in a duel than I am by far, and I assume that goes for a other dangers as well. But don't take unnecessary risks, please?"

"You either. If you don't, I don't. That's fair, isn't it?" Thessaly met his eyes, hoping it was.

"Fair." Then he took a breath, deliberately, and let it out. "You had some ideas about distracting me, yes?"

"Oh, I did!" Her voice went up, almost to the edge of shrill. She twisted, her robe falling open more than a little, as she reached for the book on the bedside table. "The bookmarks."

She didn't bother pulling the wrapper closed as she turned back, handing him the book. He, now, he was watching her, rather focused on her chest, before he looked up at her face and blushed. Then he thumbed through. "Did you have— my." Vitus stopped on the first. "I'm fairly sure you're flexible enough for that one, but I'm not certain I am." It involved her legs bent back to her ears, her hips raised.

"We can try it?" she said. "But I thought not tonight, especially if you're tired. Try the second." That had her straddling him, though this time facing away from him.

The pages turned, and he looked at her again. "I

rather like watching you. But we could start that way, you in my lap, my hands all over you. I like that idea, actually."

"There." Thessaly grinned at him. "This was the much simpler discussion. And we can change our minds and do something else if we prefer. Here, you get settled." She rolled off the bed to remove the wrapper and then consider how to remove her nightgown. She turned over her shoulder to find that he'd stripped nearly as quickly, his back against the head of the bed and the propped up pillows. He was not yet fully hard, but she was entirely certain that would not be a problem for long.

Laughing, she pulled her nightgown over her head in a billow of white cloth, before she circled the bed to perch next to him. Kissing first, then touching, and then they would certainly find something glorious together. She had every faith in that. Tomorrow would come in due course, and they would see it through together as well.

26

JANUARY 18TH AT ARUNDEL

Vitus remained entirely uncertain about this plan, but he had not come up with a better one. And he had to acknowledge that Thessaly both knew how things were done at Arundel far better than he did and was a far better strategist at speed. So now, here they were, about to go through the portal from Bryn Glas. He was wearing his voluminous cloak; she was wearing duelling clothes.

That, he had simple feelings about. Vitus found the outfit fascinating. He kept comparing what he could see of her body— feet and ankles, for example— with what was hidden behind the billowing fabric of the bloomers. Or whatever they were properly called. She had bracers on her forearms to corral the fabric from the sleeves. And she wore boots that came up her calves, laced, the sort that offered both support and good footing.

She'd also forgone any cloak of her own. He'd blinked at that, and she'd shrugged. "Warming charms. And I want to be able to move freely." Vitus had to admit that multiple yards of wool were not lightweight at all.

Vitus had presented her with a talisman that would

encourage anyone looking toward it to pass on by what they saw, or get distracted looking in the other direction. Nothing worth seeing right there. He wasn't entirely sure how it worked, actually; it was one of those methods passed down from person to person, but the accompanying theory had been lost to time.

Perhaps she could help him work it out and improve it. It must rely on at least some of the same theory as illusion work. He paused at the Bryn Glas portal long enough for her to cast a series of illusions. When she was done, he could barely see where she was, even when her hand was on his wrist and he knew.

When they came out of the portal on the far side, he was pleased to see the weather wasn't unpleasant. They'd settled on arriving at about half-three, after the Fortiers should be gone, but with enough light to get a look at the mill in daylight. Vitus nodded at the footman who was waiting, somewhat relaxed. The man jumped to attention before realising it was Vitus, who did not rate that kind of effort.

"Good afternoon. I believe Magister Montague mentioned I might be by? I wanted a look at the project we're working on."

"Sir." There was a slight nod. "As you wish, sir. Please don't enter into the estate proper. Do you know how long you'll be?"

"I wasn't planning to. And it might be an hour, it might be a few. It depends how long my measurements take, and if I find any differences once the sun has set. I brought a lantern or two for a charmlight." Vitus managed a nod, smooth enough for what was needed, and then set off. He could feel Thessaly to his left. She was keeping his body between herself and the footman. But a glance back showed the footman had sat again. He was watching the portal, rather than keeping an eye on them until they got around the bend in the path.

From there, it was a brisk walk across to the river, and when they got there, Thessaly dropped the illusion work. Vitus blinked several times, so he could more or less focus on her, despite the talisman. "This is the mill."

"The problem I have here is that I don't know what a mill is supposed to look like inside. So I don't know what might be different. Can I have a look around outside?"

"Might as well, while there's light. Then we can do inside." Vitus really wasn't sure this was a good idea now he was here. He was not designed for this sort of plot. That was becoming more and more clear every second.

Thessaly, on the other hand, bounced lightly on her toes. She set off to investigate the entire outside of the building, including climbing out on the wooden framework that held the spinning mill wheel. She spent quite a long time peering at it, while Vitus checked the measurements again. He thought from the way the readings were that there had been something active in the space a few days ago. Not yesterday, probably, but Thursday or Wednesday. He wondered what that meant, if they'd done something before having Vitus and Florent make the oaths.

Finally, Thessaly unfolded herself from where she'd been sitting. "Inside? Can you get inside, first?"

They retreated to the door, and Vitus pressed his palm against the panel that anchored the wards. He'd been attuned to it. He felt the warding magic recognise him. There was a little flicker that wasn't quite painful but like a spark against his skin in the winter. And then the door clicked, a lock turning over. He reached to turn the handle with his other hand, and the knob shifted and the door opened.

"Me first." Vitus went in, casting a charmlight and

setting it inside the lantern he'd been carrying. He looked around, considering. It was a large room, the entire size of the mill. That was not the surprising part. If a mill didn't have someone living in it, he thought that was often the case where the room would be used for storage or something like.

Instead, there was a metal construction to one side. It was not quite touching the far walls, maybe a foot or two of space around it, and Vitus blinked at it several times. It was made of a broad copper mesh, open enough that he could see there was nothing inside it bar a wooden bench or two. He held up his hand. "Wait a minute, don't come inside."

He took the second lantern, added a charmlight to it, and made a much closer inspection of the room, working clockwise from the door. Some part of him felt remarkably superstitious about it. The walls seemed to be what they looked like. At the left of the door, to the south, there was the cage. There turned out to be more room to walk around it than it looked like. The cage was also larger than he expected, as if the perspective of the room, seen from the door, was somehow altered.

The cage turned out to be about eight feet tall, a reasonable ceiling height, and a solid nine foot diameter, one of the more common sizes for a proper ritual circle. He could see lines of chalk on the floor, which was inset with slate, inside a wooden base where the cage stood. The weave of the cage itself was quite small - from outside, someone could see if there was anyone inside, but not who it was, he thought. Circling behind it, he found a dozen switches. They were labelled, but only with symbols, the sort of thing that would make sense to the owner and to no one else. One had a bee, and one had a flower of some kind. One had the image of an archway, one had a sun.

There were several other shapes he couldn't quite parse, perhaps a particular family symbology. Some of them looked alchemical, others looked like the sort of thing inscribed on mysterious stone monuments.

From there, he went around the rest of the room. He saw nothing nearly as confusing, though he was again struck by some incongruence of the shape of the room, the size of it. When he came around to the door again, Thessaly was shifting from foot to foot.

"Can you tell from there if there's an illusion on the room? Something doesn't feel right about the size or the placement." Vitus shivered once. "About a lot of things, actually."

Thessaly nodded. "Can you bring the light over near that— whatever that is?"

Vitus had a slowly dawning realisation of what it was called properly, but he didn't want to distract Thessaly. "Here?" He took the lantern over to about an arm's length from the near side of the cage. She nodded, and then concentrated.

"There's something. I don't— whoever they got to do the illusion work, I don't think they're very good? It's not holding very well. But why would they do an illusion inside a building that no one's going to look at twice, when it's also warded?" It seemed to offend her in some fundamental way.

"Explain, please?" Vitus asked. "If you would? Is, um. Is there a way you can tell if it's a new illusion or an older one? Or whether it's meant for everyone, or just some people?"

"Oh, that's an idea." Thessaly considered. "I was reading something the other day. Now, what is that? If it were cast like Aunt Metaia did for the Silence-warded places. You want magical folk to see what's really there, and the non-magical folk see whatever illusion means they won't bother to come look. Like, oh, along the visible side of Trellech from the river. It's sort of boring fields, with just enough bulls and fierce sheepdogs that you wouldn't go wandering through the fields. You'd go along the paths, far enough away from Trellech."

"Can you get a good look at it now?" Vitus was watching her, though the light was fading outside, and she was standing far enough back that the lantern with the charmlight he'd hung inside the door, on the wall, wasn't quite illuminating her face or where she was standing. Besides the problem of the talisman, which made it tricky to look at her directly.

"That's." She made a gesture with her hands, and he couldn't make sense of that either. "It's like in my dream. The one Solstice eve. Do you know what that is?"

Vitus coughed once. "Yes, but I've not the faintest clue what it means. I'm near sure it's a Faraday cage, it blocks electrical forces. You could sit in one of these in a lightning storm, and not be struck."

"But it's inside." That logic, he had to admit, was very relevant and correct.

"There's a set of, um. I don't actually know what to call them. Switches? Dials? Something. I don't want to test them, not without having any idea what they do, and they're just labelled with symbols. And this one here, with the cord attached, the lever."

Thessaly considered. "I think I'd best not come in. I can try dispelling the illusion from here. If it's cast the way I think it is, the Fortiers won't notice it's gone, at least until they try to renew it. And that might be a while, and it's the sort of thing that might fade out without a lot of warning, anyway. You write down what's on those dials or whatever they are." She considered. "Did Professor Marrington do the lecture with you in Incantation class where he talked about anchoring modes? The one he illustrated with that board of knobs of different metals?"

"Oh!" Vitus nodded, remembering it now. "He did. I can see what the materials are, that might be informative. Later, if not right now." He settled into examining each one. The identification charms shouldn't harm anything or leave any sign they'd been done. He found, in fact, that whatever the mechanism was, it was relying on multiple different metals, including, oddly, iron. Three kinds of iron, in fact, when he ran an additional test. That wasn't one he was used to. He was far more used to judging the purity of gold or silver. But the iron, some was hot forged, some was cold forged, and some had come from a meteorite. Another two were stone, one marble and one quartz. Then there was copper, bronze, one that was eighteen karat gold, and a sterling silver. No mercury, he thought, but that wasn't unreasonable. Mercury was difficult to manage.

By the time he finished with that, Thessaly was standing on both feet, looking rather smug. "There." She'd waited until he was able to pay attention. "Have a look now?"

Vitus took a few steps back, and that odd sense of the size of the building being all wrong had disappeared entirely. The cage took up a good half of the room, he could see that now, leaving a substantial space, the same wood floor with slate set inside, outside the cage. It suggested that one might want a ritual space affected by the cage and one not. But that made no sense if the goal was to create lightning or electricity or anything of the kind.

27

IN THE MILL

Thessaly stared at the room. The illusions had been rather fascinating actually, on a purely theoretical level. She wanted to discuss them with Aunt Metaia. She knew better than to discuss them with Magistra North. Using a distortion to hide a space that would otherwise be compellingly interesting was a clever sort of trick. Draw the eye to the thing you couldn't really hide. That much copper, you'd need to design the illusions specifically for that, probably in multiple distinct sets. They hadn't done that, which was also interesting.

"Tell me more about what a Faraday cage does?" Thessaly frowned, then shifted to lean one shoulder against the frame of the door, still on the outside. "I'll keep watch, all right?"

"How long do we have?" Vitus sounded bemused. "Most of it can keep. Electricity creates forces, the movement, the flow of the electricity, but there are also magnetic forces. If you make a Faraday cage, they're made out of metal, copper's a reasonable choice, you can block the electricity from affecting that space. Maybe other things as well. That's the part I can't figure out."

"I'll be quiet, then." Thessaly could feel something odd, and she couldn't pin down what it was. Part of it was nerves, she was sure. It wasn't as if she had experience sneaking around on other people's estates. Though she had, in point of fact, done a little more here than many other places, when she'd needed a little time to herself during visits.

They'd been here at least an hour, maybe rather more. The world around the mill had gone from afternoon light to twilight and now was settled into night. She could see a little down the path, from the charmlight in the lanterns, but only ten feet or so. Less, far less, if she'd been looking at the lit interior of the mill. Thessaly set herself to leaning her back against the outside wall and focused on listening to the movements around them. Some of it was the wildlife. She could hear birds, the babbling of the river. It was cold out, certainly, but her clothing was charmed for warmth and the pockets were deep enough to cover her hands past the wrists.

Vitus made just enough noise inside that she could track where he was. He spent some time over by that series of knobs, then he was walking around. She could hear the boards creak and shift slightly. In between those sounds, all of a sudden, she heard someone coming. "Vitus, look like you're doing the expected things." She hissed it out, taking a couple of steps to the left, away from the doorway and deeper into the shadows, frantically pulling up the illusion magic again.

Out of the dark came a form. The shape was cloaked, making it hard to tell any details. A man, she suspected, he appeared to have trousers, beneath the cloak. He came bursting along the path, stopping at the doorway. "You blasted annoyance. What do you think you're doing here?"

Thessaly could hear Vitus's voice, shaky as anyone sensible would probably be. "I've permission to be here. I was taking some measurements." He didn't try to justify himself, that was good. But he also didn't ask who it was.

"Away from that. Now." That came out as a growl, the sheer anger in his voice making it impossible to tell what he sounded like when not furious. "You meddle, you foul everything you're near. And you're not even anyone, are you? Just a little grasping bourgeois nothing. You don't know when to leave your betters alone. Do you really think a Lytton could ever look at you with anything other than disgust?"

Thessaly had a great deal she'd like to say to that, and she knew she couldn't, not now. She started working through what she could reasonably cast. She could not get a protection over Vitus, not from this angle and with that man between them. And honestly, she wasn't sure she trusted the effects, not inside the mill. But she could, she thought, get him from behind, draw his attention away, until Vitus could get out of the building and hide or something. Thessaly readied herself as best she could, a proper duelling stance that would let her move quickly, balanced on the balls of her feet. She was desperately grateful she'd chosen the boots. They'd be a help on uneven ground.

What she wanted to know was who this was. It could be Lord Clovis, it could be Sigbert, it could be someone in the extended family. She'd have considered one of the footmen, but not the way he was speaking. She didn't know Bradamante's sons-in-law well enough to recognise them in anger and bad lighting.

Whoever it was took another couple of steps inside. Now, Thessaly could see that he was masked as well as cloaked, choosing to obscure his appearance, perhaps even alter his voice. That didn't suggest anything good, either. Vitus had pressed himself back against a wall as the man continued ranting. "If you weren't in the picture, we'd be all set for a marriage. Not the original one, but it would do well. But no, you had to interfere. Make the chit think she could have a choice in the matter. She can't, she'll find that out. Her father's quite willing to make the arrangements."

It wasn't anything Thessaly didn't know, but hearing it stabbed like a fresh wound. Vitus, inside, managed a reply. "She has a choice, under the law." Perhaps not the sharpest rhetorical blade, but it was true.

Unfortunately, it provoked their intruder further. "Law, you talk to me about law? You're here, where you oughtn't be. And your hands have blood on them, they must. You twisted whatever it was you did for the Council. You must have, or Childeric would still be alive, shining, all set to marry and become everything he ought to have been." There was an odd note in there, something that Thessaly didn't have time to make sense of, like there was a larger goal that somehow they'd missed.

There wasn't a good reason to let this go on, and several good reasons to stop whatever it was. Thessaly considered her options. Then she pulled the talisman Vitus had given her, the one that made it hard to look at her. She shoved it in her pocket, letting the chain dangle where she could grab it if she needed to. Then she pulled her own scarf up around her face and hair, to obscure her own features, tucking the end in at the base of her neck to anchor it. Thessaly thought for a moment and then she clapped her hands twice, readying a charm as she did.

The man inside turned around, and Thessaly took several steps, dancing back. The first charm altered her own voice. It sounded odd, but it made her more a tenor than a soprano. That should be enough in the winter wind. "Is that all you can do, shout nonsense?" Taunting was a rather schoolyard approach, but she wanted to get his attention on her. She hoped Vitus would take the hint, and get out of the building, get somewhere he could get away or hide.

Before she could think beyond that, there was a roar from the doorway, and then the man was charging at her, bullish and aiming to knock her over. She was nimble enough on her feet; these were the drills she had been able to keep up, enough, the last months. Thessaly danced out of the way, treating it enough like what she'd been told of an actual bull fight. She wanted to lead him away from the mill, to give Vitus some space.

The problem was that the charmlights had gone out, and so there was near enough no light on the riverbank now. They were just a day or so off the new moon, which would make it easier to hide, but harder to keep his focus on her, without lighting herself up. She remembered something just in time, something Aunt Metaia had taught her, after talking about a particular prank she'd played in her younger years.

The charm. Could she get the charm to work? Yes. She felt the magic around her feet shift, and now the illusions were casting light, an eerie pale green flicker that was nothing like fire. It didn't make it much easier to see, but at least she might avoid falling in the river. In the summer, it might have made a reasonable escape if she could float or swim, but not in January. Before she could think about that, the man was advancing on her, and he'd finally decided on something.

Or maybe it hadn't been so long. Time moved differently in a duel. She automatically brought up more of her protections. That part of her training hadn't faded it at all, especially not with the last two week's bouts to reinforce it. He swung magic at her like a hammer, not like a blade, as if he wished to shatter her into pieces. The warding charms held, though she felt the blow and it forced her back a step or two. But that also brought her a little further away from the mill. She could see now, just barely, that Vitus was holding the charmlight, the last one, and he'd closed the door to the mill. He was out.

Another shuddering wave of magic hit her. She was braced for it better now. Before she responded, before she went on the attack, she fished the talisman chain out of her pocket, balled it up, and flung it toward the mill's door. It landed short, but not by far, maybe a few feet in front of Vitus, and she could see him dive for it.

There, now he'd be harder to spot, and she could focus entirely on the duel. So long as Vitus didn't try to help her. She sucked in a breath of too-cold air, even through the scarf, and then set to. First, to get her opponent off balance. Thessaly wanted him down on the ground, at her mercy. She wanted to know who he was, so she could figure out what happened next. And she absolutely, with all her strength and all her magic, didn't want him to come out the winner, able to hurt her or hurt Vitus.

Now, she thanked Helena inside her head for one of the tricks Helena had tried on Tuesday. They were sharp, nasty charms, the kind that stung when they hit, no matter what protections were in play. It wasn't fair, in a duel, but not all duels were fair. And this, this was not a duel. It was something far more vicious. The first one connected, she thought at his knee, and then she could drive him back along the river path, not letting him escape in any useful direction. She thought she might have felt movement behind her, but she was sure it was Vitus. She was betting a great deal that it was.

The fight was difficult, but the longer it went on, the more sure she was that she could get the upper hand. She was sure she was younger. She was more energetic. And Thessaly had a wider range of skill. Whoever this was duelled better than Childeric, but that wasn't much of a marker and it certainly wasn't terribly identifiable. She managed to get his ankle, limiting his ability to move.

He was grunting now, and there was a stream of incoherent swearing and ranting. Most of it drifted away in the wind, she couldn't make it out properly. But now and then there was a phrase about wanting revenge, about calling on his magic. Whatever he tried didn't work.

Thessaly was tiring, she could feel the limits closing in. She was not yet desperate, but it was time for something far more pointed. Emeline had taught her a lovely chain of charms, the sort of thing to use on men who wanted to take unpermitted liberties. She held her protections for a moment, keeping them steady while she positioned herself to get the right angle. It wouldn't work nearly so well if she judged the arc wrong.

A second later, the man was on the ground, groaning, both hands between his legs, as if she'd kneed him. It wasn't just the impact. The charm had a sharp streak of pain. She advanced, hoping to pin him down, but he managed to get up some kind of barrier, holding her back While she fought against it, tried to figure a way around, he pushed himself upright. Then he took off limping badly, back toward the direction of the manor house and the estate.

Thessaly was breathing hard already. She was dripping

with sweat. And as much as she wanted to chase him, there would be staff around and the estate wards besides. If they weren't outside, it wasn't actually that late at night yet, they'd be dressed and ready. She and Vitus had to get out of here, and fast.

28

IN THE MILL

Vitus had not been at all sure what to do. When Thessaly had thrown his talisman back to him, though, he'd taken the hint. He'd pulled the thick chain over his head, then tucked himself around the corner of the mill, where there was less chance of some charm going astray.

As the figure disappeared down the path, Thessaly braced her hands on her knees, glancing around.

He coughed in the dark. She jumped, and Vitus said, quietly. "When I said I wanted to see you duel, this wasn't exactly what I meant."

That, now, that provoked her to slightly hysterical laughter. It didn't solve any of their problems, but might vent some of the tangled emotions she was probably feeling. Vitus certainly wasn't sure what he felt, other than glad not to be hexed within an inch of his life, or worse.

She straightened up. "You need to beat him back to the portal. Go, tell the footman you're done. Someone interrupted you. You locked up. Something like that."

"And you?" Vitus shifted from foot to foot.

"I'll make my own way back. There's an ancient portal at Arundel Castle. I know where it is. Go home. If you need to come see me after that, take the usual roundabout way, but look like you're going home."

Vitus let out a puff of breath. "All right. See you soon." He considered, then held out the talisman. "More use for you."

She kissed him quickly on the cheek, distracted. He gathered up his satchel and went, because she was right. Best he was out of here before whoever that was coming back with the Guard or footmen or some other complexity. He thought Thessaly might have been following him along the path, at least until they were in sight of the portal. But every time he glanced around, he couldn't see anything.

The footman looked unnerved. He was standing at attention now. Vitus did his best to sound confident. "I was interrupted in the work, I don't know by who. I thought it best to lock up and let you know."

"Sir, pardon." Vitus didn't wait for the objections, just setting the portal for the one near home, and going through it. Once he was there, however, it was time to worry. He didn't want Thessaly to come home to Bryn Glas without being there to meet her. But if the Fortiers wanted to make trouble, it'd look odd if he wasn't at home.

He stopped in the house, partly to change clothing entirely, bundling up what he'd been wearing. There were ways to trace someone magically, but he'd had permission to be there. It wouldn't be a problem if that showed on his clothes. Now, he packed up his tools and a change of clothing into his satchel, nothing that would be obvious in transit. He came down through the library to find his mother knitting.

"I'm going out again, Mama." Vitus bent to kiss her cheek. "If anyone comes looking for me, if it's not Thessaly or her companion, I'm out. You think I'm in Trellech, but I said something about catching up with a friend."

His mother raised one eyebrow. "As you said, Vitus. Are you all right?"

Vitus did not know at all how to answer that. "It's complicated. Not injured, though, and I shouldn't be in any trouble."

"That's the sort of answer I expect from your brother. Will you tell me when you can?" That was what she asked Lucas, what she'd asked Lucas for years. Vitus nodded, and she smiled. "Go on, then. Take care of yourself, please."

From there, Vitus made his way through several portal loops, first to Trellech, then to London, then to Brighton. Finally, he set the portal back to Bryn Glas, hoping that would confuse anyone trying to trace or follow him enough, given the busy portals. He turned up at the house around nine at night, to find Emeline pacing back and forth in the front hallway.

"Where is she?" Emeline wheeled to look at him.

"She was walking to the Arundel Castle portal." He considered the time. "That's what, five miles? An hour and a half's walk."

"Not Arundel." There was something flat and dangerous. "You let her go on her own."

"I had to make a show of coming back. We— she— didn't want to risk being noticed. Also, I'm not going to argue with her. She's really a phenomenal duellist, isn't she?"

Something in Emeline's expression softened, then hardened immediately. "What were you doing that you saw her duelling?"

"If she didn't tell you her plans, there's a reason for it." Vitus could feel his resolve shaking, but Thessaly hadn't told Emeline, clearly. And it wasn't up to Vitus to decide to do that. "But I'll sit here and wait with you?"

"All right." There was then a good twenty minutes of awkward waiting. Emeline paced, Vitus sat, and every offer of tea Collins made was rebuffed. Around twenty to ten, the door opened. Emeline wheeled around, but as soon as she realised it was Thessaly, she was circling, checking her. "You duelled." Emeline didn't make it a question.

"Duelled and then walked five miles. I'm fine, not much connected." Thessaly sounded exhausted.

"You let me judge that. You, wait here." That was to Vitus. "You, upstairs and into a bath, once I've looked you over." Vitus opened his mouth and closed it again. Thessaly gave in, with no sort of argument.

Thirty minutes later, Emeline came downstairs, carrying an armful of clothing. "You can go up if you like. Don't keep her up." Vitus stood, rather stiffly, and she added, "She's all right. Just— ah, go talk." That was kinder, then.

"Thank you for making sure." Vitus gathered himself, his bag, and went padding upstairs. He took his shoes off, leaving his satchel in the sitting room, before going through to the bedroom. Thessaly was lying flat on her back, her feet up on some pillows, arms spread across most of the bed.

She lifted her head at the sound of him coming in, then wriggled one of her hands. "Come, please? Was it awful, waiting?"

"A bit." Vitus shrugged out of his jacket, then, when she waved her fingers again, out of the rest of his clothing, slipping into bed beside her under the covers. "I think I made the right noises at the footman at the portal, that someone had interrupted me. I locked up. I was going away now. But I didn't wait to see if he had any questions."

"That was the right choice." Thessaly shifted, and Vitus settled on his side, facing her, so he could lace his fingers through hers. Awkwardly, given the angles, but the touch mattered right now. To her, too. "It was a long walk back, but no one came after me. I'm very glad I wore my duelling boots, though. I was worried you wouldn't get away."

"Who was it?" Now that they'd covered the most essential part, mutual safety, it came bursting out of Vitus. "And that was you, following me back to the portal?"

She blushed rather delightfully. "Yes. And then I went south, cut across a few fields back to the river, and followed it to the castle. Fortunately, there aren't many people out and about in the countryside at night in January. And most of the livestock was in for the night. I might have startled a badger or two."

"And Emeline made sure you weren't hurt." Vitus asked this one more cautiously, because he was not entirely clear on how much he could reasonably worry.

"Nothing much connected. I'll have a few aches in the morning. I have a few now. That's fine." She lifted her head, stretched one toe toward the ceiling, then flexed her foot. "Moment. My feet are cold now." She pushed herself sitting, moved the pillows she'd been propping them up on, and then tucked herself under the covers, though she kept her toes away from his feet.

He nudged her foot with one of his. "I'm warmer."

"Doesn't seem kind." She immediately tucked her feet between his shins, though, and he restrained a shiver. Her feet were, in fact, still rather cold, despite a hot bath somewhere in there. "Who do you think that was? I couldn't tell."

"Logic strongly suggests one of the Fortiers," Vitus said. "A lot of that ranting was rather personal, wasn't it?"

Thessaly wriggled to get closer to him, one arm around his ribs, the other snaking under the pillows. "It was." She let out a long sigh. "It probably wasn't Dagobert."

"He's not fit for it, is he?" Vitus said. "If he is, he's been putting on a wonderful show the rest of the time."

"Excellent point. Whoever that was was free-moving. Well, until the end." She snickered once. "The last charm, um. Sort of equivalent to kneeing a gentleman in sensitive places proper modest Victorian maidens aren't supposed to know about."

That suddenly made the last part of the duel make rather more sense, and Vitus winced, then hugged her tightly. "I'm glad to know you can take care of yourself."

"You're not, I don't know. Unmanned by it?" Now he could hear she was more uncertain.

He paused before answering, kissing her hair gently, hoping the touch, his arms, his presence, would convey as much of what he felt as any words. "Not if you permit me to demonstrate my virtues at some point in the future. You're the duellist. Part of me wanted to protect you, but it's foolish when you've put so much time into your skill, and that's not what I'm good at."

"You protected me in other ways." Thessaly's voice was quiet, secure somehow, a kind of security Vitus had heard from Mama and Papa, the kind that was decades of a contented marriage. Knowing what she could expect, and certain it was hers for the asking. "The talisman. Each to our own gifts and talents."

He certainly had nothing to say to that, even while he felt he'd plunged into a large ocean with no landmarks in sight. He wanted whatever that was, in her voice, with all his heart, and he didn't know how to make sure it kept being there. Vitus took a deep breath, going on. "If it wasn't Dagobert, was it Lord Clovis? Sigbert? Someone else?"

"What did you make out of what he was saying? I couldn't hear all of it properly." Thessaly moved so he could see she was wrinkling her nose up. "I don't think it was Lady Maylis, certainly not Lady Chrodechildis, and I'm fairly sure not Laudine. For one thing, I've never seen them not in a proper gown, ever."

"Trousers," Vitus said, thinking through that. "Have they seen you in duelling clothes?"

"In the past, a couple of times. Or at least they could have. I take your point, though." Then she nudged him gently. "What was he saying?"

"Nothing kind." It had played through his mind while he was waiting. "Like he had a claim on you, like I was interfering, taking something that wasn't mine to take."

"I heard you say I had a choice. And I heard the bit about him blaming you for Childeric." Thessaly sighed. "All right. It might have been Lord Clovis. It might have been Sigbert. Only it's been too long since I duelled Sigbert to be sure. It might have been one of Bradamante's sons-in-law. There being three on offer this evening, the Percys came over from France for the supper."

"It doesn't answer much at all, except that I shouldn't show my face there without a lot of caution," Vitus said. "I'll have to talk that part of it out with Florent. You don't think it was Florent?"

"Oh, no. I've seen him duel. He drags his right foot slightly, no matter how hard he tries not to." Thessaly seemed very sure, which was a lot of weight to put on one foot. But he had to assume she knew what she was talking about. She added after a moment. "I have a little of the same problem. It's why I noticed. If I had to bet, I'd think it was Lord Clovis. A little more bulk, a little less nimble, and whoever it was didn't pull out some of the things we learned at Schola under Professor Trenton."

"Suggestive," Vitus agreed. "What are you going to do? When do you need to see them again?"

"Next week. Saturday. Supper, one of the chances for me to spend time with Sigbert and him to be persuasive." Now, Thessaly pushed up on one elbow. "He will not convince me. I want to be clear about that. Especially not after tonight."

"Especially?" Vitus could not follow that logic at all, though to be fair, it had been a rather eventful evening.

"We work well together. Exceedingly well. I don't want to form that kind of pairing with anyone else, thank you." She sounded absolutely determined about it, the absolute stubbornness of a small child who didn't know all the other ways of being in the world.

"Not going to argue with you." He might have said more, but she yawned ferociously just then. "How about we sleep? Perhaps I can demonstrate my particular kind of manliness in the morning. If you wish."

"I think I'll wish. Maybe more than once. Just to make a point." Thessaly nestled against him and was almost immediately asleep. It left Vitus to lie there, listening to her breath, and quietly be glad that nothing worse had happened that evening. Even if now he was worried about what might come.

29

JANUARY 25TH AT ARUNDEL

"Grand-mère is in something of a mood. Please do excuse her." Sigbert had met Thessaly at the portal. It was a week after her last and far more secret visit to Arundel, and her presence had been requested for a family supper. "Would you prefer a brief walk before going into the fray? The cemetery? Not at its best this time of year."

Thessaly hesitated. She did not want to thrust herself into the heart of the family just yet. A bit of a walk would delay that. And Sigbert on his own was rather more tolerable than Sigbert with his parents and grandmother watching her every move. "If that wouldn't be a bother." She was dressed for the chill, one of the very proper cloaks with a fur muff and all the charms for warmth.

"Please, then." They walked from the portal along the road.

"You should know that Father's also not in the best of moods." Sigbert said it quietly, as if he weren't sure what he could say. "He had an injury last week, and he does not take infirmity well." Thessaly held her tongue about how

Dagobert seemed to handle it somewhat better, in that case.

"Oh, I do hope it's nothing too serious." She looked away, not least because she rather desperately wanted to know what Lord Clovis had said about it.

Sigbert shrugged, opening the gate of the cemetery for her. "A minor accident. Nothing worth discussing." That, she thought, was an out and out lie, at least in terms of what Sigbert knew. He wasn't quite looking at her, he was using the fiddly parts of escorting her to avoid being specific. He was deft, but not enough to hide things.

"And your grandmother?" Thessaly asked.

"Displeased that various matters are stalled. You accepting my proposal among them." Sigbert looked at her this time, with a bit of a flush. "I've made it clear rushing you won't do." To be honest, Thessaly would at least like them to make an effort at wooing her. Sigbert was managing to be largely inoffensive. This did not entice her to join herself to him, body, oath, and magic, for the rest of their lives. "I gather she talked with your father again."

"Ah." Thessaly considered. "I have not seen my father in private since I moved to Bryn Glas. He does not speak for me, not in any degree that matters now."

"Oh. Um. I will make sure Grand-mère understands that. I did tell her that she would do better to speak to you, but I fear she's dreadfully old-fashioned. Such things should be done by the patriarch of the household."

"We live in a new age." Thessaly inclined her head. "A few moments at Childeric's grave, and do you mind if I take a few minutes at Philip's?"

"Oh, no." That, however, meant she got a solid five minutes of silence. She counted off the time at Childeric's, staring at a spot on the packed down earth, not really reading the stone, just making a show of grief she didn't feel. All she felt was pity that he hadn't made other choices while he could, and that wasn't much of an epitaph at all.

Then, silently, they went round to the far end. Thessaly had not brought anything for an offering, but here she stood and murmured in her own mind that she remembered him, that his brother would return, that his mother would join him in due course. That he was not forgotten. Then she offered her hand to Sigbert. "Do you ever think that some day, decades from now, someone will come down here and be confused, why the hieroglyphs?"

"Oh, our records are excellent. We'd pass the stories down, of course. We have the others." That got him off on a digression on some of the older graves. They began with the family who had established this manor after the Pact, when they had left Arundel Castle for the non-magical duke. That occupied them until they got back to the house. Sigbert was a tad awkward, but he told the stories with a bit of thought and care. It made her think better of him. Not so much better she intended to marry him, but enough to carry them through supper on a reasonable footing.

Lord Clovis was indeed a very poor patient. He was using a cane, and he looked pained every time he moved. Once they went into supper, he escorted his mother, looking displeased. Thessaly had pride of place next to Lady Chrodechildis at one end of the table. Sigbert was across from her, to encourage conversation. Dagobert sat at Thessaly's left, with Lady Maylis across from him, and Lord Clovis at that end. It was not the done thing, putting husband and wife beside each other, but with only six at table, there were limited options.

Especially when it was clear Lady Chrodechildis wished to talk to Thessaly and ignore both Dagobert and Lord Clovis. Lord Clovis and Lady Maylis largely ignored Dagobert. And Thessaly was entirely too well trained in the strategy of the formal table to try to include Dagobert when his family was refusing to do so.

Sigbert did his best to keep the conversation flowing, with his grandmother replying readily enough to him through the first course. By the second, however, she'd turned the table and focused on Thessaly. "Now, tell me about your intentions in the coming months."

"Oh, finishing my apprenticeship, of course. I have several projects that must be completed. And of course, the skills reward practice and attention." Like duelling, not that she'd dare say that right now, not after last week. She did not want to draw Lord Clovis's attention to that at all. "And I am still busy learning all about Bryn Glas, and reading through Aunt Metaia's library."

That got a slight flicker of something, not only from Lady Chrodechildis, but Thessaly caught more of it in Sigbert. That was interesting information. "What sort of books, my dear?" Lady Chrodechildis had shifted modes. Any child still in the nursery of a Fox household could spot that tone. It was not subtle. She was fishing for something. Did they actually think she was dim?

It wasn't like Childeric had noticed her brains. Her parents had traded on the strength of her magic, and the fact it would breed true. The intelligence hadn't mattered much. And she'd never cared about showing Childeric up. She hadn't needed to slight him. She knew her own virtues and flaws well enough. For example, a certain stubborn refusal to do the easy thing and give the expected answer.

"Aunt Metaia had a different focus with illusion work, but the house has several pieces of her work. A chance to study them, at length, even though I wish I could talk them through with her."

"And are those effects complex to do? I admit I don't know much of the field beyond the decorative." Lady

Chrodechildis made a little laugh. "And I gather there are advances, rather regularly."

Thessaly nodded, considering how to play this. She wanted her competence to be on display, but it would not do to be too competent, nor to hint at some of what she'd been reading. "There are differences if you want an illusion to be stable for an extended period, as compared to a brief one. Something on a building, for example, as compared to a dress or gown for a single night's costume. I'd been focusing on the latter, but Aunt Metaia has some fascinating materials on, oh, tapestry restoration."

"I had not realised that a topic of concern?" Lady Chrodechildis's reactions continued to seem a little odd, as if she were distracted by something else.

"Oh, well, in a restoration, often, you want to make the repairs visible, in case there is some better practice in the future. But an illusion can cover the difference, without damage to the historical piece. If the threads have faded due to the sun, the illusion can restore the original shades, or smooth over mended patches. You still need the physical restoration, of course. Illusion will not mend the damage from hanging or some misadventure."

"Indeed." Lady Chrodechildis considered that more solemnly than Thessaly expected. She then launched into a discussion of some of the features of the estate, things no one had yet bothered to explain to Thessaly. Or rather, the explanation assumed some prior knowledge, and Thessaly was torn between admitting her ignorance or seeing where it led.

Finally, she cleared her throat. "Pardon, Lady Chrodechildis, but I'm afraid I've never seen that. I don't think, well, I hadn't wanted to intrude."

It got a great deal of tsking in response, the sort that Thessaly interpreted to mean that someone had been failing to do their duty. It did not rise to calling out Lord Clovis or Lady Maylis, but it made it clear that someone had neglected a key aspect of something. As if this scolding were standing in for others, not suitable for the moment or the dinner table. As soon as they rose from supper, Lady Chrodechildis demanded that Thessaly accompany her to the west wing, and the gallery where portraits of various ancestors hung. "You stay here. Both of you men." That was to her sons. Sigbert did not even get that much, which was also curious.

Instead, Thessaly and Lady Chrodechildis went through the Great Hall, up one flight and into the little entry. "That is my private study." The next door was her private sitting room. They climbed another flight to the second floor, a long gallery stretching out over the length of that wing, with a surprisingly narrow door leading off the stair.

Thessaly sensibly kept her mouth shut, though she gazed at each portrait in due course. "You understand, of course, that we are an ancient family. We go back long before the Pact, with connections to the most noble and powerful houses on both sides of the Channel. I am in the decline of my life, but it is my hope to ensure that the family flourishes for generations more." It put the thing plainly enough, but that was nothing Thessaly had not expected.

The next sentences changed that. "Our family— you knew I was a distant cousin of Vauquelin's, yes?" Her late husband, who Thessaly had known only as an intimidating patriarch. She nodded. "We came over with William at the Conquest, and we made much of our lives here. When it came time for the Pact, there were, hmm. How shall we say differences of opinion? In the end, Richard won out, and the Pact was made. There was a Fortier on the first Council, though his portrait hasn't survived. But we have always thought it limited magic more than sense. When I look at you, I see someone who might restore some thread. You come from old stock of Albion, not so ancient a noble family as the Fortiers, but there are few who can claim that. You are pleasant to look upon, healthy. There are no defects in your extended family."

Thessaly certainly wasn't going to interrupt. When Lady Chrodechildis paused, she managed a somewhat feeble, "And of course you want the best for the family."

"It is a pity that Bradamante could not convince someone to marry in. You see my sons, both of whom have failed at tasks set to them, in multiple ways. I still hold out some hope for Sigbert, but his mother spoils him. You might, in time, provide some backbone." Then Lady Chrodechildis turned. "What would persuade you to make the agreements?"

Put on the spot like that, Thessaly swallowed. This was every bit as much a duel as the one a week ago. She was far less skilled here, against a woman who had won this sort of match over and over for decades. Finally, choosing her words precisely, she said, "Childeric told me nothing. If I am to be anything other than a broodmare for your plans, I expect something far more equal, allowing me to lend my skills to the family."

Lady Chrodechildis met her eyes, then she nodded, just once. "Do go now, Thessaly, dear. I wish to stay and consider the portraits further. Maylis will be down in the withdrawing room."

"Of course." Thessaly refrained from making an instinctive bob. She did not know how she had done in that, but at least she had said a piece of what she'd been feeling for months.

30

JANUARY 26TH AT THE FOUR METALS ESTATE

"Sure we can't lure you to supper, Vitus?" Thirza glanced up as she was sorting out what went where. They were wrapping up the experimental work they'd been doing, out at the estate. Vitus shook his head. Daedalus had gone off to pack up his various bits of equipment. Vitus, Merryn, Thirza, and Philemon were doing the rest of the tidying. Vitus had the broom and mop to properly remove the chalk marks from the floor.

Not that they'd been using chalk for the usual reason. They hadn't been doing particularly arcane rituals. Instead, the chalk had been handy in labelling the direction of the flow of the electricity they'd been experimenting with, and then the magical flow. Vitus hesitated, looking down at the floor, flashing back to what he'd seen in the mill house.

It hadn't caught him earlier, and that was a different puzzle and a different problem. He stared at it, before hearing Thirza ask again. "Vitus? Supper?"

"Oh, no. My brother's home for the evening. I want to

catch up with him." It wasn't just that, though he had a limited chance to see Lucas and more options for everyone here. "Wednesday, after the lecture?"

Thirza cleared her throat. "That is and isn't an answer. You've been distracted all evening. And more so now. Besides all the rest of it."

"Rest of it?" Vitus ran his hand through his hair, though he did turn to face Thirza. And Merryn, it turned out, Philemon and Daedalus had somehow slipped out. Merryn had something of a right to ask, especially if it might affect the Four Metals, and well, Thirza held her own sway.

"There's gossip," Merryn said. "Some about you." She perched on the table they'd pushed to the side of the room. "I wasn't going to say anything, but do you have any delicate work planned this week? You might want to rethink that."

"Am I that badly off? Visibly?" Vitus tried to gather himself, but it was difficult to do in a large workroom. There was nothing to hide behind, no chairs, so he could rearrange how he was sitting. It felt raw and unprotected, uncomfortably like the previous week. There was, he admitted, less chance of a random attack, but there was also less Thessaly to help with a solution. He shoved his hands in his pockets and looked at the floor for lack of anything else to do.

"You're not at your best, no." Thirza's voice was a bit gentler. "You were fine tonight. You didn't let us down. But you weren't as thoughtfully helpful as you usually are. We do notice that sort of thing. And we hope we're friends."

"Friends." Vitus let out a puff of breath, then looked at them both. "It's complicated. And it's not all mine to tell. Some of it I can't."

"How about we tell you the gossip we've heard, and you can decide from there," Merryn said, agreeably. "A little bird told me you're doing some work with Florent Montague, for the Fortiers. Not what, though we can guess it's talisman work. Why you? Or why'd you say yes to them? Given, well."

"Given Thessaly, and Childeric, and whatever else?" Vitus shrugged. "Florent came to me, and I was flattered. The Fortiers wouldn't usually ask me, but he insisted. He said he needed some of my knack. And some of what we're talking about here." He gestured at the floor. "In potential, circuits and connections and all that. Larger structures into which the talismans fit."

Thirza considered, then her voice got lower. "You know it's put you at risk." She didn't make it a question. She wasn't being condescending about it.

Vitus looked up, swallowed, and nodded. "Thessaly's sure something's odd there. But not any way we could take to the Guard. Or the Council, before you suggest that. Even, really, what category of wrong it is." People could legitimately build Faraday cages if they wanted to, even if how this one was built and the parallel ritual circles in the floor were incredibly odd.

"Anything you can share?" Merryn's voice was steady, reassuringly so.

Vitus shook his head. "Not right now. But it is distracting." He rubbed at his face. "What's the other gossip?"

"Whether there's something going on with the Fortiers. Or, possibly, Thessaly. After all, it's her betrothal that was the start of— well."

"Childeric Fortier was also involved in that betrothal. Why does everyone, I don't know, let him slide out of any consequences for his choices?" Vitus turned away, suddenly angry. He wasn't made for duelling, for fighting, for defending Thessaly's honour. Even here and now, he felt like anything he might try would turn into crumbling leaves, no good for anything except maybe compost.

He heard Merryn and Thirza talking quietly, and he didn't turn around. Instead, he took a few steps towards the far end of the room, then a few more. It wasn't as if walking helped, but standing still definitely wouldn't. He felt, all of a sudden, like everything wanted to burst out of his skin, all the frustration and worry and gnawing feeling that far more was wrong than he understood. Vitus wasn't just worried for himself, but even more for Thessaly.

At the far end of the room, he leaned his hands on the windowsill, staring out the window toward the woods beyond the cleared ground near the outbuildings. There was silence for a good few minutes, then he heard steps behind him, a throat being cleared, then Merryn's voice. "What can we do that might actually help?"

Vitus turned at that. "I'm not sure there's anything."

"You could ask Thessaly to come round to the club sometime. With you, as a guest." Merryn offered it cautiously. "If she'd like. If you'd like. No one will gossip about it there."

"Can't be sure of that." The Four Metals were not inclined to the Great Family sort of social gossip, the bloodsport version of it, but it only took one person saying the wrong thing.

Merryn opened her mouth. "Well. I can't say as I'd risk it either. You could have us round to your flat, though. A select group. Or somewhere else you both liked."

"Why?" Vitus leaned his hands back on the sill behind him now, more to distract himself than anything else.

"It seems to me you could use a few more friends. And maybe so could she?" Merryn's voice got more tentative.

"What's the rest of the gossip, then?" Vitus could tell there had to be some.

"That Childeric's death, something, unhinged her. That's one of the more polite phrases. Or that she'd be better off at some gently minded rural home until she feels better." Merryn added, "I'm halfway certain her father's helping some of those, actually. So you can likely read 'until she does what he wants' into it."

"What he wants is for her to agree to marry Sigbert." Vitus sighed. "I'll tell her. And."

"And?" Merryn tilted her head, just waiting.

"And I'll see about setting up something private where she can meet other people. But she— I mean, she's not a member of the Four Metals. She's always going to be on the outside. That's a lot to ask."

"Ask your brother, too, if he can get away. As to Thessaly, I'm not making any promises. But you know perfectly well we can and do bring people in as adults, if they're interesting and skilled. I've no doubts about her skill, given a little more time. And she has certainly kept your attention."

Vitus felt himself flushing. "I find her exceedingly interesting. Also stubborn and determined. And I don't know nearly enough about duelling to accurately rank her skills there, but I'm clear she has them."

Something in his tone, not just his choice of words, made Merryn laugh and relax. "There. And we'll pass on anything else, if we hear it. Note to your flat?"

Vitus considered. "Best there." It wouldn't help if something were urgent, but he might be in any of three places, and he could at least check in with the flat most easily.

"Walk you back to the portal?" Vitus nodded, understanding the hand of friendship and of letting this conversation go. He finished gathering up his things. Thirza and Merryn made idle conversation with each other that didn't demand anything of him, and he let them go first through the portal before going back home.

"Mama's napping. Papa will be back in a bit. He went out for a constitutional." Lucas greeted him immediately in the library, where the fire was going strong. "Drink?" Then his brother eyed him. "Need to work out something? There's some wood that could use chopping."

"I am not physical like you. How much wood do you chop, anyway?" Vitus asked, adding, "And a drink, certainly."

"Enough. It's a common enough punishment chore." Lucas spread his hands cheerfully. "I don't get in that much. But I supervise, and it means showing them how to do the thing. A few too many spoiled sons of the gentry who need to learn how to take orders."

It echoed some of what Vitus had been thinking earlier, closely enough that he let out a rueful laugh. "Glad someone teaches some of them." He held up his hand before Lucas put a glass there and he took a sip. "The topic of Childeric Fortier came up earlier. And I think a lot of people, him included, would be better off if he'd had someone hold him to standards of decent behaviour more reliably."

"Huh." Lucas sat down again, stretching out his feet on one of the footstools. "How is Mistress Lytton-Powell, then?"

"I didn't see her yesterday. She was invited out there again. And I was busy today. I'll see her Tuesday." Though he had an early consult on Wednesday, so he couldn't let himself be tempted to stay the night. "They're still trying to persuade her about Sigbert."

"I presume she continues to have the good sense to

prefer you. Or do I need to go have a brotherly chat with her?" Lucas asked.

"Much as the idea amuses, you wouldn't get very far. She's a fierce duellist. And while you on a horse and her on her feet might actually be more or less matched in theory, I'd hate the idea of either of you getting hurt." Vitus considered. "I'm also not sure what she'd do with you, honestly. She's only got experience with a sister. And there are cousins, male and female, but I gather none she's terribly close to."

"Not the way we are." Lucas said it confidently and comfortably. "Well. I look forward, in due course, to teaching her how to have a brother by marriage. When you get all of that sorted."

"You were warning me off the idea, before," Vitus said. "And it's like to get me into further trouble."

"Will you talk about that? And well. It turns out I might like the idea of someone who makes you that fierce. Also, she's good for your talisman work. Weren't you telling me a fortnight ago about how that conversation let you figure out three new things?"

"I was." Vitus sighed, took another long sip from his glass, letting his head fall back against the back of the sofa. "Her family doesn't approve. The Fortiers absolutely want her for Sigbert. He's being reasonable about it, or at least strategic, from what she's said, not pressuring her, but the rest of the family? Well, his parents and grandmother. Laudine and Dagobert have been far more, um. Thoughtful about it."

"Is there any risk they'd pressure her into the agreements against her will?" Lucas hesitated. "Sometimes people do."

"They'd need to bring her trustee in, and not much gets by the Scali. Especially when she's been very clear with them about her wishes in that matter." Vitus spread his hands. "She's a Fox, born into a mess of Foxes. I am badly set to argue the social warfare of it. She wants to keep playing it out a while longer, and I don't have a good reason against it."

"Except that it's putting you on edge and worrying you. Mama noticed. Papa, too, actually." Lucas shrugged. "Which is why I'm here. And I would like to meet her sometime, when I can."

"Merryn was on about that. Having a few people over, to the flat in Trellech, most likely. On the theory I need more friends. And that Thessaly might too. I don't know when, though. It'd be hard for her to get away and meet us there."

"Have you considered a talisman for her, linked to an illusion?" Lucas suggested. "Nothing, um. I don't know all the laws behind it, I know there are some, against pretending to be other specific people. But if you made something that would let her look ordinary? Some housewife, the sort with one cook-housekeeper at home, and a couple of children, that no one would pay any mind to."

Vitus contemplated that. "I'll ask her. There's no law against that, it'd be finding the right face for the illusion. And the rest of it, how she moves and dresses. But there might be solutions for it. Thank you." He lifted his glass.

"Brotherly services as required." Lucas looked a little happier. "Want to tell me a bit more about what you find so appealing, then?" He grinned, suddenly. "Not whatever you do that's private, but the rest of it."

That would take a little thought, because besides the time in bed, a lot of their other discussions had been about her relentless research. But they had talked about other things, and he could certainly talk about the house and what Thessaly obviously loved about it. "Give me a minute. Let me go change, actually. I'll come right back down and talk."

"Promise?" Vitus nodded, and Lucas settled back in his chair, looking smug about his afternoon's labours. Vitus snorted and went upstairs.

31

31ST JANUARY AT ARUNDEL

"I am so very sorry, Sigbert." Thessaly stood in the entry hall. Sigbert had come from the Great Hall. Thessaly knew that there, just beyond where she could see without moving, there was another bier, another coffin. "I wanted to come directly, given everything. It means a lot you let me know immediately." She kept her voice quiet, to the approved whisper of this household's mourning.

She hadn't known what to expect from Sigbert, given the note. An hour after lunch, Collins had brought her a black-bordered note that had just come through the portal. It was tightly written, in Sigbert's handwriting. Not his mother's florid writing, though she would be by herself, given their customs, other than whatever vigil she kept.

Thessaly had put on her blacks, told Emeline to do the same, and set off for Arundel. The note had been uninformative. Lord Clovis had died suddenly. Arrangements for the funeral would follow. If he hadn't wanted her to turn up, Sigbert should have said.

"You needn't have come." Sigbert's voice was rough. Then he glanced behind him. "Let me arrange to walk with you for a few minutes." Without waiting for her acknowledgement, he disappeared back into the Great Hall. A servant came out, almost immediately, and came back within five minutes, followed more slowly by Dagobert Fortier. Thessaly nodded at him, murmuring her condolences again, but he didn't stop.

Dagobert didn't seem upset at her. Sigbert did. Thessaly needed to find out whether she was correct, and if so, why Sigbert was upset. The cause mattered here. And whatever else Thessaly felt about any of the situation, Sigbert's father was dead and Sigbert was Lord Fortier now. The family was turned even more upside down than after Childeric's death.

After another minute or two, Sigbert emerged, wearing a cloak. "Your companion may walk behind us, if you wish." Again, his voice was tight. "The orangerie? It will be warmer there."

It had turned rather brisk, as if the end of January were in mourning as well. Thessaly nodded. "If that suits."

Sigbert twitched. "Nothing suits, at the moment. Shall we?" He offered his arm, beginning to walk as soon as Thessaly had placed her hand on his forearm. They walked in silence along the paths, Emeline a proper ten steps behind. When Sigbert opened the glass doors of the orangerie for Thessaly, Thessaly nodded once to Emeline, who went right as the two of them went left, to one of the benches. She was within line of sight, enough to be a chaperone or a witness.

"It was sudden." Sigbert barely waited for her to sit. "After breakfast. He was planning to go out riding on the estate. He stood up, and I—" His voice trailed off.

"I'm very sorry. He'd been a little unwell last week. It wasn't related to that, I hope?" Thessaly did her best to keep her voice even.

"No. His Healer came out. There was nothing a little time didn't fix." Thessaly swallowed her sigh of relief at that. She had wanted to drive off whoever she had duelled, not kill him. And she was more and more sure it must have been Lord Clovis now.

She looked down, then pursed her lips. Sigbert had removed his gloves, they were lying across his thigh. "A new ring, Sigbert?"

Sigbert glanced at his hand, stretching his fingers. "It was Father's. He gave it to me a few nights ago." Then he turned his attention to Thessaly. "There will be more pressure on me to marry. Not for some months, of course, but making it known I will, that would be a help."

Thessaly should have expected this, honestly. She let out a breath. "I am glad to discuss, once things are a little settled for you. After the funeral. I expect the Scali will not wish to rush the agreements. They were rather clear with me about not making significant decisions while grieving."

"You were grieving your aunt. And you are a woman. I am Lord Fortier. There is the land magic to consider. I cannot, I do not..." Again, his voice cut out. He went in the space of a few words from being commanding, filling the role he now held, to sounding his age and lost. It made Thessaly feel terribly sympathetic, though that was also a horrible reason for marrying someone, particularly in haste.

"I will let the Scali know you will want to discuss terms." There, she could say that, and it was not a lie. "The funeral. Do you know when yet?"

"Saturday week. There are too many families who have land obligations tomorrow or Sunday. And we need time to make certain things ready. The bees." His fingers twitched. "It has not been long since Childeric." Four months and a week wasn't long at all, no.

"The bees." Thessaly nodded. "No one explained them. That is a tradition for the family, obviously."

"One of the Merovingian customs, one of the ones we carried across the Channel." Talking about this was apparently easier. Sigbert's voice got softer and more even. "A token for the grave. The original Childeric, the one my brother was named for, king of the Franks, they found his grave in I think it was 1683. It had all manner of things in the tomb, including golden bees set with garnets. Not all of ours are gold. Gold for the men in the family, silver for the women, copper for the others." It did bring Magistra Landry to mind, how she had produced her own golden bee, though of course she had not explained what she meant by that choice, and now she was dead and even less inclined to answer queries even than before.

"And your father was Lord of a great family. There will be a lot of people who come to the funeral." The question would be whether it would be more than for Childeric, or different. Childeric's death, on the political level, had been a chance to make alliances clear. Lord Clovis's would bring people who wanted to test the weakness of the Fortiers, and the inheritance of the younger son. If Thessaly had been betrothed to marry Sigbert, this was when she'd step forward, to manage some of that, as much as the family would permit.

She was not making that offer. She wasn't sure Sigbert realised she wasn't. It was rather novel to be able to analyse the funeral that way, without feeling personal grief. Lord Clovis had people who had loved him, or who owed him loyalty. Thessaly was not one of them. She would not be rude, not for the world, for all sorts of reasons, both strategic and sensible. And because Sigbert was grieving, somewhere below the stubborn insistence that was most present right now.

He shrugged. "The other reason for the delay. The kitchens are working on the food and preparations. And Maman is in no fit state for anyone, even me."

"It must have taken her very hard. Your parents, together, had an intimidating presence, and your mother fit herself so well to your father." It must be uncomfortable to go forward now. Thessaly didn't ask how it was for Sigbert, who wasn't supposed to be the surviving heir.

Sigbert sighed, then said, ruefully, "That is a polite way of putting it. She has taken to their rooms, as I'd expect. She'll keep vigil tonight. I would ask you to join us, but I think not this time."

"I thought the same." Thessaly kept her voice even. "But please do write and let me know if there is anything I can do."

"Laudine is coming out tonight by train. She knows the household well enough to handle things for Maman." And she had not been a favourite of her brother-in-law's, even before whatever had happened last summer. "We will name Dagobert as Heir in due course. Temporarily, of course. But at least there is that line to continue, without having to consider any of the cousins."

"Ah." Another reason for the pressure to marry. And then to produce at least two children as promptly as possible, whatever else Thessaly might have wanted to do with her time. She could not argue with the pragmatism. "And your grandmother?"

"Desolate. In her rooms, of course, as well. It has been very hard on her. First Grand-père, then Childeric, and she doted on Childeric. And now Father." Sigbert looked away, over into the greenery. Without looking back, he said softly, "I don't know if I can be who they need."

Thessaly rested her hand on his, one of her fingertips brushing that ring in passing. She felt a slight charge from it, not a brief burst of the ordinary magic of a ring, but something sharper. "I think we don't know that sort of thing until we make a go of it." She pitched her voice softly. "I did not know I'd manage with Bryn Glas. We're doing well enough, though. And not all questions need answering immediately. The estate has been managed well, you have staff who know their roles. You will have some time to sort out the rest."

"Not enough time." Sigbert almost kept going, then he bit off whatever his comment would have been. "We had been working on a project. Grand-mère, Father, Childeric, and Uncle Dagobert, originally." Not any of the women, other than his grandmother, and that was telling in some form Thessaly couldn't fully analyse in the moment. There was also that 'originally' which matched up with what she'd guessed from Laudine and Dagobert. "I don't know if I can continue it."

"Is it the sort of thing that might sit for a season? Some projects are, and they are often the better for it." It would not satisfy her, but it might give her more time to find out what the thing was, or get enough evidence for someone else to investigate it properly.

"It— no, I really can't say more." Sigbert ducked his chin. "Oaths."

"Of course I won't press you." Her fingers shifted on his hand again, brushing the ring once more, and this time he looked up, meeting her eyes.

"The ring, it was Father's. He gave it to Childeric, then he'd been wearing it again, before giving it to me." He held it up, and it wasn't nearly as decorative as Thessaly had expected. It had a plain band that looked like rose gold at first glance and was more likely copper, inlaid with blue and green stone. She wasn't as good at Vitus as spotting stones on the fly, but she also suspected there was some illusion work at play, somehow.

"Does it help to wear it? I have found that wearing some of Aunt Metaia's things has helped. Sometimes, mind, it's a bit like hearing her scold me about something."

That got Sigbert to manage a small smile. "Something like that. It is, I think, a reminder of my obligations. Of what I have done, what I will do, and what that will mean for the family." There was a new resolution in his voice, and he leaned over to kiss her cheek. "Thank you, Thessaly. This has been a help. May I walk you back to the gatehouse and the portal? I should get back."

Thessaly didn't argue. She didn't think she could press any part of this conversation further, not without making her interests obvious. Instead she nodded, murmured her condolences again, her willingness to arrive early for the funeral, or if there was any other small thing she might do. Sigbert escorted her back all the way to the portal, Emeline trailing behind, and promised to convey her condolences to his family properly.

It wasn't until they were back inside at Bryn Glas that Thessaly turned to Emeline. "That was exceedingly odd."

"In several ways." Emeline did not favour many words when a few would do. Thessaly went upstairs to change, Emeline behind her to undo her buttons and help with the unlacing. It wasn't until Thessaly was in one of Aunt Metaia's tea gowns, this one in a soft purple, that Emeline said, "There is something wrong on that estate."

"Yes, but I can't name it or see it or, or anything with it. It's like smoke. Illusions. Mist. No handles." She considered. "That ring bothers me."

"I didn't hear what you said, but I gathered there was something on his hand. Perhaps Master Deschamps might have some thoughts?" Emeline offered it quickly enough.

"By which you mean it would do me good to talk to him about a range of other topics. It would." Thessaly mentally sorted through his schedule. "I expect him tomorrow, but it's still early enough he might be at his workshop. Could you get one of the footmen to take a message?"

Emeline nodded. Even better, she went and fetched the writing desk, so Thessaly could write a note without going back downstairs. She handed the note over and collapsed on the sofa to contemplate what came next.

32

FEBRUARY 15TH IN TRELLECH

It had been a frustrating fortnight, on every level except the professional. Vitus had seen Thessaly twice, but only once with any chance for conversation. The other had been at a distance at Lord Clovis Fortier's funeral. Thessaly had been with the family, though this time, Emeline was right beside her.

Vitus had made his proper bow. After all, he'd been doing work for the estate, or for Lord Clovis— that point was actually murky. No one had turned him away, but it had been only the brief and expected expression of condolences. And the tossing of the bees into the grave. At least this time, Vitus was prepared for that. He was also still offended at the quality of the making, but he was also not in any position to comment on that to anyone who might improve it.

He'd heard nothing from the Fortiers after that. There had been only a brief note from Florent that any plans were on hold for the moment until Sigbert could make some decisions. Vitus had turned his attention to other projects. Now, the requests had tipped firmly in the direction of nightmares, even though the spring rains were approaching. He was almost out of good quality topaz, and much of his current stock of amethyst was not suited to pieces to be worn while sleeping. He still had plenty of obsidian, but of course working on that was an entirely different sort of challenge. It didn't take the usual methods of inscription well.

Saturday, he'd set most of that problem aside. Thessaly had obligations with her parents, apparently. He'd spent the afternoon in the workroom on a few other pieces, before grabbing supper and going on to a lecture. This one was not electricity, or at least not directly. Instead, it was about various magical theories related to healing. On his way in, he'd seen Cyrus Smythe-Clive and his sister, but they were rather surrounded by people, and Vitus didn't go over. He had sat near the front, content to listen to the discussion.

When the lecture ended, Vitus was modestly enlightened, but it was the sort of thing where he now needed to track down someone with more expertise and ask them questions. Perhaps Andie Smythe-Clive could recommend someone, in due course. But when he looked for them, they were near the doors, still with people around. It was as if others felt some of Cyrus's magic might rub off on them, or some of his prestige.

What he did see, unexpectedly, was Dagobert Fortier. As he had at other times since last summer, he was waiting for the rest of the audience to clear out. It let him take his time and move slowly with the cane, an awkward process with the fixed seats of the lecture hall. Vitus came up to the end of the row and nodded. The other man looked faded, still, and still moved tenuously, as if afraid of a fall or some weakness.

"Vitus." Dagobert glanced around. "Were you waiting for me?"

"I wanted to offer my condolences, again, on your brother's death. I hope you and Laudine are well? And your son?"

"Ah." Dagobert paused. "I appreciate that. And the fact you'll acknowledge me in public." That was not what Vitus had expected. He would have thought the other way around. "Would you be up for a drink? Not one of the clubs, the usual bar, near the portals?"

"As you like." Vitus got the sense the request wasn't just due to the distance, but for some other reason. He waited for Dagobert to make his way up the aisle, out the door, down the steps, and then they went along to the same bar as in the past. It wasn't until they were seated, the drink orders taken and the privacy charms cast, that Dagobert spoke again. "Laudine is well. And both our sons. I appreciate you asking."

"Would I be presuming if I said that it sounds like the last weeks have been harder than expected, in the circumstances?" Vitus said it cautiously, but the funeral had certainly been odd on several levels, all sorts of silences and distances visible.

"Oh, quite correct." Dagobert rubbed his face. "I understand you were doing some work for my brother, though not what. I can't tell you anything about that, except that I assume Florent will get some answer out of Sigbert eventually about whether to continue."

"It must be a great deal to take on, and so suddenly. I hadn't heard that Lord Clovis was ill." That was not quite a lie. Vitus had known about the duel, about Thessaly's guesses, but that was not an illness.

"The Healers are baffled. He'd had an injury, but he was mending from that. They'd actually seen him several times recently. And it is something of a shock. You have a brother, yes?"

"A younger brother," Vitus said. "A different relationship."

It made Dagobert nod. "You know how your brother must look up to you, in some way. Whatever other similarities or differences there might be, that age, the expectations of age and youth, whether real or comparative, they continue to hold weight."

Vitus snorted, softly. "Oh, yes. Though Lucas and I are quite different in personality. He is endlessly patient with a horse, but never at a desk. I am the reverse. Not that I mind a horse, but well-mannered or on the other side of a sturdy pasture fence."

Dagobert managed a slight smile at that. "And you are fond of him." Before Vitus could respond, Dagobert said, carefully, "My brother and I had our differences. I miss him, but I miss what might have been more, at this point."

"I'm sorry for that." Vitus could say that honestly, earnestly, without any hint of subterfuge. "I've been very lucky with Lucas. Though he has had times when he's thought me an idiot, and recently." Then he took a breath and asked, "May I ask how Lord Sigbert is doing?"

"Ah. There are two things, one more general, and one more specific." Dagobert didn't pause, just went on. "There is some unpleasant gossip about the family. That there must be some curse, for there to be so many deaths within months. Childeric, Clovis, and some add Philip Landry and his mother onto that count. Certainly as connections of the family. Or there are mutterings about how Henut Landry was protecting the family, and since her death, she is not. That, at least, would be in line with some of the agreements I know about."

Vitus nodded, unsure what else to say to that.

"That is one line of talk. The other, I gather, is that Thessaly is a common thread, and various people wonder how much is her influence. A curse, or something of the kind. Especially since so few have seen her at anything other than the funerals."

"Ah." Vitus looked down. "And what do you think?"

"There's pressure on Sigbert to marry, and promptly. Maman is resolute about it, and there are not so many women she approves of. A matter of breeding, potential, having the proper sort of upbringing." Dagobert shrugged. "I have been happy in my marriage, with those considerations. Sigbert is young. There are younger women than Thessaly, if he were willing to wait a few years. But as Lord, that is complicated."

"Even though presumably he could name you as Heir." Vitus offered it cautiously.

"That is on the agenda, yes. It's me or a cousin, and Bradamante has been more distant." Dagobert did not explain that statement, baffling though it was. "And Sigbert is sensible, if under a great deal of pressure and expectation." Dagobert considered. "In that odd space, and you appreciate this more directly than I do, I suspect. A grown man, able in all ways of making his own decisions. And yet, a young man, who does not have as much experience of the world as he wishes. Certainly one who needs to make some decisions far more quickly than he'd prefer."

Vitus nodded. "I have sympathy. Setting up my own workshop has had dozens of challenges of that kind. I suspect that's far simpler than the land magics. Especially when Sigbert— pardon, Lord Sigbert— might have expected years, decades, to learn what he'd need."

"Just so. And like all ancient families, we have a great many traditions." Dagobert shrugged. At that point, their drinks were ready, and they paused for that service before continuing once the waiter was gone.

Vitus weighed his options, then said, "I couldn't help noting some things at the funeral. Would you indulge a question or two? You needn't answer anything private, of course. I wouldn't expect that."

"Now I am curious what you have questions about." Dagobert took a sip of his drink, then nodded. "Go ahead."

"The first was about the bees. A custom of some substantial standing, I gather? Back to the Merovingians?" Vitus offered the information Thessaly had told him.

"Yes. Gold for the men in the family, silver for the women, copper for anyone else. They're rather a bother to have made, and especially in a rush." Dagobert shrugged. "Why do you ask?"

"You might, in having more made up, look for a different crafter. They're rather poorly formed and, pardon, I don't know how much of the process you understand?"

"They are made in moulds, connected by thin rods of metal, and then those are broken off and sanded." Dagobert replied promptly enough, looking engaged in a way he hadn't so far. "You have a better idea?"

"Yes, and no. I agree the mould is likely the best choice, certainly in quantity. But the two I've handled, neither filled properly. It makes the shape lop-sided, incomplete. More care in the process, remelting any that did not form properly, that would be, er. More fit?"

"The gold and silver have been better, I think." Dagobert considered. "I will mention it. I suspect Florent could suggest someone able to make the necessary changes."

"Quite likely. He may not have noticed, of course,

seeing as he'd be counted among the family." Vitus considered. "I got the impression you get along well enough with him?"

"So long as I am treating Laudine well, yes, he finds me pleasant. He seems mild, but he can be quite fierce when it comes to his daughters. As a man should be, I suppose. You had another question?"

Vitus nodded. "I spotted that Lord Sigbert was wearing a ring, one I hadn't noted before." That neatly dodged the question of how long any of the family had been wearing it. One might not notice something. "The inlay, a gold band with what looked like turquoise and something else?" The thing of it was that once Thessaly had mentioned it, Vitus had wanted a look. And it had indeed matched the description he'd been given by Magistra Landry, what seemed like decades ago. It wasn't anything Vitus could confirm, not without a proper examination, but it was not a terribly common mode of rings among the landed families.

"My brother had taken to wearing it. A family piece, I gathered." Vitus did note that didn't specify whose family. "Not one I'm familiar with. I'm afraid you'd need to ask Sigbert if you wanted to see it. And I would not suggest that anytime soon."

"I'm sure he has a great deal to tend to. No, this is trivial in comparison to everything else, but of course I do notice rings and such. A professional obsession, I suppose."

Dagobert snorted again. "And may I ask, are you concerned about a curse, or do you carry talismans against such things routinely?"

That was a fascinating theoretical question, actually. "A bit of both. I do wear some of my own work, of course." He pulled back one of his sleeves a hair, to show the cuff link. "That's a fairly ordinary sort of protection piece, against the minor calamities of a day. I am less likely to trip on a step, risk having something dropped on my head from an upper story of a house, be nearly run over by a carriage. All handy on a day in a busy city. Less likely to be pickpocketed or otherwise taken advantage of, on a less physical level."

"Ah, that does seem practical, yes. And I assume other pieces, more private." Dagobert nodded. "I am certainly wearing half a dozen."

"Just so. Nothing on me specific to curses, but I also have a theory, not properly tested, of course, about whether some curses are situational. Something that might be neutral or even welcome to one person being a harm to someone else, where it depends on perspective."

"Huh." Dagobert looked startled at that. "I should get home, actually, I hadn't realised the time." It wasn't a smooth transition at all. "My regards to your family."

Vitus blinked several times, and then nodded. "Of course." He considered. "I'll pay the tab if you need to go." Dagobert disappeared as promptly as he could. Vitus sat in silence for several minutes, nursing the rest of his drink. It only occurred to him at the end of the glass that Dagobert hadn't mentioned anything about why he'd come out for that particular lecture, one focused on healing rather than alchemy or even electricity, on a Saturday night.

33

MARCH 11TH AT ARUNDEL

"Sigbert." Thessaly felt like she was repeating herself from just six weeks ago. Less than six weeks. Another death, on top of illness, on top of everything. Here she was, standing in the entry hall of Arundel, Sigbert in the arched door to the Great Hall. "I'm so terribly sorry."

Now, instead of a bier with Sigbert's father, it was Sigbert's mother. This time, Thessaly had received a note in the morning, though apparently Maylis had died the previous afternoon. It had not suggested Thessaly come, but it had not said she shouldn't. And whatever complexities she might feel about the Fortiers, or for that matter, her own parents, losing both parents inside of six weeks had to be a horror.

Sigbert didn't move, not in any way Thessaly could see.

"Thessaly." Then, slowly, he nodded his head once. "I'll tell Grand-mère you observed the proper forms." His voice was like nothing she'd heard from him before. It was stone, all the resonance drained out, no echo, no life, near enough.

"Is there anything I can do to help? Any preparations?"

Sigbert shook his head minutely. A negative. "Thank you, no." His voice made her shiver now, even just three words of it. There was something wrong there, and Thessaly had no idea what to do next. "We have the lists in hand." He might, a month ago, have managed a moment of dark humour, about having reviewed them recently, knowing where everything was. There was none of that.

"I hope some of the family are here?" Thessaly was thrashing around for anything. She didn't want to stop, to be here for only a few dozen words. That felt wrong, too.

"Uncle Dagobert and Aunt Laudine and Garin. For the time being, at least. And we expect Aunt Bradamante in an hour or so. We will have enough to keep vigil."

It would be a rather painfully small number for a vigil. "Let me know if I can be of any help, please." Thessaly tried to keep the earnestness front and centre in her voice. "At any time."

Sigbert didn't soften, not exactly, but he nodded once. "The proper forms." He repeated it again. Then he glanced over her shoulder. "Aunt Laudine." A second later, he added, "Uncle Dagobert."

"Might I have a word, Sigbert?" Dagobert was walking slowly, though perhaps slightly less painfully than sometimes.

Laudine followed it immediately with, "Thessaly, would you walk with me outside for a breath of fresh air? If you have a moment?"

"Of course." Thessaly ducked her chin. "Sigbert, I'll be thinking of you, all of you." Sigbert inclined his head just once, taking a step or two back offering no touch, and waiting for his uncle to cross the hall and join him. Laudine turned for the front door, and Thessaly followed her out. Once they were outside— the day was at least not raining— Laudine turned to follow the paths out to the formal garden. She was visibly pregnant now, and walking more carefully herself. Thessaly let her set the pace and decide about the conversation.

It wasn't until they were across the formal garden, well away from the house, that Laudine looked around for somewhere to sit, claiming a bench in the sun. "Do you mind?"

"Of course not." Thessaly was dressed comfortably to be outside for at least a few minutes. "May I ask how you're doing? Or the others? Sigbert was, ah, terse? Which, of course, I understand, it must be a terrible shock for him."

"Ah, the question of how we are all doing is not easy to answer, either. It is a shock for Sigbert, I am sure. And Dagobert might be his Heir, but that does not mean they entirely trust each other. One challenge among many. I'd hoped that seeing you might be a little help, but I gather not."

"He did not tell me in so many words to go away, but he might as well have. Would you write if there is anything I can do?" Thessaly glanced back toward the house. "I was thinking that it must be difficult indeed to lose both parents in such quick succession."

"There is rather more gossip today about a curse, I gather," Laudine said. "Father has his sources, and his sources have sources." She looked Thessaly up and down. "Some of that is about you, as you know."

Thessaly swallowed hard. She might still have doubts about whether any of Lord Clovis's fate was due to the duel, but she had not interacted with either Lady Chrodechildis or Lady Maylis other than in the ordinary ways of this kind of family. She had disliked the pressures to marry, and some of how both of them had treated her, but it was an ordinary grumbling frustration, not some far-reaching deadly magic. "I suppose that's inevitable. So much misfortune, all at once. It's not been six months since Childeric." She cleared her throat. "May I ask about Lady Chrodechildis? Would it be a help to have someone sit with her?"

"Ah, no. She's not able to speak, but she is particular about who she tolerates. That does not include me or Dagobert. One of two maids is with her all the time." Laudine looked out across the sleeping gardens. "An apoplexy, it was sudden. She stood up, then she fell to the ground, unable to move deliberately. The Healers have advised how to keep her comfortable." Laudine cleared her throat. "They do not anticipate significant improvement, I'm afraid."

"Oh. My." That was something Thessaly had not entirely imagined. "She has always seemed, I mean, older but active and thoroughly engaged and in control of her surroundings. That must be terribly challenging for her." Honesty made her add, "And for everyone now."

Laudine visibly appreciated the latter. "Yes. Maylis had just finished overseeing rearranging the Great Chamber, on the ground floor, to be Chrodechildis's new bedroom and sitting room. We hope that as the weather improves, she might at least come in a wheelchair into the garden on balmy days. That would be impossible from upstairs."

That implied a rearrangement of the household on all levels. "And you and Dagobert and Garin?"

"A shock to Dagobert. And Garin is confused, I think, but he does not wish to talk about it. By a number of things, the back and forth from the Essex House, about the fact he is to have a younger brother, one so much younger." Laudine considered. "This pregnancy is also something of a trial, but I cannot complain in the circumstances. Though I wish our rooms were not at the top of two flights of stairs. I can't bring myself to manage them more than once or twice a day. But it meant I was lurking in the sitting room, and could hear you talking to Sigbert."

Thessaly nodded, hesitantly. "And Sigbert, still on the first floor?"

"Yes. It may make some sense for him to move into the West Wing in due course, and turn over the first floor for our use. There's quite a bit of room there, as you've seen." Then Laudine added, "Though, I, at least, would understand if you did not wish to become closer to the family by marriage. Certainly the omens are questionable, if you believe in that sort of thing."

Thessaly firmly set the question aside for the time being. "Do you believe it is something of the kind, something beyond a run of particularly ill-fortune?"

"That's an excellent question. You realise that I count the misfortunes from June, not September. Dagobert's injuries, he is— well. Our Healer, who I trust, I was at school with him, suspects there might be a little further improvement, but not as much as we hoped for."

"I thought he looked to be moving slightly more easily, today?" Thessaly offered, cautiously, with the idea that an outside perspective might be something.

"Did you?" Laudine considered. "We've been discussing whether becoming Heir changed anything. Or perhaps being on this land. It is worth keeping notes on, at least, and seeing what changes when we are here for an extended period." She glanced down. "I would rather not have this child here, but I suppose we'll have to figure that out. Certainly, leaving Sigbert largely alone in the house is unkind. He has very little idea how to handle the ordinary household management. The staff are well-trained, but there are always matters that need a competent decision."

Thessaly nodded once. "I have been learning that.

Though in my case, I can at least ask what Aunt Metaia preferred in such cases, and then decide what I want. Here, that might not do. And, of course, not wanting to interfere with his grandmother's preferences."

"Just so." Laudine looked away again. "I admit, the loneliness is a concern. I worry about Sigbert. This is not to pressure you, but he has also not spent time with, oh, friends from school or otherwise. His interests are private, or they were shared with his father."

"And not his uncle." Thessaly hesitated. "I gathered, from the source you'd expect, that there was some project they were working on."

"Just so. If you'd pass on that, well, whatever decisions happen will not be quick. It's not something Dagobert is involved with, not at this point." Her voice became tighter, her lips pursed slightly. "And I don't know the details. May I ask, did Sigbert give any sign, the last month, of his preferences?"

Thessaly swallowed. "I told him I was open to considering negotiations in due course. I suspect that would have been, well, around now, in the ordinary way of things. To begin to put the terms together. As things are?" It was the question of what she told Laudine. "And to be honest, I am not sure he can offer terms I would agree to at this point." A great deal of that was that Sigbert was not Vitus. That made all the difference in the world. But even if Vitus was not in the picture, she would be wary. "Not because of rumours about a curse, but about what I have seen and heard."

"I must admit, I could not advise marrying into the family unless you wish a great deal of effort for very little respect." Laudine said. "Sigbert is— I think if he were in better form, he would want to do well by you. Certainly, I suspect he would do better at asking you, or permitting you to lay out your terms, than Childeric would have. But that is not much for a marriage."

Thessaly nodded. Hesitantly, she cleared her throat. "May I ask, have you been happy?"

There was, for just a moment, a radiant reaction to that, as if, whatever else was true, yes, it was a good marriage. Laudine suppressed it nearly as quickly, the sun behind the cloak of a cloud, but then she spoke. "I am fortunate to love my husband and to be loved in turn. And the fact that we're having another child is entirely my request. For a number of reasons, but in case something, if he'd taken a turn for the worse." Now Laudine looked away. "He is an imperfect man, my husband. And I am, I am certain, flawed in my own ways. People are, I've found. But our failures mediate each other, rather than being cumulative, on the whole. I have been fortunate to have his ear, his understanding, his partnership, in almost all things."

'Almost' was a key word there, clearly, but not one Thessaly could ask about. "And you do not think Sigbert would offer that partnership."

"No. He would let you build your life, at least once things settled. Have your hobbies, your interests, though of course no duelling while you were expecting or intending to be. The limitations of portal travel at such times, that is wearing. There are many worse lives, and many harder ones. But it would not necessarily produce happiness at home. Comfort, cordiality, yes. They are different things."

"I appreciate your honesty," Thessaly said finally, choosing her words precisely. "Would it help to know my intentions? So that you and Dagobert can plan accordingly?"

"I cannot promise to keep them entirely secret. If Sigbert asks directly, he is Lord of the Land, there are implications for the family, even if he does not directly call the truth magics. Tell me according to that." Laudine's voice was clear now, as if they'd ended up on ground she'd already measured and considered.

"I am open to discussing terms with Sigbert, but I do not expect we will find terms that I would agree to. Even leaving aside, erm, other considerations, other people. My parents are still pressuring me, and that might change the situation. I am glad to share more with you as more becomes apparent. How's that?" Thessaly watched Laudine carefully through all of that, to be rewarded with a slight nod at the end.

"That is more than fair, and appreciated. I will let you know if there is more I can share. Is a note to Bryn Glas the fastest way to reach you, still?"

"Yes. And the staff are checking three times a day, just in case. A few times, I've had messages outside the normal portal schedule for the post."

"Just so. Ah. Now, would you mind walking back with me? And perhaps your arm? I'm afraid he's being restless again." Laudine grimaced. "He is rather more active than Garin was, all elbows and feet, I think."

"Of course. My arm, how best may I offer you a hand up?" They sorted that out easily enough, though Thessaly felt the time duelling had improved her strength along with her agility. They walked back arm in arm, rather slowly, to find Dagobert waiting to talk to his wife. Thessaly took her leave, after one more repetition of her willingness to help. By the time she opened the portal for Bryn Glas, she hoped they would not ask, while worrying more over what was happening and why.

34

MARCH 30TH AT A RESTAURANT IN TRELLECH

"Why are you resisting this? You know your duty." Father's fingers flicked across the table, setting his fork aside and picking up the wineglass.

Thessaly reminded herself - twice - that a private room at one of Trellech's best restaurants was not the place for a scene. For one thing, it would limit her future moves in whatever this duel turned into. And for another, all the privacy protections were engaged. The only people who would see the scene were her parents.

Not even Hermia. Thessaly had hoped to see her sister, but when she'd arrived, it had just been Mother and Father. Thessaly had left Emeline to have supper in the main dining room. There were tables set aside for that sort of thing, companions or chaperones who attended upon the other guests but did not dine with them. Emeline at least had reading material to keep her busy. She and Thessaly were deep in the specifics for the creation of the duelling salle. They had to finalise the initial plans for the dirt flooring and the underlying enchantment layers within the fortnight.

Now, Thessaly took a breath. She refused to permit the first half-dozen thoughts in her head to leave her mouth. Deliberately, she folded her hands in her lap, a duellist's gesture showing she did not intend movement. Not right now. And there was the way Father would read it, that she was at least complying with the outward forms of being a modest and respectful daughter. None of the staff had entered since the main dishes were brought, and Thessaly was sure, without looking, that it was Mother's doing.

Finally, she settled on a first answer. "The situation has changed, Father. Mother. For the Fortiers and for me. And yet you press me to formalise the agreements with Sigbert. Why?"

"You know perfectly— oh, you explain it." Father jerked his chin towards Mother.

Mother at least had the good grace to look a tad uncomfortable. She might or might agree with him, but Mother knew this was not the way to get Thessaly's agreement. "There are considerations for the family, you know that." Her voice was conciliatory.

"To marry well. To have children with strong magic. To keep my marriage agreements. To benefit the family in large ways and small." Thessaly ticked them off, her voice purely neutral. "And you appear to believe the only possible solution on that front is to marry Sigbert Fortier."

"The Fortiers are a powerful family." Even as Mother said it, it came out a bit feebly.

"The Fortiers are an increasingly dead family." Thessaly would not have said that to Sigbert. She probably ought not to have said it here, but there was a remarkably satisfying intake of breath from both her parents. Thessaly would take those moments where she could, especially right now. "Parents concerned about the longevity of the family might sensibly have some concerns."

"A run of ill-chance," Father said, waving it off.

"One death out of season is chance. Childeric was, we must all admit, doing something that has dangers, known and unknown." Also, Thessaly was increasingly sure that whatever the reason he'd died, he'd brought it on himself in some form. Hubris, possibly something beyond hubris. "And Lady Maylis, that might be grief, though she never struck me as a woman who would grieve herself to death and leave her son without her guidance." If not the kindest thing she could say about Lady Maylis, it had the benefit of being true. "But Lord Clovis? Dagobert's illness? Lady Chrodechildis's? Or there are the Landrys to be considered. Perhaps there is something foul in the air or the magic or the water at Arundel. Surely that is not good for a healthy wife or a healthy babe. I am not eager to make my body an experiment."

As she said it, she began to wonder about that. The research Vitus had mentioned, the original intention had been to trace pernicious effects in the water. Was it possible something had leached into the pipes at Arundel? That would not really explain Philip, though. Certainly, she had not felt entirely well during a number of her visits. Though she hadn't spent an overnight there since Childeric's funeral, and even the silent torture of the vigil had not been as exhausting as a more ordinary weekend there.

Mother opened her mouth, then closed it. Father ignored her. "You do not have much of a choice. There is Sigbert. There is Hemlock Wilson." Who was indeed from a potent magical family, as the Lyttons counted it, but who was also approaching fifty and a recent widow from a second wife. "Clarion Hembridge." He was well over fifty, known for grasping hands and being exceedingly tight with his accounts. Even if she kept control of Aunt Metaia's gift of her own money, he would not permit her to spend it, and he would certainly not permit her to duel. "You know perfectly well Sigbert is the best of the choices. He is young, he is energetic, you get along well with him."

Thessaly took a breath. "There is Cyrus. We did discuss the possibility."

"Smythe-Clive? Oh, he has shown some promise, I suppose, as such things are counted, but the family has no staying power, magically speaking. Nothing proven. Why waste yourself there? And he already has a daughter. Sigbert is in desperate need of an heir for his own lineage."

She could not argue with that particular bit of logic. That did not, however, mean that she had to provide him one.

"Childeric made it clear, not long before he died, that he had no intention of keeping to our agreements. It has not made me eager to make more." Not with a Fortier, certainly. Her mind might drift, in the wee hours and the deep dark of the night when she couldn't sleep, to what agreements she'd like to make with Vitus.

"Sigbert is not his brother." Father brushed it off, as she expected he would. "And you do have resources of your own."

The problem was that she had a house where she could not live, not while she was pregnant, if she were carrying a Fortier. She would have dozens of responsibilities. Even if she made her primary home at Bryn Glas, it was not well set for raising small children. There was no separate nursery space where they could play and be louder without affecting the rest of the house. Vitus had been raised in such a way, she would have to ask him how it worked. But she could not raise children the way Sigbert had been raised, or Thessaly herself, in such a space.

And not that she'd seen all the private rooms at Arundel, just the second floor, where guests had rooms. But there was not a great deal of space for her and Sigbert to avoid each other, not while his grandmother had the other wing. Now she inclined her head. "Still. I am not in a rush to make promises."

"You need not marry yet." Her father's voice turned conciliatory. "But at least begin the negotiations. You have said the Scali have given it some thought. If you must have a ball or a celebration, you might do so in September." Her father's fingers twitched.

She would be bound by the agreements once they were made and the betrothal confirmed, even if they did not announce it. That was the problem. "A celebration on the anniversary of Childeric's death? People will comment." This time, Thessaly did not manage to fully repress the tartness in her voice.

Her father glared. "Do not take that tone with me. You are still a daughter of the family, an unmarried daughter, and you will behave as you have been taught. Your mother assures me that any failure is on your part, not hers. And certainly Hermia is proving more biddable."

"Where is Hermia? I had hoped to speak with her today."

Mother cleared her throat. "Dining with friends."

Before Mother could say any more, Father cut her off. "She knows her place. If you won't arrange to marry Sigbert, I will ensure she does so."

"Hermia's only sixteen!" Thessaly almost pushed back from the table.

"Stay where you are." Father's voice rang out sharply, and she could feel his magic hold her in place. She could undo that, given time, but not without being obvious. "Sixteen is old enough to marry. She's not at Schola, she doesn't need to finish at that tutor of hers. Her embroidery and painting are already sufficient. And her music."

The ladylike arts. Thessaly had done well at the painting, not so much the embroidery or music. The first was a help to illusion work, the other two were less so, and there were only so many hours in a day. She swallowed, and now she tasted bile. "What, precisely, do you want?"

"For you to agree to marry Sigbert and sign the agreements. I will not argue with when you wed, so long as it is within the year. I do not believe he would rush you beyond the point." Father leaned forward. "But he needs stability to ensure the family line. Your children would inherit the title, the properties, the accumulated library and private magics."

Thessaly was none too sure that any of those had been kind to the Fortiers, honestly. "And you have no concerns about the rumoured curse?"

"Oh, not Sigbert, surely. He is young. And even if there were, somehow, that would not mean it would touch you." Father shrugged, leaning back again now he was sure she was behaving. "You must marry. You have a choice in which of those three."

It was not much of a choice at all. The thing of it was how much she wanted to fight. Here and now was neither the time nor the place. She did not trust Mother to support her, or Mother would have done so already. Father had chosen the field. The more Thessaly thought about it, the more she was increasingly sure that her best option was to delay any sort of signing until she made agreements of her own. Presenting her marriage, or at least a formal betrothal, to her parents as a fait accompli would be tricky, but more certain.

She did not want anyone other than Vitus, but she would not risk his livelihood and passion for his work on rushing that. The scandal of it, the way people would choose sides, that could destroy any hope he had of making his name. If she thought she could hold off another six months, perhaps the landscape would change enough. She'd have to talk to Vitus about it, though, and see what he thought. Thessaly swallowed. "I understand." She did not agree, she did not concede.

Father took it for what it was, and perhaps a trifle more. He stood. "Pardon me." He strode out of the room, parting the privacy warding like a curtain. Mother looked over. "He means what he says about Hermia. Don't test him."

"Oh, I know he means it. Does she know?"

Mother's mouth twitched once. "She understands. He won't let Hermia see you until things are settled." That put another boulder in the way. Though Thessaly had a few options for managing that one, potentially. "What are you going to do?"

"Consider my options. Speak with the Scali, at some length, about what might be contractually included. Write to Sigbert. Though he hasn't replied to my last two messages, but I didn't expect it. He must be busy with matters at Arundel."

"I thought the funeral was very tasteful." Mother and Father had attended, of course, with Hermia in tow, though Thessaly had been with the family and not able to speak to anyone on her own account. She'd helped mostly with alerting the staff to various needs, to spare Laudine having to stand or walk so much. It had at least felt like something that might help someone there, since Sigbert had continued to be stone. "Maylis would have wanted things to flow smoothly, as they did."

Thessaly inclined her head. There wasn't much she could say to that.

"You know your duty. You are being asked to do as I did, as your grandmothers did." Mother spoke quietly.

"But not as Aunt Metaia did." That was the thing that kept catching at Thessaly. Aunt Metaia had given her freedom, if Thessaly could just figure out to reach for it. The trick was doing so without destroying everything else around her. Around her and Vitus and Hermia, who should all have a chance at happiness beyond duty. Then, finally, she decided to take a risk. She didn't have long before Father came back.

"Why is Father so insistent? Power, and connection, certainly." Thessaly couldn't ignore those. "But it's something more than that." She hesitated, considering Mother's dress, then what jewellery she was and wasn't wearing, what she should have been wearing with this dress from her collection. "Money?"

Her mother didn't say a word, but she couldn't entirely hide the widening of her eyes or the slight movement of her mouth. Nothing Thessaly could swear to, nothing definite, but enough. Money, then. Even with Mother's inheritance from Aunt Metaia and Hermia's, then. "I see. I will consider, Mother. I can promise that much."

Her mother patted her hand. Then there was a little flurry as the staff returned to remove the plates and bring out the cheese plates. Thessaly managed this part without thinking about it, with smiles and quiet gratitude, while waiting for her heartbeat to eventually slow after the tension of the conversation. By the time Father returned, she had pulled dignity around her again, and he kept the conversation on easier topics for the rest of the evening. He tucked in news of the Lytton cousins. There were a few plans for summer activities she might enjoy. She knew it for the illusion it was. Everything was not well, and his words could not hide that.

35

APRIL 18H AT ARUNDEL

Vitus was not at all sure what the etiquette was in this case. That was despite the fact that it was the fourth Fortier funeral inside seven months, and he was in fact now familiar with their customs. For one thing, he wasn't sure that he ought to be attending. But he'd had a note, specifically from Dagobert, now Lord Dagobert, and Laudine, asking him to attend. And another from Florent, encouraging him to come as well.

In the litany of the dead - and the causes of death - this one was even odder than usual. Sigbert had fallen from a horse, Vitus gathered, and died almost instantly. Certainly, no one could argue with that. Vitus heard a murmur, from someone near him, talking to a knot of what must have been Sigbert's yearmates, that there had a been a swarm of bees nearby, perhaps they had spooked the horse.

It was another death out of season, uncertain, and a thing of gossip. This funeral was far less well attended than either Childeric's or Clovis's had been. The mourners were cautious, quiet, and mostly those obliged by family ties or by connections. And a few too afraid of angering the remaining Fortier relations, though it was hard to count exactly who was in that group.

Thessaly was here; Vitus had seen her, lending a hand to Laudine, mostly. A handful of the Council were in attendance, though more as a nod to Sigbert's brief time as Lord of the Land. Dagobert seemed to be bearing up well enough so far, though he looked more exhausted than usual. The bees were slightly better in shape, but less detailed, as if the crafting had been rushed. Once the graveside offerings had been made, he and Laudine had both been seated at a table in the garden, and the mourners came to them. Thessaly stayed close to them, just nodding at him when he paid his respects.

Their son sat beside them, near silent, and Vitus wished he knew what to say there. It must be a tremendous amount of change for him, much of it different to explain. The adults didn't have answers. How could they tell Garin anything that made sense? But Vitus certainly didn't have answers for that.

When he was leaving, as the numbers dwindled down to the immediate family, he saw Thessaly taking Garin off for a quiet walk. It made him wonder, all of a sudden, what she'd be like with her own child. But he could not linger and watch, and instead went back to Bryn Glas to wait for her.

He had some time to wait, as it turned out, a good two hours, two and a half, before Thessaly turned up. She was trailed by Collins, who followed her into Thessaly's bedroom. Vitus could hear the sound of the bath running, and in about ten minutes, Collins came out. "I'll be bringing supper up in half an hour. Mistress Thessaly suggested some wine might be in order, if you agreed?"

Vitus was bemused to be consulted, but he nodded. "If

Thessaly wants wine, certainly. I admit that seems a good idea. I don't need anything further. I'm sure you've plenty to see to."

Collins nodded her head once and disappeared. Near enough on the thirty minute mark, Thessaly appeared from her bedroom. Her hair was in a thick braid down her back and mostly dry, her wrapper on, and she looked as if the bath had helped, but not quite enough. She opened her mouth to ask, "Food?" when there was a knock on the door and Collins brought in a tray on a cart.

"There we go. I'll be sitting up in the kitchen, should you need anything, Mistress?" Collins disappeared, leaving them to a supper of stew, good bread and butter, and yes, wine.

Vitus let Thessaly eat in quiet until she set her spoon down and blinked at him. "You're not saying anything?" Her voice was a little uneven.

Vitus shifted to offer an arm. She immediately leaned into it, her head on his shoulder. That meant he could probably ask a question or three. "You seemed to need to eat first? It looked rather awful, from what I saw. How are Dagobert and Laudine? Or Garin, I saw you with him."

"Exhausted, both of them, and worried. If there is a curse..." Thessaly's voice trailed off. "And Bradamante is apparently being difficult. An unpleasant combination of coming over big sister and would-be-matriarch. Only then her husband keeps pulling her away. I gather they're going on an Atlantic crossing, so Yves obviously plans to put distance between them and whatever curse or misfortune there might be."

"I suppose he is at least following his own dictates. And it would give Dagobert and Laudine a little space to sort things out. Bradamante isn't their matriarch." Vitus offered it tentatively.

"No, she married out. That's the point. And it's a bit late now to have Yves marry in. Like it or not, Dagobert is Lord now. He has a son. With any luck there will be another inside six weeks." Thessaly considered. "They're still in shock, honestly, both of them. And the funeral was all sorts of demands. That's why I took Garin for a walk. At least he could have a few minutes without having to be entirely proper in public." Thessaly shook her head. "Laudine trusts her Healer, and, assuming nothing else happens, she has every reason to rest as much as possible now."

"Quite." Vitus certainly felt himself unqualified to comment on what she should be doing, anyway. "And you?"

"Well. It solves the problem of people pushing me to marry Sigbert," Thessaly said, before she inhaled, the sort of sharp inhale that gave Vitus only a few moments warning. Then she was shaking, the sort of onrush of emotion she'd had, just as reasonably, a few times before. Vitus pulled his arm around her, encouraging her more into his lap, where he could hold her better, and just held on, as steady as he could.

It lasted longer this time than the others she'd let him see, until she was sniffling against his jacket, her shoulders still shivering. Vitus let his hand stroke her back, the way Lucas had taught him to stroke a nervous horse. The trick was in making long movements, nothing sudden or unexpected, the rhythm mattering as much as the touch itself.

Vitus just waited until finally Thessaly put her head up, sniffling. He met her eyes. "Bedroom? Would that be more comfortable?" Her face was blotchy. She rubbed it with the back of one hand.

"Let me, I'm a mess. Your jacket." Her words tumbled out.

"None of that matters. How about you go wash your

face, I'll bring the wine in, and the jacket will keep." Vitus was fairly sure that Collins knew some particular magic to clean such things. Or if not, she could recommend someone who did. And besides, the jacket didn't matter in the grand scheme of things.

She wiggled out of his lap, standing. Shaky, perhaps, but not for terribly long. Thessaly looked back at him from the door to her bedroom, then disappeared. Vitus poured another full glass of the wine, and brought it into the bedroom, before covering up the food and making sure the fire was behaving. By the time Thessaly appeared, he was in bed. The sheets were warmed with a charm, and he'd changed into the pyjamas he kept in the wardrobe. He wasn't sure if she'd want more intimate contact tonight or not. Now, he pulled the blankets back as she slid in.

"You didn't go away."

"Why would I?" Vitus blinked. "I don't think you're cursed, for the record. Have I said that yet? I have implied it, but perhaps it needed saying." The thought had just occurred to him.

Thessaly managed an uneven smile. "It's, I don't even know what I feel about Sigbert. Felt. Any of it."

That was also honestly reasonable. Vitus considered. "I'd be worried, I think, if you did know. It's all confusing. We don't have anything like all the relevant information. And there is honestly a lot of terrifying change going on, deaths and mysteries and more." He considered. "Tell me some of what you feel about Sigbert? It doesn't have to be all of it. Start somewhere."

"An opening move." Putting it in duelling terms helped, of course it would. She took a deep breath. "He shouldn't be dead. I mean, I don't know of any reason he ought to be. He was a good rider, on his estate, his own horse. Childeric could be reckless. Sigbert wasn't."

"In general, either?" Vitus said, clarifying.

"That." Thessaly let out a sigh and fell back against the pillows with a soft thump. "I didn't love him. I almost certainly wasn't going to marry him— um. That came out not the way I meant. I'll— that's different?"

"Come back to it." Vitus said, though he very much would like her to expand on that point. Not that Sigbert was a threat, but it was the question of what else she meant to do now that was relevant.

"He didn't deserve to be dead. Or did he? I mean, if there is a curse, it's a very precise one." Thessaly lifted a hand and let it fall. "Four. And there's Dagobert being ill. And Lady Chrodechildis."

"How is she? Did they say?" Vitus asked.

"Glaring from her bed, but that's about all she can do. Laudine and Dagobert are moving to Arundel, making over the first floor as they get a chance. There isn't really much choice, even though Laudine doesn't want to leave Essex." Thessaly added, "I did tell you what I pointed out to Father. What if it's the estate? I mentioned that to her. She said she'd had the same fear. She's having things checked out thoroughly, but she doesn't think it's that." Thessaly sat up. "Maybe she knows it's something else?"

"What makes you think that?" Vitus hesitated, then went on. "I'm not arguing, but I didn't see or hear whatever makes you think that."

"I don't know. Just the way she said it. And the way she looked at Dagobert. It was before everyone arrived this morning, just before all the expectations landed on everyone. But what? I mean, if she knew what it was, why isn't she doing something? Or is she doing something, and it's not obvious?"

"Maybe it's not something she can control? Or not something she understands fully? Or something like that?"

Vitus was trying to think through the implications. "There's a lot of that in talisman work."

Thessaly twisted to face him, now sitting with one foot tucked under her thigh, knee bent. "Tell me about that?" She had the quality of a child wanting one more story, one more joy before sleep. Vitus was taken again with how eager her passions were when she could let them show.

"Talismans, sometimes we're making them. Oh, Niobe calls this closed and open, though there are better technical terms. Closed, you're working in a system where the factors are known. The charms against lightning, for example. You know precisely what you want to prevent or discourage or avoid. It can be named, magically, in the description - lightning, plague, specific illnesses. Unwanted relatives, so you don't run into them casually."

Thessaly snorted at the last one. "Does that work?"

"Depends on who designed the talisman. Mine work fairly well, so far, based on observed data." Vitus was rather proud of that, actually. They weren't easy to do, especially with expansive families or sets of people. "And open talismans are more dependent on other factors. The one for Carrington, for example, that's interacting with the environment in the moment. The state of the wearer, what is going on around them, if there are other circumstances. So it might be something where Laudine understands some of what the effect is. But not all of what's going on, or how to change it. Just what experience suggests is affected and what is not."

"I don't know that we'll ever know. Or be able to ask." Thessaly sighed, and rearranged herself to settle on her side. "Can you talk through examples of talismans with me? More of them, I mean? When you have time?"

"Oh, ask me to talk about a subject I love with a person

I adore? Whatever shall I do?" He hit the teasing note right. He saw her smile properly.

"Silly." Thessaly took a breath, then said, her words coming out in a tumble. "Sigbert should have had more of a life. And he was trying to be decent, and mostly he was managing it. But I want, I want things that are about a future with you. Not anyone else. I don't know how to get from now to there, though. Not without risking your work, your reputation. And I'm afraid Father's going to, um. Be difficult again about marrying me off, sooner than later. Within a month or two, probably. Given prior evidence."

Vitus swallowed hard. "I want a future with you, too. And together, we'll figure out how to get there." He considered. "Would a betrothal protect you enough? Even if we didn't marry for a bit, until I'm more established?"

"Maybe." Thessaly looked up. "If I could avoid shouting on the street about how much I want to marry you." Her mouth curled up slightly.

"You're doing remarkably well at that so far," Vitus said. "I will dream of a day we can walk down the street in Trellech arm in arm, then." He let out a huff of a breath. "And now?"

"And now, I want. I want a night with you. Without expectations looming, or fears, or any of that."

"I will apply myself to that bit of magic, then. Not quite a talisman, but I think I have some relevant skills." Vitus reached out, letting his fingers trail across the back of her hand, a pattern that hinted at much more to come.

She laughed, nudging him. "Less in the way of clothing, then. And less light?"

"Both can be arranged." Vitus set himself to those particular problems, as well as making sure the wine glass was well out of the way. It did not solve any of their large problems, but those could wait for a night. Today had held plenty.

36

MAY 20TH AT ARUNDEL

"We do appreciate you coming." It was Dagobert who stood to greet Vitus as he entered the parlour. Vitus had never seen it before. He'd never been invited so far into the house. Laudine was settled on the chaise under the window, with other chairs pulled around in a conversational grouping. The entire room was what Vitus had expected from the house. Dark wood panelling with shades of purple, along with touches of gold, including gilt bees climbing the edges of the mantlepiece.

Vitus nodded, shaking Dagobert's hand and then sitting in the indicated chair. "I. Erm. Yes?" It was certainly not his most suave. "You mentioned you'd prefer sooner than later."

"Oh, that's mostly in case Isembard is in a hurry." Laudine spoke more lightly about it than Vitus had expected, and it was the first time Vitus had heard the name. That must have shown on his face, because Laudine added, "It is a Fortier custom to tend toward Merovingian names. In this case, Isembard— well, one of them— was a vassal of Charlemagne, well-regarded in battle. It means either iron-bright or iron-axe."

Who was not Merovingian? That was part of the point of the Carolingians. Vitus wondered, entirely inside his head, how deliberate that choice was. Though presumably there might have been other people, back further in time, who were named Isembard. "I hope all goes well, and that he lives up to the hopes for his name." Vitus considered. "I'm familiar with Isambard Kingdom Brunel, the engineer. That seems a hopeful sort of precursor, too. Axes being slightly less in demand these days for many people."

Laudine favoured him with a smile, one he thought might be truly sincere. "We appreciate your good wishes." She shifted slightly, and it became clear that she, not Dagobert, was going to be the one doing most of the talking for the moment. "We would like to commission a talisman, a complex one, and a highly personal one." She lifted her fingers. "I have reasons for not asking my father."

It was and wasn't what Vitus had expected. "Pardon, Lady Fortier?"

"None of that, either. For one thing, I'm not at all used to the name yet." Laudine looked Vitus square in the eye. "Let me lay out the parameters, and then you can tell us what you think is possible. It will require innovative work."

Vitus nodded. They had, in fact, paid a generous consultation fee up front for this time, and he bore these particular Fortiers no ill will. They'd been thoughtful and helpful to Thessaly, which was also a mark in their favour. "Please, go ahead. May I take notes, or would you rather not?"

"I'd prefer not, for the moment. And I will ask for oaths on what is shared here. Though I'd prefer to make them once you decide if you will accept the commission, since that may affect the terms. We trust your discretion in a general sense, but there are nuances that are complicated."

Vitus nodded, folding his hands. "Please, go on."

Laudine let out a breath that was near enough a sigh. "My husband and others in his family were involved with a project of substantial magical scope and innovation. I am not able to speak of the details, neither is he. At a particular point in time, he came to realise that it was a poor decision." She glanced at her husband appraisingly.

"More precisely, a sequence of increasingly bad decisions." Dagobert spoke quietly, as if some doom were still lurking over his head. "I was cursed for my disagreement by two people, and the combination has been lasting."

"Specifically, my husband tires far more easily than he ought, and our Healer, excellent though he is, has been able to mediate it only so far. Being here, on the land, as Lord, has been some help, but not as much as we hoped. I have been able to assist, to some degree, but not while expecting, and likely not with a young child. Or at least not in an uncontrolled setting, the sort of ordinary daily interaction of vitality between people who are close."

Vitus realised they were not touching, that he had not seen them touch other than in formal ways in some time. That was another thing he absolutely could not inquire about, except, well, they had opened a door to it. "I presume that you have noticed the vitality as a concern in ordinary daily contact?"

Laudine pursed her lips. "Yes." She glanced at Dagobert, one of those unreadable silent conversations, then added, "We often used to share a bed, and that is… not a good idea. Not for the entire night. And yet, we rely on Dagobert's tending of the land, of the land magic. And his ability to join me for a meal, or spend time with Garin. Or Isembard, in the near future. And more than anything, I want to protect them from that drain."

"It is like water, flowing away, too fast to dam up sometimes." Dagobert's voice was even more of a whisper now, a roughness to it. "And I will not hurt my family. I would stay away from them if I had to, but that will hurt them. Does already." He said the last part rapidly, as if his wife had indicated something.

Vitus nodded slowly. "And the goal would be a talisman that would dam the flow, stabilise it. And also something that you, Laudine, could add to, in a controlled manner?" He was thinking already how it would need to be two pieces, matched. Even cuff links, if he could get the form needed small enough. One to stem the drain, the other to provide something to draw from.

Laudine nodded precisely. "Just so. Paired pieces, or something of the kind."

"I was thinking paired, yes, but where you would wear one of them for a time. Perhaps a week, a fortnight, a month, depending on how it works in practice. And then swap. Something suitable to wear on a watch chain or a brooch or something of the kind, hidden or obvious." Vitus was, he admitted, already deeply intrigued by the challenge inherent in the project.

"You think you can do the work? Not immediately, if that would help. We understand that you would need to research, design a proposal, and then look for a proper time to implement it."

"I would also need to ask some rather personal questions. A full astrological chart, naturally, but then additional questions to take your native inclinations into account. Strengthening the places there is already suitable potential is easier, and more natural, than creating it out of nothing."

"And the stones?" Dagobert leaned forward. "We understand this will have necessary expenses. Your time and magic, as well as the materia."

Vitus nodded. "I am thinking rubies and pearls - the former from elsewhere, obviously, but British pearls if I can find suitable sets, to anchor them nearer home. Likely other materials as well, and I expect extensive inscription work. I may need to lease a suitable ritual space for a week or two, depending on the specifics, to allow the work to be done over a period of days at a propitious time. I'll have to look at the charts in detail once I have more specifics, but it may be necessary to do a temporary piece or pair of pieces if the best days are not soon."

Laudine snorted; something in her had relaxed during Vitus's explanation. "That is all understandable. We will want the steps laid out, you understand. Not your crafting secrets, but what each part is designed to do."

"Certainly, my lady, you have more than enough understanding to follow." The honorific came out easily this time, and Vitus glanced at her, suddenly wondering if that form were more palatable. "I have two prying queries to begin with."

"Yes?" Laudine took a breath. "We had best know what they are."

"First, I will need a list of the other household talismans, architectural magics, and so on. Anything that needs routine upkeep or renewal, whatever those lists include, as well as personal jewellery items you wear regularly. Let's say once a lunar month or more."

Laudine's eyebrow arched at that, and Vitus added, "It is a tad cautious. But I've found that Philodorus Minor's investigations of the impact of talismans in the same geomantic location have been more reliable than either William the Elder or Honoria Bessette's."

"At some point when I can focus on it, we might argue about the Bessette, but no, I see your point." Laudine nodded. "I will look forward to that debate in due course. It is pleasant to have something to anticipate."

Vitus smiled suddenly, before he said, "The second point?"

She nodded. Dagobert leaned forward. "Go on."

"I would ideally need to know the date and time of the curses. I can guess near enough to within a few days, but a precise chart would be far better." Vitus said it as evenly as he could, because he could think of a dozen reasons why they would not tell him.

"Last summer solstice." Dagobert gave it quietly. "I would have to— Laudine, would you?"

"I'll have to check my notes on the time, but I can likely get it to within an hour, possibly closer. Is that sufficient? Not long after midnight, at the latest."

It wasn't as if people normally kept track of that sort of thing in the moment. "I might need to consider rectification against the ebbs and flows of the effects. More prying questions, I'm afraid." At least they were not horrified at the idea. Laudine had been trained well, and her father had obviously shared a lot about the general expectations for these kinds of pieces. Though that raised a question that Vitus very much wanted answered.

Laudine nodded. "I will have some notes for you promptly. Or as promptly as I can." She grimaced, and Vitus suspected that Isembard was perhaps being active or somehow uncomfortable. "You had further questions?"

"This one is prying, but also— um. Relevant?" Vitus swallowed. "May I ask why your father is not consulting? I would have thought that in terms of prying questions, he might be perhaps more comfortable. He is obviously fond of you, as his daughter."

"Ah." Laudine glanced at her husband again, then went on with barely a pause. "My husband's oaths on the matter explicitly excluded speaking with any of the family by blood or marriage who were not involved. You do not qualify." She waved a hand. "Neither does Thessaly, I should note. Betrothal and marriage being two different magical rites."

"I did not expect to speak to her about it. With your permission, that I was doing work for you, but that is all, in keeping with the Guild's standards of confidentiality. I maintain a private workroom for a number of reasons." Vitus attempted to sound proper.

Laudine shook her head. "That is fine. Just— we could not ask Papa. Even for recommendations, without revealing the scope of the problem. I know he has guesses. If he asks you directly, you may use your best judgement outside the specifics covered by the oath." With that, she took a couple of pieces. "Here is what I would like you to swear here and now. And here is what I would like you to agree to, in the contract, witnessed by representatives for each party. Your solicitor, a representative from your bank, whoever you prefer on your side. That gives no details, simply confirms the contract as made in agreement with the documentation." She waved a hand. "The top oath now, the other when you have presented a complete proposal."

The oath for the moment was what Vitus had expected. It had the terms of a confidential consultation, not to be shared with others without permission from all parties, with a release at death. It obliged him to take the usual precautions for such things with his papers and notes, and to store them in a locked vault once the work was completed. Nothing there was unusual, and Vitus made the oath promptly.

"There." Laudine grimaced this time, as if something in the magic had upset some balance in her own system. Dagobert, too, had begun to look rather faded. "If you do not mind, we should rest. Can you find your way out?"

Vitus stood, promptly. "Of course. I'll send a note round when I've got a proposal in hand." With that, he excused himself, and a footman walked him out to the portal in silence.

37

MAY 20TH IN THE EVENING, AT BRYN GLAS

Thessaly took one look at Vitus and said, "Come to the grove?"

He blinked, stopping where he stood. "Are you sure?"

"Mmm." She gestured. "Can you grab that blanket?" It wasn't yet six. They'd have a good two hours or so of light.

Vitus did not argue, which Thessaly considered a particular virtue of his. She went down the stairs ahead of him, pausing to let Emeline and Collins know they'd be outside for a bit. Supper around sunset would be grand. Neither of the older women asked her what she was up to, which was good, because Thessaly wouldn't have known how to explain.

She wasn't sure she could explain it to Vitus, honestly, and he had more right to know. But she could read the shifts in his magic, the way something had flickered into focus in him. And also, she was desperately curious about the appointment. He hadn't come straight back, she thought, but had taken time to make notes or whatever it was he did.

Once they were in the centre of the grove, Thessaly let out a long breath. She settled down on the blanket and made sure her skirts didn't take up the entire space. Vitus settled next to her, though turned, so that he could face her more easily, reaching for one of her hands. He laced his fingers through it, then he also let out a slow breath. "All right. Here is the right place, maybe."

Thessaly squeezed his fingers back. "You went somewhere else, between?"

"To talk to Niobe, and run through what information I'll need to ask them." Vitus swallowed, visibly. "Discretion with clients matters. Both the reality of it and the show of it. I can't tell you much. Though they said I could tell you I was working on a piece for them."

Thessaly nodded. "I understand that. It happens with illusion work, too. If I take up consulting, I'm sure there will be commissions I take on I can't talk to you about." She saw that hit him, that this was fair, that it was going to be fair going forward. That she certainly wasn't someone who'd pout and fuss about not knowing everything he did. She added, "I'm glad you went to Niobe, and I like that you tell me that sort of thing? But if you'd ever rather not, I understand that too."

"I should at least have written to you and let you know when I'd likely turn up. Rather than leaving you to guess," Vitus offered, grimacing.

"That would be a kindness. I spent the last hour reading the same three pages over and over. Or not reading, as it were. Not the worst hour I've spent in the recent past, not even in the top hundred. But I'd rather do other things." Thessaly patted his hand. "What can you tell me?"

"I'd like to talk out the larger implications, honestly." Vitus tugged her hand into his lap, cupping both of his around hers. "They asked me to make a talisman for them.

Or more than one, probably, for what they want." He lifted one finger from where it curled around her hand. "I asked why they weren't having Laudine's father do it. There's a matter of oaths."

"And that's the part you want to talk about." Thessaly tilted her head. "Related to whatever is going on at Arundel?"

"Mmhmm." Vitus looked down at their hands, speaking slowly now. "Dagobert's curse dates to the night your aunt was killed. Not from her, from others in the family. I don't think it's what they intended."

"And you won't speak of the details. That's fair. And the talismans are for some ongoing aspect?" Thessaly added, a little dryly, "People don't usually invest in your sort of talismans for something expected to resolve promptly. For one thing, there's the time needed to make the thing. You've explained enough of that."

It made Vitus chuckle. "No, that's logical enough. Yes, something ongoing." He considered. "I think they're concerned about the show of the thing, as well as the reality."

"That, now, I know something about." Vitus blinked up at her and Thessaly let her smile broaden. "Illusionist, remember? Our entire art, sometimes, is drawing the eye to one place to do something elsewhere. That's a lot of what Aunt Metaia did with the protective illusions. I really find it quite interesting." She flicked her fingers. "Not so interesting I particularly want to hire out to the Great Families. Not any time soon. But enough I might ask about learning more about it, and the places that ordinary people could use a bit of illusion."

Vitus blinked at her several times, and then leaned forward to kiss her, taking his time about it, one of his hands coming up to cup her neck. She had, in fact, brought them out here so that they would not get too distracted by the physical instead of talking. That, however, did not mean she didn't enjoy the kiss, want more of it, and looked forward to what they might do when back inside. When he pulled back, his hand went around hers again, warm and right there.

"You should do that. When you're ready." Then he flicked a finger. "Anyway. There will be oaths, but Laudine showed me the shape of them. Proper documentation with the Scali and all that. I just made the provisional ones to allow for the planning today. That's ordinary."

"Quite." Thessaly considered. "I suppose you can't answer anything about if it's about the mill. Or anything else."

"Actually." Vitus tilted his head. "That didn't come up directly. It might later. They're under oaths, Dagobert specifically, about what they can and can't say. And those included not talking to anyone related by blood or marriage. It's why Laudine can't consult her father, but she could with me, even if there are parts she can't discuss."

"And, ugh. I can't keep track of this without a chart. They must know you were doing work for Lord Clovis and Sigbert." Thessaly started there. Vitus nodded once. "And that you'd seen the inside of the mill." He nodded again and Thessaly went on. "And that you had talked some of it out?"

"Laudine made a point of noting you were not included in the group she could not talk to. Betrothal and marriage being rather different on that point," Vitus said. "And besides, the betrothal would have broken, anyway." He shrugged once. "But I don't see how that helps. I don't know the way to read the history of magic cast in a space. And honestly, I don't even know that the Penelopes would get much from it, if they tried." As he spoke, his eyes widened, like he'd realised something.

"Yes?"

"I explained a Faraday cage to you, I know." Vitus was leaning forward.

"And then you loaned me a fair bit of reading material, most of which I have looked at it. Some of the details lost me. I have a list of questions in the library." Thessaly's training was not remotely designed for complex diagrams of wiring. She was neither a talisman maker nor a ritualist by preference.

"The thing is that it removes a space from interaction with the electrical forces in the room. I could arrange to show you a small one. There's a common enough experiment." Vitus wriggled his fingers. "But I don't know what it does here."

"Does Dagobert, do you think?" Thessaly asked, chewing on the problem a little.

Vitus stared off over her shoulder, chewing on his lip. "I think he knows what their original goal was. I don't know how that changed. You said, pardon." Vitus looked at her, earnest now. "You said Childeric changed once the betrothal happened. Is it possible that whatever they were doing was part of that? I'd have worried that it was something in the research. Only Dagobert made it clear his own problems were a specific curse." Vitus twitched his fingers. "Or there's a question of whether there's a larger curse."

"I keep coming back to thinking about that. It's groping around in the dark, isn't it?" Thessaly shook her head, a bit of hair coming loose and down her cheek. "It's a hard idea to ignore, at this point."

"So many deaths out of season. Particular ones. On an estate that you'd think would be firmly set about with all sorts of protections." Vitus agreed with that. "But it's a cause and effect problem, perhaps? What was it like, early on? Before your betrothal?"

Thessaly grimaced. "Being around Childeric was tiring, a great deal. More after the betrothal than before, but before we were mostly out together in company. A supper, a concert, a gala. Later," Thessaly paused, obviously sorting through memories. "I couldn't tell, at the time, how much of that was him and how much was the situation. But I was going through my notes again earlier today. And I don't think I had the same feeling with Sigbert. Or even the days before the funeral. I didn't care for it. Those days, they were demanding in half a dozen ways. But I didn't feel faint, I didn't feel like my knees would give out, or just that I wanted to lie down and sleep." Just thinking back to those feelings, how she'd made space for feeling awful, gave her a stomachache or something akin to it.

"And you did, with Childeric?" Vitus said. "You hadn't said."

Thessaly's chin came up. "Women put up a with a great deal of discomfort on the average, and we're expected to do it without letting it show. I thought it was mostly that until he turned awful. And then he was awful. Of course, I felt horrible after that. It would have been remarkable if I didn't."

"I do hope you do not feel you must hide any of that with me." Vitus squeezed her hand. "I suspect not, given your clothing choices at home."

"Oh, there are uses for a corset and a bustle. And if they fit well, they don't limit most movement. How you bend, yes. Whether you can, no. Not really. Well, bending sideways is a bit of a trick. You can't hinge at the hip." She waved a hand. "Anyway. At the time, I thought it within the expected range. But what if it wasn't? What if something was—"

Before Thessaly could continue, Vitus smacked his forehead with his free hand, fast enough to make a loud and startling noise. "He's the right age, too. He was. I don't have my lists." Then he blinked at her, several times, rapidly. "I told you I was looking at the number of people who didn't complete apprenticeships. Niobe confirmed some of those lists for me, too. Sigbert was younger than the people listed. I'm older."

"And Father has kept going on about some of the men my age not being up to snuff." Thessaly let out a low whistle. "Do you think there's something to it?"

"I'm not sure there's any way for us to know. I can't imagine it's a topic Laudine and Dagobert want to talk about much. And we don't even know if Childeric realised anything, or if his parents had concerns, or any of that."

"He was the golden boy." Thessaly shook her head. "And it's not like we can ask any of the professors at Schola. They'd turn us away and be right to. It's not right to pry into someone else's records." Then she coughed. "Even if you very much want to." Then she swallowed. "But there's me. There's Cyrus. There's you. It can't be everyone in those years."

"Talking it through with Niobe, she didn't think so. No one's looked at all the information together. Well, maybe Schola has, but if so, they're not talking. And it's certainly not the sort of thing families would reveal even if they knew. But think about it. Can you imagine Childeric admitting it? Any of the Fortiers? Other families might have known, but had different responses. Support for their children, for one thing. Training to use what they could do better."

"Not really." She leaned back, her head on Vitus's

shoulder. "Cyrus's magic is hearty, we know that. And recently tested. Mine is, bar some bobbles for being out of practice. And that's so much better now." Thessaly shook her head. "I— look, that part, I don't think we can sort out ourselves. And while I think it probably is a Council matter, I don't even know where to start with it."

Vitus nodded slowly. "Look. How about we ask Thirza and Merryn to come talk? Here, if you'd rather, where you can be sure it's private. They both know a wide range of people, and they'd likely have an idea who to bring it to, or how."

"And," Thessaly's voice went soft, "you like them. I like Thirza, what I know of her, though we've never talked privately." She halted, uncertain. "Would it be uncomfortable for her to come here? Where she visited Aunt Metaia?"

Vitus hesitated, then stroked her hand with his thumb, reassuringly. "How about I ask? If she'd prefer somewhere else, we could talk at home. Or my office, with a bit of illusion to get you there without people noticing."

"All right. Let's do that. This is, this is too big, too many, too much to figure it out all by ourselves." Thessaly nodded once. "Shall we go back inside, and you can write to them and then we can find something distracting to do?"

"Oh, I was thinking something involving a great deal of intimate focus?" Vitus offered, but then he was standing up, offering Thessaly a hand. "That sounds grand. Just what I want in my evening. Though I'd best not stay over, I have work to do first thing in the morning."

"Some night soon, then." It meant Thessaly would have something delightful to look forward to. Vitus gathered up the blanket and brought it back, as they talked through their respective commitments for the week.

38

MAY 22ND AT BRYN GLAS

"You could say no, even now." Vitus glanced over at Thessaly, from where they were waiting by the fence. Emeline was further back, about ten feet, with a good view of people arriving from the portal. Thessaly had chosen green today, not her aunt's favourite teal or peacock green, but a deeper emerald. Exactly the right shade to go with the stone Vitus had been working on, which meant he could not stop watching her and thinking about that.

Thessaly shook her head. "There are all sorts of reasons to have this conversation. And Aunt Metaia trusted Thirza, I know that." She hesitated, reaching for a word. "This is too big for us to figure out by ourselves."

"That does not necessarily mean you must trust my friends." Vitus pointed out, as gently as he could manage. The fact she did, the way she had offered the invitation once she'd slept on it, had startled him.

The thing he was learning about Thessaly is that she picked her moment. Once she had a decision, she acted on it. Not precipitously or foolishly, but as a duellist, seeking the right response in the moment. For someone like Vitus, who could second-guess himself for hours or days or weeks, it was startling. Good for him, most likely, certainly an excellent complement to his tendencies. But startling. Before he could say anything more, the portal opened, and two figures came around to the fence.

Thessaly inclined her head. "Magistra Remerton, Magistra Penforth. Be welcome to Bryn Glas." It was a nice nod to the formalities, including acknowledging that Merryn had earned her proper full mastery two months ago.

"Oh, please. Thirza and Merryn, please." Thirza waved off the formality. "Thank you for being willing to host us."

Thessaly ducked her chin. "You're my first guests here other than Vitus, actually." She laid her hand on the fence, shifting the warding, and then opened it. "Please, do come in. We've tea waiting in the library."

"Thirza was telling me a little about the house and the care your aunt took with it." Merryn came through the gate first, Thirza a little more slowly. Vitus gestured toward the house, leaving Thessaly to walk with Thirza. They began talking quietly, and Merryn was obviously giving them space for that. When they paused by the door to the house, for Thessaly to open the warding again, Merryn stepped to one side.

Once they were all in the library, though, Merryn turned around, delighted. "Oh, this is truly lovely. A place that's alive. Thirza had mentioned the colours, but a grand effect."

Thessaly ducked her chin. "I'm thinking of some adjustments upstairs, keeping the style but changing some of the colours. I'm not quite so fond of peacock green as Aunt Metaia was. I'd like a little more range. But I have no plans to change the library. Except perhaps finding some more places for shelves." They were rather overflowing, with no space to add more books. "Please, do sit." Merryn's comments had done the trick, though, easing things into a more conversational mode. Thessaly and Vitus claimed the sofa, with easy chairs for their guests on either end, which made it easy for Vitus to pour tea and make sure everything was handy. In more ordinary custom, Thessaly would have done this, but Vitus had offered. It made a point about his comfort in the home, and it left Thessaly's hands free.

Once everyone had tea, Thirza tilted her head, taking the lead. "I'm sure Vitus has mentioned, but Thursdays is when we often chat at the Four Metals. I hope he's also mentioned that you'd be welcome to join us as a guest at some point."

"He did." Thessaly's voice was clear and steady, but Vitus felt her take his hand an instant later, and he squeezed back. "I admit I'm finding the idea of talking with more people a trifle..." She shrugged. "Duelling is one thing. We all know how the interactions go there, and people are private about who they're duelling with as a rule."

"Ah. And we are rather a crowd of chaotic commentary at times." Merryn nodded. "We'd be glad to see about finding some like-minded people for quieter settings. A private dining room. Or Thirza has a little room for entertaining." Merryn added, sounding amused, "I have rooms in Trellech, but the sitting room is usually covered in books. And Vitus has room for what, four comfortably?"

Vitus nodded. "Which I would be glad to do, but it limits the invitations. Only four chairs in the place besides my workbench."

"And we can't possibly move that," Thessaly agreed. She'd heard his comments on the precise way it was aligned and adjusted before. Then she took a deep breath. "Thank you for the offer. Let me consider what I'm comfortable with?" She went right on, her voice careful and precise. "Thirza, I know Aunt Metaia thought extremely well of you. And Merryn, your name turns up in some of her notes."

"She was one of us, as I'm sure Vitus has mentioned by now." Vitus caught the note of something so complicated in Thirza's voice, and he suddenly wondered exactly how close Thirza had been to Metaia. "We do have some experience with complicated magical exploration and the risks. You needn't tell us any details you're not sure about, and honestly, we'd rather not know. But we can talk about the process of what needs to be handled by someone, and who that someone might best be."

Merryn picked up, as if they'd practised this, and they probably had. "We gather you have some information that you think an appropriate authority needs to know. But that also has risks. One aspect of that is to place you both under oath, so that you cannot convey how to reconstruct whatever the problem is, either by direct action or by implication. It's a trifle tricky, the wording, but I brought copies of several variations. The Scali can certainly advise on a ritual specialist suitable to the problem."

Thessaly nodded. "That's one concern. I can't help thinking of angles of attack. I don't think there's a particular danger from the people who know more than we do. But if someone found out about it and wanted to create such a thing again, anyone with more information might be at risk."

"The oath will handle a fair bit of that, yes. And the forms I have include a modification that would, more than likely, send you unconscious if forced to press up against the oath, rather than other harm. Not that it's not a risk;

it's rather a feature of certain kinds of penny-dreadful tales." Merryn tutted at that. "It is not an unknown problem, at least."

Thessaly nodded slowly. "I am, I admit I am out of my depth here. In duelling, of course, there are all sorts of standards and agreements. And equally, those go out the window if there is an actual fight or a need to defend oneself. And in my own line of magic, the methods for illusion work do go through the Guild."

"Because the Guard and such have some need to be able to tell where they are placed, and how, for safety reasons," Thirza said. "Metaia talked me through those at one point. I never got as good as she was at spotting one had been cast. And that's part of your oaths as an apprentice, yes? To keep to those agreements."

Thessaly nodded. "Made at our apprenticeship, renewed when we become journeymen or women, and yearly afterwards, to make sure we're aware of any adjustments. There's a summary each of us has to read and swear to."

"Decidedly more formalised than our usual line of things," Merryn said. "All right. The thing about experimentation is that you get a range of results. Some of them are, we hope, the ones you were looking for. But others will be all over the place. Sometimes it's something you never want to repeat. Sometimes it wasn't what you were intending at all, but it opens up an entire other line of investigation. That sequence we were talking about last month, Vitus, I ended up applying a sliver of it to a different kind of warding problem. Someone wanted to keep their young children from the poisonous plants in the garden. There are a host of standard solutions for that, but we're fairly sure we've found another, and perhaps more stable."

Vitus beamed. "Oh, grand. That's a useful one. Making a circuit of it, then, so it's self-sustaining?" Merryn nodded, and Vitus waved a hand. "We can get into that later." He chose his next words carefully. "Part of the challenge here is that we aren't entirely certain what was intended. And I don't know that we'll ever know. But we are wondering if part of it was to cover for, what's the word..."

"Fragilities," Thessaly said, decisively. "Or maybe it's better put as a gap between Childeric's actual magic and competence and where he and his family thought those things ought to be."

"And there's no way to find out more now?" Thirza leaned forward.

Thessaly spread her hands, slowly. "Laudine and Dagobert are bound by oaths. And he was excluded from matters after last summer. So yes, I expect he knows more than he's told us, and I can gesture faintly at the shape of it. And it also doesn't entirely matter. What does matter is whether it continues and what to do about it."

"And it definitely had to do with the demesne estate?" Thirza said. Thessaly nodded once, silently. "I think your best course is to take it to Hereswith. And whoever else she chooses to talk about it with." Thessaly's chin came up, and Thirza asked, "You think not?"

"Aunt Metaia didn't bring it to her." This was true, and also it was a somewhat fragile point to argue from.

"Metaia didn't have all the information you have, yes?" Thessaly had to shake her head at that. "And Metaia had her own approaches to investigation. Do you have a reason to distrust Hereswith? Or your cousin, for that matter?"

Thessaly shook her head. "No. They've both been very clear about their support and action. But I also know they've been terribly busy. Out of season busy."

"The two things might, in fact, be related. I'm sure I couldn't figure it out, but bringing it to them is all the more relevant." Thirza leaned forward. "You have many skills, Thessaly. And you'll have more, given time. But Hereswith has a different set, and more to the point, she can draw on the entire range of expertise of the Council, their various allies and experts, and she can speak directly to the Guard and Penelopes in confidence. Or whoever else she felt needed to know."

"And I cannot." Thessaly let out a puff of breath. "I'll have to think about how to bring it to them. But I suppose you're right. I just..." She glanced around the room, ending up looking at the fireplace. "I'm afraid they're going to bury it, never talk about it again, that families will keep doing this, and people will get hurt again and again."

"We are human and made of flaws. The Great Families especially, I expect. Though I don't have as much direct experience as you have." Thirza's tone turned a little confiding and also sharper than Vitus had heard her before. "The Council might bury it. But they might well bury it after ensuring it cannot continue. And I am not sure you'll get that far from anyone else."

Thessaly shivered, and Vitus promptly moved to put his arm around her, deliberately. "I suppose. It will take me a few days to come round to the necessity. And there is not as much urgency as there might be. There's about to be a new baby in the household, and I'm certain that will keep them too busy for any further plotting. Even if they were inclined. And I, I think I trust Laudine and Dagobert, in what they've said. And what they haven't said."

"Then take a couple of days if you need to." Thirza glanced around, then took a deep breath. "May I ask if you think there's anything about a curse?"

That brought up something Vitus and Thessaly had

been discussing that morning. He cleared his throat. "Laudine sent around the notes on the estate's standing enchantments and protections. Most of them are within the range I'd expect, of course. There were additional protections, using techniques not common in Albion that are noted but not detailed, done by Henut Landry."

"And those, presumably, ceased at her death. So are the deaths among the Fortiers just due to those protections failing?"

"It would suggest a great deal of enmity directed at them that was not dealt with by the other warding. And the deaths, other than Childeric's, were all on the estate proper. I would have expected elsewhere, if it were something done by someone outside the family, against the family."

"Thessaly, you're trained to be sensitive to this sort of thing. It's common for duellists, I know." Thirza spoke carefully. "What did you feel from the estate? A sense of some lurking danger, or something wrong on the estate? Did that feeling change at any particular point?"

"I have been going back through my notes. I was trained to keep them, you understand. Any social event I attended, even nominally informal ones. Who was there, what I wore, which topics were a focus. And then there are other notations, for the weather, how I felt overall." Thessaly turned her palms up. "My notes say I was often tired after spending time with Childeric, and not so much after his death, even when I was on the estate for some time. I had more nightmares there, but not more than I would expect, under the circumstances. And in my stretching and other magical exercises, whenever I snuck them in during the day, I did not see changes which didn't have some obvious cause."

Thirza snorted. "I am impressed by your level of

detail. May we, perhaps, prevail on you to join us to take notes for our experimentation, at some point? I think you might well have useful suggestions, but your record keeping would be invaluable. I suppose you do something similar for duels?"

"I do." Thessaly shrugged. "It's not something people talk about much. But others notice if you wear the same dress with the same group, or talk too much about one or two topics. And now, looking at the patterns." She shook her head. "But I wouldn't have felt something that was targeted at them, as specific individuals. Vitus was explaining to me about open and closed approaches to talismans. This would have been a closed one, maybe?"

"If so, it raises the question about whether Dagobert has been spared - and Laudine - or not, doesn't it?" Thirza grimaced. "I'll have to think about that one. I'll let you know if I have any ideas of what to look at more closely. But I'd recommend sharing whatever you can about the observed patterns with Hereswith." She considers. "It's the problem of the scientist, really. You can observe something in the world, but you do not yet know how to study it. How do you deal with that in a duel, a new opponent?"

Thessaly leaned against Vitus a little more. "In the duelling salle? Try a few things, and see what the responses are. Reading the reactions as best you can, both the feel of the magic and what someone does. Though of course, there are a number of standard approaches, those are somewhat neutral. Not as telling. Then, once you have more information, you can form a strategy better. Quickly, of course."

"Ah. Here, you can observe, and then plan your initial actions in advance, it sounds like. Your hypotheses to explore. Moving on promptly if one doesn't seem to bear fruit, of course. Think about that, as you think of the next step." Thirza spread her hands. "Now, though, may I look at the shelves, and perhaps show Merryn a few things? Or if you'd rather I not handle anything..." She let her voice trail off.

"Oh, no, please. I've moved some things upstairs, the ones I'm working through in more detail." Also, Vitus knew, the more intimate private sorts of books, because those were currently on a shelf in the bedroom for mutual exploration in comfort. Thirza stood, pointing out a series of the details in the decoration to Merryn. They were talking not only about the design, but about the illusion and charmwork and magic that had gone into specific aspects. The green of the vines, for example, and the way the colours subtly shifted, or how to get that particularly vibrant sheen to the blue geometric decorations.

The shift to talking about the library brought a smooth enough transition. Once Merryn had been shown a good number of things, they could settle down into a more ordinary sort of conversation for Vitus on a Thursday. That involved batting around some different ideas. Thessaly didn't have all the background, of course. But she made several thoughtful suggestions about particular choices. Twice she asked particularly relevant questions that gave Vitus half a dozen new ideas to explore. He considered it an evening well spent. They walked the two older women out to the portal later, and Thirza took a moment to speak to Thessaly privately. When she came back, Vitus slipped his arm around her waist. "All right?"

"She was very clear that Aunt Metaia would be very proud of me. Had always been. But that whatever I was doing, it was going in the right direction. Care and something generative. Broadening. Not narrowing."

"There you are, then. And you enjoyed talking to both of them, yes?"

Thessaly stopped, bemused, turning to peer at him. "Are you worried I didn't like your friends?"

"Erm. Yes?" Vitus felt himself blushing. "If it's a bother, I'll make sure you don't feel obliged."

"I enjoyed the conversation. I want to learn more if we do that again. I felt like a dunce several times. And I'm not sure how to, how to have that kind of friendship? Not really. Though I'm getting there, a little, with Cyrus and Andie."

"But friendships with others in Fox House always has a calculation in it?" Vitus offered.

"Yes." Thessaly nodded. "And I'm not sure what I'm missing here. Or if I'm not actually, I just think there should be six more layers."

"Ah." Vitus chuckled. "We are more properly igneous rock, I suspect, and Fox is sedimentary, at root, layers put down. Or perhaps metamorphic, the layers warped by a vast surge of incredible power. And pressure."

"Oh, definitely that one," Thessaly agreed. "All right. Come inside and tell me about metamorphic rock, so I understand the implications better."

39

MAY 27TH AT DINAS EMRYS

"We appreciate the time." Thessaly had just settled in the chair when Vitus spoke. Cousin Owain was hosting. This was the sort of matter that required privacy, but going to the Council Keep might be noticed. They were up in Cousin Owain's sitting room, the same one they'd used previously. Though this time, Emeline was downstairs having a couple of tea, rather than guarding outside the door. "I gathered from Thessaly that you've been exceedingly busy."

"Yes, far more than usual for the season." Magistra Hereswith inclined her head, spreading her skirts out a little with one hand as she sat down. "But you implied you had important information."

"A week ago, Laudine and Dagobert consulted Vitus on the creation of a talisman. The details, of course, are confidential, the usual sort of oaths, but he was permitted to tell me that much. And we've been discussing it since."

Magistra Hereswith nodded. "And you have something specific?"

"Yes, and no." Thessaly pulled her notes closer, though

they were cryptic to the extreme. "First, I heard this morning, they sent a note round first thing, that Laudine and their newborn son are well and recovering. So, whatever else, we may reasonably assume the family will have other occupation for the moment. Distraction."

"The remaining family." Cousin Owain said it quietly, but it was what they were all thinking. "What do you think of her, Thessaly? Of both of them, actually."

Thessaly inhaled. "Laudine was more honest with me, and more helpful, than the rest of the family put together, I think. Though it's tremendously difficult to weigh that, given the number of secrets that weren't shared. Sigbert was trying better, before." Her voice broke off. "They asked Vitus for help, and I think that shows some degree of good sense."

"You are biassed." Vitus sounded almost amused. He'd been nervous about this meeting. He was far less used to talking in this manner. Thessaly wasn't a great deal more experienced, exactly, but she had learned from Aunt Metaia that Council Members were also people. Some of whom she liked, and some of whom she did not.

Now she smiled at him. "I am, but it is a measured bias. May I ask, Cousin Owain, about the quality of the problems you've been keeping busy with? Something with the Fatae, with the land, something else? The broad category? You'd said that the Fatae were ill at ease in your ordinary negotiations." She was trying to feel her way through what to say next.

The two Council members exchanged glances. "The Fatae are unsettled, in ways they have not been able to describe. It is nothing that is yet an abrogation of the Pact, but it feels like it might come to that. Or it has. It does not seem to be entirely localised, which is part of the confusion. We have had a range of odd events. Bright blue roses popping up." Blue in that hue was an impossibility with ordinary flowers. Even those of Albion, without help from illusions or charms. "A swath of a beach turned to shimmering mother-of-pearl, and then it washed away. Rumours of black beasts on the moors— oh, those are common enough, but these sounded like ancient elk. Possibly also sightings of bears and a pack of wolves, maybe a lynx."

"It's more usually large cats or hounds, isn't it?" Vitus asked.

"Oh, yes, and we have checked the usual reason for that, and come up with nothing." They didn't explain it, of course, and Thessaly filed that into Council business not discussed with outsiders. Cousin Owain glanced at Magistra Hereswith and added, "The timing does not seem to fit any ordinary ritual cycle, not in aggregate. A few points do match up with specific events, including the last two solstices. Others do not, especially more recently."

Thessaly nodded. "And has the frequency increased or changed, or whatever the useful measure is there, I'm not sure what?"

They exchanged another of those glances. Magistra Hereswith said, slowly. "Increasing frequency until recently, the last month or so. But we're not sure if there are what you might call ripple effects."

"A change sent out into the world continues to create change," Vitus said, speaking up. "The amplitude may change over time, the strength. Sometimes things get stronger."

"Just so, " Magistra Hereswith said. "You're asking questions with a particular purpose."

Vitus cleared his throat, and Thessaly let him speak. "I have suspicions about something. I cannot discuss them, as things stand. I may be able to investigate and get additional information. This past week, some other relevant discussions suggested a way to look at some of the notes that Thessaly's Aunt Metaia left."

"What sort of suspicion, in a broad sense?" Cousin Owain leaned forward.

"Thessaly and I have observed, though not observed in use, a device that is intended to manipulate magical fields and possibly others. Electrical, magnetic, but in ways that aren't the usual sort there. The space in question was visibly designed for ritual use to some degree. It may be entirely within bounds, it may not be. And I strongly suspect that anyone who knows what it actually does can't speak of it."

Thessaly and Vitus had sorted that wording out. He had argued, given the oaths they'd had him take, that Dagobert was sworn not to speak of whatever the devices were. Lady Chrodechildis couldn't even if she wanted to, that much communication, that nuanced, seemed beyond her. And there was no one else left, more than likely, who knew. Alexander might have, but he'd been at school until the middle of June. It wasn't as if they could ask him directly for some time, whatever he knew.

Logic had winnowed down the options. Logic and a series of deaths that, stacked together, seemed tremendously telling.

"That makes it difficult to investigate." Magistra Hereswith's voice was dry. "I presume it's well warded, whatever you suspect?" Vitus nodded, though Thessaly had wondered about the warding. It had been Lord Clovis and Sigbert who had given Vitus permission. They were dead. It would depend how the warding was designed, how lasting it was. On the other hand, while it wasn't on the Arundel estate proper, it was within steps of the boundary, and that counted for quite a lot if Dagobert exerted himself.

"Yes. And there's still no conclusive evidence that could be brought to the Penelopes or the Guard. Nothing like that."

"Or the Council." Cousin Owain was even more dry, if such a thing was possible.

"We are speaking with the Council," Thessaly said. "Quod erat demonstrandum. It is possible we, mostly Vitus, might be able to arrange additional information or access or investigation. We honestly don't know. But if there are techniques we could use, in that investigation, asking seemed relevant. Samples to take, identification charms."

"We can teach you a few things. Thessaly, you might have an easier time with them, if you can gain access as well. Several of them need a delicate touch with the enchantment."

Thessaly nodded once. She waited for the two Council members to whisper to each other, and for Cousin Owain to make a few notes. When he looked up again, she said, "I still haven't sorted out Aunt Metaia's notes, not the coded ones. But I think it's possible she was searching for the same thing. I haven't found anything that disproved it."

"And yet no proof?" Magistra Hereswith sighed.

"It's the sort of thing where when— if , when— I figure it out, I'm going to be cursing myself for how long it took, I'm sure. It has that feel of it, like one of her puzzles." She added to Vitus, "She'd set me scavenger hunts with riddles, and this feels just like that. Why she was doing it in her own personal notes, I don't know, except that maybe it amused her."

"Or maybe she was afraid of someone getting access to her notes. Someone besides you." Magistra Hereswith considered. "You've tried looking it as proper cryptography, I suppose?"

"Nothing that simple, that patterned? And I considered some plausible dates. Nothing made sense there. Or, no. There was one encoded bit that basically said 'wrong idea, try again'. Which was, well, I laughed hysterically for a good half hour. It was late at night. And then I tried something else the next day."

Vitus had not been around for that, and he raised an eyebrow at her. She shrugged. "I tried a lot of things over a couple of weeks?" She then contemplated. "I haven't actually gone through pigment reactions, or the lore attached to some of them, to chain ideas together. I'll try that. It's not the language of flowers, I tried that. Or any of the Powell traditions. Those were the second thing I checked."

"What was the first?" Magistra Hereswith asked it almost idly.

"Oh, when I was tiny, she gave me an alphabet. Sewn, one of those banners with pockets? And she made stories out of the animals, but it wasn't, it wasn't a Powell tradition. It was something she'd come up with when she was tiny, herself." Thessaly shrugged once. "I don't know. I keep wondering if there's something there, but it hasn't yielded." She let out a breath. "I'll try again. And Vitus and I will see if we can find out anything else. Just, it seemed a time to tell you."

Magistra Hereswith nodded. "We can't ask you to take the risk. But as you said last time, we can't stop you. If you do find something concrete, we would very much like to know as soon as possible. The effects we've been dealing with are worrying in a number of dimensions." She rubbed her nose, looking rather tired. "I am pleased to say that introducing Cyrus to his duties has been easier than it might be. He is a quick learner, I've found."

"It seems like it's been doing him some good? I've enjoyed picking up with duelling." Thessaly did smile at that. "He's not the best in the salle, and he knows it, and he doesn't mind. He wants to get better, though, and often in the ways that make a more sensible duel, not always the ones about winning."

Magistra Hereswith tilted her head at that. "FitzAlan said something similar. I asked him to see about arranging a paired bout at some point, or rather, a sequence of them. I'm curious what Cyrus does when working with a partner." She contemplated. "I've told him this. It's not a secret from him. I'm training him up on the diplomatic angle and to take that on when his daughter is a little older. Not frequently, for a while. But it's often helpful to have someone who is presentable in public, easy to get along with. And especially someone who understands how to lose in the moment to win in the end."

That put an interesting picture on it. She nodded. "I like him. I've enjoyed spending more time with him, and with Andie. The rest of society, pah." She grimaced. "That's been mostly awful, and even more so since Sigbert's death. Not that I was getting a great many invitations to start, but even fewer now, and not from anyone I actually want to spend time with. Other than the direct personal ones. The duelling, present company, and so on."

Cousin Owain cleared his throat. "We are always glad to see you. Though admittedly not exciting company. And we have been rather busy."

Thessaly stood, coming to kiss his cheek. "You are very pleasant company, Cousin, and we should arrange supper or something sometime. But now, I suspect we should let you and Magistra Hereswith do whatever plotting you need to do. Can you show us those charms here, or downstairs in your ritual room? And Vitus, a walk before you need to go home?"

Vitus took the hint. Of course, they'd discussed that in advance. Part of this was making sure they made their exit before anyone thought of more questions, ones that might be more difficult to dance around. What mattered is that she and Vitus had permission to continue considering the problem, and with any luck, Vitus could get more information.

The charms were in fact fairly quick to learn, though Thessaly did pick them up faster. They were rather like one of the more archaic sequences she'd learned for detecting illusions, and for good reason, they almost certainly sprung from the same source. She'd have to chase that through Aunt Metaia's library when she got a chance. That was for later. Right now, she wanted a little time with Vitus, before diving back into mysteries.

40

JUNE 7TH AT ARUNDEL

"What can I do?" Vitus looked up from where he was squatting, peering at the floor. It had taken a week to prepare, but they were out in the mill, entirely legitimately this time. Or at least, as legitimately as possible given that Dagobert was dancing around the edges of oaths made previously. He had not been able to explicitly grant them permission to come to the mill, but he'd been able to say they had permission to go anywhere on the estate or the Fortier properties.

And no one had removed Vitus from the warding. If the Lady Chrodechildis were bothered by someone crossing the wards, well, that couldn't be entirely helped.

Thessaly and Vitus had arrived with baskets full of equipment. Vitus hadn't exactly been able to ask his fellows in the Four Metals for advice, but Thirza had turned up a day after their conversation with Hereswith Rowan and Owain Powell with half a dozen uncommon volumes, a set of working notes for investigating odd magical contraptions, and two dozen bits of relevant materia, all of which she put at his disposal for the duration. With instructions not to skimp on using the consumable parts. If she got nothing back but the books, that was fine.

He'd stared at her, but he hadn't argued. He and Thessaly had stayed up late the next nights, working through what they could and should do. They knew the basic layout of the building. They had an idea of the structures, Vitus had been reading up on Faraday cages. Neither of them needed to understand exactly how all of it worked. But they did need to understand what it was intended to do, and how it might be permanently disabled. Vitus was increasingly sure it was disrupting something fundamental in the magic around Arundel and maybe far further afield.

Vitus took a breath. "Do you feel confident checking for resonances yourself? Via Appian's methods, like we talked about? I think that suits better than Glock Minor."

Thessaly nodded. "The corners, then, and by each side of the door and windows. I'll be staring at this mess of wire and coils and switches."

The problem— well, one problem among many— was that they didn't dare turn the thing on. Some of the connections were visible. He could at least make sense of the patterns there. But others weren't. And if it used magical vitality as a key aspect, parts of it wouldn't interact without that. But Vitus had pencils, plenty of paper. He could scribble as many notes as he needed.

He set to work making a sketch. Now was when he blessed Niobe's initial training. She had argued, vehemently, that an essential skill of a talisman maker was as a draughtsman, able to make technical drawings with precision. She'd taught him, of course, with the aim of working at a tremendously small scale, for gems to fit on brooches and pendants and rings. But the techniques applied here. Vitus sat on the floor, carefully away from anything he might accidentally touch, and sketched, using his hand to measure proportion.

Thessaly began on the left side of the door, working her way clockwise. Vitus heard her quiet murmur of the resonance testing, a mix of incantations and low pitches. She paused here and there to make her own notes, to repeat a step to confirm something. She was as cautious and diligent as Vitus could hope for, and that part of this abysmal situation felt good. He could trust her as a partner. Thessaly had protected him by duelling when that was called for. When the work needed her steady hand and her clear voice, here they were. It didn't jar him from his work, and he didn't think he was disrupting her.

By the time she'd made it to the third window, Vitus had sketched everything he could without standing up. Now it was time to stare at the wall with the switches and see how the things leading into the box connected. Once he sketched, he considered the box itself. Logic suggested some way to open it. If they'd planned to use the device for long, they ought to have planned for needed replacements or evaluations. Any stone, any gem, any piece of materia could fracture or be damaged.

"When you're done, I could use a hand." Vitus kept his voice moderate.

"Five minutes. Maybe ten." Thessaly's response was clear. Vitus took that as a good reason to go take a break, and he went outside, to where they'd left the smaller basket with food and drink. They had a couple of flasks of lemonade, sandwiches, and a few smaller items, enough to sustain them if this took all day.

It was nearer fifteen minutes, but Thessaly came out to join him, setting her notes down. "I have measurements, but I can't see anything out of the ordinary immediately. And the space is odd, magically. It feels like it's been disrupted. Metamorphic rock. But I don't feel any sense of threat. Or even, really, much sense of magical pressure. I'd have expected more of that, like a ritual workroom, and there isn't."

"If we're theorising right, no one's activated this since, well. April. At the latest." Sigbert's death. "Six weeks now. I want to look behind the panel, but I think we need four hands to release it and lower it without jarring anything. Which part would you rather do, unfastening it or lifting?"

Thessaly didn't answer immediately, thinking about it. He passed her the lemonade, then half a sandwich. After she'd had a bit of both, she swallowed. "Unfastening, I think. You've height on me, and shoulder width, I think you should be able to hold it steady. If it lifts off cleanly, I can duck under your arm and give you space to move it."

It made perfect sense. She'd dressed to move easily, too. Not her duelling gear, that would have been a bit obvious, but a walking skirt, cut to fall close to the body, with barely any bustle or padding. Vitus nodded once, and they went on in silence for another few minutes. She cleared her throat eventually. "Did you find anything you want to talk about yet?"

"Want is not the word. A lot more questions than answers, but I have plenty of notes." He then stretched, feeling it in his shoulders. "Shall we? Or are we sitting here and putting it off some more?"

That made her laugh, amused. "Let's go ahead. Make the most of the strong light, for whatever you find." Vitus nodded, twisting to close up the food basket. Then he pushed himself standing, before turning to offer her a hand up.

Once they were back inside, Vitus peered at the edges of the panel, holding up his light talisman to see better. "I think there are latches here and here." He pointed. "Do you see those?"

Thessaly ducked under his arm, leaning in, then nodded, moving her fingers as if to undo the latches without touching them. "Both at the same time?" she asked.

"I don't think that's essential, but together as much you can seems a good idea." It took a couple of tries, before they rearranged themselves better. Vitus stood behind Thessaly, his arms reaching over her shoulders, hands gripping the case. Her hands rested on the wood, just in front of where the latches were. He counted, and on three, she moved to flip the latches. He heard the shift just before he felt the weight of the cover, and he stepped back, holding it as steady as he could. Thessaly ducked under his arm, nimble as anything, to be at the side. Vitus pivoted, setting the cover down, leaning against the wall where no one would knock into it, and then looked at what it had revealed.

There were half a dozen switches, but as he'd thought, each had a small metal container of materia. Gemstones, mostly, though he wouldn't lay bets that it was only gemstones. They'd likely been prepared in some way, or had other materia added. He could see, in fact, little bits of ash, as if some parts had burned up at some point. It didn't appear to be some deliberate component, at least.

What he hadn't expected was a ring, tucked into the corner of the box, a flash of copper and turquoise. Thessaly saw it a moment after he did, and she breathed out, "Philip's?"

"I think so." Vitus took a breath, not wanting to touch it. "We'll— it shouldn't stay here. It should go back to Alexander, surely. I've a case in my bag we can put it in." And the silk to avoid touching it, too.

"That." Thessaly sounded far more decisive than Vitus felt. "The rest of it?"

Now, looking again, he could see the precise connections between the various wires and tubes and other pieces. Thessaly silently handed him his sketchbook and pencil. Vitus set to work drawing a complete schematic, following it up with notes about each of the switches and what they held. Vitus had been at it long enough for his fingers to cramp and his shoulder to ache when he had to stop. "Don't touch it, but can you have a look and see if you can identify anything? I don't want to risk charms near it, focused on it."

"Is there another part, somewhere?" Thessaly said, finally. "I feel like some of these imply a pairing with something else, don't you? A mirroring?" Fundamentally, there were three unusual spaces in the room. The panel, the Faraday cage, and the ritual floor in the other half of the room. Both of them looked first at the one, then at the other. Thessaly cleared her throat. "You look at the cage more, you know what they're supposed to look like. I'll check the floor. Fortescue's First and Second. I won't try anything beyond that." Those were basic identification charms, the sort that didn't disrupt anything around them. Vitus nodded, and they both set to work.

Vitus finished first, largely because as far as he could tell, the Faraday cage was, in fact, a cage of metal and wire. Whatever magical elements were inside it must have been brought in, as pendants or talismans or something of the kind, or other objects. The only magical aspects were in the setting of the floor. He went back to their bags, bringing back a case and silk handkerchief and carefully easing the ring into the case for safe storage.

Thessaly took a lot longer, sitting on the ground and moving around to peer at the corners, the sides, and to test everything repeatedly. When she finally stood again, she shook her head. "I don't understand it, but I have a lot of notes. Is there anything else we can reasonably look at?"

He moved to sit on the ground, in an open space. What he had in front of him were two sets of circuits, mirroring each other. One, he was almost certain, was the slate-floored space out in the open. Though it would take destroying the floor to check on the stones at each compass point, anchoring the magic. The second set, the Faraday cage, was more puzzling. Partly because Vitus didn't think the thing worked. Not as designed.

He tapped the sketch, finally, well after Thessaly had sat down next to him. Without looking at her, he said, "This makes no sense, not as it is currently set up. And I'm assuming they don't have talismanic pieces in there, just cut stones and other materia."

"Why do you say that?" Thessaly said, leaning over to peer at his sketchbook. "Though you're right, I didn't see any signs of inscriptions. And there's no hint of illusion work on the workings that I can spot without more invasive testing."

"Well, for one thing, if they had another talismanic expert on tap, we'd likely know. No one with that kind of expertise has died in the last year. I'm almost certain they didn't ask Florent, given how he reacted to some of our work. They didn't ask Laudine, the way she's worded things. Dagobert might have got some general information from her, but that wouldn't create proper talismans. And, as you say, no signs of inscriptions." Then he tapped the paper. "What did you get of the other materia, please?"

"Rowan," Thessaly said promptly. "Quite a lot. And elder. The pieces in the two halves are from the same tree, both of them. And there's dried berries, I think under the floor, they came up as little circular shapes. And several of the other stones, they're specific to the Pact and the Fatae." Then she flicked her fingers through the rest of her list. "Powdered stones, maybe. Wait." Her voice cut off sharply.

Vitus held still, silent, not jostling her. It took her a good minute, one finger marking her place on the list, before she pulled a small notebook out of the bag and peered at it. "I'd have to look in more detail. But some of these. they're the same things on some of Aunt Metaia's notes were focusing on. I thought they were about her investments, though, the ships coming and going."

"And that might give you a way to learn more about what it was supposed to do. Or the rest of her notes?" Thessaly nodded, and Vitus went on. "So, posit a device to …" The brunt of it hit Vitus, and he grunted. "Something to go around the Pact. To step sideways from what the Pact dictates. Make a space where it didn't bind. The thing doesn't work, I don't know if it could work. But this doesn't." He gestured feebly. "Like a portal, but it made a room instead of a door, maybe?"

"It doesn't work. But trying is, is it treason? I don't know that I've ever heard of anything like it." Thessaly was gnawing on the problem. "And if Aunt Metaia was getting glimpses of it, it explains why she was so careful. It is exactly a Council problem." Thessaly then looked up. "Lady Chrodechildis mentioned something, you remember when I was at that awful supper where everyone else seemed in disgrace? That she thought the Pact too limiting. They couldn't have found a way around that, could they? With this? It doesn't look, well. Enough."

"Honestly, it really needs the Penelopes. But that, again, is the Council's problem." Vitus felt he was in that liminal state where staring at it would just make things worse. "Help me put things back together?"

They repeated the dance with the cover and the latches in reverse, which took a little longer. Vitus's shoulders were beginning to ache by the time he heard both latches snap closed, then he finally stepped to the side. "Let's go— go."

"Home," Thessaly said. "Do you think of Bryn Glas as home, then?" Her voice was suddenly hopeful in a way Vitus hadn't expected. It was a pure illuminated joy, the way the sun caught amber or citrine and everything glowed gold.

"I do. Let's." They packed everything up, each doing one more scan of the room to make sure they hadn't left anything behind. Then they went out, pulling the door closed behind them. They were perhaps a third of the way back when they met up with Garin, who was in one of the side gardens. No one seemed to be with him, not a nanny or governess or tutor, certainly not his parents.

Thessaly nodded. "Garin. Good afternoon. How are you doing? We've permission to be here." She didn't explain, of course she didn't.

Garin looked her up and down. "Were you over by the river? Father said it's not safe there. People get hurt."

Vitus did not know what to say to that. Thessaly took a moment. "We were careful. Do you know about people getting hurt there?"

"I kept dreaming about it. For a bit. Not so much recently? But Isembard's in the nursery, he wakes me up in the middle of the night." Garin shoved his hands in his pockets, which was certainly not the sort of thing a nanny would approve of.

Thessaly grinned. "Ah, but having a younger brother, or sister, I have a sister, gets better. The crying is a lot, though. I hated that. I bet you're old enough you could have your own room with a charm, so the crying didn't wake you. It's the sort of thing people sometimes forget would be a help. You ask your nanny or, um. The housekeeper?"

Vitus nodded. Garin looked at them, rather dubiously, but then he shrugged. "I can ask. Will you come back sometime and show me more duelling? In the salle here?"

Vitus heard Thessaly inhale. "Maybe. I can't make too many promises right now, and I don't want to break one to you. But if I can, I'll sort it out with your parents. All right?"

It got her a considering solemn nod, then Garin said, "I'd walk you to the portal. That's polite, isn't it? But Nanny said I was supposed to stay on this side of the gardens."

"Then that's what you should do," Vitus agreed. "Were you bored?" Garin shrugged, very much put upon. Vitus considered. "What you could do, if you wanted, is get a list from the gardeners or the housekeeper of the plants that are out here, and one of the guides for identifying them, and work through. It's a good time of year for it, things flowering properly. You could even start making sketches. If you want to go into alchemy like your father, it's good to know the materia. Thessaly and I both do, for the magic we do."

"If you say so." Garin said it with a grand dubiousness, which was about what Vitus expected at his age. "It's better than playing with a hoop, though. Or tin soldiers. And Maman would like it if I asked about a good book, I think, or Father."

"There you go. And if they get a few minutes, it would give you a chance to come out in the garden and talk about something together. I think they'd like that." Thessaly gestured. "We ought to get on. Have a good afternoon."

Garin stood at attention— Vitus looked back at the

garden gate, the path that cut across the back of the house — until they were out of sight. "He's a very serious child."

"I think he understood that something has been very wrong, but he has no idea what it was or is. And it's not our place to tell him. For one thing, we don't actually have answers yet." Thessaly paused. "I'll write to Laudine, though, and mention keeping him in informative books."

That was what they could do at the moment. Vitus offered Thessaly his arm, escorting her to the portal and then back to Bryn Glas. Which, yes, had somehow shifted to being home inside his head, all without him noticing.

41

JUNE 14TH AT ARUNDEL

"I am glad you agreed to this conversation." Magistra Hereswith folded her hands. Thessaly kept quiet. Her role here was— well, it was complicated. They were in the ritual workroom at Arundel, with all sorts of enchantments in play, few of which Thessaly entirely understood. They were not quite the ordinary judicial enchantments, but they touched on that.

It was not the truth-telling magics in play, not exactly. As Lord, Dagobert could call them. But as Thessaly understood it, the Council had not asked for that. Perhaps because they knew he'd be no good for the conversation if he did. As it was, Dagobert looked pale. They had brought a sofa in. He and his wife were seated on it, their hands barely touching. Magistra Hereswith and Council Member FitzAlan had their own chairs, as did Thessaly and Vitus. Cousin Owain stood by the door, keeping watch on the space, she thought, rather than participating in the conversation proper. There were small tables with glasses of water, but no other items, not even a notebook and pen.

Vitus, for his part, looked cautious about everything. If

she hadn't been in any gathering like this before, Vitus certainly hadn't. And Thessaly at least had some experience with FitzAlan now. Though in this moment, there was something sharply honed about him. He was all work and formality, with none of the good humour and love of life he showed during duelling sessions.

"I know that we did not precisely have an option. Or rather that the other choice involves a full investigation by the Guard, the Penelopes, and who knows what else." Dagobert's voice was quiet, but steady enough.

"Just so. FitzAlan is here in that role, as the Council's point of contact with the Guard and the Ministry. He has not heard the details we'll be speaking of, and I also wanted his judgement coming to it fresh." She then nodded. "And for the record, Thessaly Lytton-Powell and Vitus Deschamps are here as witnesses. They are the ones who have significantly aided in bringing this to what we all hope will be sufficient resolution. We may have need of their information, stated again."

Dagobert flinched at that, though Laudine didn't move. Thessaly shifted just enough to take Vitus's hand. If they weren't doing truth-telling charms or something like that, it wouldn't matter. Or rather, it did matter. She found it reassuring, and she was certain Vitus did as well.

Magistra Hereswith went on. "You may, any of you, formally request us to stop speaking. But in that case, yes, our next step would be bringing this to the Courts and the full weight of the Ministry. And we have reasons to avoid that, of our own." She inclined her head once. "If you would state what your oaths permit and give as much explanation as you can in your own words." That was directed at both Dagobert and Laudine, though Thessaly noted they had not been named, not since the ritual circle had been called into place around them.

Dagobert cleared his throat. "There are limits to what I may, oaths made that still— if I tried, I would." His voice faltered, then he began again. "There are matters I may not speak of. Before I say what I can, I wish to express my regret for the deaths I had any hand in: Metaia Powell's and Philip Landry's. Not directly, either of them. It was not my hands, but I hold blame." He did not look up as he said the names, and Thessaly did not know how to react in that moment. She had not expected that. Vitus squeezed her hand, and she looked at a spot on the floor. Anything else would be far too revealing.

She heard Dagobert's voice go on. "My family had an idea. Not all of us. Bradamante still does not know the scope, I am sure of it. Nor her husband or children or any of them. But my mother, my brother Clovis, and his sons, Childeric and Sigbert. All of us were active participants. Clovis would not have told Maylis much about it, bound by oaths and by habit. I did not tell Laudine any of it, beyond the fact Maman had a project, until after last summer solstice. And she still does not know many of the details, since I was bound to keep them secret." Thessaly heard his voice shift, a note she couldn't understand. She glanced at him, at that, to see him looking relieved. "I am glad that it has been discovered. I do not want it to be continued, but I cannot be the one to end it, not by myself. I am not able." His voice quavered slightly as he continued, "I made the attempt to try to, to do something about it, but in my— in my frailty I could do no more than discard the ring they stole from Philip Landry after his death there, as if it were wergild."

Thessaly looked away again at that. The sound of it was too raw. Magistra Hereswith spoke, her voice a blade that cut cleanly. "And the other deaths?"

"I do not know the cause or the means. But I worried,

until her death, that Magistra Landry would find her revenge. I worried that what we were doing had consequences none of us understood. I had no part of it after summer solstice, you understand? Even if I could speak of it, I would have no information for you from that time."

"What can you tell us?" Magistra Hereswith brought him back to the topic, like someone bringing a rambunctious hound to heel.

"The project, it, I worried that I had said something, let something slip, last summer. We left Dinas Emrys. We discussed, mostly Maman and Clovis discussed, and they sent me off with Philip, to speak to Metaia. I don't know what they expected. I honestly don't know what I expected." He cleared his throat. "He said he had information for her that she needed to know, er. Something was going on that she needed to know about. She opened the gate, and came out into the road, to speak to us outside the immediate wards. There was a brief conversation and Philip told me to go back and wait by the portal. I don't know what he did, I don't know how he did it. I went, and I waited, and a few minutes later he joined me."

"And then?" Magistra Hereswith's voice prodded things along when Dagobert's words trailed off. There was something ferociously distant there now, a column of power and restraint, because continuing mattered far more than whatever she felt about it.

"There was a disagreement. About when I realised what he'd done, I was certain the entire Council would search out what had happened, and make sure the matter was dealt with." That, or perhaps the earnest fear that came out there, got a sound of some fierce amusement out of Magistra Hereswith, FitzAlan, and Cousin Owain, a chord in perfect unison. "My mother and brother both cursed me, at near enough the same moment, and I do not remember anything else from that point for a fortnight."

Laudine picked up, her voice precise. "Childeric and Sigbert brought him back to the house. I took him home, and it was a fortnight before he made much sense. High fevers, delirium, though as far as I can tell, even then he did not speak of the truth of the matter, of course the Silence oaths held. He was able to tell me the, what shall we say, shape and size of the problem. None of his family showed any particular care for his recovery, or for his opinions, thereafter. My husband agreed that he had been a fool, dangerously so, and put much at risk. We were aware they continued with their project, with their research, but I suspect, from bad tempers on a number of occasions, that they did not find much actual success."

"And then there were other deaths." Magistra Hereswith's tone was studiously neutral. "Do you have thoughts about that?"

"The only logical assumption is that one or more of them caused Philip Landry's death, left his body." Laudine replied promptly enough. "And that Henut Landry figured out who was to blame. Or at least, sufficient of the blame. And yet, it makes no sense. Surely her competence did not stretch to the Challenge, and she herself died before Clovis, Maylis, or Sigbert. Or before Chrodechildis's apoplexy. And Maylis was not directly involved in the other, well, project."

Magistra Hereswith wiggled a hand. "I am making no assumptions about that point. But you had no direct information on that count. No note or communication or oracular dream, anything of that kind."

Laudine shook her head. "I have no answers on that point. And I do not know why we were spared, comparatively speaking."

Thessaly suddenly recalled the dream she'd had the night Magistra Landry had died, but she held her own counsel. She might tell Magistra Hereswith in private, later, but she didn't think it was relevant to the particular question.

"Indeed. Thessaly, if you - or Vitus, if you prefer - would summarise what you found?" Magistra Hereswith spoke more warmly.

"It had become clear to the Council that my aunt Metaia had been investigating something before her death. She had hidden her notes, as well as encoding them. It has taken a great deal of work to decipher them. She identified the Fortiers as exploring paths that— one of her notes suggests was they were outside the Pact in some substantial way, but not how. Vitus was granted access to a space, outside the estate wards, to assist with something, by the late Lord Clovis and Sigbert. Since that access had never actually been withdrawn, we investigated the space last week."

Thessaly did not mention the secret investigation. She had told Magistra Hereswith and Cousin Owain, but the remaining Fortiers did not need to know that. Certainly not right now. And how she felt about Dagobert, in particular, was exceedingly complicated, given what he'd said about Aunt Metaia's death. "What became clear when investigating the space was that it was an attempt to manipulate the bounds of the Pact and the Silence through the use of magnetic and electrical fields. In both some mechanical form as well as magical ones. We did not attempt to engage the devices, of course. And we are not remotely experts, but Vitus does not think they could have worked as designed. We do believe we understand how to disassemble them safely."

"Do that. Please." Dagobert's voice was louder now.

"Burn the place to the ground if you need to. I want nothing more to do with it. I don't want anyone to be tempted by it, ever again."

Magistra Hereswith coughed. "Then we are down to negotiations." She set out to do that, laying out what the Council would demand in order to keep this private. The mechanisms fully disassembled, of course, the building taken down to the bare walls and the floor entirely replaced at a minimum. They would need to ensure that all notes related in any form were destroyed and make oath on it.

Laudine spoke up then. "My husband continues to suffer the impact, the weakness, of the curses. Being on the land, being Lord of the land, seems to help. But we cannot be sure there is not some lasting impact. If all possible notes are destroyed, and some aspect emerges in a decade, five decades, ten - how will anyone know what happened?"

"Do you have some proposal, then?" FitzAlan had been quiet all through this, but he spoke now.

"Private notes, sworn to be held only in the private family library. Not enough to reconstruct the mechanism, but enough that someone diligent could learn of the impact, the deaths over the past year, the consequences. Or what has been a help, should others in the family be affected?" Laudine glanced upward, toward where the nursery was, in the east wing. "I am thinking of my sons, and those who inherit the land magic in due course."

It was a potent enough argument. Everyone in the room except perhaps Thessaly and Vitus was primed to think not just of this moment, but all the ones to come. That was part of what the Council did. And whatever else Laudine valued, the wellbeing of her sons would be at the top of that list.

"We could have such materials in the Council library, well warded," FitzAlan pointed out.

"And the family would not know to look there. And might not, shall we say, trust the Council if they went looking. A great deal can change, year to year, generation to generation. I do not know what that will look like. More importantly, I— we— do not know what will be needed in the future."

Magistra Hereswith considered. "Vitus, you have perhaps the best sense. Is this acceptable to you to mitigate dangers in the future?"

"I believe so. Perhaps Laudine and Dagobert might include in the other oaths they make a commitment to explain what is included, what will not be included, and provide samples for review?" Vitus came out with it slowly, but the others nodded.

"Fair. We will lay out the oaths and arrange for someone to administer them properly. It may take a week or so. I assume you can come to Dinas Emrys for it - not at the Solstice Rites, but perhaps the afternoon before?"

That took a little more negotiation, then Magistra Hereswith nodded. "Thessaly, Vitus, you are welcome to depart." And, from her tone, ought to. "We will be in touch about a number of remaining matters." Thessaly had expected this; Magistra Hereswith had clarified that one of the oaths she'd be requiring was that none of the surviving Fortiers put Thessaly or Vitus at risk through action or inaction. Negotiating that would be delicate. She stood, nodding slightly, and then Cousin Owain let them out of the ritual enchantments and out of the room, before going back to his role.

She walked in silence with Vitus back to the portal and back to Bryn Glas, utterly unsure what to think about some of the revelations, or the fact that the lurking fear seemed to be largely ended.

42

JUNE 15TH AT BRYN GLAS

"Your mother was very—" Thessaly stopped, then tried that sentence again, as Vitus opened the door to her sitting room. They'd just returned from supper with his family. Mama and Papa had been very welcoming, and Lucas had been utterly charming. He'd filled the awkward moments with stories, teasing Vitus and, more importantly, making sure Thessaly relaxed and laughed.

"Mama has been wanting to meet you for months," Vitus said. "May I unlace you, or do you need Collins?" He had become somewhat more competent with lacings over the past few months, but Thessaly had dressed with particular attention for this supper. He wasn't entirely sure what that meant for the underpinnings.

"See if you can manage?" Thessaly went ahead of him into the bedroom, dropping her gloves on the table by the door, then reaching up to undo the pins in her hair. Vitus had to pause. He loved the moments, rare as they had been so far, when she shifted from her public face to her private, how she let him see that.

He followed her, stripping out of his jacket and

removing his cravat, before coming around behind her to see how the dress fastened. "Mama approves. If you weren't clear. So does Papa. I'm sure I'll hear more this week, but I have no doubt about that."

"And Lucas." Thessaly let out a breath. "Your parents welcomed me. And I don't know how to feel about that. Not the part that's about them, the part that's about my parents."

Who had not welcomed Thessaly, and who certainly showed no sign of welcoming Vitus or anyone like him. Vitus knew she'd had some conversations with Magistra Hereswith and her cousin in private while they'd been setting up yesterday's meeting with the Fortiers. Thessaly hadn't wanted to talk about it. Now Vitus cleared his throat. "Any thoughts about that?"

"I don't precisely have an actual answer, but the Scali confirmed that Mother and Hermia's inheritances from Aunt Metaia are well protected. Father's put up quite a fight about both, but apparently Aunt Metaia was meticulous about the arrangements. The only thing I'm sure of is he's desperate for money, not why. Debts of some kind, the kind where my marriage would have both solved the money and made him someone others wouldn't threaten. Or he thought so, anyway." Thessaly was none too sure that would actually have worked.

Thessaly sighed, but she didn't turn around, letting Vitus continue with undoing the various fastenings. "Cousin Owain is applying some pressure. They're not certain, but there's some suggestion Father knew about what the Fortiers were doing, at least the outline of it, something that would ensure their power. And of course, now, it'd just be Garin left, and no."

Vitus let his hand rest on her hip, over the layers of fabric. "What do you think of that?"

"If I weren't thinking about what it meant for you, your work, at all, I'd want to be married." She jerked her chin. "To you, to be clear. So that they couldn't come up with someone else. But it's, I don't want to hurt your business." This conversation might in fact be easier with her facing the other way.

He leaned forward to kiss the base of her neck before going back to his work. "Shall we talk about that? I haven't wanted to press." He swallowed. "I want to get interesting commissions. That seems likely to continue now, whatever the gossip does. There are enough people who know better, or who think my work's worth it. Niobe's made a few referrals, as have the Carringtons. So has Cyrus. I haven't even finished the piece for his sister yet. I need to do the last piece of that solstice morning, and dawn."

"And the income? You know I'd, I mean, money isn't a problem on my end."

"I want to make sure Mama and Papa are comfortable. Maybe see about Mama taking a trip, a month or so, to one of the healing baths on the Continent. And that sort of spending, that's something to talk about. But it seems to me, that's a kind of thing we could work out. Especially if, I mean, there's this house."

Now Thessaly twisted around, her dress gaping at the back as he got the last of the hooks. She wriggled out if it, leaving a pool of blue silk on the floor, followed by the bustle. She stepped out of it, moving to one side. "What do you think about the house?"

"For one thing, you have a portal. It's quite stable. I can live anywhere, especially if I can sleep in the workshop on the rare nights the timing is horrendous." Vitus had thought this one through. "I love the house. The colours, the decorations, the way everywhere you look, there's something delightful. I want to see what you make of it, over time. It's quiet, peaceful. Restorative." He hesitated, then added, "I don't have strong opinions about the decorations and such, but I'd like to be here, with you, choosing things. Admiring them. Whichever made sense."

"We could build you a workshop here as well. Better protections, maybe?" Thessaly offered. "More space. Though maybe not better light, that depends on the weather. Or you could keep your flat. There's no reason you couldn't."

"And no reason we need to decide anything about that tonight," Vitus agreed. "What about the rest of it?" He felt her shoulders tighten under his hand, then he added, "Let me get you out of the corset and petticoats. We will be more comfortable in bed."

Thessaly made a low sound in her throat, a sort of snort, but she turned around again to let him loosen the corset. It took him a moment to work through the knotted bow. "I'm furious at Dagobert. And Laudine, but mostly Dagobert."

"Your aunt." It wasn't a question, it couldn't be a question, of course Thessaly felt strongly about it. "And Philip?"

She was quiet at that, long enough for him to undo the bow, loosen the laces, and give her enough room to undo the hooks at the front. He let his fingers linger for a moment. He'd not expected, months ago, that they'd have this particular kind of intimacy, the quiet moments of having gone out together, come home, and undressing without any rush. They knew what would follow. He delighted in time in her bed, and he had no doubts about her affections.

It wasn't until she'd undone the hooks at the front busk, laying it aside on the dressing table stool, that she turned. "Philip's dead. And Dagobert didn't say, I don't think he can, but I can only assume that's the Fortiers, their doing. I don't know how to feel about him. I don't think I know enough to know how much to blame him. I don't like leaving it there, but I don't know that answers are a thing we can have. Not there."

"Yes. A family who kept their secrets well." That had been nagging at Vitus for the last day, too. "What do you want, if you could have anything?"

"Never to deal with them again." She said it, fast and fierce, as strongly as she'd duelled. "I just want to wash my hands of them all. Of all the Great Families, most of the Council." She hesitated. "There's Cousin Owain. And Cyrus has been very decent, and I do like the duelling."

"All right." Vitus turned around, sitting on the edge of the bed to undo his shoes and work them off his feet. "You can do that, you know."

He looked up to find her staring at him, hands on her hips, her petticoat twitching slightly with the sudden movement. "I can't."

"You can. You could be here as much as you like. See who you wanted."

"And as soon as I show my face in Trellech, people will talk to me. Worse, they'll talk about me. Mother and Father would know. All of that." Thessaly said.

Vitus grinned. "I have a very clever brother. Besides him being charming." He spread his hands. "Lucas wondered, we'd been talking about finding time for you to meet more people, people you might actually enjoy being around. He wondered if it would be possible to set up a talisman that would hold a steady illusion. A face, something ordinary. As Lucas said, a woman with a few children at home, a cook-housekeeper. No one of particular interest, just going about her day. I checked the laws. I'd need your help to design the talisman, but I think it's possible."

Thessaly took a few steps, first sitting on the bed, then falling backwards on it. "That's really something I could do?"

"Mmhm. You could go to your duelling. Merryn and Thirza have both encouraged me to invite you round to the Four Metals a bit, if you wanted company without bother on the street.." He hesitated. "And there's the question of names. If we marry, you could be Deschamps. Much less likely to draw attention than Lytton-Powell."

It made her laugh. "True." She let out a long sigh. "My sister?"

"Ask your cousin about that. And Magistra Hereswith. They owe us rather a lot. I suspect they could work something out. Set up your sister to be a companion to someone who could mentor her properly, get her away from your family. Especially if there's any leverage over your father. And then, of course, take some steps to avoid your father marrying Hermia off without her permission." Thessaly made a thoughtful sound at that. Vitus added, "Talk to them about it, anyway. See what they think."

Thessaly was quiet, long enough for Vitus to finish stripping out of his clothing. He tidied her gown and corset to where they could be tended in the morning, then offered her a hand up so she could get out of the remaining petticoats. "You really think it could work?"

"I think we won't know unless we try. Unless we ask for what we want." Vitus let out a puff of breath, then held out his arms to her. She stepped into them. He let his fingers run against her skin. "I want to make a life with you. I want the people we care about to be happy. The rest of it will come."

"Children?" Her voice was quieter now. "Commissions?"

"Do you mind if I take commissions from the Great

Families?" She shook her head. "More reason to keep the flat, or something like it. A neutral space, nowhere near here. I can be entirely mysterious about my beloved wife, who keeps busy with her own interests. My work does sometimes involve a dinner invitation or something like that, but it won't be a problem to go by myself. Niobe's never had that problem."

"Huh." Thessaly took a step back, closer to the bed. "You didn't answer the other."

"Children? If you are willing, I'd love that. I kept thinking, seeing you with Garin, what kind of mother you might be. What kind of father I might be? And Mama and Papa would be delighted, though they'd be the first to say such things should be our choice."

"Do you, wait? I don't know how to say this." Her voice cracked. "Do you think they'd help me figure out how to do it properly? Warmly?"

Vitus turned to kiss her, taking his time with it. "I am certain Mama would be delighted. She always wanted a daughter. And she knows, a little, about how much it hurt you, people not telling you important things, not asking about them. I'm sure she won't."

"She was very kind at supper. Checking in advance about the meal, about what would make me feel at ease." Thessaly pulled back again, just enough to look at him. "And she's like that all the time?"

"Oh, yes." Vitus grinned. "I'll talk to her. And if you wanted to be somewhere else for a bit, while everything settles down, perhaps you and she could go to one of the baths and have time to talk, in a relaxed way. Away from Albion. Or not." He wasn't at all sure how Thessaly would take that.

"You worry about her." Thessaly hesitated. "I don't know how to worry about someone, kindly, like that?"

This, now, required another kiss, and Vitus nudging her to settle in the bed, the rearrangement of blankets and sheets and pillows. Once they were properly sorted, him leaning on his side, he said, as firmly as he could, "I am certain you know. And can learn more. You've done well worrying about me. Do you really think your family means you can't?"

There was one of the longest silences yet. Finally, she just nodded.

"Your aunt was warm, your aunt loved you, your aunt worried about you and your sister and her friends. I am certain she taught you a great deal of that, by example. Mama— and Lucas, and even Papa— will be glad to help more. And I am quite able to tell you what I want, or if you do something I don't like. Let me prove it to you?"

Her breath caught at that. "It's just. I don't want to do that. What I was raised to. I want to do something else. I want, I want something solid, stone and metal and the earth under my feet. Not illusions, not pretty words, not the show covering up chasms."

"We'll find that together." Then Vitus grinned, suddenly. "And perhaps for the moment, a bit more earthy pleasure?"

It made Thessaly giggle, just as he'd hoped, the tension popping like a soap bubble. "Did you have something in mind, sir?"

"So many things it will take us a lifetime." Vitus began with a kiss as his hand shifted between them, to arrange body against body. He planned to take his time, to work her to such delight she couldn't think, before he fed his own desires. He'd wanted it since they left for supper, in fact. Before that.

EPILOGUE

SEPTEMBER 3RD AT THE POWELL ESTATES AND BRYN GLAS

It was not how Thessaly had imagined her wedding day, back when she expected to be marrying Childeric. It was, in truth, far better. But it had taken her time, months, to get her head around the idea of something that wasn't entirely to the Fortier customs.

That had apparently been something of a feat. Magistra Hereswith had confided privately to Thessaly and Vitus that it had taken every one of her diplomatic skills and a scattering of chosen threats to bring Thessaly's parents into compliance with the plans. In the end, they'd arranged for the wedding itself to be in the gardens at the ancient Powell estate. Vitus and his parents had been consulted about the customs they most cared about.

One argument had been about timing. Thessaly's preference had decidedly been for an autumn wedding. Vitus expected to be particularly busy with items for holiday gifts in October and November, along with some work for maintenance talismans for the Council keep. Planning the whole thing in two months had meant no one could come up with ridiculous and unnecessary celebratory ideas.

Perhaps most relevant, the sooner they married, the sooner the threat of being forced to marry someone else would evaporate.

And, to be honest, doing it while Dagobert and Laudine were still in formal mourning simplified things no end. There was not a precise number for 'mourning one's nephew, from whom one had inherited the title', but Thessaly had gathered they were using six months as a reasonable count. Which meant marrying before mid-October was preferable. For her, at least.

She had not seen them since that meeting, though Vitus had, of course, continued with the commission for them. He had told Thessaly that it seemed to be working as intended. A few months space had brought Thessaly to a point where she wished them no ill. But she also wanted them at a substantial distance, both physical and emotional.

Thessaly might also have once wanted a life where she could teach Garin a bit of duelling. Where conversations with an extended family, each with their own gifts, could be shared, not seen as something dangerous. She hated leaving him alone that way, it wasn't his fault. But she could not bear to be near his father, or at Arundel, and that mattered more.

September had also been just enough time to make the changes in the house Thessaly had wanted. She'd consulted Vitus, of course, about what he wanted in a workroom. But it had been Niobe who had overseen the work to ensure all the necessary enchantments and charms suited. And then there had been making over rooms in the house. One for Hermia, whenever she wanted to visit, two others for eventual children. And this past week, she had somehow made it through without Vitus visiting. That had given her just enough time to make over the sitting room and bedroom into something they could share. And to move her own work to the study and workroom downstairs.

The grounds, too, had been adjusted. The new salle was settling in nicely. And now, once or twice a week, people came up and through the portal for a bout or three. They'd arranged it tucked in behind the portal. That way, people didn't have to enter the rest of the wards. It made Thessaly feel more free about inviting people she didn't know as well.

All of that had meant a busy summer, between the changes on the property and planning for the wedding. Now, the day was here. Today was for her, for Vitus, for celebrating with the people who wished them well, and for doing the proper rituals to anchor their marriage the way they chose. In the end, that had shaped everything else.

She and Hermia had spent the night with Cousin Owain and his household. There had been a lovely meal last night, stories of happy marriages in the family, and of making a good life without a marriage, as well. Mother would have disapproved, but Mother disapproved of most things right now. Mother had also absolutely not been invited, and no one had commented about it.

On the other hand, Aunt Tegwen had invited Vitus's mother out for the meal. At the end of the evening, Mistress Deschamps had asked Thessaly to walk her back to the portal. "This is the evening where, technically, some matron is supposed to give you advice about the marriage bed. I gather, without having asked for any details, that you seem to be managing that quite pleasantly. But I hope that if there is any small thing I might help with, you will feel you can come to me. And we may perhaps look forward to having you join us regularly for suppers at home?"

Thessaly had been charmed, honestly. "I wouldn't

think of keeping Vitus from time with you. Or his father or brother." Her mouth curled up. "Perhaps especially Lucas. I would hate to make him unhappy."

"Goodness, thank you. Lucas unhappy is like a wet dog, it gets over everything. And we would be delighted to come to you, if that is more convenient at some point." That was a delicate nod at an eventual pregnancy of her own. Thessaly was not ready to drop the contraceptive charms just yet. There had been so much swirling change in the past year, most of it challenging. But in due course, yes. She'd smiled and made it clear they'd sort things out.

The celebration itself had been simple. Mother and Father had turned up for the ceremony itself. Before that, Thessaly and Hermia had walked down to leave flowers at Aunt Metaia's grave, along with a small libation. That wasn't their usual custom, but it felt right. Then Thessaly had gone back to the house, dressed in a simple gown. White had become the custom among the non-magical, but Albion did not follow the fashions of Britain's queen. Thessaly's dress had, instead, been the peacock green that Aunt Metaia had particularly loved, with decorations of British pearls. It made Thessaly feel gorgeous, in a way she hadn't expected to.

The ceremony had been elegant and brief. Hermia had been her attendant, in a dress of pastel blue-green, and Lucas had stood beside Vitus, in his formal cavalry uniform. It gave the whole thing an element of proper show. Mother and Father had been quiet, but impeccably behaved. Cousin Owain had been keeping an eye on them, making pleasant conversation but not leaving them alone, she gathered. There were, of course, Vitus's parents, a number of the Powell family, Father's brothers and their wives.

And then there had been a few others. Magistra

Hereswith and her husband with her companion Bess making sure everything went smoothly behind the scenes. A number of people Vitus was closest to in the Four Metals had come, the ones who were becoming Thessaly's friends, too. Cyrus and Andie Smythe-Clive. And of course both Niobe, for Vitus's apprenticeship, and Magistra North, for Thessaly, along with her husband. And several of the Scali had come with Emeline in company. She was about to take up a new position as a bodyguard, now that threats against Thessaly seemed rather less likely.

She and Vitus had sworn their oaths on their magic and on the Silence. Instead of the plain gold band she had expected, Vitus had slipped a ring onto her fingers. It was a broad green emerald that felt like perfection on her finger, with tiny pearls set beside it. The ring did not sparkle with the many facets of diamonds; it did not draw the eye. It felt, instead, like her feet were firmly planted on ground she loved. She would ask him, later, what he had chosen for it, but she knew it was perfect. And he had made it, with love and care and understanding. The details mattered, and they did not.

From there, things had come out smoothly. Mother and Father had stayed through the luncheon, the early dancing, and then had quietly excused themselves, as had some of the other guests. Others had stayed to the end. Niobe had drawn both Vitus and Thessaly into some of the country dances, along with Aunt Tegwen and Cousin Enfys and some of the other Powell relatives. Lucas had swung Hermia around in a waltz, and then picked up some of the dances along with Niobe, escorting her with glee through the steps and turns.

Finally, they were escorted back to the portal and welcomed by the household staff. "All is ready, Mistress."

Collins came forward, her eyes gleaming. "And we wish you and Master Deschamps very well."

Thessaly beamed at them, then tugged at Vitus's hand. "I have things to show you before the bedroom."

"Not for terribly long before the bedroom, I hope?" He laughed, but he let her pull him across to the smaller barn. She opened the door easily; the door had been hung perfectly, it swung open without a sound. Then she nudged him inside. "We can change things if you wish, of course, but Niobe made sure all the functional parts should suit." The room was a creamy white, to reflect the light with a worktable in front of the window for the best light. Cases of shelves, designed to pull out from the wall for access, lined the back wall, an abundance of storage space. "And there's space there, for your wheels and such. The floor's charmed to collect all the dust, that method you had been admiring in Harley's Mechanicals."

Vitus turned around, his mouth open. "I will not explore every detail, Not now. Maybe not even tomorrow. We have a wedding to celebrate." Then he picked her up, swinging her around. "And you'll tell me all the details?"

"I will." She flicked her fingers, bringing up one of them, a set of coloured designs along the ceiling, perhaps a foot below. Then she flicked her fingers in a different pattern, and another, and they changed colour each time. "So you can have the room echo what you're working on. Naomi was rather smug about it. The enchantment work there is mine."

"Ah." Vitus kissed her. "You are a gem among women. May I demonstrate?"

Thessaly laughed, and let him lead her back out of the former barn, to the house. He picked her up to carry her over the threshold, but sensibly put her down to walk up the stairs and into their rooms. There, he stopped, blinking.

She had kept the effect of Aunt Metaia's love of colour. Along the main wall, she'd painted a fresco into the plaster. She'd drawn on the local wildlife - foxes, badgers, a shoreline with seals, perching birds, mountain ponies. Then she'd set illusions so that the sky behind echoed the time of day. Just now, it was a glorious sunset, all golds and purples and pinks shading the room with light.

"And tell me about that, in due course." He took her hand in his, kissing the ring. "And I should tell you about the ring."

"Unlace me, and tell me in bed?" Thessaly suggested. She was looking forward to this evening. She came to her marriage bed not a nervous virgin, depending on her husband to ensure a good time. They were doing this together, knowing more than enough about each other to make sure the night would match the day in pleasure and comfort and mutual delight.

Vitus pulled her close, guiding her into the bedroom. Here, she'd drawn on the tumble of gemstone colours, the glowing reds, blues, greens, golds, and sparkling clarity. It was accented here and there with an illusion for what paint and plaster could not do. It was like living inside a jewel box in the best possible way. She felt as if the colours enlivened her soul. Vitus spun in place, taking in the choices in the curtains, the pillows, the bedding. "I do not deserve your eye."

"Oh, you inspire." Thessaly turned her back, so he could unlace her. She took a moment to step out of the dress and leave it in the sitting room for Collins to tend to. She came back in, closing the bedroom door behind her. By the time she had, Vitus was largely undressed, and was sprawling on the bed. She joined him, holding out her hand. "The ring?"

"When Niobe introduced me to her gem seller, they

had an emerald. I didn't think, then, that I'd ever be able to give you such a thing, but I've been working on it for—well. I began it last October. It is a talisman for loyalty in love— my loyalty— and for abundant pleasures. Wisdom and harmony. And the pearls bring joy and harmony."

"And you don't hold with the lore about emerald preferring chastity?" Thessaly asked, teasing.

"I do not. Loyalty, faithfulness, yes. But I don't think we'll have much trouble with that, do you?" Vitus raised himself up on an elbow. "I have had no eyes for any but you since we met. And you have chosen me over several others."

"None of whom matched your standards," Thessaly said, leaning to kiss his nose. "Let us test this out, then, to make sure all is well."

Vitus laughed, moving to place hands on either side of her shoulders and bend to kiss her. She slipped her hands down his chest, to his hips, pulling him closer. They were going to have an excellent night indeed. And whatever the days of their marriage might bring, she was sure they'd face the challenges together and delight in the joys.

Thank you so much for joining Thessaly and Vitus on their journey! Reviews (wherever you get your books or look for reviews) are a huge help both to me and to other readers. They don't need to be long or complex to help people find books they'd love.

Read on for more about the Fortiers, the Landrys, and some historical details. That includes *Grown Wise*, coming in May 2025, that picks up some remaining threads of what the Fortiers were up to and the generational consequences.

AUTHOR'S NOTE

Thank you for following me - and Thessaly and Vitus - through three books of challenges! Now they can build a life together.

My thanks in so many ways to Kiya Nicoll, my editor and friend and other half of my brain, who put up with my having new thoughts about this trilogy at all sorts of points in the process. And my thanks to Elise Matthesen, for ongoing excellent comments about stones and their properties.

I have plans for some extras for this book. Keep an eye on my newsletter and website!

The Fortier and Landry families appear in many other places in my books, later in the timeline.

Grown Wise, Ursula Fortier's romance in 1947, revisits some of the events of this trilogy and the impact on the family. It'll be out in May 2025. Ursula is Isembard's daughter, Laudine and Dagobert's granddaughter. By 1947 she's been named Heir to her Uncle Garin.

Otherwise, here are some key titles for the family:

- *Eclipse* finds both Isembard Fortier (born in this book, in his 30s) and Alexander Landry (in his 50s) as adults, when Alexander comes to teach at Schola in the 1924-1925 school year . It's a friends to lovers staffroom romance between Isembard and Thesan Wain, Astronomy professor.
- Alexander is the focus of *Best Foot Forward* in 1935, as well as *Nocturnal Quarry* in 1938 (a character focused novella that includes a bit more of Alexander's family.)
- *Old As The Hills* has a key event in Garin's life, and some of the aftermath, though he's not a main character there.
- *The Magic of Four* includes Isembard's son Leo as one of the main characters.

You can find Niobe Hall, Vitus's apprentice mistress in *Facets of the Bench*, much later in her life in 1927. And Margot Williams, Thessaly's cousin, appears in *Bound for Perdition* (in 1917) and *Three Graces* (in 1945).

You can find more about Cyrus and his sister in *Sailor's Jewel*, *The Hare and the Oak*, and an upcoming book (set in 1928) with his daughter Gemma's romance.

I've also been sharing sequences of extras related to the Fortiers and to Cyrus on my Patreon at patreon.com/celialake. The relevant sets include A Fox Hunt (Ursula and Garin going into her romance in 1947), Schola Tales (Leo Fortier and others in 1946-1947), and Ritual Time (following Cyrus year by year after he becomes Head of the Council in 1932).

On to the content notes!

There is a tremendously long history of using specific gemstones and talismans for magical purposes. The primary resources I drew on include *A Lapidary of Sacred Stones: Their Magical and Medicinal Powers Based on the Earliest Sources, Includes More than 800 Gems and Stones* by Claude Leconteux as well as *Stars and Stones: An Astro-Magical Lapidary by Peter Stockinger*. The former - as you might guess by the title - is extensive. The latter is more focused, but goes into more detail in some places.

As I noted in the author note for Enchanted Net, lore also has a lot to say about inscriptions for specific purposes. For example, there's this description (taken from the Lacon-teaux book): "etched with the moon and sun and hung about the neck with hairs from a synocephalus and feathers from a swallow, it protects one from evil spells. Magical properties are increased if set in gold or silver and if a man on horseback holding a sceptre is carved on it." If that seems like a lot to put on a gemstone, yes, I thought that too. (A synocephalus has the head of a canid.)

Vitus and Niobe take something of a middle road here when it comes to design: pieces are created at magically relevant time (astrologically/astronomically speaking), using materials that associate in particular ways. They're also imbued with magic by the creator, enabling them to do the desired function. It's a little like building a computer and coding with it after building it out of raw materials.

Chapter 3 : Albion - like Britain, historically - has a number of varied **guild systems**. Some guilds are fairly free-form, or they rely on individual evaluations. The Talisman Maker's Guild obviously has a specific process for evaluation by members, with Vitus's final exam here. (As Vitus notes, he's already met the requirements to be a journeyman member of the Gem Cutter's Guild, since that's a precursor for much of the talisman work.)

Chapter 7 : **The parson's cat** is a Victorian game (also known in some places as the minister's cat). In it, you go around the room and give the cat an adjective in alphabetical order. If you hesitate, you lose the round. It can also help you keep your calm during a difficult conversation, as Thessaly demonstrates here.

Chapters 9 and 10 : The **All Hallows** customs here are drawn from northern Wales, with a mingling of things that might have come into the family over time. The dangers that Thessaly notes - Gwyn ap Nudd with his hounds, voices calling out, dangers at crossroads - are all commonly referenced culturally. (Gwyn ap Nudd is ruler of the Otherworld and associated with the Wild Hunt.)

The traditions around cracking nuts and reading the future in them is also common in various parts of Great Britain.

Chapter 11 : As noted above, **Cyrus and his sister** also appear in a number of other places. Cyrus eventually becomes head of the Council in 1932, and he has a steady hand there. Andie, his sister, takes on a new name in 1901 (just as *Sailor's Jewel* takes place), Rhoe. That's because she's taken on a new position in the Temple of Healing, as the senior Healer in charge of the ritual healing baths.

Chapter 27 : I did some research to figure out if I could do a Hound of the Baskervilles trick here with **phosphorous**. Unfortunately, phosphorous was known, but not in this kind of use, and the related approaches with radioactive substances weren't figured out until 1896. A little too late for this book!

Thank you again for joining me for this story. Again, if you'd like a bit more about aspects of what happened that Thessaly and Vitus never see, some of those will be explored in *Grown Wise*, out in May 2025.

My newsletter has all my updates and news, as well as additional information about where I am and what I'm doing online. Until next book, happy reading!

ENCHANTED NET SUMMARY

Enchanted Net, the first book of the Mysterious Fields trilogy, begins with **Thessaly Lytton-Powell's** betrothal to **Childeric Fortier** in March 1889 at his family's demesne estate, **Arundel**.

The betrothal is the event of the season, a gathering attended by nearly every powerful person in Albion (Britain's magical community), and everyone the Fortiers want to impress. Along with members of Albion's **Council**, the guests include many allies of the Fortiers such as the formidable **Henut Landry** and her sons **Philip** and **Alexander**. Henut and Philip are established magical specialists, while Alexander is almost finished with his time as a student at Schola, about to depart on a Grand Tour.

Thessaly comes from good families with powerful magic - the Lyttons and the Powells - but neither have the same kind of social power. Marrying the golden son of the Fortiers is quite a step up. Thessaly's willing. She understands the family expectations and obligations - or at least she thinks she does. Her apprenticeship in illusion work is going well, even if Thessaly does not expect to need to make her living at it. Besides, she's also a duellist, skilled in using her magic and her wits to reach her goals.

Marrying into the Fortier family is a particular kind of challenge, though. They are a family of strong magic and stronger opinions. The Dowager Lady **Chrodechildis** still rules the family with a strong hand, even though Lord **Clovis** and Lady **Maylis** Fortier's sons (Childeric and **Sigbert**) are young adults. **Dagobert** (Chrodechildis's younger son) and his wife **Laudine** maintain a little more space from the family, but are at all the necessary events with their 9-year-old son **Garin**.

The Fortier marriage agreements are clear about what is and is not permitted and expected. Thessaly is committed to marrying Childeric and doing her best to provide him with children, but other relationships that do not interfere with that are possible. Certainly, Childeric's taking advantage of that clause.

Vitus Deschamps comes from a less distinguished family, with his father acting as a man of business for various Fortier client families and his brother **Lucas** serving in a non-magical cavalry unit. Vitus has been travelling on the Continent, learning from talisman makers and gem cutters as he comes to the end of his apprenticeship as a talisman maker. His apprentice mistress, **Niobe Hall**, welcomes him back warmly, wanting to set him up to succeed for the future. His return also lets him reconnect with the **Four Metals**, a secret society focused on crafting and innovative magic.

When Vitus meets Thessaly at a costume gala, they immediately find each other to be kindred spirits, interested in exploring the artistry that magic makes possible, as well as the function of different enchantments and forms of magic.

As spring turns into summer, however, there are some worrying signs. Childeric alternately ignores Thessaly and becomes increasingly controlling of her behaviour. Both Vitus and Thessaly have also become aware that a number of people around their age are not fulfilling their magical promise the way anyone expected - there are failed apprenticeships, complications for expected marriages, and more.

Vitus spends his spring developing his own connections, both within the Four Metals and consulting with Philip Landry about a particular technique. He knows what he needs to do to conclude his apprenticeship: gather a few more key examples of his work to present to his guild. Vitus also needs to set up his business and ways to establish his skills and differentiate himself from Niobe.

As Thessaly and her beloved aunt **Metaia** (a member of Albion's Council) are getting ready for the Council rites on Summer Solstice, Metaia asks some probing questions and shares her worries about Childeric, as well as making it clear Thessaly has her support. The evening is a shining show of magic and prestige, as expected, but Vitus and Thessaly do get a chance to dance together.

When Metaia is found dead the next morning, Thessaly - and her family - are shocked and grieving, especially Thessaly's mother **Sioned**, Metaia's older sister. More puzzling, there's another death, that of Philip Landry. Thessaly is desperately trying to figure out what happened and what it means, and Vitus offers what comfort he can - if constrained by proper behaviour and his own social station.

The funerals raise questions, odd moments of behaviour that don't make sense. The Fortiers have retreated into their estates, barely making the necessary condolence calls. Vitus and Thessaly both notice several odd reactions at Philip's funeral. Vitus begins to try and figure out what might be going on, even though he has very little information to work with.

Ten days after Metaia's death, Thessaly is summoned to Arundel with no explanation. She's shocked to hear Childeric announce that he intends to challenge for Metaia's open seat on the Council. She's rightfully upset that he didn't discuss it with her, or give her any warning of what he had planned. And yet, while she's furious, she can't go against him - not in public, and not in private.

Vitus has his own unexpected conversation when Henut Landry asks if he would take over the lease on Philip's rooms, solving his search for his own professional space. He agrees, once she makes clear what the catch is. Vitus is, after all, more likely than a stranger to let her know if some odd object or paperwork turns up. He also takes on a commission from **Theo Carrington**, another of the declared challengers for the open Council seat, for a talismanic piece that will support his magic.

At the end of the book, Thessaly and Vitus manage to get a chance to meet and talk. When Vitus admits he wishes he could kiss Thessaly, she agrees that she wishes he would. They kiss, but almost immediately are discovered by one of the worst gossips. Vitus walks away in order to offer Thessaly the scant protection he can.

Now you're ready to read Silent Circuit! (The link will take you back to chapter 1).

SILENT CIRCUIT SUMMARY

Silent Circuit, the second book in the Mysterious Fields trilogy, opens with **Thessaly Lytton-Powell** doing her best to navigate the expectations of the Fortier family.

It's going badly, especially since there is nasty gossip about Thessaly's friendship with **Vitus Deschamps**. **Childeric Fortier**, Thessaly's fiancé, makes it clear – backed up with threats – that any further similar behaviour will have severe and unpleasant consequences. It means Thessaly can't get support or kindness from Vitus, the one person who's cared most about her through the loss and grief of **Enchanted Net**.

Matters are also unsettled in Thessaly's own family. Her aunt **Metaia's** murder in June changed the balance of family power. Now Thessaly's father and his family want more control and influence, especially over Thessaly and her sister Hermia's choices. Thessaly's Cousin **Owain** – also on the Council, as Metaia had been – keeps a watchful eye out and lends his support quietly.

Vitus, for his part, is busy establishing himself as a talisman maker as he finishes his apprenticeship. He's taken on a commission for the upcoming **Council** Challenge, making a piece for **Theo Carrington** as well as assisting with some pieces for the Council itself. He's also continuing to strengthen his friendships within the Four Metals, one of Albion's secret societies particularly interested in innovative magical crafting.

As the summer rolls into autumn, there are a series of worrying events. The Lammas rites at **Arundel**, the Fortier demesne estate, have a host of bad omens. Childeric's aunt and uncle – **Laudine** and **Dagobert** – seem to be excluded from a number of family decisions, with no obvious reason. Thessaly has an unpleasant conversation with several Council wives, making it clear exactly how closely people around her will be watching for any flaw or misstep.

Finally, Thessaly gets a chance to talk with Vitus in the main library. He suggests some materials that might explain why her family has been behaving so oddly about Aunt Metaia's will. The next day, she finds out why. Metaia left the bulk of her substantial estate, including **Bryn Glas** (a home in northern Wales) to Thessaly. It's hedged round with protections and trustees to make sure neither Thessaly's parents nor the Fortiers can take it away.

Thessaly immediately moves there, retreating to a place of safety she never expected to have. It also finally gives her a space where she and Vitus can speak privately, without fear of gossip or confrontation. Even though her marriage agreements with Childeric allow for friendship with others and even a lover, Childeric has made it clear he will have none of that. He intends to control every part of Thessaly's life. Neither Thessaly nor Vitus see any real way forward.

Besides the personal issues, there are larger problems at play. The Council is concerned about what led to Metaia's murder, and there are unusual magical reactions in play. People Vitus knows are seeing something similar, odd readings on a new magical device intended to help deal with industrial pollution. And Childeric's behaviour is more and more worrying, including direct threats to Thessaly and to Vitus if she even considers stepping out of line. **Henut Landry**, (whose son Philip died mysteriously right around the same time as Metaia) is lurking at Arundel, with her own particular self-assigned tasks and goals.

As the Council Challenge approaches, various people make final preparations. Theo Carrington tests the talisman Vitus has made, and is delighted with the effect and work. Thessaly has dress fittings that make it clear how little her opinion counts for anything. There's a little gossip about the other challengers, including **Cyrus Smythe-Clive**, who was a yearmate of Thessaly's at school. The Fortiers are preparing for a grand celebration, certain Childeric will triumph.

On the autumn equinox, four people enter the Challenge chamber at the Council Keep. One more turns away before entering. A short time later, Childeric's body – marked with a few odd wounds – appears on the stones outside the door, dead. **Hereswith Rowan**, Head of the Council, draws the Fortiers into a private room to tell them, and Childeric's mother refuses to believe what's happened. Thessaly strategically chooses to faint, rather than be pressured into something worse. She wakes the next morning at her Cousin Owain's home, finding herself suddenly able to make more choices than she'd expected.

Childeric's funeral is laden down with family customs, from silent vigil and the sewing of a shroud to a procession. Each person attending adds a small token – a metal bee – to the grave. The attendees include various members of the Council, including the successful Challenger, Cyrus

Smythe-Clive, who awkwardly offers his sympathies to Thessaly.

Once Thessaly is able to be home at Bryn Glass in private, she refuses any sign of mourning, wearing bright and joyful colours rather than the dull black that's expected. Thessaly and Vitus can begin to think about a different future than they'd expected, but it's still not a simple problem to solve. A wrong move could jeopardise Vitus's future career and cause ongoing problems for Thessaly that money alone can't solve. As the book ends, Vitus admits to his mother and brother that he loves Thessaly, whatever that ends up meaning for them both.

Also by Celia Lake

The Mysterious Fields Series - Victorian

Enchanted Net

Silent Circuit

Elemental Truth

The Mysterious Charm Series - 1920s

Outcrossing

Goblin Fruit

Magician's Hoard

Wards of the Roses

In The Cards

On The Bias

Seven Sisters

The Mysterious Powers Series - 1920s

Carry On

The Fossil Door

Eclipse

Fool's Gold

The Hare and the Oak

Point By Point

Mistress of Birds

The Mysterious Arts Series - 1920s

Bound for Perdition

Shoemaker's Wife

Perfect Accord

Facets of the Bench

Charms of Albion - Victorian standalone

Pastiche

Sailor's Jewel

Four Walls and a Heart

Land Mysteries - 1930s and 40s

Best Foot Forward

Nocturnal Quarry

Old As The Hills

Upon A Summer's Day

Illusion of a Boar

Three Graces

The Magic of Four

Other stories

Complementary

Winter's Charms

Forged in Combat

Learn more about the world of Albion and future books at my website, celialake.com. Additional information linking characters, places, and timelines is available at my authorial wiki at bit.ly/celia-lake-wiki (or get there from my website under the menu that says "more information").

Sign up for my newsletter to be the first to hear about future books and learn about fascinating bits of research. Happy reading!

gramcontent.com/pod-product-compliance
g Source LLC
TN
0921080826
LV00001B/160